HIGHEST PRAISE
FOR HOMESPUN ROMANCES:

We at Jove Books are thrilled by the enthusiastic critical acclaim that the Homespun Romances are receiving. We would like to thank you, the readers and fans of this wonderful series, for making it the success that it is. It is our pleasure to bring you the highest quality of romance writing in these breathtaking tales of love and family in the heartland of America.

And now, sit back and enjoy this delightful new Homespun Romance . . .

SUMMER LIGHTNING
by Lydia Browne

Praise for Lydia Browne's previous novels:

S0-BZH-474

Titles by Lydia Browne

HEART STRINGS
PASSING FANCY
WEDDING BELLS

SUMMER LIGHTNING

LYDIA BROWNE

JOVE BOOKS, NEW YORK

SUMMER LIGHTNING

A Jove Book / published by arrangement with
the author

PRINTING HISTORY
Jove edition / July 1995

ISBN: 0-515-11657-2

A JOVE BOOK®
Jove Books are published by The Berkley Publishing Group,
200 Madison Avenue, New York, New York 10016.
JOVE and the "J" design are trademarks
belonging to Jove Publications, Inc.

PRINTED IN THE UNITED STATES OF AMERICA

10 9 8 7 6 5 4 3 2 1

1

OVERHEAD THE VAST arch of tiled ceiling supported crystal and brass chandeliers. The floor was of Vermont marble, as fine as what Michelangelo employed. The oil paintings that hung along the walls were all of great men: Washington, Lincoln, Grant. Always on entering the great hall, <u>Edith</u> felt she should take off her hat or kneel for a moment in silent reverence to the power of the United States Post Office.

As usual, however, she simply paused as she came through the open brass doors. The coolness breathed out by the marble and highly polished woods fanned her overheated face. St. Louis in August was hot enough to melt bone even without the layers upon layers of clothing a properly dressed lady must wear. Slowly, lingering in the peace and quiet, Edith walked to her own postbox and twisted the small brass knob in the center of the wooden door.

The square hole was empty. Though she knew no other box would open to her combination, she pushed the miniature door half-closed so she could glance at the number. 1563. The space was still empty. No letters at all.

Suddenly the serenity of the post office could no longer reach her. Edith's gloved hands trembled as she closed the postbox door. There had to be letters, there must be letters. Moving as though in a bad dream, she took her place in the line to reach the service window.

"Excuse me," she said to the bored, mustachioed face behind the grill. "There are no letters in my post box. Number Fifteen-Sixty-Three. Could you see if they haven't been delivered yet?"

"It's nine-thirty, miss. All the mail's been delivered."

Aware of the press of the line behind her, Edith put one hand out to tremulously touch the gleaming grill. "Please, could you check for me? The name's Miss Edith Parker. Farmer and Maid Matrimonial Service."

The bored civil servant blinked at the name. Edith met his eyes, knowing her desperation must be written on her face. After thoughtfully sucking his teeth, he shouted over his shoulder, "Hey, Charlie! C'mere."

But the answer was as hollow as the empty box. "Nuthin'," Charlie said, slouching back. "Nuthin' nowhere."

"Maybe later. There's another delivery at four."

"Thank you," Edith said. "I shall certainly come back at four o'clock." Lowering her veil to hide her frightened face, she turned abruptly, tripping over the festooned chain-links that kept the public in its place.

"Whoa, there," a masculine voice said as a hand shot out to take her arm. Edith saw a flash of tan summer suiting, a brown face surmounted by fair hair, and a pair of warm brown eyes looking back at her with pleased attention.

"Pardon me!" she said, jerking away. Her large hat slipped over her eyes. Shoving at it in embarrassed agitation, she dropped her bag.

The man swooped down to get it. His face was dark from the sun and his eyes crinkled at the corners as though he were used to smiling. Mistrusting his charm on sight, Edith was barely able to thank him civilly as she took her bag back. Men, as her late aunt had frequently told her, could only be trusted at a considerable distance.

"You're Edith Parker, aren't you?" he asked.

Knowing he'd heard her tell the clerk the name and was now taking advantage, she instantly denied it. "No, you've made a mistake. Good day."

She left the post office without glancing behind her. But she knew the man was following her. Stiffening her back and walking faster, Edith purposely robbed her walk of any swing or seductiveness that might have inadvertently escaped her rigid training. She'd been told all about mashers and white slavers—how they approached innocent girls in public places and led them into lives of infamy. Of course, her aunt had always stopped before describing such a life.

Edith slowed as she entered the mysteries of the seraglio. *Beautiful maidens dressed only in filmy veils reclined on dangerously soft couches. Strange, sweet incense filled the air as husky men lifted huge feather fans in hypnotic rhythm. And she, her Western clothes torn and tattered by the rough treatment of the heathens who were her captors . . .*

"Miss Parker, I'm Jefferson Dane. I wonder if we might go somewhere and . . ."

"Kindly leave me alone," she said, her daydream breaking like a soap bubble. "Or I shall call a police officer."

Leaving the man behind, baffled in his pursuit, Edith continued on her way, head held high. She crossed the paved street, certain he would not trouble her again. The last thing she needed to add to her day was a common masher. She'd shown him that she was not receptive to the liberties his sort took!

Outside Chicksaw's Tobacco Shop, she caught Tommy's eye. With the tiniest lift of her hand, she summoned the boy to her side. Though she could ill afford it, she felt she must purchase *The Horse and Stockmen's Quarterly Bulletin*. It would never do for a lady to enter a tobacco shop, however.

"That's okay, Miss Parker," Tommy said cheerfully, when she offered him a nickel. "Pa says I can give you a copy, seeing as you're an advertiser."

"That wouldn't be right. It's defrauding your father."

But Tommy impudently stuck his hands behind his back when she tried again to hand the coin to him. "Take it, at least, and buy yourself some licorice."

Though she saw temptation and virtue war on the boy's

imperfectly washed face, he still refused the money. "My pa says that if gentlemen can't help a poor fe . . . I mean, he says poor folks should stick . . ." The dirt was drowned in a vivid blush.

Edith accepted the *Bulletin* without further quibbling. As she continued to walk on, she straightened her back until it ached. Burning with mortification, she wondered how many of the tradesmen were looking at her as she went by, pity in their eyes, charity in their hearts. What was it that Tommy would have said? That gentlemen of business must help the less fortunate. That a poor, solitary female can't hope to survive in business. That every woman should have a husband.

She tried to fight it, the urge to glance back to see who was staring at her. Like an itch that must be scratched, the urge grew worse with each passing second. Edith glanced as casually as possible over her shoulder, glad that her spotted veil hid her features so well.

The tall man in the tan suit stood talking to Tommy on the steps of his father's store. She saw the man laugh, reaching out to ruffle the boy's black hair. Something that flashed in the sunlight was passed from large hand to small. Then the man continued to follow her.

Edith faced front with an almost audible snap of her spine. Her walk military in its correctness, she approached her boardinghouse. Looking up at the squalid building, she sighed, her steps dragging, her pride deserting her. There had been no letters. No letters meant no clients. No clients meant, inevitably, no money. And no money meant another confrontation with Mr. Maginn, her landlord.

The building seemed to lean toward its near neighbor, its respectability peeling away like the old paint. Edith knew she was giving way to sentimentality in continuing to live here, instead of closer toward the center of town. This, however, had been the last home she had shared with her aunt, the late Edith Susan Parker, founder of the Farmer and Maid Matrimonial Service.

Also, in order to move she would have to come up with capital. And of capital she had thirty-five cents in an old tin box under her bed. It was enough to feed her for a day or two, upon eggs and weak tea, but not enough to pay her rent. Rent already three days overdue.

She thought longingly of the hundred-dollar bill that also reposed in the tin box. Firmly, she suppressed all such weakness. That money had been her aunt's nest egg since her own mother's death, and she had impressed upon Edith from childhood that the bill was inviolate, to be used only in the direst emergency. A temporary embarrassment of funds couldn't really be call dire—not yet.

With infinite care, Edith turned the handle of the front door and crept over the threshold. "Miss Parker!" called the stranger's voice from behind her.

"Miss Parker . . ." drawled a new male voice, slurred by excessive alcohol.

She closed the door firmly, right in the tall man's face. He'd taken his hat off and the last sight she had was of his blond hair shining in an errant beam of light piercing the gloom of the dingy street. Though she knew it was unreasonable, she felt as if she'd closed the door on the last free breath of fresh air in St. Louis.

Whatever the reverse of fresh air was, it stood before her. Mr. Maginn, in a filthy union suit and torn checked trousers, waited between her and the stairs, ogling her. His eyes were bleary, the whites yellow where they were not bloodshot.

"You got my rent, sweetheart?"

"I regret to say, Mr. Maginn, that I do not. However . . ."

"Yeah, it's been 'however' for a while now. You can't say I been giving you a rough time about it."

"No, and I appreciate your forbearance. In a few days, no doubt, my financial situation will right itself and you will receive your rent, with the extra added, of course."

Mr. Maginn missed the newel-post the first two times he tried to rest his elbow on it. He succeeded the third time and said, "You sure use your mouth pretty when you talk. I bet you can use it mighty pretty in other ways."

If it were not for his drinking, his untidiness, and the sour odor that surrounded him, Mr. Maginn might have been an attractive specimen. His dark hair had a wave in it and, before he'd become so fat, he'd undoubtedly had a striking physique.

Not even her imagination could stretch to consider him as anything but repellent.

Licking his cracked lips, Mr. Maginn leaned forward. "What about havin' a li'l drink with me? We can, er, talk about your rent. Wouldn't you like a free room, huh? I'm willing to be reasonable, if you'd be . . . willing."

He continued to lean forward, forgetting how precariously he was placed. As he toppled, Edith passed him, sweeping her skirts behind her to avoid touching him. By the time he picked himself up, cursing, from the floor, she'd escaped to the first-floor landing. She could hear him roaring a bawdy drinking song up the stairwell as she reached her own landing, the fifth.

A pathetic whisper reached her as she opened her door. "Can't you keep that bird quiet? I have such a headache. . . ."

"I'm sorry, Mrs. Webb. I'll cover Orpheus at once."

Her neighbor's door softly closed.

The bird sang even more brightly at the sight of Edith. She knew keeping a pet was a fruitless extravagance, but his yellow feathers and lively eyes were the only cheerful things she saw on most days. Knowing Mrs. Webb must be wincing at each trill, Edith picked up the cover and apologized to her canary.

"It's Mrs. Webb, Orpheus. She has another headache. They never last very long, so I'm sure you won't mind."

Reluctantly, she placed the twill cover over the cage. After a single protesting chirp, the canary went to sleep. Edith hoped Mrs. Webb would do the same.

Sitting on the bed had been an unpardonable sin when her aunt was alive. After her death, however, the armchairs had been sold at the same time Edith had moved out of the three rooms they'd shared on the second floor up to this single room. Mr. Maginn's mother had owned the boardinghouse then. She had gotten married and moved back East around the same time that Aunt Edith had been struck in the street by a brewer's wagon.

Even before removing her hat or gloves—another sin— Edith lay the *Bulletin* out on her pillow. The masthead of the magazine was boldly patriotic. Red, white, and blue banners billowed across the top, with Old Glory stuck in at various corners of the first page. The name of the publication was so ornate as to be almost unreadable. The motto proclaimed, *For Home, For Family, For Freedom*. The rest of the front cover was occupied by an engraving of a bull, as aristocratic in bearing as any duke or earl.

It was a thick publication, a special edition for the approaching breeding season, full of valuable advice and helpful advertising. But Edith passed by the notices for better breeding stock, for Jersey stock at cost, for Studebaker buggies. Not even a serious discussion of inbreeding kept her from paging on.

Usually her advertisement appeared toward the back. A small picture of her late aunt staring sternly yet benevolently through her steel-rimmed spectacles, a modest headline asking "Are you lonely?" and the text describing the service. At the bottom, in bolder type, "Write detailing your requirements with a photograph, if possible. Kindly send one dollar earnest money."

Edith searched hastily, then slowly, then with painstaking care, studying each page. Finally, she put the pages aside. The unthinkable had happened. The advertisement had not run.

"It must be there," she muttered. "I've just missed it, that's all."

Once more Edith paged through the magazine. Not once in all her twenty-three years had the Farmer and Maid Matrimonial Service advertisement failed to make its appearance in *The Horse and Stockmen's Bulletin*. She felt as though Matthew or Second Kings had suddenly gone missing from her Bible.

A tiny skittering sound made her glance toward the shrouded cage. She had hardly looked down at the *Bulletin* again, when she heard a soft brushing against the panels of her door. "Who is it?"

"Look under the door," a muffled voice replied.

On the bare wooden floor, half under her door, lay a sheet of speckled paper. Edith picked it up. On one side it was a laundry list—three shirts, a coat, and several unmentionable items belonging to the male sex. On the other side, written in smooth black ink, was a letter.

To Whom it May Concern:

Jefferson Dane is a decent, hard-working man. He has no vices, other than a drink on social occasions. A widower, he has two daughters, a fair-sized cattle ranch, and lives with his father, a war veteran. He has never, to my certain knowledge, murdered, assaulted, or spoken roughly to any woman, regardless of provocation. Sincerely . . .

The signature at the bottom of the sheet was as plain as washday cake. Jefferson Dane, Richey, Missouri.

Edith couldn't help smiling at the novelty of this reassurance. Before she opened the door, however, she hastily assumed her usual solemn expression. She must still be on her guard. A white slaver must have some charm, she reasoned, or no woman would ever go with him.

"You can't come in," she said before he had a chance to speak. "It's against the rules of the house."

"But we can't talk in the hall. I have personal matters to discuss with you and . . ."

The door opened a crack. "Please, Miss Parker! My headache," Mrs. Webb said. The single eye at the opening, all that could be seen of Mrs. Webb, looked Mr. Dane over thoroughly.

"Best thing for a headache is fresh air," he said. His grin was so impudent that Edith was shocked. That was no way to treat an invalid. But Mrs. Webb had almost smiled in answer, a thing that had never happened before.

Edith said, "I'm sorry, Mrs. Webb. Please come in, Mr. Dane. We shall just leave the door open for propriety."

Jeff halted as soon as he stepped in. If he'd stretched out his arms, he would have touched both stained walls before his hands were at the level of his shoulders. The odor of a thousand years of cooked cabbage lingered in the hot, stale air. He could feel sweat starting to prickle his skin.

Though there was a window at the end of the room, it did not appear to have ever been opened, for thick paint held it fast. It was so grimy on the outside that little light could penetrate.

Nevertheless, he saw that the little bits of furniture were threadbare and could never have been plush.

Loosening his collar with one tugging finger, Jeff said, "I'll get right to the point, Miss Parker. I'm in a fix, and I'm hoping you can get me out of it."

"What is the difficulty? You're not a former client of mine . . . you're not dissatisfied . . . ? But no, your note said you are a widower. I cannot be held responsible for anyone's . . ."

"No, I've never used your services, Miss Parker. It's really my father's idea that I'm here at all. When he saw I was having trouble deciding . . . well, he pointed out your little ad and wondered if you'd make a house-call."

"A house-call?"

He heard the suspicion reawaken in her voice. Though her veil had obscured her face in the sunny streets, and the light was bad here, he knew she must be near forty, if not more. The sort of scrawny, unappetizing bird who no doubt considered her long existence on the shelf a tribute to her choosiness, rather than admit that no man had ever wanted to catch her.

"You see, Miss Parker, I'm thinking of marrying again. And there are three women in Richey who would make good mothers for my two girls. But I can't make up my mind which one to take."

Well, he didn't think too highly of himself, Edith fumed. Which one to take, indeed! As though the objects of his matrimonial plans had nothing better to do than to wait until he deigned to decide. Why didn't he just marry each one in turn? Other men had. Bluebeard, and Henry VIII for example.

"No!" brave Lady Jessica said to the fat, leering king. "I shall never wed a man whose hands reek with the blood of his murdered queens."

Henry rubbed his ringed hands. "Marriage or the block, Lady Jessica! I'll leave the choice to you."

"I'm sorry?" Edith said with a clearing shake of her head. The oak-beamed baronial hall faded, his majesty's voice changing from a bass rumble to a medium baritone, with no trace of an English accent.

"I said, I have no problem in leaving the choice up to you. They're all nice women, good with the girls."

"Yes, you mentioned daughters."

"I've got two of 'em. Maribel, she's six, and Louise." He gave a rueful smile. "She's eight and a real handful. To tell you the truth, Miss Parker, it's because of Louise that I'm taking this step. She's growing up wild as a flag iris and I think she's going to be just as pretty. What's she going to do without a mother to tell her what's what when the boys start coming around?"

"Surely if she's only eight, you have time. You needn't leap into matrimony. It's a very serious measure."

He nodded. "I know it. But I want the girls to have time to get to know their new mama. If I bring in somebody when she's sixteen or so, there's no way Louise is ever going to listen to her or trust her."

For the first time, Edith put aside her bias against Mr. Dane. She looked at him, looked deeply. She saw a man who'd loved one woman profoundly. Her death must have beaten him in a way no living person could have done. He'd probably been so confused and hurt that he'd been unable to give his daughters the attention and affection they deserved. Now he was trying to make amends.

Edith also saw a good-looking man. Most likely still under thirty. His hair was bleached from the sun that had tanned his face. The broad shoulders under the new suit were the kind a woman could lean on and find comfort. His voice had a calming note. She thought he must be good with animals. Anything that had been hurt would turn naturally to him, knowing it would find in him the strength to do what must be done and cherishing after.

"I don't think I can help you," she said slowly. "I usually only work with letters."

"You have my letter."

"Yes, but the ladies haven't written . . . I need both in order to make a match. You see," she gestured toward the cabinets that filled one corner of the tiny room. "Someone sends me a letter. Perhaps they are . . . Well, take the last couple for whom I arranged an introduction."

Seeing interest on his face, Edith went on, only vaguely noticing that she'd suddenly become very comfortable with Mr. Dane. "He wrote to me, asking for a nicely bred girl, used to farm work. That's a fairly typical request. But Mr. Hansen wanted her to like cows. Really like them—their characters, their fondness for the people who care for them—not merely tolerate them because they are a useful animal."

"I have to admit most cows are likeable. You found someone for him?"

"Oh, yes. I'd received a letter some weeks ago from a girl, a regular churchgoer. Miss Fiske asked me to help her find a respectable husband. She was living not far from here but what she really wanted to do was get to the country. She'd lived for a time in Pennsylvania and she said her favorite part of farm life had been working with the dairy cows. She wrote so beautifully about them, I knew she would do for Mr. Hansen."

"So you work by happenstance."

"Sometimes I am very lucky."

It was more than luck, though no one ever believed the truth. Not even Aunt Edith, though at times Edith could have sworn she saw the same strong intuition at work in the older woman. Aunt Edith always claimed to have an extra-good memory, her explanation for the nearly magical way she had of matching two people exactly.

"They were married two weeks ago," Edith said. "I think they'll be very happy."

"For the first two weeks, anyway."

"Please don't be cynical. That's a very bad way to start."

Her tone was so serious that Jeff had to respect her for it. "I'm sorry," he said. "I believe in marriage. It's the happiest way to live. People weren't meant to live alone."

He glanced once more around the appalling little room. There wasn't even a carpet on the floor, or a decent picture, nothing like the gew-gaws most women collected. No luxury or ease, only a bird cage hanging from a hook. What must it be like to live in such a bleak emptiness? He hated to think how cold it must be in the winter, for he saw no way of heating it.

"By the way," he said, "we haven't talked about your

compensation. I realize you probably have a lot of calls on your time, Miss Parker . . ." Jeff hesitated for a moment, then boldly doubled the price he'd meant to pay her. "So what do you say I give you fifty dollars for the week, to make up for the other clients you'll lose. Oh, and room and board's included, of course. My dad's a heck of a fine cook."

Fifty a week? That would pay her rent in a far better boardinghouse for five months, four if she wanted to eat well. She could get away from Maginn and from being stripped naked by his eyes. At the same time, however, a warning bell sounded in her mind. "If a thing is too good to be true," her aunt had often said, "it undoubtedly isn't true."

Fifty a week was an unheard-of sum. Edith doubted the governor made that much. It was fairy-tale money, a pot of gold, and as likely to vanish with the dawn. A man determined to carry a girl into infamy might hold out such golden promises.

All her suspicions returning, Edith let her common sense override her intuition about his decency. "I'm sorry, Mr. Dane. I cannot help you. You will have to decide by yourself." Orpheus twittered as if in protest.

Mr. Dane accepted her refusal with an understanding nod. "I guess it was a lame idea, anyway. Nobody could expect a nice lady like you to travel off with a stranger. I didn't even think about a chaperone . . ." he gestured faintly toward her.

"Thank you for asking me." She put out her hand, a proper businesswomen concluding a candid discussion. Mr. Dane's handshake was firm, his fingers warm through her cotton glove.

Edith tottered when she felt the surge of energy ran up her arm. Nothing in her experience could compare to it. It was like a flash racing through her body, as though lightning had struck her. She tingled down to her toes. The excitement burned brightest in her breasts and beneath her skirts. She jerked her hand free of his engulfing one.

"Are you all right?" Mr. Dane asked.

A slow tide of color came and went in her cheeks, as though she had been swallowed and released by a wave. "Perfectly fine."

He seemed unchanged, untouched by any strange emotional experience. She watched him go out. In the hall, he stopped and turned back. "Listen, I'm staying at the St. Simeon. If you change your mind, you can get in touch with me there. I hope you will come, Miss Parker. I need somebody on my side."

"Your side?"

"Everybody else . . . those that know about it . . . everybody's got their favorite horse running in the Dane stakes. I can't get an honest opinion from anybody, not even Dad. If I got an impartial judge, maybe I could start wooing wholeheartedly."

"I'm sorry," she said mechanically. "It's not possible."

After he was gone, Edith tried to busy herself with little tasks, sewing on buttons, filing, writing notes of reminder. She knew she would have to go down to the *Bulletin* and face Mr. Steadman, to confront him on why the advertisement she relied on was missing from this quarter's edition.

Her heart failed at the very idea of going all the way down to Grand Boulevard instead of dealing with the problem by mail. There wasn't time to use the mail, though. If Mr. Steadman was fair, he might refund part of what she'd paid. If he wasn't, she could always sit on his doorstep and waste away.

Edith straightened her hat to a nicety in the crooked mirror. Trying to wear her aunt's sternest expression, she went down the stairs. Stepping as quietly as a cat, she edged past Mr. Maginn's open door. The landlord sprawled in a soiled armchair, his head back and mouth open. A few flies hung over him as they would hover over refuse in the street.

A board creaked beneath Edith's foot. Maginn's snuffling snore broke and she heard him grunt. As quietly and as quickly as she could, Edith escaped before he awoke from his stupor.

To take the omnibus meant paying the fare. If she walked to the *Bulletin*'s office she would save two precious nickels, but she'd surely use a quarter's worth of shoe leather. Her lips tight, Edith chose the cash.

Despite her concentration on surface matters, Edith knew that deep down her mind was busy with something else. What had been that strange connection she'd felt to Mr. Dane? Her hands still felt sparkly, like the Fourth of July. He was in her mind during the entire walk to the business district, more vivid than any champion her imagination had ever created.

2

"IT'S THIS NEW management," Mr. Steadman said, blowing an exasperated puff of air through his bushy mustache. "They don't know what they're doing yet."

"I see. Still, Mr. Steadman, that doesn't . . ."

"Several of our advertisers had complained about it. One feed company had their headline matched up with a recipe for mixed pickles. They became awfully shirty about it."

"At least some portion of their advertisement ran, sir. Mine, on the other hand, wasn't even there incorrectly."

He only shrugged.

"I have paid in advance, Mr. Steadman, for a service which I have not received. Surely you can refund some of what I paid."

"All I can offer you, Miss Parker, is a free ad next time. I'm sorry, but our cash picture's pretty bad right now. This new management, like I said. 'Course, you could take us to court and try to recover damages, but after all, Farmer and Maid and the *Bulletin* have been working together for twenty-odd years. It'd be a shame to ruin that association over a simple mistake."

Edith saw the justice of the managing editor's viewpoint. Not to mention that there was no way she could afford an expensive court case. She stood up from the hard wooden chair he'd offered her when she'd come in. "Thank you for your time, Mr. Steadman. I trust this mistake will not happen again."

"You be sure and come to me if there's ever another problem. I had a lot of respect for that aunt of yours." He transferred his smoldering cigar from his right hand to his left and took her by the elbow. "I'll show you out."

To Edith's burning shame, her stomach growled loudly as they walked into the lobby. Immediately, she began to talk, to cover up any further embarrassing noises. "Your life must be very interesting, Mr. Steadman. I know all my clients look up to the *Bulletin* and feel it's an important part of their lives. Tell me, how do you . . ."

Despite her efforts, the rumbling that echoed through the lobby had the effect of thunder. She felt as though every head in the place must be turning in her direction.

"Look at the time," Mr. Steadman said. "Can't I make it up to you, Miss Parker, by taking you to lunch? There's a nice little place around the corner."

The thought of food was enough to make Edith's head swim. But to enter a public restaurant with a man she hardly knew smacked of that dishonorable life her aunt had always warned her against. One false step, apparently, was all it took.

"You're very good, Mr. Steadman. But I have an appointment and am already late. Good day."

The acoustics in the lobby of the *Bulletin*'s office must have been especially good, for even though she was some distance away, she clearly heard the editor murmur, "Poor little lady." Her cheeks were crimson for half her walk home. Had Mr. Steadman seen through her pretense?

Mr. Maginn's absence from his usual perch by the stairs seemed to indicate that he was supervising his seldom-seen sister in the cooking of the noon meal. Not having paid her rent, Edith was naturally cut off from dining at the communal table. Though the food was mostly thin soups and watery porridge, the dirty, sticky table seemed like an oasis of fine cuisine, forever beyond her reach.

The stairs were impossibly steep. She rested at the third landing, her gloved hand against the wall. Her knees felt weak, and her head went round and round like a calliope. She could almost hear the cheerful, vulgar organ music. Knowing she mustn't collapse here, she staggered up the last two flights of stairs.

Though she longed just to lie down for a little while, Edith knew she must not take the risk of falling asleep and missing the four o'clock mail. All her hopes were pinned to that delivery. She owed three dollars for rent, but even a single new client would mean she could eat, and eat well.

The dry soda crackers that she shared with Orpheus—his cage open since Mrs. Webb never missed a meal—were a poor substitute for a luncheon. Eating them with pride made them no more palatable.

She wondered what Mr. Dane would be eating. The St. Simeon Hotel was known for the excellence of its table. Or perhaps he was having a business meeting at one of the fine restaurants by the river. Edith suppressed a groan and tried to think of something unconnected with food. But as all roads lead to Rome, all subjects, sooner or later, led her to meals.

After the three crackers, all she dared take from her store, Edith took up some of the letters she had in her files. Men and women wrote to the service in about equal numbers. As things had turned out, Miss Fiske had been the last unmatched client in the files. Otherwise, Mr. Hansen would have had to wait for some lonely girl to write in before finding his mate.

The letters were all the same. The circumstances might vary widely, from orphans to the overlooked child in a large family, from independent persons to those who were forced to rely on the largess of some relative, from the frantically youthful to the ripeness of maturity—which did not necessarily indicate the age of the writer.

All the letters had at their heart the feeling that the world was meant for couples. Whether the letter stated that the writer was looking for a spouse or a parent for children (already gotten or yet unborn) a lover or a housekeeper, each made clear that the loneliness of the writer was increased by the observation that every being on earth went more happily as one of a pair.

The time until three-thirty passed pleasantly enough. She meant to leave in plenty of time, for she would have to walk very slowly to keep from exhausting herself. It was only when Edith tried to stand that she found the weakness in her legs had not passed off. Sitting on the edge of her bed, she felt so weak that she leaned her head on her hand and closed her sore eyes.

In the dungeon beneath the castle, the only light came from smoking torches in the wall. The captive maiden would have been glad to shout defiance to her guards, were they not, like all the inhabitants, feasting in the great hall above. Now that there was no one to see, she could give way to tears. One by one they dripped from between the fingers that hid her eyes.

When Edith looked up, the small wooden clock on the wall told her it was five minutes past four. Distressed, for the post office closed at five o'clock, Edith knew she'd have to hurry. In her haste, she half-fell down the last several stairs, twisting her ankle. She hopped on her other foot for a moment, biting her lips to keep back a cry.

The crash brought out Mr. Maginn, like a malevolent cuckoo from a shabby clock. Edith realized he was at least partially sober and she bit her lip. While he was drunk, she could deal with him fairly well. Sober was another matter.

"Well, well, Miss Edith, you won't flee so easy this time."

"Mr. Maginn, you'll have to pardon me. I'm late and I . . ."

"Mighty hoity-toity, aren't you—for someone who's owing back rent? Come on in here, and let's have a little talk about that . . . and other things."

"Really, Mr. Maginn, I can't right now. If you'll just let me go, I'll have your rent when I . . . at least, I hope I will."

But he stood in the doorway, staring at her. He beckoned her over by crooking his fat white forefinger. Edith felt she had but two choices—to go to him or to run away. As each step was a shooting pain, she had in fact no choice at all.

Trying not to limp, she walked into the bright, seemingly clean apartment. Despite the fact that each surface was dusted and every pillow plumped, a smell lingered in the room, as though the exhalings of Mr. Maginn never really faded. The smell caught Edith by the throat. She tried to breathe shallowly.

"What am I to do with you?" he asked, coming closer. His tone was a travesty of the paternal.

"I hope to pay you this afternoon, Mr. Maginn. I am on my way to the post office and I feel confident . . ."

He ran his hand down her arm, insinuating himself closer. "You're a lovely thing, me darlin'. All ripe and delicious, like peaches and cream."

"You're too kind," she said, recoiling. One of his teeth must be rotten. His breath would choke a horse. "As I said . . ."

"Now, it don't seem right that you should have to struggle so. I've had me eye on you for some little time, sweetness. Things are bad with you. I could be willing to make life that much easier for you."

His arm was about her waist. Despite her hand firm against his shoulder, his strength was slowly but certainly bringing her closer to his spongy body.

"Say you leave your door unlocked tonight," he whispered wetly in her ear. "Say you be happy to see me. Then I'd be more than happy to make your dreams come true. It's not right such a beauty should be sleeping all alone."

"Please, Mr. Maginn. . . ."

"Oh, yes, my lovely, you'll say please. And thank you, Ringo, you'll be saying pretty as you can."

She was bending away from him as completely as she could, her body stiff and tight. The sound of his tongue churning across his thick lips filled her ears and his moon face was so close to hers she could have counted the pockmarks. Hardly knowing what she did, she clouted him on the side of his head.

With a yowl, he started back. Edith fell, further jarring her bad ankle. As she pushed up painfully from the polished floor, she saw his face go crimson. "I'll pay you back for that," he swore, rubbing his ear. "Tonight, I'll pay you back."

A timid voice called from the back of the apartment, "Are you all right, Ringo?"

"Mind your own business, Evvie."

Edith heard the slap of carpet slippers fading along the hall. She brushed off the back of her full skirt and straightened her hat. Looking at her landlord with all the haughtiness she could find, she said, "I have nothing more to say, Mr. Maginn. I shall have your rent this afternoon."

"It don't matter now if you pay or don't," he panted. "I'll be outside your door tonight. You better let me in, if you know what's good for you."

"What you suggest would not be good for me, not in the least. I will not open my door to you."

"You'll do it, my lovely." He didn't try to touch her again, for which she was grateful. She already felt as though slime covered her skin.

"I don't think so."

"You'll let me in . . . let me do whatever I want, or you'll be on the sidewalk come Monday."

Edith tried to keep her fear from showing in her face, but she knew she failed when she heard Maginn's hateful chuckle. He threatened her with the one thing she feared above all else. To be on the street, destitute. She could imagine it so clearly.

He smiled like an inferior devil. "Now you know I wouldn't want to evict you. See reason and I'll let you stay. That's fair, isn't it? You scratch my back . . . who's to say? If you're nice to me, I might be tempted to make it legal. You and me . . . I could see us living down here, all right and tight. A nice little wifie's better than an idiot sister any day."

Maginn didn't try to stop her when she walked out. She returned to her room, her ankle bothering her less than her conscience. She argued that this was as dire a moment as she'd ever faced. Trapped between two downward paths, surely it would be all right to use the money. She took it out and tucked it away in her bag.

Much ashamed, Edith admitted that if she must prostitute herself, she would rather it be to the handsome Jefferson Dane than to the repulsive Maginn. If only she could be sure that Mr. Dane's proposal was authentic, she would seize upon it in a moment. She thought of his warm brown eyes and almost believed. Shaking the thought away, she blessed the hundred-dollar bill.

Though her aunt had told her again and again never to use the money, Edith doubted such a situation had ever come up for her. A solid woman, a Christian woman, but not ever one to tempt the male sex, as she herself had admitted.

"You are a different story, Edith," her aunt had often said. "The gentlemen admire the slender yet elegant figure. And you do have pretty hair. I tell you these things not that you should be vain of them, but so you will be wary. Do not talk to strange men in the street. Don't tempt them with sly looks or a seductive walk. A lady keeps her eyes on the street and her feet on a narrow path. Men are such . . . susceptible creatures."

Edith had followed all her aunt's advice. Yet it seemed she had tempted Mr. Maginn. Though Edith felt sure he had not had very far to fall.

She wondered again about Mr. Dane. Did his pleasing exterior hide a heart of gold, or of clay? Did none of the three ladies of his choice tempt him to fall? What was the matter with them that they didn't take advantage of the ease with which a man could be fascinated?

At the post office, her heart leapt high when she saw the sharp edge of an envelope through the small square of glass. In her eagerness, she misdialed twice before she got the right combination. Withdrawing the letter, heedless of decorum, she ripped open the letter. No money fell out. She shook the page vigorously, and then the envelope. Nothing.

While waiting in line to break her hundred-dollar bill, Edith read the letter. It came from a client, now happily married in Topeka. For once, the joyful contents had no power to raise Edith's spirits.

The clerk at the counter was a different man, with scraggly side-whiskers and a frown. He barely glanced at the highly engraved piece of blue paper.

"No good," he said. "Next!"

"What? No . . . no good?"

"The Braxton Bank of Louisiana closed five years ago, lady. That's nothing but waste paper now. Next!"

The woman behind Edith elbowed her way forward. "Two stamps, please."

Edith couldn't move. Her aunt must have known about the bank. How could she leave a worthless inheritance? Edith didn't want to think all her legacies might be valueless.

The woman turned from the counter, nearly running over Edith. "Really! Eavesdropping on my business!"

The tone, rather than the words, reached Edith. Hardly knowing what she did, she stumbled away from the counter.

Walking home, her ankle aching bitterly inside her high-buttoned shoe, she felt raindrops fall out of a clear sky. One by one, they spotted the bosom of her dress. It was only when people turned to stare after her on the street that she realized she was weeping in public. She clawed down her veil.

Her head spinning from hunger, Edith climbed the worn steps to the peeling front door of the boardinghouse. A sour smell of burnt potatoes reached her and made her mouth water. Even something charred would be better than nothing.

She paused by the Maginns' door, which was slightly ajar. As she raised her hand to knock, she thought, "I can't do what he wants, but I could beg. . . . Evvie likes me; she's talked to me once or twice. She told me about the boy who wanted to marry her. Maybe she'd give me something."

On the other side of the door Mrs. Webb said loudly, "But you promised me!"

Mr. Maginn laughed coarsely and cruelly. "You didn't think I meant it? I knew you were stupid but not that stupid."

Edith shrank back, her fist pressed to her chest. She couldn't believe what she was hearing.

"It's that girl in the room next to mine, isn't it? Her and that miserable canary. I should have known. First you leave Carrie Nester for me and now me for . . . her."

"Well, it's not the canary. I can tell you that. Besides, what makes you think good old Carrie was the first? There's lots of chances for a fella living in a place like this. Lonely women . . ." There was something so hatefully superior in his tone that Edith was not surprised to hear the sound of a slap.

The snarl that followed the impact sent a thrill of fear down Edith's spine. In a voice scarcely human, she heard Maginn say, "Don't you . . . don't you . . ."

"Stop! You're hurting me," Mrs. Webb sobbed. Perhaps she stumbled, for she gave a half-scream suddenly cut off. Edith looked up and down the hall. Should she go for help? Should she break in and save Mrs. Webb?

There came some soft, confused sounds next. Edith couldn't make out what was happening. Then she heard Mrs. Webb's pouting voice again. "You almost broke my arm . . . brute."

"Ah, but you're a rare armful, m'lovely."

"And you're not interested in that stuck-up snip, are you?"

"Never mind about her."

"But Ringo . . ."

"It won't make no difference to you and me. So long as your husband is gone for good . . ."

"I can divorce him any time, and then we could make it legal." She seemed to be offering some rare treat.

"Legal? I can't marry any divorced woman. The Church . . ."

"Why do you care? It's this you should be wanting."

Ringo Maginn's voice thickened. "I do. God, shut the door if you're going to . . . Oh, God."

Edith fled.

It seemed only a few minutes later that she sat up in her bed, the clothing she'd never removed twisted about her body. She had no memory of lying down, only of dreaming she was on board a ship. The bed seemed to mimic the motion of a ship even now, heaving high and dipping low. She put her feet on the floor and groaned, her eyes burning.

Orpheus sang loudly, despite his covered cage. The frantic note in his song penetrated her exhausted sense. Coughing, Edith tried to stand. A haze lingered before her eyes. There had been cannons in her dream, white-hot mouths belching forth smoke and deadly iron. Was she still asleep? For she could still see the smoke.

As her little bird sang furiously, Edith realized that this choking smoke was no phantom following her from a nightmare but harsh reality. The boardinghouse was on fire.

3

JEFFERSON DANE AWOKE to someone knocking at his hotel-room door. "What is it?"

"Mr. Dane, sir? It's Josh. The hall boy?"

Sighing, Jeff sat up, disoriented. He could distinguish the light curtains fluttering in the breeze from the opened window but that was all. It was enough, though, to lead him to the door.

He jerked it open. "If this is the way your hotel treats its guests, I'll be pulling out in the morning."

Seeing the hall boy blinking at him in alarm, Jeff moderated his tone. "What's up, Josh?"

"Please, Mr. Dane, sir, Mr. Dilworthy sent me up, sir. He's in an awful stew, sir."

"If he's drunk it's no reason to wake up half the hotel. Tell him to sleep it off. Or pour a gallon of coffee down his gullet. It's nothing to do with me."

The image of the austere desk clerk stewed to the gills brought an impudent smile to the hall boy's round face, as Jeff had meant it to. "I wish he was tight—I shore do. But that's not what's the matter. It's this crazy girl."

"What girl?"

"She's down at the desk. And, boy, she's something. Looks like she was dragged around some, and her hat's on backwards, smuts and soot all over her, and . . . oh, yeah . . . she's got a canary in a cage. Keeps asking for you."

"What time is it?" Jeff yawned, glancing over the boy's head at the flickering gas jets that illuminated the hall.

"'Bout half-past twelve. I was just about to get some shut-eye myself. So, you going to come on down, sir? Mr. Dilworthy says . . ."

"I can guess," Jeff answered, having taken the desk clerk's measure when he'd checked in. Officious, nosy, and suspicious, Dilworthy would be just the fellow to take care of a drunk or a lunatic. The hour was late, and he could feel sleep tugging at him like an impatient woman.

"Tell Dilworthy to slip the gal a couple of dollars. She'll probably take it and go. I'll give it back to him tomorrow."

"Okay," Josh said with a nod. "He was getting ready to call the police but he figured maybe you knew her."

"Doesn't sound like it. Good night."

"Good night, sir." The boy, absurd in his tight waistcoat and too-long pants, headed down the hall.

"Hey, Josh? Don't wake me up again for anything less than a war or an election, okay?"

Closing the door, Jeff stretched for a moment before padding back to bed. The talk about the Texas cattle fever had gone on since lunch, his fellow Missouri cattlemen ranting and raving about the general cussedness of the Texan in general. He himself had always run a clean herd, mostly by keeping the Texans out of whatever means necessary, even with a gun on occasion. He thanked providence and his parents once again for putting his ranch halfway between Sedalia and St. Louis. It didn't often pay the Texas men to come that far out of their route—not yet.

Jeff lay his long body down on the bed, his arms flung wide. Try as he might, however, he couldn't find a comfortable spot. He'd slept better in the woods, with the owls hooting and the nightjars rattling. There'd been that time he'd awakened in the peace of a perfect, dew-moist morning, only to have a rising crow shoot a stream of foul . . .

Turning onto his side, Jeff wondered why he couldn't stop thinking about birds. Where had he heard a canary today? A canary in a cage. He couldn't recall, but it probably wasn't important anyhow. Not as important as sleep.

Five minutes later, fully dressed, Jeff stepped into the small lobby. "Where's the girl?"

"Really, Mr. Dane, I must protest. We are a respectable hotel with a high-class clientele. Asking me to pay off a . . ."

His words were cut off by a brown fist suddenly tightening his skinny tie. "Where did she go?" Jeff asked, spacing each word out.

"Over there," the man gasped, his hands flopping like dying fish.

Dropped none too gently, Mr. Dilworthy said, rubbing his throat, "Really, Mr. Dane! Roughhousing is not admired at *this* hotel. And as for your lady 'friend,' she really can't stay in the lobby all night. You'll have to ask her to go elsewhere."

But Jeff was already looking down the lobby. Miss Parker had her back turned, but he recognized the covered birdcage. Something had driven her out of her boardinghouse and into the night to call on a man. Jeff knew it had to be something big.

"Miss Parker?" he asked, coming up behind her. "What's the . . ."

He almost bit his tongue. When the girl turned, he beheld a wide pair of eyes the color of twilight in a spiritual face that could haunt a hardheaded man's dreams. As for the rest, she was pale and thin in her gray dress with the ugly pattern, her dark auburn hair pulled ruthlessly into a low tight bun. A few strands of hair had escaped and trailed in her reddened eyes. One small hand held the birdcage by the ring in the top.

"I beg your pardon," he said, backing up. "I thought . . ."

"Oh, Mr. Dane!" She flung out her hand as though in supplication, her voice rough. When she closed her eyes, Jeff could tell she was struggling to regain some composure.

"Here now," he said, catching her hand and chafing it gently. "You come over here and sit down."

She let him lead her to a plush sofa before she pulled her hand away. "I mustn't. My dress . . ."

"What is all that?"

"Soot, I think."

Jeff saw that what he'd thought was a pattern on the gray stuff of her dress was in fact a scattering of tiny holes burned into the fabric.

"Never mind the damn sofa," he said. "What's happened to you?"

As calmly as though she were discussing ancient history, she said, "My boardinghouse has burned down. Orpheus awakened me in time. I don't really remember how I got . . . out."

"My Lord," he said, shocked, urging her once more to seat herself. "Hey, Dilworthy," he called, turning his head to glare at the desk clerk. "Bring me a shot of something strong. Whiskey, brandy, whatever you've got. Hurry up."

Mr. Dilworthy pursed his lips as though quelling thoughts he dared not utter. However, he brought out a bottle from beneath the counter and poured a liberal dose into a clean glass. "Not a saloon," he muttered as he put the tray down on the table.

"Here, now, Miss Parker. Get that down."

"Oh, no, sir. I promised my aunt I'd never touch spirits."

"It'll do you good." He held the glass out.

Edith took a taste, then licked her lips like a cat. "It's dreadful!" she said in surprise. "I always thought it must be marvelous, so many people indulge in it to excess."

"It's only nasty going down. On the inside, it's fine."

Screwing up her face, Edith tossed back the liquid in a single, burning gulp. She strangled, coughed, and wiped her burning eyes. After a moment, she became conscious of a glow like a hot coal in her interior.

"I do feel warmer. When the fire engines came, I got sprayed and I thought I'd taken a chill."

"Tell me what happened. How did your home burn down?"

Edith felt oddly moved by his concern. She had not even dared to hope that Mr. Dane would receive her kindly. But there had been no other place to go. "Evvie—my landlord's sister—said it was a grease fire in the kitchen. It started so quickly she didn't have a chance to ring the alarm bell. The firemen think everyone escaped."

"When was this?"

"About ten o'clock."

"Wasn't that kind of late to be cooking?"

"She said her brother liked to eat fried potatoes in bed." Edith shuddered delicately.

Jeff saw her reaction and hid a grin. "But you're not hurt. You must be born lucky, Miss Parker."

"I don't feel lucky," she said, catching back a hiccup that was nearly a sob. Pressing her fingers to her lips, she looked at him in alarm. "I beg your pardon," she murmured.

"Never mind. I guess most of your stuff is . . . gone?"

To her shame, tears came into her eyes. All the letters, everything she had of her aunt's, even her attempts to write down her daydreams, all gone in the roaring inferno that carelessness had made of a decrepit building.

Edith thrust her chin out and said resolutely, "If your offer is still open, Mr. Dane, I'd like to accept that job."

"That's very good of you. But we'll talk it over in the morning." He stood up. His legs seemed to go on forever, the tall boots he wore extending almost to his knees.

Edith didn't move. After one quick glimpse up the length of his body, she looked down at her clasped hands. "I'd prefer to discuss our business now."

"It's late, and you've been through a year's worth of trouble. I'll get you a room and. . . ."

It would be so easy to let him be masterful, to give all her troubles over to him. But she couldn't possibly allow him to take on her as a responsibility. She must stand for her own.

"I don't wish to be stubborn, Mr. Dane. But I would prefer to discuss our business now."

Jeff smiled, though she didn't see. The little thing was as nervous as a bird at a convention of cats on reducing diets. She was pretty, far prettier and much younger than he'd guessed at their first meeting. Her thickly lashed eyes were slightly slanted, wider at the edge than near her nose, giving her a startled look.

He studied her. Surprising himself, he found a gradual anger washing over him, getting worse by the second. What had the girl been doing to herself?

She was not naturally this thin. Her skin was stretched too tightly over her cheekbones, and he'd seen wristbones that stuck out like hers before. She couldn't be more than twenty. The desiccation he'd assumed to be the natural look of a dried-up spinster was plain ordinary starvation. If Miss Parker had eaten a square meal within the last week, he would breakfast tomorrow on his plainsman's hat, without gravy.

"All right," he said gently. "You're going to come to Richey with me. I reckon we'll say you're my distant cousin, come out to look after the girls."

"I don't care for subterfuge," she began. When he started to explain it was to save her reputation, she said, "I appreciate that. In this instance, I will agree to mislead people."

"Good. 'Course, once I ask the girl to marry me, you can head on back here. I'll pay your fare both ways, naturally."

"That seems acceptable," she said, surprising him by not arguing the point. Jeff saw her sway, worn to the bone no doubt. He wanted to pick her up—she plainly weighed less than an orphan calf—and carry her away to a place of safety and comfort. His hands fairly twitched with the yearning.

Then she seemed to snap to attention, driving exhaustion back by an effort of will. He had to admire her, even while he deplored her stubbornness. Any other woman would have fallen apart by now. He almost wished she would crumble. It would be much easier to sweep up the pieces than tiptoe around the cracks.

"I wonder . . ." She hesitated, and flicked her eyes up to glance at his face. "It is a great imposition, Mr. Dane, and I apologize for the necessity. Might I have an advance on my compensation, do you think? I have no clothes now."

"My pleasure, Miss Parker. But that'll have to wait 'til the bank opens."

"Oh, dear, I didn't think of that. And tomorrow's Sunday." She glanced down at her spoiled dress, and Jeff leaned forward, certain her tears were about to flow at last. Instead she glanced up with something like bravery and said, "What cannot be cured must be endured, eh, Mr. Dane?"

She swayed again and blinked rapidly. "Alcohol is very curious. I'm glad I had the chance . . ." Without changing expression Edith slid slowly off the sofa.

The sun was on the wrong side. Edith wondered if she had somehow turned herself completely around so that her head now lay at the foot of her narrow bed. But how she could have managed it without falling off and waking herself up was a mystery that she could not solve.

Orpheus sang in the sunny window with a merry abandon that Edith did not recall ever hearing from him before. She turned her head to see him. The pillowcase beneath her cheek did not scratch, or smell like the raw yellow soap Evvie Maginn used for the tenants' laundry. In the window was a rosy red lamp, the edge of the shade alive with hanging prisms that sent rainbows dancing and dodging around the cheerfully papered walls.

Edith lay still and stared in wonder. An angel must have transported her from a dingy boardinghouse room to a chamber straight out of a fantasy. "If this is a dream," she said out loud, "the next thing I hope to smell is bacon, eggs and coffee. And if there should be strawberry preserves for the toast, I shall know that I have died and gone to Heaven."

It could not have been more than a moment later that a rap sounded on her door. When it opened, the first thing that entered was the soft smell of eggs and the stronger, exotic fragrance of China tea. The bacon was there too, still sizzling.

"Over by the window, then, miss?" asked the bright-eyed boy carrying the tray.

"Thank you," Edith answered. She'd never expected her angel to have freckles. Before she could ask any questions or even sit up, the boy opened the wardrobe. Edith could see a brown dress hanging there.

"I hope the clothes are going to be okay," he said. "I borrowed 'em from my sister and she's barmaid at the General Washington. They pick their barmaids by the pound down there." He grinned, showing a gap where his eyetooth ought to be, as he sauntered toward the door.

Before he vanished, he said, "Mr. Dane said I'm to take care of you personal. So, you need anything, just holler down the hall for Josh and I'll be right 'long."

"Thank you, Josh," Edith said, but he was gone.

As she pushed back the covers, she realized it was a good thing she'd not sat up. The only item between her and the bedclothes was the petticoat she wore next to her skin. She had no memory of where her other two might be, though she hoped they might be with her dress. She also noticed that she was clean, all the ashes and soot washed away.

Though she knew she should solve the mysteries of this wonderland, Edith counseled herself that she could just as well puzzle out the answer while she ate. The bed seemed reluctant to allow her to leave the solace of its softness, for she must have been caught back three times before she finally freed herself.

It was not the fire or her losses that she recalled first. Rather it was the remembrance of considerate hands, male hands. They had been beautiful and long fingered, like a prince's. But a prince who had come down in the world and been forced to make his own way: they'd been rough with calluses and marked by scars. Edith remembered vague images of kissing those hands in gratitude as her tears splashed on the brown skin. But no . . . that had to be part of a dream.

After eating everything but the design on the china, Edith washed her face and hands with the water in a rosebud-pink ewer and basin. The towel was as soft as the bed linen. She realized this was a very good hotel, dedicated to their guests' comfort. There was even groundsel and clean water in Orpheus' cage.

Tired out from dressing, Edith sat again on the deep armchair near the window. Her head felt light, and she lay back to watch the crystals dance in the sunlight.

"Hey now, are you asleep?"

Mr. Dane stood over her. Edith started, and sat up. "I didn't hear you come in."

"I stood outside and knocked for what must of been five minutes. Are you okay?"

"Yes, I'm fine, thanks to you." He looked away as though to refuse her thanks, but Edith persisted. "If you hadn't been so kind last night, I don't know what would have become of me. You must have guessed that I had fallen into rather dire straits."

"You mean your boardinghouse burning down? That might have happened to anybody."

"Yes, but . . ."

"Besides, you thanked me plenty last night." He tugged on his earlobe as he smiled sideways out the window. "There were some complaints about it."

"Complaints? You are joking, of course."

"Nope. You see, it was kind of late and you were singing. A few folks stuck their heads out and asked me to ask you to . . ."

"Singing?" Edith stared up at him, astonished. "You *must* be joking, Mr. Dane. I don't sing."

"I don't know much about music, but you sounded all right to me." Jeff looked down and saw she was seriously distressed. "It's all right. Everybody understood."

"Understood what? That I was intoxicated?" Edith stood up and stared straight into his amused brown eyes. "I never touched liquor before last night, Mr. Dane. I trust that is clearly understood. I would never have tasted it at all if not that in my distress I drank it without realizing what I was doing."

Though she was still far too thin, Jeff was amazed at the difference a good night's rest and a little food made in her. Her cheeks were naturally meant to be as rosy as they were now with the flags flying in them. Her eyes had snap and sparkle that lent a new dimension of charm to the deep blue. And her voice was not actually a meek whisper but full of mellow, well-rounded music. Any other woman might have made her lightest word an invitation with such a voice, but Jeff couldn't imagine Miss Parker leading a man on with it. She probably didn't know how.

"I know you don't drink, Miss Parker. And you didn't do anything under the influence that could be called into question. You thanked me for my help and went right off to sleep."

"Ah, yes," she said, her eyes cast down. "How did I . . . this morning I awoke wearing nothing but . . ."

"I helped you out of your things," Jeff said. "And wiped you down with a damp towel. You didn't seem to have any burns. You were lucky."

Her eyes flashed up again. In them, he could read doubt and alarm, the same expression they'd worn during his first interview with her. Remembering, however, the emotions that he'd known when seeing her patched undergarments, he had no qualms about saying, "Don't worry, Miss Parker. I'd have done as much for a sunburned cowhand. Besides, I've been married."

"I haven't been." Edith was mollified by his comparing her to a cowboy, until she thought about it for a moment. Though she knew she was no beauty, she didn't appreciate being likened to a saddle tramp. A little stifled enthusiasm on Mr. Dane's part would at least salvage her pride.

"What song?" she asked suddenly.

"I'm sorry?"

"What song did I sing?"

"I don't know," he said, lifting his broad shoulders. "It was in some foreign language. The only word I got was '*amore*' 'cause you kept on repeating it."

"*Amore?*"

"That means 'love,' doesn't it?" At her thoughtful nod, he said, "You were singing pretty loud. I liked it, though, no matter what those ladies had to say about it."

"Ladies? Never mind," she said, holding up her hand. "I don't really want to know. It's just odd that . . ."

"What is?"

"I've been told I cannot sing. My aunt loved music and thought . . . she even sent me for lessons. But I have no voice."

"Sounds all right to me."

She shook her head. "No singing voice. No magic. That's what the teacher said. No magic."

For weeks after that insult, Edith had busied herself with dreams of standing on a stage, bowing to the plaudits of an enraptured audience, and then tossing her flowers into the lap of an ancient Mr. Fowler. He would have to admit at last that he was wrong. But he had been right.

"Whiskey does strange things, Miss Parker."

"I never intend to find out more than I have already. So tell me," she said suddenly, finding this conversation to have become unpleasantly personal, "what are your plans now?"

"Well, I think the first thing should be to get you some new clothes. Then, we'll get on to Richey in a day or two."

"A day or two? We're not leaving at once?"

"I still have some business to get through. I would also say that you need a rest."

"I?" she asked. Jeff tried not to let her see how much it tickled him when she drew herself up to her full height. No more than five foot five in the barmaid's shoes, she only came up to the buttonhole in his lapel. "I assure you I'm perfectly well."

"Maybe. But I've seen people through something shocking like a fire before. You may find out you get out of sorts and tired easily."

Recalling how much dressing had tired her, Edith closed her lips tightly over the protest she was on the point of making. With a half-smile, she admitted, "To be perfectly frank, all I really want to do is tumble into bed again."

Even that, Jeff noted, had been said in perfect innocence. She hadn't flirted with her eyes, making more of the words than a simple declaration of fact. She wanted to get into bed and never hinted that he might be welcome to join her.

"Go right ahead," he said. "I've got a few things to do yet this morning. What do you say I come back around eleven? There's got to be a store open someplace, even on Sunday."

"I'm afraid there won't be. The laws . . . These clothes will do me until mine are laundered."

For the first time, Mr. Dane looked embarrassed. He rubbed the back of his neck under the sharp edge of his blond hair. "I'm afraid your dress . . . fell apart when Mr. Dilworthy took it to be washed. Your other stuff . . . petticoats and stuff . . . will be ready later today."

"I see. Well, it was rather old." Inwardly, Edith found herself rejoicing. Never to have to see that old gray dress again! Never to have to take it in or let it out! Never to have to make it over and over so that the dingiest places were hidden!

She had worn it for seven years and hadn't liked it when her aunt had paid to have it made up. Gray was serviceable, and always appropriate, she said. The fact that it drained all the color from Edith's eyes and gave her hair a greenish cast was a plus rather than a minus in the elder lady's view.

Even as she sighed in relief, Edith knew her aunt's wisdom would prevail. At the department store tomorrow she might look with longing at dashing silks and brilliant satins, and think of herself arrayed in a velvet gown, a long train sweeping behind her. In the end, though, she would undoubtedly find herself once more with a gray poplin dress, with neither ribbons nor frills to soften its hard lines. After all, she would have to spend only what Mr. Dane agreed to advance her.

She was bringing up this subject when he glanced at the gold railroad watch he'd hauled up from his vest pocket. "I'd better be getting on," he said.

Edith held out her hand. "I want to thank you again for your kindness to me."

"Pshaw," he muttered, looking down at the little fingers resting in his rough paw. "I'll see you for lunch, all right?"

"I'll be ready."

"I bet you're always punctual. I'm usually late, so don't bother coming down. I'll call for you." He paused in the doorway. "Get some rest, Miss Parker."

She nodded brightly, her figure in the too large dress appearing even thinner than it was. The color had already faded from her cheeks, though the shadows under her eyes had lessened with the morning. Jeff went out and closed the door. For a moment, he remained there, his hand still on the doorknob.

He remembered with what radiant eyes she'd looked at him last night, her silky hair fanned out across her pillow. Maybe it was the whiskey that had turned her blue eyes to fire. She'd murmured something about not minding his being a white slaver, words that conjured up images he tried to forget.

His self-control and his scruples had held strong while he undid the row of buttons that ran over her front. He'd given her petticoat-muffled body no more than an idle glance, yet the look in her eyes, the softness of her full-lipped mouth, had nearly overmastered him. It had been worse when he'd run a wet washcloth over her limbs and face.

Miss Parker, spinster, had not known she was all suggestion as she lay there, but Jeff had known it. His long-celibate body had urged him to act. He had fought that impulse with cold water once in the safety of his room.

He'd do his best to forget the way she looked then. Yet, as he walked down the stairs, he knew he'd relive in his dreams the moment when he'd felt her soft lips moving on his hand. It tingled even now. He thrust it deep into his coat pocket as though that could extinguish the memory.

4

THE WHITE BOXES arrived at ten-thirty. Josh brought them up, his hands by his waist, his lantern chin holding the topmost box safely down. Moving only the upper part of his face, he asked Edith, "Where do you want 'em?"

"Want what?"

He raised an eyebrow. "This stuff, course!"

The boxes in the middle shifted. As though propelled upwards by a powerful shove, the boxes flew out of Josh's hands. Falling, they disgorged tissue paper and cloth.

"Tarnation! Well, here they are. I'll go get the rest."

"Wait! These can't be for me," Edith said, kneeling to pick up the jumble.

"Your name's on 'em. Look."

Her name was written in neat black print on the lid Josh shoved under her nose. She recognized the name Milvoy and Fitch, one of St. Louis's leading department stores. Yet she knew, as did all the world, that they were never open on a Sunday.

She rested on her heels, a cream-colored silk blouse in one

hand, puzzling over the curiosity. Josh tapped his foot. "So you want 'em, or not?"

Edith wondered if this was one of the temptations her aunt had considered when warning her against the blandishments of the faithless male sex. Yet, though she knew she should sternly refuse the clothes, a devil's voice whispered that it could do no harm just to look. . . .

"Very well," she said. "Bring up the rest."

All the necessities of the toilette: delicate shoes, beautifully embroidered lawn petticoats, silken stockings, a figured sateen corset, and two nightdresses that were mere drifts of batiste. A whole vein of hats to be mined. Undergarments of pink gauze and white silks. Edith felt her face grow hot at the thought of Mr. Dane's big brown hands tossing over these dainty confections, choosing them just for her.

Opening the last and largest box, Edith's heart stopped at the sight of gray. Her lips wrinkling in distaste, she withdrew a dress of light poplin. Obviously, Mr. Dane had in mind to replace her old dress as nearly as possible. And yet . . .

Edith rose from the chaos of paper and boxes all about her. A small mirror hung on the wall beside the bed. Kicking off her shoes and holding the dress to her body, Edith climbed up on the bed to try to see as much of herself reflected as she could.

The dress was of so soft and insubstantial a gray that it might, in some lights, be thought white. Like moonlight, the color changed by enchantment the objects it covered. Her hair looked almost mahogany instead of red by contrast with the smooth fabric. Her skin glowed a pearly white. She had to try it on, despite knowing it must be returned.

Primping was a sin. Edith primped. She tried her hair up and falling in a cascade of waves. She pulled up the white lace collar she'd pinned around to fill in the jacket-like collar of the dress, and then changed it for a scarf of apple green silk. It all looked wonderful.

Secretly, she'd always wondered if, in the right clothes, she might not be . . . acceptable. In these wonderful things, she could almost believe she was pretty. She wasn't vain enough to believe it, but she almost could.

She spent so much time in front of the little mirror, what

with climbing on and off the bed and making alterations, that Mr. Dane's arrival took her by surprise. And after letting him praise her punctuality!

"Just a moment!" Where were her borrowed shoes? Here was one nesting in a box with a pair of scornfully elegant pumps.

"You okay?"

"Fine, just a moment!" Her voice was perhaps garbled, as she was on her hand and knees, the bed covers draped over her head as she dug beneath the bed.

Nevertheless, she heard his laugh plainly. Sitting back on her heels and throwing off the coverlet, she glared at him over her shoulder. She knew she was a sight, and only realized then how much she'd wanted to surprise him with her newfound fine feathers. Her hair was all whichaway, for she'd never returned it to its simple bun. Hurrying to her feet, she gathered it up and stuck pins in it at random.

"Are you always going to enter uninvited?" she demanded, her elbows still raised.

"I'm sorry. I guess I was worried. You did come mighty near to fainting last night."

Instantly, Edith drowned in guilt. This was after all the man to whom she owned unreturnable bounties. To mistreat him was not only rude, it was ungrateful.

Before she could apologize abjectly, he looked past her at the mayhem strewn around the room. "Good, all that stuff came. What do you think?"

"It's all wonderful, but you know I cannot accept it," she said, turning from the mirror.

"Kind of thought you might feel that way. But . . ."

"For one thing, I can't afford it. All I have in the world is what you will give me for this business. And, Mr. Dane, I'm not even sure I can do what you want."

"You won't know 'til you give it a try." He bent and picked up the barmaid's second shoe. "Are you going to wear this? Or one of these other ones?"

"Those, of course. These others will have to go back." She couldn't help sighing over the pale gray shoes with the pink rosettes that would have so well set off her dress. "If you'll give me a moment to change, I'll be with you at once. Oh, I must pack all these things into their boxes again."

Hurriedly, she picked up one of the nightdresses. She tried to smooth out the wrinkles it had collected while lying on the bed. "Oh, dear. Perhaps Mr. Dilworthy can find someone to press it."

Jeff took the dainty thing from her. "Never mind that. Look, you have to keep these things. A couple of nice, Christian ladies picked 'em out and you can't throw their kindness back in their faces. I know you've got your pride . . ."

"Nice ladies?"

"Sure. *I* wouldn't know what to buy you. Gwen used to tell me I was no more use than a steer when it came women's stuff. Even when she'd described what she wanted right down to the ruffles, I'd still come home with the exact wrong thing."

Edith realized she should have known better than to let her imagination get away from her. Of course Mr. Dane had not wasted his morning selecting which garments would flatter her most. He'd turned the matter over to clerks.

"So any way, I mentioned to Mrs. Waters what had happened to you . . . I mean, the building burning down and all your worldly goods gone to smash. After that, I just got out of her way, like I would have if she'd been a runaway train. She grabbed her mother, told her the whole tale, and next thing I know, they're off to the store, gabbling away like mad."

"But the stores are all closed on Sunday. They couldn't have gotten in, let alone . . ." Edith waved her hand at all the "worldly goods" piled up on the bed.

"Considering that Mrs. Waters' father is Mr. Milvoy and her uncle's Mr. Fitch, she didn't have much of a problem. Mrs. Milvoy got the key and shoot—they were gone."

Edith put the back of a shaking hand to her temple. "To think that two wealthy women would do this for a stranger, utterly unknown to them. I just can't take it in."

Gently, Jeff said, "Maybe you should write them a little note or something."

"Yes, I will. At once."

She turned to approach the small writing desk in one corner

of the room. Jeff reached for her arms to stop her. She quivered at his touch and held still, her head half-turned.

He glanced over her from behind. The loose knot was far more appealing than the tight bun she usually wore. Some tendrils had sprung free to tease the nape of her neck. Jeff's hands tightened above her elbows. A violent desire to press his lips against the white skin before him alarmed him with its primitive strength.

Sternly, he reminded himself that he had been a widower for too long. These feelings, this heat, arose only from his celibacy. Added to his abstinence, the romantic circumstances of their meeting made for a hell's brew of lust. It had nothing to do with Edith Parker, pitiable, penniless and patently virginal.

He forced his hands to open. "There really isn't time for you to write now, Miss Parker. I've reserved a table at Mr. Waters' restaurant, the Beauville down on Chouteau, and we best be getting along."

"All right. I'm ready." Going to a restaurant with Mr. Dane didn't feel like going out with a stranger.

He glanced over her as she turned again to face him. As his lips twitched into a grin, he felt the carnal fit pass off. Her dainty feet in white stockings peeked out from beneath the hem of her simple dress.

"It's up to you, but do you really want to go barefoot?"

She stared at him, puzzled, then glanced down. "Oh, my."

"I'll wait outside."

When she came out, she was as neat as a window dummy. There could have been nothing more correct than her hair or more tidy than her clothing. It almost hurt his eyes to look at her.

He left her standing in the lobby while he went to check the desk for letters. He hadn't thought to stop before going up to see her. He'd just headed at once for the stairs, taking them two at a time.

The day clerk handed him three letters. Two went right into his pocket. The one from home he kept in his hands. "I've got a cab waiting," he said, coming back to her.

"Don't mind me," Edith said, glancing at the letter.

"It's all right. I know what's in it."

He escorted her outside. As they went through the wide doorway, Edith glanced back into the lobby. Several people must have risen from their chairs the moment she and Mr. Dane had left. They stood together in a knot, the desk clerk raising the large access panel in the counter to get out and join them. As she peered at them as she walked away, she saw them staring back. One raised a hand, not in a wave but in a fist.

Climbing into the cab, Edith debated mentioning the odd incident to Mr. Dane, sitting opposite her. But he had opened his letter and was apparently engrossed in it. Once in a while he chuckled.

"Was it what you expected, Mr. Dane?"

He glanced up, his eyes smiling, flecked with gold. "My girls like to write to me. But as both of them are a little shaky in that department, I get to help them. And, of course, to get in here before I leave for home, they've got to mail it before I *leave* home. So it's always what I expected, but never just the same as I remember it."

Glancing down, he read the end again, grinned and shook his head in wonder. He folded the page and stuck it in his pocket. Foolishly, Edith felt excluded, like a dog left out in the yard.

After all, she scolded herself, staring unseeingly out the window at the passing city scene, his children were nothing to her. Mere names without substance, not vibrant little girls with interests and excitements she knew nothing about. She would meet them for a week, and no doubt they'd be scrupulously polite to her and then forget her the moment she boarded the train. That was how it should be. Edith ignored the way her hand had itched within its glove, itched with the longing to read those words of love and farewell.

The restaurant was all fumed oak and brass. The saloon on the other side was open to the restaurant but shielded by an etched glass panel. Raucous laughter penetrated the dark interior as men ate a free lunch while drinking their five-cent beers. After Jeff and Edith sat down, a waiter approached, mustache well waxed, his round tray tucked under his arm.

Jeff asked, "Should I order for you?"

Edith nodded. "Please. I've only rarely eaten in a restaurant before." Going to a restaurant with a stranger, a thought that had scandalized her yesterday, seemed an unimportant detail today. She'd already drunk whiskey, sung in public, and accepted the charity of strangers. In short, she'd experienced more variety in twenty-four hours than in twenty-three years. What was a mere restaurant after all that?

After he'd given their order, Jeff faced Edith, his elbows on the square table. His dark eyes studied her. "What did you do after your aunt died?"

"I went on with the service. Hardly anyone noticed that the torch had been passed on."

Sitting up more correctly in her chair, Edith concentrated on his questions. He hadn't really interviewed her before and she was sure he wanted to check her credentials. After all, she was coming to stay in his house with his two no-doubt impressionable young daughters.

"You really enjoy your work."

"Yes. Yes, I do."

"Now explain here. Say I write you a letter, telling you what kind of girl I'm looking for."

"Go on and tell me," Edith said, satisfied. Two could interview each other at the same time. She wanted to know more about his "choices" and more about him. Though certain now he was no white slaver, she still wanted to be sure everything was aboveboard. Telling herself it was part of the job lessened her shame when she realized that all she really wanted was to hear him go on talking.

That, and the steak spluttering on the grill. Edith kept swallowing to prevent the overflow from the juices that filled her mouth every time she thought of that steak. How long had it been? Six months? A year? Turning many a hard-boiled egg into a pheasant supper with her imagination was a simple matter, since she had no idea what pheasant actually tasted like. It might very well be egglike. But once having supped on reality, no imaginary wizardry could turn any lesser food into a beefsteak.

"What do I want in a wife?" He tipped back his chair and studied the ceiling. "I'd like her to be kind of sassy. A little spark keeps a man's interest. Young is good, but not too young.

I don't want her to be some featherbrain. And she should have some experience with children. Mrs. Green would be good for that. She has two boys—fine strapping cubs both."

"Mrs. Green being . . . ?"

"She's one of the three ladies—you know—back in Richey. Her husband was a good friend of mine. Asked me to keep an eye on her and his boys."

"And you have done so." She knew without being told that he'd been the soul of charity.

"I've done my best."

"And the other two?"

"Oh, yeah." He rubbed his left eyebrow vigorously. "Look, can't this wait until we get there? Names aren't going to tell you anything."

Edith smiled enigmatically. "Please continue. The more I know about each lady the easier I shall find it to be fair."

"Okay," he answered, shrugging his big shoulders in his pale jacket. "Miss Climson has never had a man to call, never called on a man, and has never once been chased into the berry bushes during the Founder's Day picnic. She's the school teacher."

"Ah, that would explain it. She had to adjust the tableaux that follow the parade. At least, that is what my teacher always did, and there were lots of men waiting in those rose bushes behind the school."

"And then there is Miss . . ." He glanced at Edith. Had she just made a joke?

"Wait! What about Miss Climson?"

"I told you everything."

"No, you haven't," she protested, leaning forward to catch every word. "How old is she? What does she look like? How does she dress? What are her dreams, her hopes? What does she see herself doing in five years' time?"

"Good heavens, I didn't know that much about my wife!"

"Were you happily married?" She hadn't meant to ask that. The words just slipped out.

"Yes. We were very happy. For a while, after she died, I didn't think I'd ever be happy again."

"How long ago . . . ?"

"Three years. She never recovered her strength after Maribel was born. Gwen just kept getting weaker and weaker. Dr. Samson never could tell me why." He gazed off at nothing and seemed to be speaking more to himself than to her. "For a while there, I lived on black coffee and grief. I hated to go to sleep, 'cause I'd always find her in my dreams. Pa took care of that, in his own way."

He smiled at her, his eyes coming back to the present. "He poured a slug of laudanum into my coffee and I dropped where I stood. Slept for three days and got a heck of a talking-to when I woke up. He reminded me that my girls needed me. I still remember him saying that life won't let people get in the grave with their dead. It keeps tugging at you, making you live, forcing you along until you give in."

Edith felt the message Mr. Dane was trying to convey. Obviously, he thought she'd buried herself with her aunt. Edith had to admit the justice of his judgment. How long had it been since she'd had a rational conversation with another person? Dream people didn't count, although she'd enjoyed talking to them. Perhaps she'd enjoyed it too much. The kings, queens and harem girls had become more real to her than any living person.

"You said your father lives with you?"

"Good ol' Dad. You'll like him, Miss Parker. But don't believe half of the stories he tells. He didn't really save General Grant's life, or lead the charge at Gettysburg. He was shot by a woman while scavenging meat for his troop."

"For which side did he fight in the late war?"

Jeff scratched his head, giving a slow grin. "That's not real clear. Sometimes he says it's one, and then the next thing you know it's the other. I remember him going off in a blue uniform, that's all I can tell you."

He glanced up. "Here comes our food. Now, you tuck into that, Miss Parker. You still look kind of peaky."

Though the steak smelled delightful as it spluttered next to the white mounds of potato, the flavor was gamy and the texture tough. Edith's jaw ached after the first bite. Nevertheless, she nodded her approval when Jeff asked her how she liked it.

"Well, you're wrong, Miss Parker. This is no good."

He raised his hand to summon the waiter. "Lookee here, son. You go and tell the cook to put these steaks back under his shoes. What's the matter with 'em? Well, I'll tell you. I respect old age too much to want to eat it for lunch. And this young lady was looking forward to something a sight tastier than this old boot."

The waiter blustered a little and then said, "I'll get Mr. Waters for you, sir."

"Good, you do that."

Edith whispered, "It's all right, Mr. Dane. I don't mind. There's no need to make a fuss."

"Never you mind, Miss Parker. It's an insult to serve meat like this to a God-fearing cattleman."

But when Mr. Waters, a florid gentleman with a stomach his watch chain almost failed to span, came over, Jeff stood up, his grin spreading. Shaking hands, he said, "Here I am again, Nick. And ready to prove my point."

"You don't give up easily, Jeff. I respect that in a man. What's the trouble?"

"Sit down and take a bite, man."

His cheeks abloom with confidence, Mr. Waters did as Jeff asked. Like Edith, he soon began chewing more and more slowly, each grind of his teeth a greater effort. He fought to swallow his bite. "So all right, that particular steak is a mite . . . stiff. But I'm sure . . ."

"You want to try the young lady's?"

"As they came from the same side of beef . . . But you get the occasional tough cow from the wholesaler. Could happen to anyone."

"And your cook takes the tougher stuff and gets a kickback from the supplier, or charges you for the prime stuff and puts the difference in his own pocket."

"That happens too."

Some vulgar shouting echoed from the saloon, words no gentleman would utter. Mr. Waters glanced at Edith, a frown drawing down his heavy brows. "Beg your pardon, miss. Gotta take care of that one of these days."

"Look, Nick," Jeff said in a reasonable tone. "You want to attract a better class of customer, right? You want the society ladies to eat here, and to bring along their high-rolling husbands. You want the businessmen, the big boys, to make their deals here and drop the cash they carry around."

"Sure, that's what every restaurateur wants."

"So stop serving meat that the customer needs to cut with a hacksaw. This cow's been driven from Texas, losing weight and fat with every step. He's lean, so lean that all the flavor's gone, 'cause all he's had to eat is scrub."

"True."

"Now take one of my beefs. He's been living on lush Missouri grass for two years, never having to walk further than the stream running through the bottom of the field. Then for the last six months of his life, he lives like a prince on the finest grains and corn. He's fat, Jack, fat and contented."

"I kinda of envy him," Jack said, his broad hand resting on his stomach. Edith nodded in agreement.

Jeff went on, "Then he takes a little ride on a train. The track's laid, you know. Then he's put down humanely at my brother-in-law's place at the St. Louis stockyards. Harlan also takes care of the aging, and he'll see you get what you pay for."

"That'll make a change, all right."

Jeff put his hand on Mr. Waters' shoulder and gave him a searching glance. "And when you serve your customers," he said, "they'll get a steak so juicy, so tasty, you know they've got to come back for more. 'Specially as every other restaurant in town's still serving Texas beef."

"All right . . . all right." Mr. Waters pushed himself up from the table. "You've sold me. But I want exclusive rights in St. Louis. Let's say, for a year. By that time, either I'll have the best place in the city, or be bankrupt. And dang me, if I don't close down the bar!"

The two men shook hands again. Mr. Waters nodded to Edith before returning to his office. Jeff sat down. "Sorry about that," he said, shaking out his napkin. "Shouldn't deal in front of a lady."

"Don't apologize. I was fascinated. Is that why you came to St. Louis?"

"I've had this idea for a while. But I've been stymied by the greed of men like Waters who want to hang on to a dollar.

Longhorns are big critters, cheap to raise, and so cheaper to buy. On the other hand, that Texas beef is usually as bad as can be. That's why you've got to stew so many cuts of meat to make it eatable. Either that or see a dentist regular."

The waiter came back, carrying two new platters. "Here you are," he said, laying them down. "You should have told me you were friends of the boss."

In a very few minutes, Edith laid down her knife and fork. Sitting back in her chair with a soft sigh, she smiled dreamily at Jeff. "That was wonderful."

Jeff glanced at her plate, empty and shining, then down at his own with half a steak to go. His eyes showed his mirth. Edith snapped upright. "I beg your pardon. It's dreadfully rude to gallop through a meal."

"Not at all. It's a pleasure to watch a lady enjoying her food. Most just pick and nibble, you know."

Edith launched upon a more elaborate apology. She did not want to admit to Mr. Dane how deep her hunger ran. Actually, she could have eaten another steak with all the trimmings and never have felt a moment's discomfort. After a moment, Edith realized that she had lost Mr. Dane's attention.

Knowing it was rude, she turned in her chair to look over her shoulder. What was he staring at?

A blonde girl, tall with an elegant figure, was speaking rapidly to Mr. Waters. Edith stared at the girl with as much attention as Mr. Dane did. A goddess could not have been more lovely, with her beautiful figure, fine bust and swanlike neck. Under her draped mantle, she was dressed in the extremely tight clothing that the latest fashions dictated, with the lashings of ruching and feathers that only the most majestic figure could carry off.

Edith glanced toward Mr. Dane. "She's lovely. Is that Mrs. Waters? If so, I must thank her personally for her kindness."

"What? No, that's not, definitely not Mrs. Waters." Miss Parker's interested eyes drew more from him against his will. "Her name is Sabrina Carstairs."

"Do you know her?"

He didn't want to lie, but he wished he hadn't gotten started.

"Oh, yes. That is, I knew her once. Briefly. Hardly spoke at all."

The blonde threw her hand in the air, obviously exasperated. She twirled away from Mr. Waters and began to walk as rapidly as her tight skirt would allow, with the plain intention of never darkening this door again. As she passed their table, Jeff ducked his head, becoming blatantly interested in his meal.

Edith, however, openly watched the girl as she stalked past. She'd never seen so truly beautiful a girl before, though she'd often wondered what it must be like to be one.

Suddenly, the girl stopped, as if she'd thought of several good things to say to Mr. Waters. But instead of walking back to him, she said, "Why, Jefferson Dane, is that you?"

"Hello, Sabrina," Jeff said looking up.

5

"BEEN IN TOWN long, Jeff?"

"I'm here on business. I'll be going home in a day or two."

"That's too bad. I would have liked to have seen more of you. Talk over old times." Her smile was slow, deliberately intriguing. Jeff shifted in his chair and rubbed the back of his neck. He avoided glancing at Edith. What she must be thinking!

"I've found a new place to live, on Elm. Not so fancy as the place I was in when you and I were . . ."

"Times are hard," he said, cutting her off quickly.

"Seems that way. 'Cept in the cattle business. It doesn't look like that boom will ever end."

Jeff remembered that Sabrina had possessed, in addition to an inviting body, a sharp, almost male mind. She certainly understood the laws of supply and demand. "Like everything else," he said, "it has drawbacks."

He saw that Edith's bright eyes flickered between the buxom blonde and himself. She seemed as excited and involved as though she were watching a play. He only hoped she was too innocent to guess what his friendship with Sabrina had been.

"You know, of all the things I miss . . ." Sabrina started to say, putting her hand on his shoulder.

The waiter had come over to clear the plates. Reaching for Edith's plate, he knocked over her cup of coffee, sending the spray across the statuesque woman's light-colored wrap. Miss Carstairs leaped backwards, brushing at her mantle frantically.

"Oh, you . . . you silly . . . God, what a mess!"

Edith snatched Jeff's napkin from under his hand and, with her own, began to mop at the gleaming silk and beading. "It's all right—I don't think it will stain."

"Not stain! Are you kidding?" She threw off her mantle and thrust it into the apologetic waiter's hand. "You're going to have to buy me a new one."

Still helpful, Edith said, "Perhaps you can dye it brown."

"Brown? I wouldn't wear brown if it was the last color. . . ." She twisted to look down the rear breadth of her skirt. "Oh, good, at least it didn't splash my dress."

Sabrina snatched her mantle back from the waiter's hand. "Never mind. I'll give it away. It was getting old anyway."

The waiter nodded dumbly, even his mustache drooping in his misery. He slunk away without a backward glance. Sabrina stared after him in exasperation.

Jeff said, "I'm glad you weren't hurt, Sabrina. Good thing that coffee was cold."

"Ah, heck. It's not worth fussing about. Kind of thing that could happen to anyone." She glanced after the waiter again. "Poor dope."

She spent a few more minutes at their table. To Jeff's relief, they talked about her royally pampered cat, and her new house, not about the past.

Always aware of Edith listening, after a few minutes Jeff said, "Interesting. Well, we have to be going."

"Wait for the bill, boy. Can't rook the waiter. Look what he did for me." She patted the puff of hair behind her head.

As he stood, he said, "You always look fine, Sabrina. No matter what."

"Why, thank you, Jeff. I've often thought you were the finest gentleman I ever met up with. You know, I wrote you a letter not too long ago."

"I never got it."

"I figured that. A gentleman like you would have answered, one way or the other. But if you happen to get it, do me a favor and rip it up. It's not important now."

"All right. I will. Well, we better be getting along."

Sabrina glanced at Edith. "Thank you, whoever you are. You mopped that coffee up right nice."

"My pleasure, Miss Carstairs. I'm sure it won't stain."

Edith stopped him from calling a cab, saying she'd enjoy the walk. She said nothing else, and Jeff didn't break the silence. He tried to think of a way to reassure Miss Parker that he wasn't a heartless libertine, using a woman only to discard her when his appetite had been satisfied. It was just his bad luck, he decided, that sent Sabrina to Waters' place while he was there.

Miss Parker was probably planning to back out of their business deal at this very moment. All her doubts about his intentions must have come back. The thought filled him with discontent. She might be a naive, funny little thing, but somehow he had faith in her. Besides, she needed him a whole lot more than he needed her. The same instinct that made him collect strays was working on her behalf.

Edith sighed and Jeff looked at her with an apology on his lips. "I'm sorry about that. Miss Carstairs . . ."

"Isn't she beautiful? All that golden hair . . . she seemed very good-natured too, which is not, I believe, a usual thing with really lovely girls. So often they become proud and vain."

"Uh . . ."

"It's become so warm now, I don't think she'll need her wrap after all."

"Look, I don't want you to think . . . I don't mean to . . ."

He received the full impact of her happy smile. It staggered him to realize she hadn't been worried about his evil intentions at all. "It was so *nice*, I thought."

"What was?" Was she being sarcastic?

"The waiter and Miss Carstairs."

"Having coffee spilled over you is nice?"

"No, of course not. I mean, they're so terribly in love. It's nice. Not the sort of thing one sees every day, not even in my line of work."

Despite the people jostling past them on the sidewalk, Jeff stopped. The brisk clip-clop of the passing horses and the shouts of the drovers faded. He could even ignore the newspaper boy yelling his head off a few feet away.

"What? That's nonsense. Sabrina wouldn't give the time of day to a man who couldn't afford to give her the best."

"The best?"

"Jewelry, furs, horses . . . the best of everything. You should have seen where she lived before. It's a good thing I only knew her for a month or she'd have driven me into the poorhouse."

"I suppose she felt she had to look out for her future. I have often thought a life of shame must be a precarious one. Of course, my life has been thoroughly proper and yet it turned out to be risky in the extreme." She gave him a direct look. "That keeps me from looking down my nose at Miss Carstairs."

Jeff was left gaping. He never thought she'd look at it like that. Any usual woman would have been having hysterics at actually speaking to a "fallen angel."

Edith tugged lightly at his arm. "We are blocking the sidewalk, Mr. Dane."

He walked a few steps on. "Wait a minute. What about the waiter? You don't mean that Sabrina and that . . . I can't even remember what he looks like. There's no way those two are . . ."

"But of course they are. It stands out all over them."

"You can't know that for sure."

It had been like a halo shining around the two of them. A brightness that hovered a few inches above the heads of the dazzling blonde and the younger waiter. The closer they'd been to one another the brighter it had grown.

"Any woman," she said, settling for a mundane explanation, "who just received a cup of coffee over what was obviously a brand-new mantle and who didn't instantly crush the offender must be in love."

"Maybe she didn't want to cause a scene," Jeff said and immediately reversed himself. "No, Sabrina *likes* scenes. The louder and more public the better."

"Love has the power to change people."

"Well, maybe you're right," he admitted. "Maybe she has settled down with a waiter. That would explain the cheaper rooms. But she was still flirting with me . . . wasn't she?"

"I imagine it must be something she can't help. Some girls are just born knowing how to flirt." Edith wondered what it would be like to squeeze—ever so lightly of course—the firm muscle beneath his sleeve. But her upbringing forbade any such act.

When they reached the hotel, Edith said, "Thank you again for lunch. Please don't forget to give me Mrs. Waters' address so I can write to her."

"I'll bring it to you in a few minutes."

She nodded and headed toward the mahogany-railed staircase that swept up from the lobby. Passing two dignified older women on the stairs, she nodded and smiled. In return, she received a set of glances so frosty that the humid summer air seemed to harden into a winter's chill. They seemed almost to switch their skirts out of range of some contamination.

Pausing on the stair, Edith turned to watch the ladies descending, a puzzled frown puckering her brow. Had she accidentally offended them? How, when she'd hardly stepped out of her room? Perhaps her singing in the night had disturbed more people that Mr. Dane had told her about.

From here, she could see him at the desk. Suddenly, he pounded his fist against the blotter. A faint ring sounded among the thudding, as the blows moved the summoning bell. Wondering, Edith started down the stair.

Jeff met her halfway across the lobby. His tanned face showed red as an Indian's, his brown eyes hard as horse chestnuts. "Come on," he said in a grinding whisper. He took her arm and turned her again toward the stairs.

"What is it, Mr. Dane?"

"The management has asked us to leave."

*   *   *

"Damn and blast them to hell," Jeff said, striding along the hall. He still towed her along by the arm, though he seemed to have forgotten about her. "It's a fine thing when a man can't even do right by a fellow creature without a bunch of prudish old women . . . that Dilworthy . . . he *saw* the state you were in last night! What could any decent man do but make sure you were all right?"

He stopped outside her door. Edith felt as though she'd been dragged along behind a runaway train. He held out his hand for her key. "Pack up your things, Miss Parker. I'll get my grip and we'll shake off the dust of this place in two hoots."

"Surely there's no reason to leave so abruptly, Mr. Dane," Edith said, digging in her bag for the key. They were the first words she'd been able to slip in.

"I don't stay where I'm not wanted, Miss Parker. They've made their feelings clear on the subject."

"But all I have to do is explain . . ."

"I'm not having my business told to a bunch of busybodies just to stay *here* another night. It's not worth it."

Mr. Maginn had been threatening but he hadn't stormed as impressively as this. Jefferson's responsive face had become stony, only his hot eyes showing his anger. His voice was tight and hard as he thoroughly castigated everyone in the hotel, excepting only the young hallboy and herself.

Yet she wasn't afraid as she had been frightened of Mr. Maginn. She knew instinctively that Mr. Dane would never harm her. "So, what hotel will we go to next?"

"We're not." He took the key out of her hands, turned it quickly in the keyhole and pushed open her door. "I've got Waters' word that he'll take the meat. So we're going home."

"All right." The way Mr. Dane combined the two of them into an "us" warmed her as though she had entered a room and everyone had turned to welcome her. "I haven't a bag to pack my new clothes in. Do you think you could advance me a few dollars?" Asking him for more money brought a hot blush into her cheeks.

"I forgot." The anger seemed to die down in his eyes. "I'll

run out and buy you one. Get your stuff together to be ready to go when I come back."

"Thank you, Mr. Dane. Shall I pack for you?"

"I'll take care of it. I don't travel with much."

In her room, Edith wasn't sure she'd made it clear that Mr. Dane was to be repaid for the valise. She considered going down to catch him, but the idea of passing before all those critical eyes turned her knees to water. Coward though she might be, Edith shrank from that ordeal.

After laying out her new clothes neatly on the bed, Edith remembered she had not yet written to thank Mrs. Waters and her mother for their charity. Fruitlessly opening and closing the desk drawers, Edith realized that there was not a scrap of paper to be had in the room. And the only pen she found had a broken nib.

Twice she walked to the door. Twice she turned back. Orpheus gave an inquisitive chirp. "I know," she said, shutting her eyes. "I'm as spineless as a jellyfish. It's not as though they're going to eat me, and I must write Mrs. Waters. I can't be so basely ungrateful as not to reply to her kindness."

The hall of the castle was lit only by flickering torches. The shadows fought the light as Lady Jessica crept down the stairs into the great cold hall. The secret papers were in the mighty hewn oak table that Sir Ivor used when holding his corrupt Court of Justice. She halted on the rough steps as two guards, their swords clanking against mailed legs, passed below her. Lady Jessica longed for the safety of her tower room. But no . . . Lord Jeffrey's life depended on those papers! She would not fail him.

"Pardon me," Edith said, her voice tiny.

The clerk did not move. He thrust letters into the guests' boxes with unnecessary violence.

"Might I trouble you . . ."

Shoving in the final letter, the clerk turned. On seeing her, his bony nose wrinkled. "What do you want?"

"You're the man who was on duty last night?"

"Yes, young woman, I am. Really, haven't you caused enough trouble? Are we to have a scene?"

She recognized him now. Not so much by his sour face but

by the faint, smudgy glow about him. Concentrating, she saw that someone loved him devotedly, though the reason was not easy to see. He didn't deserve to hear what she had to say. Edith fought to keep the words back, but they could not be denied.

"What's your name?"

"Dilworthy, as if that's any of your business, young woman. Now, please . . ." He shooed her away with a flapping hand as though she'd been a stray cat. "Your 'friend' will be back soon and then you and he can do as the management of the St. Simeon has asked. This is a respectable . . ."

"Listen to me, August. It's important."

"Threats don't mean . . . how did you know that?"

Edith leaned forward to give her words more emphasis. "Does someone meet you every morning when you go home?"

"Kindly tell me how you know my name."

"Is there someone like that? Always there when you come home and at other times too? Does she take care of you in little ways that maybe you don't notice? Clean laundry, your favorite kind of cookie . . ."

The fussy little man primmed his mouth as though wild horses wouldn't make him speak. Then he said, "My landlady's daughter makes me breakfast."

"That would be . . . ?"

His small eyes grew narrower still. "Are you some kind of fake spiritualist? This is worse than I thought. Immorality is one thing; blasphemy is another. I'm going to call a policeman, young woman. Trying to flimflam decent . . ."

"Listen to me," she said again.

Reaching out, she placed her hands over his. As the connection was made, Edith saw everything very clearly. The girl loved him but was beginning to despair, certain the object of her worship would never look at her. If the situation didn't change, August would lose her, growing ever more bitter until his soul could never be untwisted.

"It's very important, August. Tomorrow when you go home, you've got to notice her. Ask her about her interests, find out what she likes to do. Be good to her."

The desk clerk stared past her shoulder as though he'd gone

absentminded. "I've heard her mother call her Katrine. When I left for work today, Katrine gave me a bun warm from the oven for my dinner pail."

The glow around the clerk had brightened noticeably. If it went on like this, soon other people would see it. Edith hoped they'd be kind. Some people would find ridiculously humorous the thought of this bellicose little man being involved in a romance.

Mr. Dilworthy was still too dazed to comment when she asked for writing paper. Going back to her room, Edith felt she'd done some good. She sat down to compose a suitable note of thanks to Mrs. Waters and her mother.

When she heard a knock, she called for the person to enter and went on writing. After a moment, the knock sounded again. "Come in," she said again, more loudly, turning in her chair.

Another knock. Sighing, Edith got up and went to the door. Jefferson grinned at her when she opened it. "I didn't want to barge in and get bawled out again."

"I shouldn't have snapped at you. I can only repeat . . ."

"Come on, Miss Parker. It was a joke."

"Oh." Obligingly, she smiled.

Jeff saw she had no idea how to respond to his teasing. She was grateful to him for his aid and the job he offered her. The advantage was entirely on his side. He had to remember to play fair. Yet all the while, the sweet, furtive dimple that came and went at the corner of her lush mouth tempted him to kiss her. He backed off, fast.

"Here's a couple of grips, Miss Parker," he said, holding up the leather cases. "Let me know when you're ready to go. I'd like to catch the eight o'clock train. It's a sleeper."

"I only expected *one* case, Mr. Dane. And I will certainly pay you for it."

"'Course you will," he said, humoring her. "And I got two so you wouldn't have to cram all that stuff in one. Oh, and here's Mrs. Waters' address. It's over on Forest Park. Nice houses in that part of town."

"Yes, I know." They had often fueled her dreams, especially the ones like medieval castles with stonework and oriel windows. "I'll finish writing at once, then pack. I shall be ready shortly."

Jeff went into his room and shut the door, though he knew she still stood in her own doorway. Looking at his reflection in his shaving mirror, he said straight out, "It's bad enough you've ruined her reputation in this hotel . . . I catch you spoiling it in Richey and I'll ride you out of town on a rail. Down boy!"

He thought about the three women waiting for him. Decent, hard-working women—at least two of them real lookers. If he didn't marry one of them, he'd be the laughing stock of the town, as it had been obvious for some time what he'd been thinking of. And as for them . . ."It's not every man who has the potential to ruin four women's reputations at once."

The problem with him, he knew, was that he was a romantic. Gwen used to tease him about it, saying that he'd read one too many Sir Walter Scott novels as a boy. And he had.

There was something about all that chivalry that made a man feel good about his sex. He had, after all, saved Miss Parker, if not from blackhearted evil, at least from the terrors of destitution. Naturally, he'd think about doing more than saving her. After all, even in the old days, the boys in the tin suits didn't rescue princesses for the heck of it. The princesses usually wound up showing their gratitude.

Jeff fired his hairbrushes into his valise. No sooner did he drive out the thought of making love to Miss Parker than it came back, more vividly. On this trip he'd spend a lot of time in the smoking car, exclusively a men's province. As she'd never just take fifty dollars without earning it, he couldn't leave her here. The best thing to do, therefore, was to go through with hiring her, but remember to stay away from her.

That should be easy, he told himself, taking a last look around to see if he'd left anything. After all, he'd never clapped eyes on her before yesterday. She hadn't cast a spell over him. His thoughts, feelings and actions were still under his complete control. And it wasn't as though she were standing outside his door, pleading for his touch.

"I'm ready if you are," she said, standing outside his door. She let fall the hand she'd raised to knock. Meekly, she let him take her cases and followed behind him, carrying Orpheus' shrouded cage, as he set off down the stairs.

His thoughts were obviously occupying him to the exclusion of all else. She did not break in on them. Perhaps being thrown out of his favorite hotel had cast a damper over his spirits. She could sympathize. Even in her fantasies, she'd never been thrown out of a place, scorned by society.

Lady Jessica walked with her head held high, disdaining to notice the jeering populace. On a platform, the stake rose high and austere above the piled kindling. As she ascended the steps, she turned scornful eyes toward the judge who had condemned her. Sir Ivor dropped his eyes beneath her proud glance. He had called on her in the dungeon, offering her life in exchange for her virtue. "Better the stake!" she'd cried. "If you martyr me, I shall be a saint in heaven. And Lord Jeffrey will surely avenge my death with your own!"

Meeting the eyes of the executioner at the foot of the stake, Jessica stared in wonder. Though the greasy cloth that hid his features burned a pair of brilliant eyes . . .

Edith didn't even notice the whispers of the hotel guests as she walked out behind Jeff. She was far away.

6

Dawn turned the sky pink as the long train pulled up to the brick depot in Richey. The uniformed porter helped Edith down the iron steps. Steam puffed around her as she looked at what she could see of the town. It had a respectable, conventional look, with well-kept storefronts and a sprinkling of narrow houses. A few people were astir, and lights in windows told of more citizens awakening with the day.

As the porter pocketed the folded money Jeff held out to him, he said, "Thanks, sir. Maybe I'll see you on your return trip, Miss Parker. And I'll be taking your advice."

"I'm glad, Mr. Vincent. She must be a very nice girl."

"That she is." Seeing that their bags had been unloaded from the second to last car, the porter waved his dark hand at the engineer, leaning out of his window. As the whistle shrilled Mr. Vincent swung back aboard.

Edith waved and, as the train rolled past, she gave Jefferson an uncertain smile. He had seen her comfortably bestowed in first class and then had all but disappeared for the remainder of the trip. He still smelled of pipe and cigar smoke.

She'd seen him once, when he'd taken her into the hotel car to share a dinner with her. She couldn't complain of her treatment—the Pullman Palace car she had slept in had been more like Versailles than a box on wheels—but she wondered at his unexpected reserve. Perhaps he was tired. He hadn't come into the sleeping car. She'd watched for him until her heavy eyes had defeated her.

"You must be fatigued, Mr. Dane. Is it far to your home?"

"I'm well, thank you, Miss Parker. And no, it's not far but too far to walk. I'll get my buggy from the livery stable."

He took her arm and walked with her into the depot. They were the only passengers stopping in Richey, and the interior was deserted, very different from the bustling noise and confusion of the St. Louis station. Jefferson asked her if she'd like to rest on one of the benches while he went for the buggy.

Edith agreed gratefully. Though the train had been the epitome of comfort, it had still traveled at a speed of close to forty miles per hour while swaying from side to side. Edith could still feel the motion when she closed her eyes.

She opened them when she heard a noise. Glancing around, she saw that the roller shade behind the cashier's window was flapping slightly, as though in a breeze. Edith rose to study the train schedule posted behind a glass. In the reflecting surface, she saw a pair of spectacled eyes peering at her from beneath the shade the way a lizard peers from beneath its family rock.

Edith felt acutely uncomfortable under this secret stare. Trying to be casual, she picked up her new alligator handbag from the bench and slipped outside to wait for Jeff.

He came back quickly, driving a bay horse between the shafts of a shiny black buggy. As soon as he pulled up, a middle-aged man in a tight blue coat came out of the station, placing his peaked cap on his balding head. Climbing down from the springy seat, Jeff said, "Hey, Arnie. How's business?"

"Pretty good, pretty good." Behind rimless glasses, the station master's slightly protuberant pale blue eyes fixed on Edith. Now she knew who had been so furtively watching her.

Jeff wrapped his hand around her elbow, pulling her closer to his side. "Arnie Sloan, this is my cousin, Miss Parker, from St. Louis."

"Morning, ma'am," Mr. Sloan said. His eyes took in her clothes as though he were memorizing them. Edith's face burned, but she forced a smile.

"Want some coffee before you head on out to Jeff's place, Miss Parker?"

Jeff answered for her. "Right nice of you, Arnie, but we best be getting along. Dad's bound to have breakfast going."

"I'll give you a hand with the bags," Mr. Sloan volunteered. Edith saw how he examined the labels of her luggage and ran his hands over the leather as though appraising how new it was.

"I bought them before I left St. Louis," Edith said to him. "I've never traveled anywhere before. Being on the railroad, you must have many chances to travel."

"No, ma'am. Plenty to see and do here at home. Been station master nigh on ten years, ain't never been bored yet."

"I'm sure you haven't been." She held out her hand. "Nice to have met you, Mr. Sloan."

Jeff helped her into the buggy. "See you at the meeting tomorrow, Arnie."

"I'll be there. 'Bye now, Miss Parker," he called, as Jeff slapped the reins over the bay's back. They set off down the road, Edith holding her hat against her head.

"He's the biggest gossip in town," Jeff grumbled. "Some he knows; a lot he makes up."

"Then I'm glad I was polite to him. Though I don't like deceiving anyone about my relationship with you. And your family," she added. She didn't want him to think she had begun bracketing the two of them together.

"I don't like it myself. I like to be beforehand with the world. Saves trouble. But in this case . . ." He shrugged. "It's for your own protection."

They were already out of the small town. The land rose and fell gently beneath the horse's hooves. Everything was green and pleasant, the crops in the fields high and lush. Early as it was, a certain moisture in the air prophesied a hot and sticky day ahead. Yet the freshness of the air and the lack of crowding buildings made even a muggy day one to look forward to. Edith felt a pain in her breast, as though her heart had expanded for the first time, snapping some confining bond.

"So," Jeff said, keeping his eyes on the road. "What was all that with the porter?"

"What was what?"

"What advice did you give him? And why were you talking to everybody and his Aunt Lucy aboard that train? You wouldn't even say 'boo' to me when I first met you."

Edith looked at his frowning profile. "There is a difference between chatting to people while sharing a common experience and speaking to a man and a stranger in the street."

"A man who has accosted you in the street, you mean."

"I suppose I do."

"Very well. And the advice? Something about a woman?"

She hoped he had forgotten. "We were . . . talking about his mother."

Jeff drew back on the reins. The living silence of the Missouri morning surrounded them. The wind rustled the tops of the trees while the cicadas sang their monotonous song. A few birds looked curiously at the people before returning to their search for breakfast.

"His mother is a 'very nice girl'?"

Edith stared down into her clasped hands. A hardheaded businessman like Mr. Dane would never believe the truth. Perhaps she could bend her words to fit the listener. Lying, it seemed, was a practice hard to resist.

"We spoke for a moment last night about his lady friend. That's all. Really."

He nodded and slapped the reins over the horse's back. "You're a lousy liar," he said evenly. "I'll remember that."

Edith felt compelled to explain, stumbling over her hasty words. "I haven't had much practice. But I thought . . . you did hire me for your problems, Mr. Dane. I thought you wouldn't like it if I gave advice to someone else, on your time."

"Do what you please, Miss Parker. I've hired you. I have not bought you, body and soul."

Edith felt a shiver at the base of her spine. What would it be like if he had bought and paid for her? She dragged on the reins of her runaway imagination. "In that case, I will tell you that Mr. Vincent was hesitant about proposing matrimony to a young lady he'd only known for a few weeks."

"I haven't known you that long, but I know what you said."

"Naturally, I told him not to go too fast. He might frighten her if he suddenly laid his heart at her feet. Or what is worse, she might not think him sincere."

"I lose my bet. I would have guessed you'd tell him not to waste any more time but get on with it."

"That would have been most imprudent."

Edith turned her head as though the fence they drove beside was the most interesting thing she'd ever seen. Perhaps lying was a skill that improved with a little practice, for he hadn't noticed her untruth this time. But how amazing that Jeff Dane should come to understand her so quickly. She had, in fact, given the porter that exact advice. The glow about his frame had been as brilliant as the sun, for the love between Mr. Vincent and his lady was shared fully.

In a little while, Jeff drew up before a two-story white farmhouse. The roof of the porch that ran around the front of the house seemed almost to reach the ground. A walk led up to the front, waist-high masses of rose shrubs bordering the crushed white stone. Their heavenly fragrance rose to meet Edith as she stood to get down from the buggy.

"How beautiful," she sighed as Jefferson lifted her down.

Looking up into her face, as she gazed at his home, Jeff had to agree. Quickly, he swung her down. "Those are my father's doing. He loves his roses. I'm not allowed to touch 'em. Cows I can manage but I just kill plants."

"I've never been lucky that way either."

He'd walked ahead down the path, carrying Orpheus, leaving her to follow. "I wonder where everyone is," he said aloud. "Usually, when I come home, they come charging out like . . ."

"Daddy!"

From two directions, little comets hurled themselves toward their father. One caught him about the waist, the other about the knees. As he began to sag, he threw Edith a laughing look, holding out the birdcage. With an answering smile, she took it.

Instantly, Jeff bent and scooped his two daughters up in a giant embrace. The larger girl chattered away, seemingly intent on filling her father's ear with all the happenings of the week in the shortest possible time. The little one just giggled.

Without putting either girl down, their father juggled them around so that they were each tucked under one of his arms. He carried the laughing girls up the stairs to the deep, cool porch.

Sitting down on a hard chair, Jeff brought the girls upright to sit on his knees. "This is Miss Edith Parker, girls. She's come to stay with us for a while."

Two pairs of eyes, matching hazel, looked up at her. Except for their eye color, the little girls were as different as could be. The little one's hair curled riotously above her baby-plump face. Her nose was tiny and her mouth a tight rosebud of light pink. It was impossible to say how she would look when older.

Louise's face was more defined with a short snub for a nose and a chin astonishingly determined in one so young. She seemed all too intelligent. Her bright eyes flashed on Edith and in an instant, Edith felt as though she'd been examined to her boot soles and backbone.

"Hello," she said timidly.

It was Maribel who spoke first. "What's that?" She pointed to the cloaked cage.

"This is Orpheus." Edith pulled off the covering. The little yellow bird gave her a reproachful look, his head tipped to one side. Then, as though testing his voice, he chirped once or twice. Maribel squealed in delight and squirmed off her father's lap. Kneeling, she peered into the cage.

"Does he sing?" Louise stood by her sister.

"When he wants to," Edith said.

She slipped a glance toward Jeff. He leaned forward in his chair, his powerful hands spread wide on his knees. As if feeling her look, he met her eyes. Boldly, he winked. Edith jerked her attention back to the children.

Maribel poked a chubby finger between the bars. "Here, birdie."

Orpheus tipped his head back and sent a shower of golden notes into the air. Then he flipped his wings as though waiting for applause. Maribel clapped twice. "Sing!" she commanded. Orpheus obliged.

"You're a dreadful show-off," Edith said indulgently.

Jeff stood up. "Let's put him up here." He lifted the cage to a hook in the crossbeam of the porch. The early morning sunlight did not reach directly in but the beams were bright enough to turn the canary's feathers to gold.

Orpheus began to sing what was obviously an ode in honor of the morning. The sudden crowing of a rooster didn't make him break off. Rather he seemed to take it as a challenge and increased the beauty of his aria.

"He'll need water," Edith said. "And I have his seeds in my luggage, if you girls would like to help me feed him."

She'd prepared on the train to meet tears or shyness. After all, the girls wouldn't know who she was and she'd been bashful with strangers all her life. Now she had only to meet Jeff's father. If she could survive that ordeal . . . but no, Jeff had said it had been his father's idea that she should come.

She heard the tap-drag of the elder Mr. Dane's footsteps before she saw him. The girls spun around from contemplating the bird and danced to the door. "Gran'pa, Daddy's home!"

One attached to each of his hands, they dragged him onto the porch. "Howdy, son. Didja . . . ?"

"Yeah, Dad. This is Cousin Edith, from St. Louis."

"'Course it is. I'd know you anywhere, cousin. And you'll have to call me Uncle Sam. Well, maybe not. Sounds a little too Yankee for me. Just call me Sam."

His grin was the same as his son's, only not quite as broad or infectious. The big shoulders were like Jeff's too, only weighted by an extra twenty years. It was his left leg that dragged. His eyes were deep-set and his blond hair showed touches of frost. Despite that, the two men looked more like brothers than father and son.

When Edith shook hands with him, she felt no electric tingle as she had with Jeff. However, she was aware of the faintest glimmer about him, almost imperceptible even to her sharp sense.

"Don't leave our cousin standing, son," the older Mr. Dane said. "Breakfast'll be ready in two shakes." He glanced at his granddaughters. "Get washed up, my beauties."

"Yes, Gran'pa," the two girls piped and ran off.

Jeff said, "I'll get your luggage, Miss Parker."

"Perhaps . . . if I could go to my room first. I'd like to take my hat off."

"That's right, son. First things first. Speaking of which, my pie's about ready to come out. 'Scuse me, miss. I mean, Cousin Edith." He grinned.

Jeff and Edith followed Mr. Dane into the house. "Dad's one of the best cooks around. We used to have a bunch of ladies coming around after Mother died, bringing all sorts of food. Maybe he should have married one of 'em but he said he'd rather learn to cook than replace Mother."

"When did she pass away?"

"Two years ago. Here you are."

The rooms they'd passed through had been neat without being finicky. She noticed the mantels and tables were bare of knick-knacks, not even pictures. However, there were a great many books, both on shelves and scattered freely around.

At the end of the upstairs hall, Jeff swung open a door and stood aside to let her enter a good-sized white room. Instead of the heavy curtains, beaded, bobbled, and fringed, that her aunt had always hung, thin muslin covered the windows, draped back to let the full sunshine in. The brass bed was neatly made, the candlewick spread flat and nearly smooth. A mirror above a plain pine dressing table showed Edith her own tired face.

"What a pleasant room," she said, reaching up to take out the hatpins that seemed to have dug through to her skull.

"Thanks, it's mine."

Edith's hands stilled. "I beg your pardon."

"This is my room. I'll be bunking in with Dad while you're with us. Don't worry," he said in response to her startled look. "It's no trouble."

"But I can't . . ." He was gone.

Edith looked at the big, deep bed. It seemed to grow larger as she stood there. She'd never slept in a bed that belonged to someone else nor ever even shared a mattress with a friend. Her aunt had been horrified by the thought of such moral decay.

Searching her spirit for some hint of true distaste, Edith was startled to find none. She reminded herself that this was a *man's* bed, a very attractive man's bed. This is where he laid

his head every night. Possibly he'd shared it with his wife—
Gwen. Edith knew that married people usually slept in a
common bed though she didn't imagine it could be very
comfortable.

Laying her hat down on the pine bench at the foot of the bed,
Edith smoothed a single wrinkle out of the white spread. She
followed the crease up to the pillows, the minute dots of the
pattern tickling her palm. The pillows were down, deep and
soft. Edith fought the urge to put her cheek tenderly against
one.

After all, it couldn't hurt to sleep in a man's bed as long as
the man were sleeping somewhere else. Jeff wasn't likely to
lose his way in his own house, or to absentmindedly return to
his former room by mistake. Such a thing would be absurd.

*The darkened room showed only a glimmer of moonlight
through the translucent curtains. Long ago the house had
quieted and now the few sounds that reached her wakeful ear
were of the house settling. Then, faintly, she heard a footstep in
the hall outside her door. Propping herself up, she looked
toward the sound and saw the white china knob of the door
turn. A slice of darkness grew as the door opened. Soft as a
whisper, Jeff called her name. "Are you awake, my dear?"*

*Frozen, she didn't answer. She heard him sigh and the creak
as the door began to close. "Yes, I'm awake." He came back
into the room, closer and closer. . . .*

Edith sat up, pressing her hands to her cheeks. Her heart beat
very fast and her lips were strangely dry. Perhaps she'd fallen
asleep and dreamed. . . . No. That fantasy had been produced
by her waking mind.

Swinging her feet off the bed—another sin to be counted
against her, shoes on a clean counterpane—Edith vowed to
take this fantasy as a warning. She would lock her door. Not so
much to safeguard against Jefferson, but as a defense against
her own worst nature.

A few minutes later, she stepped into the wide hall. Following her hunger, she found her way to the kitchen by the smell
of warm biscuits. Both girls were there, their hair wet from
splashing their faces. Mr. Dane, a red gingham apron contrast-
ing with his blue jeans, worked at the big black stove.

"There you are. Just in time." He placed a towering stack of pancakes on a plate and put it down at an empty chair. "Now don't say you can't eat all of these. They'll just go cold if you don't pitch in."

"Oh, I should be happy to eat whatever you set before me, Mr. Dane." She sat down and poured pure amber honey over the stack. The pancakes looked wonderful, high and moist. "Your son said you were a fine cook."

"He did? Shucks."

Though his expression changed little, he flipped a pancake high in the air, catching it in the pan. Maribel laughed. "Do it again, Gran'pa."

He obliged and then said, "That's enough. I want to eat 'em, not play with 'em."

Every moment, Edith expected Jeff to walk into the bright kitchen and seat himself at the round oak table that gleamed golden in the sunlight. She found herself eating more and more slowly, to give him time. The little girls had no such restraint. They ate with relish, sometimes seeming to put more in their mouths than they could hold.

Mr. Dane said, around a mouthful, "Won't be much left for your dad, Louise, the way you go on."

"Um, where . . . ?" Edith began.

"You can't expect that son of mine to sit down to eat before he's checked the stock. Not after being away for a week. But then, he does the same thing every morning the Lord sends."

"Commendable," Edith replied. All at once, she began to eat more quickly, certain she was merely trying to get ahead of the children. After all, she had a lot of meals to catch up on, and at their rate of speed, there'd be no second helping if she didn't hurry.

She looked up to find Louise gazing at her. Edith became a little nervous. The child's look seemed to be largely composed of speculation and surprise, as though she were wondering what strange kind of insect she found in the yard. Sternly, Edith told herself that she was far older than Louise and should easily be able to manage the child. Yet when she tried to meet her steady gaze, it was Edith's eyes that fell.

"If you're done eating," Louise said, "I'll be glad to show you 'round, Cousin Edith."

Mr. Dane frowned. "That's right nice of you, honey. But I bet she's worn out from traveling, aren't you, uh, Edith?"

"Actually, I slept very well on the train. Thank you, Louise. I'd appreciate a tour."

"Okay." The girl took her plate to the sink. "You ready?"

"Me too," Maribel cried, climbing down from her chair.

Like Louise, the younger daughter of the house carried her plate to the sink, although she demonstrated greater care, holding the rim tight in her fists. Edith felt it wise to follow the little girls' example and also put her sticky plate into the cast-iron sink.

"Why, thanks, cousin," Mr. Dane said. "Girls, you run on out in the yard. I want to talk to Miss Edith a minute."

With some alarm, Edith resumed her seat. She folded her hands primly in her lap and looked up at the older gentleman, trying to disguise her apprehension. He leaned back in his chair to glance out the back door. Edith peered past him and saw that both girls were running around the yard, aimlessly.

Mr. Dane brought all four feet of his chair back to the ground. With a mysterious air, he drew a small clipping out of his apron pocket and unfolded it. His deep-set brown eyes looked at the neatly torn piece and then locked on hers.

"You don't resemble your picture much. You sure that son of mine brought home the right party?"

He handed the paper across. It was her own advertisement from the *Bulletin*, from the last time it ran. Edith had never noticed before how sharp and narrow her aunt's gaze was behind her black pince-nez. Perhaps it was her own guilty conscience that made it seem her aunt was giving her a most criticizing look.

At the same time, however, Edith recalled that Jeff had mistaken her for her aunt when first they'd met. She cringed at the thought. Surely, she could not look so stern . . . so . . . incurably virtuous.

"That's my late aunt. I'm running the service now."

"You must be pretty busy. Jeff must have been kind of pushy to get you to come all the way out here."

"I didn't have very much choice, I'm afraid."

"You mean he *made* you throw everything else up? That doesn't sound like Jeff."

"Oh, no," Edith said, hurrying to adjust Mr. Dane's wrong idea. "He was courtesy itself. It was just that . . . well . . ."

Without knowing quite how, Edith began telling the older man all about her troubles with her empty post box and her demanding landlord. "Really, I was at my wit's end."

"So when my son offered you a job, you jumped at it?"

"No, she didn't. That's the last thing she did."

Edith turned around in her seat. Jeff Dane leaned against the kitchen door frame, his arms folded across his chest. She had no idea how long he'd been standing there, but he surely must have heard every word, even when she described him as "a gallant knight riding to her rescue."

He pushed lazily away from the upright post and entered the room. A long brown dog followed him in. The animal stopped and raised its head. Edith found herself looking into the sad face of what was probably the ugliest dog she'd ever seen in her life. His face was all wrinkles and his ears were long lappets.

"Down, Grouchy," Jeff said, shaking the coffee pot.

The hound slumped against the ground, gazing up at her out of pouchy red-rimmed eyes. Cautiously, Edith extended her hand. The whiplike tail thumped against the boards of the kitchen floor as he lifted his pointed face to sniff. He whimpered as his wet nose nuzzled her hand.

"What kind of a dog is it?"

"A hound dog. Got a first-class smeller there. Track anything over any kind of ground, won't you, boy?"

The small eyes rolled ecstatically at his master's voice.

Sam said, "Would you believe that dog slept outside your door at night, Jeff? Wouldn't budge much in the daytime either. I think he was worried. Since one master left him, I mean."

"Left him?"

"His owner died last year," Jeff said. "He left Grouchy to me in his will."

"I see." Moved, Edith took a piece of bacon off her plate and offered it to the dog under the table. As nonchalantly as a baby,

Grouchy stood up, stretched and yawned, showing a dark tongue. Then, as if he were thinking of something else, he filched the tidbit and gave her hand a quick swipe in thanks before lying down again. Edith met Jeff's eyes and had to smile when she realized he'd seen the whole thing.

"Did you ever have a dog?" he asked.

"No, I wanted one but I had enough trouble convincing Mr. Maginn that I should be allowed to keep Orpheus."

"You've missed a lot."

"Perhaps."

He sipped his coffee. "Remind me to pay a call on the landlord of yours next time I'm in St. Louis."

Sam said, "Maybe I'll go along next time. Sounds to me like the fellow needs a little lesson in how to treat a lady."

7

EDITH LOOKED BACK and forth between the two men. "It's all right," she said, not sure if they were serious or not. "I imagine Mr. Maginn has other things to think about now. After all, his home did burn to the ground."

"What do you remember about the fire?" Jeff asked.

"Nothing, really. I took Orpheus and . . . of course, the stairs weren't burning yet, just the lower landing. . . ."

"You were lucky not to be burned in your bed," Sam said.

"Everybody got out, I think. I remember standing in the street with lots of other people. Mr. Sandrow—from across the street—I didn't know he was bald. And Mrs. Webb . . . I'd never seen a red silk nightie before."

Jeff coughed and she raised her eyes to him. "I'm sorry," she said, "I'm running on and you must want your breakfast."

"Never mind. I meant to ask, how is it that you came to me? Surely you must know people in St. Louis . . . relatives?" He smacked his hands together. "I should have asked you that before. I can send a telegram to anyone you want me . . ."

A silent shake of her head silenced him, for she looked as

though this refusal were the most prosaic thing in the world. His father leaned forward and said, "There must be someone who needs to know where you are."

"No, my aunt was my only relative." She smiled, that elusive dimple peeping out for a moment like a shy child. "Until now, that is. I think I'm going to like being your 'cousin.'"

Standing, she said, "I've forgotten about Orpheus. He must be so hungry. He wouldn't eat on the train."

The two men watched her go out. Jeff sipped his coffee, his thoughts wandering down unaccustomed and frightening pathways. Though he'd had a variety of adventures before settling down at last on the family ranch, he'd always known that the love and strength of his family were behind him. He cherished memories of an openly affectionate mother and a father whose manliness had never been threatened by a hug. Those recollections served as a cushion against the rough, sometimes brutal world. What would it be like to have no one? No one at all?

Sam said, "That's a brave gal."

"No argument. But I didn't know things were so bad with her as that. Losing everything you own is one thing. Not having anything worth missing is something else."

"Maybe, son, you could manage to take a bit longer than a week to make up your mind about the ladies. After all, we can't send that little girl back to St. Louis with a lousy twenty-five bucks in her pocket."

"Uh, I promised her fifty."

"Fifty!" His father leaned back and made a long arm for the coffee pot. He tipped a generous measure of the thick, hot brew into Jeff's cup and then into his own. "That's a lot of money. Are you sure she's going to be worth it?"

"I don't know. She seems to have . . ." He shrugged. "If she can't help me, then she'll go home with fifty dollars. We can just call it charity."

"Things are really that bad for her?"

"You should have seen the room she was living in. My shack when I worked on the Trinity had a more homelike feel. A good, big fire was the best thing that could have happened to her boardinghouse."

"Why do you suppose a nice girl like that would live in such a place? She is a nice girl, isn't she?" Sam narrowed his eyes at his son.

"Don't worry, Dad. She won't teach the girls five-card stud or how to swear." He examined the formidable face of the woman in the advertisement. "Ask yourself what kind of girl this lady would have raised and you'll see why I'm so sure."

A little while later, Jeff stepped out onto the porch. He glanced up at the little cage and saw that the bird was drinking, his head tipped back and his tiny throat working. When the bird saw the man, he flirted his wings and cheeped.

"Sociable little thing, aren't you? Where's your mistress?"

He stepped off the porch, setting his broad-brimmed hat on his head. It was good to be back on his own ground. Without thinking too much about it, he inspected at the house, checking the paint and the roof. He kicked a few white pebbles back onto the path and snapped a drooping flower off the honeysuckle vine that sprawled on a trellis at the front of the house. Gwen had loved honeysuckle. Though the fragrance clung to his fingers, it was not of his late wife that he was thinking as he came around the corner of the house.

He saw his daughters grubbing in a depression in the ground. A recent rain had left this spot soggy and the girls were squatting down above it, intent on their play. Several rocks served as bases for their mud cookery. Edith stood in the shadows of the house, watching them.

Before she could speak, Jeff strode forward. "Louise, Maribel! Is this any way to behave before our guest?"

Their startled faces jerked up at his first words. Now Maribel's lower lip began to quiver and her eyes filled with tears. Louise, her left cheek smeared with rich brown mud, sent a resentful look toward Edith. "We didn't know she was there."

Edith hesitated no longer. She stepped forward and said, "Excuse me, Mr. Dane . . . I mean, Cousin Jeff. There's no need to be cross. I don't . . ."

"You're very kind, Edith, but they ought to know better. Now march inside and get washed up."

"But we're not finished . . . ," Maribel began to protest.

"Yes, you are."

She turned her swimming eyes up to her father, her baby lip pouting. Ediths' heart turned to butter, though she saw Jeff standing firm, his hands resting on his hips.

"Don't cry," she said. "Your pies look good enough to eat. But you know, they really should bake a while. You go in and wash as your father wants you to, and I'll watch over these so they don't get too brown. I mean . . . any browner."

Maribel's eyes cleared as though by magic. Louise, already halfway to the back door, turned and looked back. Edith expected to have to work hard to build liking in the older girl's heart, but she saw no hostility there now. Louise gave Edith an easy smile as she waited for Maribel to waddle over to join her. As they went inside, their heads were together, Louise whispering to her young sister.

"It wasn't necessary for you to stand up for them, Miss Parker. I'm not a brutal father."

"I know it." She looked down at the mud circles she'd seen so carefully placed and patted until they took on a favorable appearance. The edge was even crimped by Louise's fingers in imitation of real pastry crust.

"But I insist on decent behavior in front of guests. They have to learn to be respectful. I can't have them growing up like wild Indians."

"Of course not. I can see you must do your duty."

Edith unbuttoned her gloves and stripped them off, tucking them into the belt at her waist. Gingerly, she bent her knees and sank down above the mud puddle. With care, she arranged her skirt, turning a breadth up to keep it clean.

Looking up, she saw him standing in amazement above her, his well-shaped mouth open. "I always wanted to do this," she explained. "My aunt never allowed it. I hope you don't mind?"

"Mind? Uh, no."

He watched her take a handful of the solid mud. With care she brushed off the twigs and bits of grass that blemished the surface. Weighing the clod in her hand, she peered around for a suitable rock, exactly like a woman in an unfamiliar kitchen.

"Here."

Jeff walked to the flowering border beside the house and

pulled loose a more or less square gray stone from the edging. He knelt, one knee in the grass. With a solemnity that did not feel at all out of place, he handed her the stone.

"Thank you."

Copying the children, Edith reversed her hand, placing the mud with a solid plop on the stone. It was a peculiarly agreeable noise. With a stick, she scraped the sides so they were even with the stone, flinging the excess mud back into the wallow. A few white pebbles arranged in the center for effect and Edith nodded her approval as she dusted her dirty hands.

"That looks nice," she said, turning her head toward him. Her happy smile wavered at the expression in his eyes.

Suddenly, she realized how completely insane she must appear. Hastily, she began to stand up. She stepped on her skirt, hearing an ominous rip. Trying to stand and step back at the same time, Edith tripped over her feet. She felt herself falling, destined to land in the mud at her feet.

Then his arms were tight around her. She staggered, only his solid strength keeping her upright. "Whoa there. Hold on."

His voice was in her ear, thrilling with its deep register. Across her breasts lay one of his heavy arms, his hand squeezing her upper arm. His other arm clasped her waist. She had never felt so safe. And yet . . . Edith knew she was on the brink of a great danger. Was it brave or foolhardy to dare it?

She turned her head to look into his eyes, so close that she could see the golden flecks in their depths. "Thank you," she whispered, not moving.

That strange look appeared in his eyes again. Edith saw that she was making a fool of herself. Surely by now he was ready to put her on the next train out of Richey, even if it went to the moon or the Badlands. She dropped her gaze and lifted her arms to free herself.

In his arms, she weighed no more than a fine porcelain figurine, liable to break at an irresponsible touch. As though she had rocked upon her shelf, Jeff very carefully released her.

"I'll have to get some fill dirt to dry up this spot," he said, clearing his throat.

"Must you? The girls were enjoying it so much."

"I guess I don't have to do it right this minute. But it'll have to be done. Any more rain and we'll have a sinkhole big enough to lose the wagon in."

Edith nodded gravely. "Yes, a farm like this must be a great responsibility."

She moved away from him, wishing her heart would return to its usual place. At the look in his eyes when he held her, it had leaped up into her throat.

"If you don't mind my changing the subject," she said, "I wonder when you would like me to begin working. The sooner, the better, as my aunt used to say."

She did not explain that her aunt had used this chestnut only in reference to an unpleasant task. Pleasure could always be deferred. The disagreeable must be done at once.

"You shouldn't worry about it today. After that long train ride, you should rest. Take a day or two to just kick back."

"No, that would be stealing your time, Mr. Dane. Let's plan on driving into town a little later today. If you will introduce me to your candidates . . ."

"I have a better idea," Jeff said. "Tomorrow there's a sewing bee for one of the preacher's girls, Dulcie. She's getting married and all the women have been cutting out this and that. You know, women's stuff."

"Yes. Perhaps it would be best if I met the ladies under the appearance of a social call. After all, it would be impolite to let them know they were being looked over."

She furrowed her brow, as she thought of a delicate question. "But what should I bring to the bee? It would be very rude to arrive both uninvited *and* empty-handed."

"You can sew, I guess?"

"Yes, I can, but I have nothing prepared."

"Seems to me there must be a couple of half-finished things of my mother's around. She didn't often get to finish the fancywork. There was always a button I was missing. And Dad's awful hard on the elbows of his shirts."

"But I couldn't take something of your mother's. You should keep them. I know I'd give anything to have something that belonged to my mother."

"Do you remember her?" Jeff stirred the top of the mud with the toe of his boot.

"No. I was very young. But I sometimes dream about her. At least, I think it may be her." She knew the loving presence that hovered over her as she slept was definitely not Aunt Edith.

"What . . . ?"

The banging of the door broke into what he was going to ask. The two girls came tearing out of the house as though hornets were after them.

"We're clean!" Maribel shrieked as the girls began to dance around the grown-ups. Water sprayed them, thrown off by Maribel's wringing wet braids. The collar of her dress dripped diamond points of water. Louise looked a little better, with only a large water stain spreading out from her abdomen.

"I can see that," Edith and Jeff said at the same time. They gave each other a smiling glance.

"Are you ready, Cousin Edith?" Louise asked.

"Ready?"

"You wanted me to show you around, remember?"

"Oh, yes. Please."

"Come on, then." Louise took Edith's hand and began to walk away. Perforce, Edith had to follow, with Maribel dancing alongside to a song of her own making. Jeff took a step after them, unsure whether he wanted to accompany them or to keep Edith by him another moment.

Edith looked over her shoulder at him. He was staring down ruefully at his boots, sunk to the ankles in mud.

Behind the house was a lazy, looping path that ran through a large garden before opening out into fenced pastureland. Edith would have liked to stop to admire the flowers and vegetables but Louise kept a steady drag on her hand. Once clear of the garden, Louise abandoned the path to cut straight across the grass toward the large barn.

The two girls chattered about everything, hardly stopping for breath. Maribel was excited about starting school in a few weeks. Louise, an old hand at school, was more interested in the fair that was to take place at the end of the week.

For some moments Edith had been bothered by an impossible sight. She had casually dismissed the large black objects in the pastures as monolithic stones. In the back of her mind, she had wondered if this part of Missouri was volcanic or had been patterned by some sort of Druid of an earlier age. Now, however, she turned uneasily to watch the "stones." Had that one moved?

Close to the fence, a "stone" turned its hefty head and mooed. Edith stared in openmouthed wonder. Cows couldn't possibly grow this big!

More like shifting slabs of night than beasts of the field, they had coats that reflected a high gloss. They showed not a spot of white, nor even brown. Seeing that Louise observed her amazement, Edith said, "I had no idea they'd be so huge."

"Shucks, Aberdeen Angus aren't *big*. Daddy says they're compact, compared with the longhorns or the . . . the . . ."

"The Herefords," Maribel piped up.

"That's it. Mr. Rivers got some Herefords. They're great big . . . bigger 'n' ours by . . . I don't know. A whole lot."

"These will do just fine for now," Edith said.

Still awed by the fact that anything that big could move at all, she was in no hurry to see greater wonders. The black cattle had blocky bodies that looked as though someone who had never seen a cow had tried to sculpt one. The fine detail was absent. And they were so black they might have been made of the jet mourning jewelry Aunt Edith used to wear.

Down at the big barn, the two girls took her to meet the dairy cow. After seeing the massive beasts in the field, Edith felt quite safe with the almost insignificant creature. A mild brown eye regarded the children indulgently as the jaw moved pensively. The white tip of her snout made her look as though she'd been dipping into her own milk pail.

"I got to milk her," Louise said. She went forward to walk the cow into the shed, laying a hand on its rear quarters for encouragement.

Involuntarily, Edith exclaimed, "Do be careful, dear!"

"It's okay, Cousin Edith. I been milking Tammy since I was Maribel's age. She sometimes kicks the bucket over in flytime, but she's never kicked me."

In a moment, the milk was falling into the wooden bucket with a musical beat. Peering over the gate, Edith saw the little

girl with her head pressed against the large animal's flank. Her
thin arms pumped up and down to the rhythm of milking. The
splashing was almost hypnotic as the blue-white milk fell.

Looking up, Louise asked, "You want to try, Cousin Edith?"

Edith shook her head. Then she realized how preposterous it
was to make mud pies eagerly but shrink from the real work
this girl did every day. "All right, if you'll show me how."

The teats hanging from beneath the full udder were firm and
warm. Edith winced when she took one tube between her
thumb and forefinger. "It feels so alive," she murmured.

"'Course," Louise said, giving her a perplexed frown.
"What did you think?"

"I can't say I've ever thought about it very much. In the city,
we buy our milk in bottles."

"Well, you knew it came from a cow."

"As I said . . . I never thought about it. The bottle was just
there on the doorstep, every morning."

Maribel shrieked with laughter. "Daddy," she said, running
out of the barn. "Cousin Edith thinks milk comes in bottles!"

Jeff came in, Maribel carried in the crook of his arm. Seeing
Edith still sitting on the milking stool sent the little girl off
again. "Bottles, Daddy. Milk in bottles."

Louise looked fiercely at her sister. "Hush, Maribel. It's not
polite to tell someone how stupid they are."

"That's right," Jeff said, putting the little girl on her feet.
"Besides, some places milk comes in a bottle. I've seen it
myself. A man comes around with lots and lots of bottles in a
big white wagon and drops a bottle off at each house."

"Oh, Daddy," Maribel said, clearly doubtful.

Edith had sat up straight when Jeff came in, letting go of the
teat. It seemed somehow indelicate to milk a cow with a man
watching. She preferred to concentrate on the children, even
though she began to feel as stupid as they thought her.

She said, "The milkman has a white horse, to pull his wagon.
And you have to get up very early in the morning to see him,
because he has to go to all the houses before the people are up."

Two pairs of hazel eyes studied her with pity. "That's okay,
Cousin Edith," Louise said. "You don't have to make up 'the

milkman' for us. We don't even believe in Santa Claus anymore."

"Not since we were little," Maribel said, sucking on the tip of her braid.

"That's right," Jeff said again, but Edith noticed something sad at the back of his eyes as he looked at his daughters.

Giving himself a shake, as though he were waking up, Jeff walked over to stand above her. "Doing the milking for us, Miss . . . Edith?"

She looked at the cow, who regarded her over her shoulder as though to say, "What is the hold up?"

"Louise was planning to show me how, but I think now . . ."

"Oh, I'll show you." He reached over and took her hand. "It's simple enough, really. You just reach . . . you have to be relaxed. Gentle. You're all tense. Let your hand go floppy."

He shook it mildly as though to work free all the tension. Edith knew it came from his touch and it wouldn't subside until he let go. Instead, he reached up, still holding on, and placed her fingers around the teat.

"Start up high, and pull straight down. Remember, gently. Take it slow."

When the milk splashed into the bucket, Edith laughed in surprise. "Gracious!"

"There you go. You've got it now. Try two hands." He straightened up and stepped back.

"Why is Daddy's face red?" Maribel wanted to know. Louise hushed her.

Edith sat up. "It's very interesting," she said. "Why don't I let Louise do it, though? She's so good at it."

"All right," Louise said, sitting on the milking stool. "Though I guess you'd get the hang of it pretty quick."

Jeff said, "Dad's probably rooted out those bits of sewing I told you about by now. If you want to go take a look . . ."

"The girls want to show me around. Don't you?"

"Sure," Maribel answered. "Come look at the baby chicks. Louise is going to show 'em at the fair."

"So you said before. But what fair is this?"

"The big fair." Maribel lifted her arms to show how big.

"Cows and chickens and sheep and goats and . . . ice cream!"

Jeff explained, "The county fair travels around the county and this year it's here again. Starts on Friday, officially. We hold it in Richey's Meadow out beyond the town. And Maribel's right. There's livestock judging and plenty to eat. Dad always enters his roses, though he hasn't won a prize yet."

"But they're so beautiful!"

"Yes, well . . ." Jeff rubbed the back of his neck and looked at her sideways. "It's like this . . ."

"He was robbed!" Louise said, grinning over her shoulder.

Her father returned her smile. "That's right, honey. You keep on being a smart girl and you'll go far in this world." To Edith, Jeff said, "Dad's got a competitive nature, that's all."

"He seems very nice."

"Yes, he is. But crazy as a bedbug."

"Crazy?"

"Completely! At least on the subject of flowers and cattle. It got so I had to quit entering my prize bull, the Black Prince. Dad would sulk if we lost and turn boastful if we won."

If Jeff thought his father was crazy for that, what would he think of her if he ever found out the truth? Could Jeff believe in her powers? Edith doubted it. He was as attractive a man as she'd ever seen but he was still a man.

Her late aunt had held no very high opinion of the flexibility of the male mind. Edith herself hadn't enough experience to know if Jeff was one of the rare few who could accept the mysterious at face value. She decided to use her power for him, if she could, but never to tell him. After all, she was hoping to hold on to Jeff Dane's good opinion for the length of her stay.

"Where are these chicks?" she asked.

8

"MAYBE THIS ISN'T a good idea," Edith said, hesitating on the wooden walk.

"Don't worry. You'll like them."

"I'm sure I will." But the question in her mind was, Will they like me?

Lady Jessica stood outside the throne room. Within, Her Royal Majesty would soon choose her ladies-in-waiting. Splendid in a white ruff and farthingale oversewn with ·brilliants, Lady Jessica looked as magnificent as any of the other virgins who were vying to serve the Virgin Queen. She wondered if their knees were knocking as hard as her own. All depended on the vital first impression. A stammer, a misspoken word and she would be banished again to frigid, lackluster Northumberland.

Jeff lifted the basket out of the buggy, telling Grouchy to stay put. "The ladies of Richey, I have to say, can hold their heads up with as much pride as any queen."

That didn't make Edith feel more confident. She could imagine all the women huddled in the corner, looking at her with contempt. They'd whisper behind their hands, criticizing every detail of her clothes and hair.

Jeff took her elbow. Though his touch was warming, she gazed up with apprehension at the house next to the church. A vivid garden hardly left room to walk to the door but served to disguise the foursquare style of the house.

"Don't get Mrs. Armstrong started on her flowers," Jeff said. "She's as wild for them as Dad is. When they get together, that's all they talk about."

"That must be nice for your father."

"It would be, if they didn't argue. Dad likes things neat and Mrs. Armstrong—well, look around."

Brilliant orange lilies bloomed on top of blazing red asters. Yellow roses poked out from the cone-shaped flowers of a thriving dark purple butterfly bush while blue lobelia warred with a flourishing red phlox. Up the porch supports clambered a screaming yellow and green trumpet vine while a gentle pink clematis made a curtain across the front.

"Well, it certainly is cheerful," Edith said.

"Yes. Cheerful is what I'd call it."

Before he could knock, the front door opened. A very tall, blonde girl, her figure as fully developed as Sabrina Carstairs', stood on the threshold, her hands outstretched in welcome. She had a warm, happy smile that seemed, like the sun, destined to beam on everyone. It showed her slightly prominent front teeth more than a prudent girl would have allowed.

"Hello! You must be Mr. Dane's Cousin Edith! I'm Dulcie. Come on in." She stepped back, nearly knocking over a white Devonshire vase, filled with every color of gladiola.

"Oops," Dulcie said, grabbing and righting it. She moved very quickly for a large girl, especially one who seemed all legs and arms. Edith was reminded of the large daddy longlegs that used to inhabit the attic at a former flat of her aunt's.

Jeff held out the basket. "Here's some things from Dad."

"Isn't Mr. Dane the sweetest thing?" Dulcie asked Edith.

She smiled, hoping she wasn't committing herself to an opinion. It all depended on *which* Mr. Dane Dulcie meant.

"I mean," Dulcie rushed on heedlessly. "For a grown man to spend his life in a calico apron . . . that's sweet!"

"He seems to enjoy it," Edith said, now certain.

"Oh, I don't see how he could. I hate cooking."

Since Edith had already been awakened by Sam's joyful, tuneless yodeling while he baked, she felt sure he enjoyed doing the baking. And when she'd seen his high, light meringues, garnished with blackberries and mint leaves, she had known he loved it. He'd whipped a pint of fresh cream to be served alongside the delicious circles of sweet puffs.

Dulcie peeked inside the basket. "Ooh!" Turning her head, she called, "Mother!"

"Yes? Coming."

The woman who came through the arched doorway did not present the image that Edith had expected after seeing her garden. Mrs. Armstrong dressed with Quakerish plainness, as befitted the wife of a preacher and the mother of hopeful girls. But on closer inspection, Edith saw that her hazel eyes had the same zest for life that her garden expressed.

She greeted Edith and said, "Arnie Sloan has told me so much about you, I feel like we're friends already."

Edith had never been greeted with such warmth. She couldn't quite meet the Armstrongs' eyes. To know she was there under false pretenses was as embarrassing as the time her garter fell in the greengrocer's.

She said, "You have a lovely garden, Mrs. Armstrong."

Jeff heaved a sigh. "I'd better be going along to the meeting, Edith. You're going to have a fine time. I'm leaving you in the best of care."

"Ooh, you darling!" Mrs. Armstrong flung her arms around his waist. "You can't go 'less you give me a little kiss. Just a little smooch . . ."

"Why sure, you beautiful creature, you."

To Edith's surprise, Jeff swept Mrs. Armstrong into a bear hug while Dulcie turned her dark brown eyes up to the ceiling in exasperation. "Mo-ther!"

At the end of the hall, a man appeared who looked more like a blacksmith than a preacher. "What?" he bellowed. "My wife in the arms of another!"

Edith backed up, her hand fumbling for the white vase. Was she about to witness a sensational scene of adultery revealed?

She couldn't quite believe it of Jeff, yet the evidence was before her very eyes.

He put the preacher's wife behind him, valiantly. "You've surprised us, sir."

"And in front of my daughter!"

Edith decided the vase wouldn't stop such a big man from tearing Jeff into little bits. Blindly, she sought behind her for the cast-iron fruit bowl also on the table.

The preacher walked forward and sadly shook hands with Jeff. "If you want her, my son, you must have her. I'll want five dollars and a good cow."

"Oh!" Mrs. Armstrong shrieked, stepping out from behind Jeff and punching her husband in the upper arm. "Is that all I'm worth to you? After twenty-four years of marriage?"

"Has it really been twenty-four years?" her husband asked wonderingly. "It seems like yesterday you were batting your lashes at me."

"I never . . ."

Mr. Armstrong peered into his wife's eyes. "Why, you're mighty pretty, Miss Drake. I think I'll follow Jeff's example."

Once more Mrs. Armstrong was swept into a strong embrace. This was no mock kiss, however, but a thoroughgoing effort. On both sides.

Edith took her fingers from around the foot of the bowl. Obviously, this melodrama had been a joke. She turned her eyes to Jeff, who winked at her. Instantly, she dropped her gaze. Would he be insulted that she had thought the worst of him?

Dulcie said, "Fa-ather! Really!"

There was a loud *smack* as Mr. Armstrong came up for air. His wife looked dazed and she held onto her husband's thick arm as though to keep from going over weak at the knees.

Jeff said, "Oh, woman, woman. Faithless . . . I go my way. Brokenhearted."

He dragged his feet all the way to the door, while the Armstrongs laughed at him. "Alas, cruel fate," Jeff moaned. "Edith, I'll pick you up at four o'clock. If I don't drown my sorrows in the watering tank first."

"I hope you won't," Edith answered with a smile. "I'd hate to walk all the way back to the ranch."

He gave her a quick, frowning glance as he opened the front door. Mr. Armstrong said, "Wait a minute, Jeff. Are you going to the fair-committee meeting?"

"Yes, sir."

"Let me come along too. I've heard a distressing rumor about the games of chance—that whiskey is to be one of the prizes. Now it's bad enough that the Red-Eye will be open during the fair hours but we mustn't allow . . ."

Jeff held up his hand. "You don't have to convince *me*. Come along to the meeting. I'm sure the boys will hear you out."

"Thanks. Let me get my coat. I'll meet you out front."

As the door closed behind Jeff, Edith felt as though she'd been abandoned by her last friend. She looked toward the Armstrongs, trying to smile.

Mrs. Armstrong said suddenly, "Gracious! You must be thinking we're all touched, Miss Parker. Such awful behavior in front of a stranger!"

"I thought you were wonderful!" She relaxed. Maybe it would be all right. A rush of enthusiasm carried her into making an impertinent suggestion. "Have you ever thought of taking that performance on the stage?"

Mrs. Armstrong shook her head, a motherly smile on her lips. "We don't believe in acting in public. And no dancing."

"Mo-ther," Dulcie said. "Miss Parker isn't going to kick up her heels in the hall!"

"It's best she should know these things. And shouldn't you be doing your hair? The other guests will be along in a moment."

"Am I early?" Edith asked, instantly sure she was imposing dreadfully upon this nice family.

"Oh, no," Mrs. Armstrong said. "Everyone else is late."

"Jeff said . . ."

"Men!" Mrs. Armstrong looked lovingly up as her large husband came into the hall again, working his arms into the sleeves of his black coat. "They always think things like this start on the minute, as though we're running a railroad. And as for you, Ezra Armstrong . . ."

"I'm going, I'm going." He rolled comical eyes at Edith and hooked a thumb at his wife. "You see who's master in my house."

"We said a long time ago that you've got the church you can be boss of. The house is my business so git!"

"Yes, madam trail boss." He snapped off a salute as he left, his wife and daughter gazing after him lovingly.

Edith left her eyes stinging, and didn't know why. She blinked the water away fiercely. "Is there anything I can do to help you get ready?"

"Lands sake, child, no. You're our guest. Go and have a sit-down in the parlor. I'll come in a minute. Got to get those children washed."

Obediently, Edith went into the rose-pink and wisteria-purple parlor. It was hot there, for the morning sun illuminated the triple windows at one side. She wished she hadn't put on that extra petticoat, but had thought "better safe than sorry."

A small, uncomfortable-looking chair beckoned to her. She moved it into a corner and sat down. It gave way beneath her.

Unable to jump up in time, Edith crashed to the floor. The fall rattled her right to her teeth.

The Armstrongs came rushing into the room. There were a lot of Armstrongs. Three boys, ranging from a young man to a tow-headed boy with two missing teeth, pointed at her. Two young girls, one with slightly lowered skirts and one still in pigtails, giggled. The oldest boy of the group, tall and dark, shook his head. He came over to offer her a hand and hauled her up out of the destruction. All that remained of what had been, no doubt, a treasured relic of the house were a few pathetic sticks.

"I'm so sorry," Edith whispered. She wanted to rub where it hurt but she folded her hands instead.

"Are you all right?" Mrs. Armstrong asked. "I should have warned you. That old chair isn't fit to sit on."

"Wasn't fit, Ma," the young man said. He must have been nineteen or twenty. "I don't guess it can be fixed now."

"I'll be happy to replace . . ."

Mrs. Armstrong shook her head. "Can't be done, Miss

Parker. Wouldn't be worth it, anyway. Piece of old junk. Put it right out of your mind."

"But really . . ."

She wasn't allowed to finish her offer. Her hostess led her by the hand to the plush settee. "You just sit down. I'll get you a cup of tea. You must be shook from head to foot."

"I am, a little. Thank you."

Edith sat and sipped her tea, ignoring the younger children who peeked in the window, discussing her. The young man came in to sweep up the pieces.

"Don't worry, Miss Parker," he said. "This old thing needed repair anyhow. And I didn't want to do it."

"You would have done it?"

"Sure." He shrugged as though it were an everyday accomplishment. "I like to make stuff. I carved that bird behind you on the wall."

The bas-relief songbird looked as real as Orpheus, though still the native brown of the wood. She almost expected the bird to flap its wings and fly away. "It's very good," Edith said. "You're obviously talented."

"If you don't mind . . . I know we just met an' all, but could I do a carving of you?"

"Of me?"

All the members of the Armstrong family were tall, though most of the children were blond. While his hair was a dark, curling mass, his eyes were an intense blue she hadn't seen in his parents. His arms dangled out of their too short sleeves, his hands surprisingly delicate in form. She could believe he was an artist.

Edith decided he'd probably done likenesses of all his family and friends. Perhaps he'd even made a carving of Jeff. She'd like to see it, if he had. A new face, even one like hers, must be welcome to an artist's eye.

"What's your name?"

"Gary. An' if you want, I could get the materials right away. I've got a couple of nice blocks all sanded and . . ."

"Now isn't a good time, Gary. There's the sewing circle. I'll be in town for a week though, at least."

"Sure, sure. I know. It's just . . ." He blushed, the color

coming and going like a tide. His hands twitched as though they already held his tools.

Edith gave an encouraging smile. Artists were often shy, she'd read, and being shy herself, she knew what it was like. She would have been hard-pressed to say which of them jumped higher when the first knock sounded at the front door. A gabble of female voices began the moment Mrs. Armstrong opened it.

Glancing around to address a word to Gary, Edith found she was alone in the parlor. But not for long.

A phalanx of women entered, all friends. Edith could tell by the warmth that flowed around them. It was as strong as love, though of a different order. She had no hope that she could ever be part of such a group.

They looked at her with curiosity gleaming in their eyes. She rose to her feet, shaking out her skirt, and offered a calm smile. They couldn't tell how her heart was beating, or that the tea in her stomach had suddenly turned sour.

"Now, girls," Mrs. Armstrong said, bustling around to the front. "This is Miss Edith Parker, Jeff Dane's cousin. She's come to stay with them for a little bit."

At first, there had seemed to be dozens of women crowded into the parlor. Soon, though, Edith realized there were only five, including Mrs. Armstrong. Two names caught her attention.

"I'm Miss Climson, the schoolteacher."

"And I'm Miss Albans. Vera Albans. I do lots of things. Make hats. Sew. Anything, really."

"Vera," Miss Climson said. "You mustn't say you would do *anything*."

"Pretty much, S.J. Pretty much." She looked at Edith with an inviting glance, one eyebrow raised above a blue-gray eye. Her hair was like hot gold, caught in a smoothly bulging style.

Edith felt compelled to speak. ."I . . . I . . . make things too. Um, flowers. I make paper flowers. And fans."

Mrs. Armstrong looked up brightly from her conversation with the other two ladies. "Did someone mention flowers?"

"What a pity you don't trim hats," Miss Albans said. "I was hoping to hear what the latest styles really look like. They can't be the way they're described in the magazines. They just couldn't be!"

The ladies all laughed at her mock dismay. Edith joined in, a half-second behind. Secretly, she sighed in relief. At least she'd scraped through there, though why she hadn't simply said she had private means? Perhaps because she could be plausible as someone who lived by selling paper flowers whereas she *never* could have passed for an heiress.

A belated knock at the door sent Mrs. Armstrong scurrying off again. Miss Albans leaned over toward Miss Climson. "That'll be Mrs. Green, S.J."

"Undoubtedly."

Miss Climson had brought out an elegantly embroidered pillowcase. Spreading it carefully across a tea towel laid over her dark brown skirt, she began to attach blonde lace to the edge. Her stitches were tiny and meticulous, for which she donned steel-rimmed glasses that she'd also removed from her work bag. Glancing at Miss Climson's work, Edith could see that each stitch was precisely the same size as all the others.

"Isn't that beautiful!" Edith said, reaching out to touch the elaborately entwined design of birds and vines.

"Please don't," Miss Climson said without missing a stitch. "I am trying to keep it clean."

Edith recoiled. "I apologize."

This was one of the women Jeff had in mind. How could he consider her? She'd always be telling Louise and Maribel not to touch things.

Miss Albans leaned closer to Edith, whispering, "Don't mind S.J. She's . . . particular, that's all. But nice, once you get to know her."

Out in the hall, a woman's voice was engaged in a lengthy explanation. "So I went back for the pound cake and forgot my sewing. Then the dog shook himself all over the clean floor and you know how water spots ruin varnish so the only thing to do . . ."

Miss Climson set another stitch. "Mrs. Green does occasionally take a breath," she commented quietly.

She glanced up. Edith did not need her special sight to

recognize in the teacher a capacity for laughter like a spring of joy. "She . . . she does?"

"Oh, yes. However reluctantly."

Mrs. Green was still talking as she came in. She broke off in the middle of a rambling story about what her youngest had said to come up to Edith. "I've heard so much about you. I couldn't wait to meet you. Tell me, is it true what they say?"

"About what?" Edith asked.

"About the county fair, of course."

"The county . . . ? I'm afraid I don't know anything . . . when Jeff comes back . . ."

Miss Climson stepped in. "You know we're having the big fair here in Richey this year. I hope the weather will be fine for it. The children are so excited about it all."

"The weather will be fine, S.J., but what about the fair? Is it true that there will be professional horse racers?"

"What?" the other ladies asked, turning from their work and their own conversations.

Mrs. Green nodded emphatically. "Yes, I heard it yesterday from Mr. Bradley. He swore to me that it was true. Professional riders, that's what he said. He referred to them as 'jockeys.'"

Edith spoke above the resulting babble. "I'm sorry. I don't know anything about it."

"Impossible," Mrs. Green said. "Perhaps you just missed hearing about it because you were so busy with the rest of the organizing. I'm sure you're doing a fine job but if you need any help, feel free to call on me."

Edith's head swam. She stammered out a polite "Thank you."

Vera Albans came to her rescue. "No, no, Adelia," she said, patting the plump redhead on the arm. "This isn't Leena Michaels from Cat's Wallow. This is Miss Edith Parker . . . you know. Jeff's cousin. Arrived yesterday."

"Oh, of course. I'd heard from Arnie that you'd come for a visit. I'm a scatterbrain. Do please forgive me."

Mrs. Green had a smile that lit up the room like a candle on a frosty night. Actually, with her deep bosom, bright red hair, and comfy build, she would be able to keep Jeff warm without a blanket on the coldest night Missouri could throw at them. But what about summer? He couldn't have two wives—one for snow and the other for summer?—could he?

A cool, collected brunette like Miss Climson would make an excellent antidote to Mrs. Green's exuberance. But what about poor Vera Albans, left out? Perhaps she could take spring, for she was pretty as a rose. Pity there wasn't a fourth candidate to occupy and console Jeff's autumns.

Edith shook herself, realizing she'd gone too far. She was to help Jeff Dane to find a wife, and she'd already married him off to four women, one of whom didn't even exist.

Mrs. Green looked around the room, greeting everyone. When Mrs. Armstrong came in again, bearing a fresh pot of tea, Mrs. Green asked, "Where's that nice little chair? Have you finally decided to have Gary fix it?"

Mrs. Armstrong put the tea tray down on the table. "Miss Parker, shall I freshen your cup?"

"Yes, please."

Mrs. Green said again, more loudly, "Are you having Gary fix the general's chair?"

When the preacher's wife began to talk to the other ladies about their sewing projects, Mrs. Green turned to Edith and said, "Mr. Armstrong served under General L. L. Polk in the late conflict. He was there when the general was killed at Pine Mountain. He kept the general's little campaign chair as a memento. No one ever sits on it, but I'm just so envious of them for having it. *My* husband sent a substitute to the war, for which I'm very grateful but still . . ."

Edith was dumbstruck with guilt and shame. She sat in the corner, feeling miserable. Once or twice she raised the apron she was working as though to look more closely at the stitches, but really to block a welling tear.

When Mrs. Armstrong again went into the kitchen, Edith volunteered to help. "I want to say . . ." she began.

"Now, you're not to mind what Adelia Green says. God just plain left the tact out when He made her."

"I'm grateful to her. Now that I know I have ruined a cherished memento, I will certainly . . ."

"No, you certainly won't." The preacher's wife cut her off. "But you could do me a favor."

"Anything!"

"That girl of mine is like to drive me wild! Here, this party's all for her and she hasn't stirred a step outside her room. Be a dear. Go make sure she hasn't set herself on fire trying to curl her hair."

"About the chair, Mrs. Armstrong . . ."

"Coming!" she called in response to a hail from the parlor. "It really doesn't matter, Miss Parker. First door on the right as you go up," she said, nodding toward the small stair that rose in one corner of the kitchen. "Tell her how rude she's being. They want to see her, even if she isn't perfect in every detail."

Having destroyed a valuable heirloom, Edith couldn't very well refuse her hostess' commission. Though knowing nothing of young girls, Edith felt she could at least deliver a simple message. On the way up, however, Edith decided to soften Mrs. Armstrong's command.

She rapped on the white door in the hall. "Dulcie?"

A muffled reply reached her ears. It sounded distressed.

Edith knocked again, and the door opened. "Dulcie? Your mother asked me . . ."

All Edith could see of the girl was her bustle. The rest of her was leaning out the window. "Go away," she said.

"All right." Edith began to withdraw.

"No, wait." Dulcie drew her head in and turned.

Edith gasped and covered her lips with her hand. Dulcie Armstrong had gone positively green.

9

HER FACE WAS thickly coated with a bright-green paste. Tears cut white tracks through the compound. With her nearly white hair and deep brown eyes, Dulcie looked like a wild ghost-witch preparing to cast an evil spell. Especially with the desperately angry look haunting her eyes.

"What is that on your face?" Edith asked, closing the door instinctively.

Dulcie pointed toward her dressing table. A bowl of the gluey substance sat on a towel. At Edith's approach the boggy surface shivered as though alive.

Next to the bowl sat a magazine which Edith recognized at a glance as the last issue of *The Horse and Stockmen's Quarterly Bulletin.* It lay open to a page headlined, "Aunt Hermione's Beauty Cures."

The letters were nearly all complaints of love unrequited. Most of the advice was the same—to be sweet and patient while waiting for the desired object to see one's sterling worth. Edith had received many letters from "Aunt Hermione's" disappointed correspondents who had seen their beloved drift off on the arm of one not so worthy, but far more active.

However, "Aunt Hermione" occasionally broke down and offered concrete solutions to tough questions. This one was on "Clearing the Complexion." Reading the ingredients, Edith realized that *concrete* was the proper term for this solution.

She read the ingredient list again. "Equal parts alfalfa and clover hay, linseed oil, and gluten. Stir well. Apply regularly to the face. Morning and noon feedings stir well into nine pounds of corn and oats, equally mixed."

A fearful suspicion took hold of Edith's mind. "Oh, dear. Did you read these instructions all the way through?" Dulcie nodded. "But what about this last sentence? About morning and noon feeding?"

Shrugging, Dulcie made a strangled sound. Edith interpreted it as "misprint." "I'm afraid you're right, but that's not the misprint. It's the part about apply this regularly to the face. The *Bulletin* has been having trouble getting things right lately." She looked at the magazine again to confirm her guess.

"What you have on is a special feed for calves. At the bottom of the page begins 'Mr. Hollister's Scientific Remedies.' He suggests a milk and honey mask for one's young bulls."

She glanced in sympathy at the young girl, whose face was now as fixed as a granite statue's. "I'll get your mother."

Dulcie waved her arms frantically and shook her head. From a bedside table, she pulled out a white-backed Bible. Staring at Edith, she thumped the book several times with her fist.

"I'm sorry, I don't understand."

Tossing the book aside, Dulcie's eyes rolled. Edith felt stupid. Then Dulcie lifted one finger as though to say, "Ah!"

Exaggerating every motion, she curtsied, then held up her arms as through expecting to be swept of in a waltz. She danced once around in a circle, nearly knocking over the washstand.

Facing Edith once more, she put one hand on her hip and shook a finger of the other as though forbidding something. Edith realized her own face was suddenly saying "Aha!"

"Your parents wouldn't approve of this," she interpreted.

"They'd think it was vain and silly like dancing. Well, they're right, you know. My aunt . . ."

Dulcie said without moving her lips. "Help!"

Edith tapped Dulcie's cheek with her finger. Then she tried to scratch it with her nail. Water made no impression. An experiment with some hoarded eau de cologne brought a little green off on the dampened handkerchief but didn't even begin to remove the thick layers.

"Dear me, it's really stuck. Are you sure you only used what the recipe called for? I wonder if lining a young bull's stomach with cement is really a good idea."

Dulcie pointed to a nearly empty bottle also on the dressing table. Picking it up, Edith was at once struck by a strong smell of spirits of hartshorn, a well-known thickener. "I'm getting your mother," Edith said firmly, starting toward the door.

The young girl grabbed Edith's arm, halting her. She shook her head frantically.

"We must do *something*," Edith said. "You can't stay like that. Besides, everyone is waiting for you."

Dulcie began to cry, all the harder when she realized that not even tears could now melt the plaster on her face. Then Edith said, "I have an idea. Wait here."

Dulcie indicated with a look that there was little else she could do.

A few moments later, Edith opened the girl's door again and stood back. Gary walked in, a tan bag in his hand. "Good golly," he said. "What a mess!"

"Please don't gloat, Gary. We don't have time for that," Edith said, shutting the door. "Just go to work."

He set the bag down on the dressing table. Snapping back the locks, he removed his carving tools. Dulcie shrank back. "Now don't worry," Gary said, patting her shoulder. "You know my hand never slips. But you better hold still."

Forcing herself to smile, Edith came over and picked up Dulcie's hand. Holding it awkwardly, she said, "I'm sorry, but he was all I could come up with. Are you sure you don't want me to tell your mother about this?"

Gary answered for his sister as he picked up his smallest

chisel. "Don't even think about it, Miss Parker. My folks are about as easygoing as you can imagine but they're death on vanity. Why, they made my little sister Annie wear a big plaid bow on her hair most of last winter, just 'cause she said it didn't become her. They don't want us thinking about our outsides, when it's our insides that matter."

After fifteen wincing minutes passed, most of the green had fallen in chips to the floor. Gary broke off in the midst of a tuneless whistle. "That's the best I can do. Say, if you can make me up some more of this stuff it sure would make a great medium for modeling. It handles really nice."

"Oh, get out, Gary," his sister said. "No, wait. I'm sorry. You've been a big help. I wouldn't have gotten out of this mess without you."

Gary bundled his tools back into his bag. "Don't mention it. And you better get washed up. You still look kind of green around the gills."

Edith let go of Dulcie's hand. The marks of the girl's nails were driven into the side of her palm. Once or twice it had seemed certain that Gary's hand would slip.

"He's a very good carver," Dulcie said, after the door closed behind him. "And I thank heaven for it. If he'd cut my face . . . I already have buck teeth, you know, and a scar wouldn't make me look any better."

"Your brother is right. You are still greenish," Edith said, not knowing how to answer. Dulcie's front teeth did stick out and not all the polite nothings in the world would make them go in. "Where's that cologne? Maybe if we scrub extra hard with that . . . it took some off before."

"I can only thank you again. I was so mortified for anyone to see me like that!"

"Oh, well," Edith said, pouring cologne on a handkerchief. "I'm not anyone."

Downstairs, the ladies were working hard on the delicate underthings and bed linen that a new bride required. Mrs. Armstrong, her starched apron brilliantly white, fussed over the refreshments in the dining room. "There you are, Dulcie. What a time you've been! Thanks for getting her, Miss Parker."

"It was a pleasure, Mrs. Armstrong. Can I help you with . . . anything?"

"No, no. Go along and talk with the others. Dulcie, be nice to everyone. They're working for your sake, you know."

"Oh, Mother! I'm not going to snap their noses off, for goodness sake."

Dulcie nudged Edith who stood with her mouth open in the middle of the doorway. "C'mon. I want to see what I'm getting."

Haltingly, Edith followed as Dulcie went ahead, prattling. "Of course, it's very good of them to do nice things for me, but I want to get married without all this fuss. After all, people get married every day. And if you really love someone, you don't need linens and aprons and pillowcases and all the rest, do you?"

She held the door open for Edith to follow. Her tender smile firmly in place, Dulcie said, "Hello, everybody!"

Edith sank into a vacant chair near Mrs. Green. She blinked and passed her hand over her eyes. Then she stared, fixing her inner vision strongly on Dulcie. She failed to make out the slightest glimmer or glow about the young bride-to-be.

As a test, Edith looked at the others in the room. Neither Miss Climson, Miss Albans, nor Mrs. Green gave off any light at all. Several of the women with rings on their third finger, left hand, had a certain incandescence about their figures but it was by no means brilliant.

Her gaze dropped to the carpet. Edith's chest felt hollow, as though something were missing. It was as though she'd been suddenly struck blind. Surely, a young lady approaching the height of her existence must be sending out rays of light radiant enough to dazzle even casual observers.

Then Mrs. Armstrong entered and it was as if a comet had blazed around the room. Edith sat upright, wishing she had a pair of glasses with smoked lenses to protect her outer as well as her inner eye. Knowing a relief that left her limp, she basked in the glow of Mrs. Armstrong's affection for her husband.

"Thank goodness," she whispered.

"I beg your pardon," Mrs. Green said.

Edith merely smiled at her in meaningless apology. If her "vision" hadn't been working properly, she would, of course, have had to resign immediately from Jeff Dane's employ. The risk of matching him with an unsuitable lady would have been too great. She could not act without seeing the hidden emotions of others.

Actually, she had matched up letter writers without using her talents, and those matches had, apparently, worked as well as those she'd "helped" along. Yet a regular choice would not do for Jeff. Edith knew she'd not be satisfied until he and his children were completely happy with the perfect wife and mother.

She glanced around. Miss Clemson continued setting stitches with machinelike precision. Miss Albans had laid her work aside for the moment, deep in conversation with two other ladies. From the way they held up their hands and exclaimed, Edith guessed they were discussing scandal. Mrs. Green was also sunk in conversation with a married lady. They had a comfortable look, as if they were talking of cake recipes and furniture polish.

Then her eye fell upon Dulcie, who was showing off her amethyst engagement ring to her friends. The only glow Dulcie wore came from the tiny gem on her finger. Edith feared that a merely material flash would not outlast the bridal year.

Dulcie sat beside her. "What an elegant apron. I'll save it to wear it for company, or when Mr. Sullivan calls."

"Mr. Sullivan?"

"My fiancé. Victor." Dulcie dropped her eyes, her lashes shading her cheek. If Edith had been a normal person, she might have sworn to Dulcie's blush. As it was, however, she could only marvel that such acting talent ran in a family determined not to use it for profit.

"Have you known him long?"

"Oh, no. Ours is what you might call a 'whirlwind' courtship. He only came to town two or three weeks ago. It was love at first sight. For both of us."

"Was it? I believe that's very rare." Edith turned the subject back to the apron she was working. "Most of this was made by the late Mrs. Samuel Dane. I'm just finishing it so you can have it."

"Really? I liked Mrs. Dane a lot. I'm glad I'll have something of hers."

Tending closely to the heart of one of the embroidered flowers, Edith asked, "What was Mrs. Jefferson Dane like?"

"Didn't you meet her?"

"No, never."

Dulcie said, "I liked Gwen. She seemed like a real happy person, always laughing and flirting."

"Flirting?"

"Oh, yes," Mrs. Green entered their conversation easily. "Gwen Dane was a dreadful flirt. She must have had half a dozen beaus on her string before Jeff came back."

"Came back? Where had he been?"

"Like so many young boys, he was lured away from home by temptations we women never suffer. What, dear?" Mrs. Green rose to answer Mrs. Armstrong's summons.

Seeing perhaps that Edith looked shocked and intrigued, Dulcie laid her fingers on Edith's arm. "I heard that Jeff Dane went to a gold strike on the Trinity River in California when he was eighteen. To hear some of these folks talk, you'd think that was a sin. I think it's an adventure. I'd love to be able to just pull up stakes and chase a dream. Wouldn't you?"

Edith didn't mention that she rarely had to chase dreams. Usually, she had to frighten them off. Even now, as she worked her needle through the fabric, she was thinking of dawn above a silvery river. *The rampant scents of wildflowers filled her spirit as she opened her tent flap and stepped out into the cool lushness of a California morning.*

Wildcat Hawes they called her, as quick on the draw as any man jack. Little did the grubby miners know that under her buckskin vest beat a heart ablaze with love for only one man, the man she'd followed to the primitive conditions of the gold-fields. She fought to conceal her love, knowing that he didn't want her as much as he wanted that gleaming devil, gold.

The time passed quickly, as it always did when she was lost in daydreams. Wildcat was just showing her beloved the error of his ways when she looked up to find Jeff grinning down at her.

"Where are you?" he asked. "A million miles away?"

Edith looked around. Half the ladies had left. She only hoped she'd been civil in her farewells. Sometimes when she was lost in thought, people could speak to her and she wouldn't hear them. Like Mrs. Webb, several people in the boardinghouse had considered her insufferably stuck-up when she'd only been fighting Tartars during dinner, or taming tigers at noon.

She tied the final knot in the last flower. "I'm ready," she said. "Just let me say my good-byes."

Jeff waited for her until the bracket clock on the mantel chimed the quarter hour. Then he went in search of her.

He heard the bass rumble of the preacher's voice before he entered the kitchen. Pushing open the door, he heard, "To cling to possessions is folly, Miss Parker. Some of the best men who ever lived have taught us that."

"That's true. But there is a difference between sharing your goods with the poor and having them smashed to bits by clumsy guests."

Jeff thought, What's up now?

"The message is the same. I should remember General Polk for his faith and good works rather than for his talents as a military leader. That chair was the wrong thing to remember him by. I can see that now."

"Don't tell me . . ." Jeff muttered.

Edith said, "Will you tell me more about him, Mr. Armstrong? I should enjoy learning about such a noble gentleman. Maybe if you share your memories, you will keep them all the brighter."

Mrs. Armstrong said, "There now, Ezra. Stop making the girl feel guilty over a chair."

Jeff coughed and walked in. "If there's anything I can do . . . Maybe I can fix it, though if Gary can't, I guess my skill won't pay toll."

"I'm afraid I've wrecked it utterly, Cousin Jeff," Edith said,

hanging her head. She would have told Jeff about her mishap
once they were private. Then only she would see his disappointment. Perhaps he would decide he didn't want such a
bumbling nincompoop handling his delicate liaisons. If that
were the case, she'd want to hear her dismissal in private too.

"The chair was old," Mrs. Armstrong said. "And it didn't go
with any of the furniture."

"I think," Mr. Armstrong replied, "that will be the last word
on the subject. Jeff, do you want some coffee?"

"No, thanks. I'd best be heading back. Lots to see to when
you've been gone a week."

"I bet those pretty girls of yours seem to have shot up since
you left."

"They sure have." Jeff turned to Edith. "You won't believe
it, Edith, but they were just babies last week."

After some more good-byes and Dulcie's surprisingly warm
farewell embrace that left Edith shy and bewildered, Jeff and
Edith walked out to the street. Standing by the boardwalk, Miss
Albans and Miss Climson had paused to talk privately.

Jeff tipped his hat as he opened the gate. "Good day, ladies.
Hasn't the weather turned sunny?"

Watching carefully, Edith saw no sparks fly between Jeff and
either of the two young women.

Miss Climson said, "I'll want to have a talk with you about
Louise, Mr. Dane. We really can't have her running wild about
the schoolyard like she did last year. And your younger child
will be starting this fall too, won't she?"

"Yes, Maribel will be there. And Louise has grown up a lot
since that little incident with the firecracker."

"I'm glad to hear it. I'm all for patriotic fervor but not five
months before Independence Day."

"I agree completely, Miss Climson."

Miss Climson said, "It was a pleasure to meet you, Miss
Parker. I hope to see you again soon. Good day." The school
teacher began to walk away.

Miss Albans said, "My best to your father," before she
followed her friend. Mrs. Green had evidently gone hurrying
home to her sons. Edith wondered if sparks ever flew between

the warmhearted matron and the widowed man beside her. She was ashamed to admit, in the secret, darkest depths of her soul, that she hoped they did not.

"I want to stop by Mrs. Green's a moment," Edith said. "She promised to give me a pattern for a new style of rose."

"A flower?"

"For embroidery." She sat on the edge of the buggy's seat, pressed into the rail at the side, recalling from the earlier ride how close his thigh lay next to hers on the seat.

"All right, but please don't stay long. I've got to get back. Chores can't wait for gossip."

"I don't know enough about the townspeople to gossip."

"Mrs. Green does."

As soon as the buggy drew up in front of the small house, Mrs. Green waved from the window. Then she came out, empty-handed. "I'm so sorry, Miss Parker. I've looked but I just can't find . . . everything's topsy-turvy. The boys were playing 'fort' while I was gone and they've turned the settee upside down and were using the legs of my desk as a mock turnspit. I can't find anything!"

Jeff offered, "Do you need help to move the furniture back?"

"Oh, no, I've managed nicely. The boys are really good-natured about putting things back, once I remind them. But I'm afraid you'll have to wait for your pattern, Miss Parker. I could bring it by later; I'm sure it won't take me a minute to find it once I've set my house in order."

"How would it be if I call for it, later on?"

"Yes, perhaps that will be best." Her red hair was brighter than ever in the sunshine for she'd run out without a hat. Her skin had that beautifully clear, almost translucent quality, that only red-haired people possess. Even in the strong sunlight, she seemed to have no wrinkles. She also seemed to have missed the liberal sprinkling of freckles most red-haired people fall heir to.

Yet even with such a flawless face turned up, Edith saw no sparks fly between Mrs. Green and Jeff. There wasn't enough glow between them to attract an unfussy firefly. Not even the sharp, harsh light of mere physical infatuation.

Much perplexed, for her work had just gotten more difficult, Edith sat in silence as they rode out of town. The haze that blurred and gentled the air, giving the landscape the look of an old-master painting, left her unmoved. What could she do? Her task was now not only to find Jeff Dane a bride, but to make him fall in love with the lucky woman.

10

"SO," JEFF SAID as they drove to the ranch. "How was it?"

"I had no idea people still did such lovely handwork. Miss Climson's workmanship was especially impressive."

"That wouldn't be the reason I'd choose her to marry. But what I mean is, how did they treat you? Earlier I got the idea that you were a little worried about that."

"Oh, no. Everything went swimmingly," Edith said, not really attending.

"Come to think of it . . ." Jeff peered around the brim of Edith's hat. "You still look worried. Did something happen? Nobody was rude to you. I know they couldn't have been."

Edith watched the red earth spin away beside the buggy. How much could she tell him?

Edith said slowly, "I am a little concerned about Dulcie. When I first met her, I didn't realize she was the bride-to-be."

"That's right. Nobody thought anyone would ever fall for her. Maybe you noticed her teeth . . . ?"

"They're not *that* bad," Edith said, defending her newfound friend. "Everyone seems to think she'll start gnawing at the trees to build a dam. Yet I have arranged matches for several young ladies who were much less comely than Miss Armstrong. After all, she isn't wearing a wig or false padding."

"You don't have to worry about Dulcie. Her fiancé doesn't mind her teeth, so why should we?"

He glanced at her. She toyed with her glove, tugging the fingers out of shape and then slapping it into the palm of her other hand. She wasn't watching the road, as he'd thought, but seemed to be looking inward.

Jeff stopped the buggy. Edith straightened up to face him. "What are you doing?"

"You're really worried about her. Why?"

"Are you going to stop a buggy every time you want to speak to me? We shall always be late."

"But what interesting talks we will have had." Jeff dropped his hand over Edith's. "Come on," he said, "Spill the beans."

Quickly, she slipped her tingling hand out from beneath his. "Don't do that!"

"Do what?" His face hardened. "Touch you?"

"Excuse me, Mr. Dane. I'm not used to it." She folded her hands, controlling her sudden need to touch him to dull the sharpness of her rebuke. "I am not a demonstrative person."

"No, I don't suppose you've had much encouragement."

"It isn't a matter of encouragement. A lady should have no need to touch anyone, except with a parasol."

His smile came back. "What do you do with it? Whack them over the head?"

Edith pulled her lips in tight against her teeth. When she'd fought down the bubble of her laughter, she said sedately, "Of course not. A lady should only . . . poke."

Jeff chuckled. "Right in the back."

She didn't like that cold mask to drop over his features. It was more comfortable to think of him as a happy man than to see the dark emotions he possessed, as did all humanity. Edith would have preferred the whole world show her only its contented side. That way she had no responsibility.

Jeff lifted his hand as though he'd touch hers again. Instead, he cleared his throat. When he had Edith's attention, he said, "You still haven't told me what is troubling you."

She had to tell someone or the burden would be too great. "It's Dulcie. How well does she know this man she intends to marry?"

"Victor Sullivan only came to town a couple of weeks ago. They met at a church sociable a few days after he got here. I reckon he's a fast worker."

"What do you think of him? Personally, I mean."

"Nothing, so far. I haven't had much to do with him. He's popular enough, from what I've heard. Why?"

Edith hesitated. How much could he—could any man—believe? "I don't feel Dulcie is really . . . in love with him."

"What? Did she say something to you?"

Edith shook her head.

"You saw something while you were at the Armstrongs'? Was she kissing somebody else?"

"Of course not. Not if she were promised to another."

"Well, then . . . ?"

"I just . . . feel it. My feelings are never wrong about things like this."

"Oh, is that all?"

Jeff shook the reins and started the buggy moving again. Grouchy sat down in the back, satisfied they weren't getting out.

"Is that all?" Edith asked, shocked.

"Yeah. Just because you've imagined a 'feeling,' you're getting all worried. That's pretty foolish, don't you think?"

"Certainly not! I rely on my feelings."

"'Course you do. You're a woman. Gwen was the same way. She'd get a creepy feeling and stop dead in the middle of whatever she was doing. Once she told me the henhouse was haunted. She didn't dare go in. Took me two weeks to convince her there was nothing wrong."

"How do you know there was nothing wrong? She might have been right."

"Don't tell me you believe in spooks? That's . . ."

"What? Ridiculous? Asinine?" Edith began to feel very warm. A strange jumpy sensation in the middle of her stomach made her understand what the expression "making my blood boil" really meant. His calm dismissal of one half of human existence was enough to send her into a passion.

"Yes! Damn it, every time a woman wants to get out of trouble, she talks about her 'feelings' or her 'nerves.' Men don't play that kind of game."

"No, men simply dismiss anything they don't understand!"

"We don't invent ghosts that aren't there, that's for sure."

"How do you know there weren't any? If you can't see them, how do you know they aren't there?"

"What?" He shook his head as though to clear it after a punch. "This is too stupid to talk about. How did we get into whether there are ghosts are not?"

"I don't know. But personally, I'd rather believe Gwen's feelings than yours! At least she had them!"

They rolled into the farmhouse drive. Edith did not wait for his help to climb down. Putting her nose in the air with a sniff, she walked quickly up the path.

Jeff caught up to her in the cool porch. He seized her by the elbow and turned her around. "Look, Edith, I'm sorry. This 'feeling' obviously upset you. Sit down and we'll talk it over."

"There's no point," Edith answered, irritated further by his so obviously humoring her. "You aren't about to believe what I say merely because I have a feeling about Dulcie and this man."

"Would it make you feel better if I found out a little about Sullivan? I could go to the Red-Eye and talk around some."

"The Red-Eye?"

"It's a saloon. Sullivan has been spending time there in the evenings."

"A drinker?" she exclaimed, repelled.

"Don't look like that. A man likes to take a drink now and again. Even I . . ."

"You're a father. You shouldn't be going into saloons."

"I'm a father, not a saint."

Lifting a stray strand of hair off her forehead, he tucked it under the brim of her golden straw hat. It seemed like the same loving attention he'd given his daughters that morning, but it felt far different. Jeff wanted to pull free the comb that trapped her hair and thrust his hands into the soft, free waves.

"Edith, men and women are . . . different."

It might have been wiser, Edith thought, to go directly into the house. It was certainly far from wise to look up into Jeff's face and murmur, "Different? How?"

He leaned down slowly to brush the corner of her mouth with his. Her skin was as soft and sweet as the first peach of summer, and Jeff knew a surge of hunger. But he controlled himself, waiting for her to scream, to slap, to run away. Instead, a tremor ran through her as her eyes closed. Ever so slightly, her chin lifted.

Edith's knees were trembling. It spread through her body, leaving her too weak to turn away. His scent, so virile and real, filled her senses and made her head whirl. As he cupped her face with his roughened hands, she swayed toward him.

His lips were warm and soft as they nudged hers. Edith held very still, hardly breathing. He withdrew the merest fraction as though waiting for something.

Her own lips felt so dry she had to lick them. She chose to do so at the exact moment Jeff kissed her again.

"Edith!" he said with his chuckling laugh. Then he pulled her close. His mouth, resolute now, swept over hers. Her knees weaker than ever, she clutched his shoulders as he bent her slightly back.

She didn't know what to do except hold on. He teased and taunted her, kissing her delicately, then abruptly harder, only to draw away as she pressed closer. A new feeling, something she'd never known before, welled up inside her. Impatience. Blazing impatience.

Edith kissed him back. She didn't really understand what she was doing, he knew that, but when she leaned into him, her hands tightening, her inexperience didn't matter. He wanted to teach her. "Open to me," he whispered.

Her modesty made her hesitate but her newfound heedlessness drove her on. She didn't know what this would lead to. She realized that at this moment she didn't care.

The firmness of his tongue seduced her. She gasped, a tiny noise that seemed to inspire him. As he pulled her nearer still, one of his hands slipped down to cross her waist, pressing on her lower back. Without a second thought, she urged her body against his. From his body, she felt something surge forward that she instinctively both feared and longed for. The fear increased more quickly than the yearning.

She ripped away, her breath too fast, feeling as though she'd leapt out of the heat of a living fire. With the back of her hand against her lips, she stared at Jeff. His broad chest rose and fell to hurried breaths. She saw he stared back, with as much bewilderment in his eyes as must be in her own.

"Oh, my God," he said.

Her fingers crept to her crimsoned cheeks. "This is dreadful. I don't know what came over me. Please accept my profoundest apologies, Mr. Dane."

"Apologies? Edith . . ."

"I should not have tempted you."

"Edith," he said again, stepping forward.

Just as rapidly, Edith stepped back. "Obviously, I did something to tempt you, or you never should have behaved so. A lady will always be treated as a lady so long as she deserves to be. I have failed . . . somehow." She hung her dark head in shame.

"You're joking, right?" Her scarlet face told him she was not. "Listen, Edith, you're not responsible for . . . what just happened. It was me. I . . ."

"You're very good to take the blame, Mr. Dane."

"Jeff. Please remember to call me Jeff, from now on." He longed to hear her sigh it, to breathe his name in his ear as he buried himself in her. Jeff clenched his shaking hands. He'd never had his imagination run away from him like this before.

Everything was so clear. He could almost feel it, her white arms entwining around his neck to pull him down, to rest his head against her roundness, urging him on with those arousing whimpers at the back of her throat. And he'd give her such pleasure . . . to drive her wild in his arms so when he at last . . .

Jeff tried to listen to what she was saying, to empty his mind of the riot of carnal images that filled it. "Please, repeat that."

"Yes, Mr. Dane. As I was saying, it's good of you to take the blame. It is what I would expect of a gentleman such as yourself. But I acknowledge my own fault. I shall try not to tempt you again."

She saw that his gaze had dropped to where her hand was attempting to still the furious beating of her heart. She took her hand away as quickly as though the ribbon at her throat had turned into a band of fire.

Sputtering, she said, "I . . . I think I should return to town later to investigate the ladies more closely. The sooner we make a decision the better, Mr. Dane. I mean, Jeff. It may be difficult to decide. I like them all."

"My father's going later on. You can ask him to take you."

"Yes, yes, I will. Very difficult," she added as she hustled indoors to find his father.

Difficult, Jeff thought, wasn't the word for it. The half-frightened, half-pitying look she threw him as she left told him what she thought. So might she have glanced at a famished dog to whom she'd thrown a needed if skimpy bone. Clearly, she wished she could do more but had nothing else to offer.

Jeff ran an unsteady hand through his hair. She had much more to offer than she knew. The untapped passion of her virgin kiss dazzled him. A man could die of such a woman, die happily.

Later Sam Dane showed some surprise when Edith asked him to let her drive along with him. "You were just there this morning. I wouldn't have thought Richey had so much to show a lady that she'd head back so soon."

"She's a hard worker," Jeff said from the next stall. He stood up and looked over the dividing planks.

Edith tried to pretend he wasn't there, shirtless. She saw his bare shoulders when he stood. The telltale heat of a blush crept up her cheeks. She addressed herself solely to Sam.

"Your son has told me, Mr. Dane, that my coming here was your idea. I want to get my work done as quickly as I can."

"All right. I can respect that. But I have to warn you . . . I'm just taking the wagon. It's not very comfortable."

"I'm sure it will be fine."

"Okay, then. We'll get going in a bit."

"Thank you, Uncle," Edith said, catching a glimpse of one of the girls out of the corner of her eye.

"Oh, yeah. I almost forgot . . . ," Sam said, then broke off to cough, covering his slip.

Little Maribel came around the corner of the barn, a long black cord trailing from her hand. When she saw the adults, she grinned, showing the gaps among her teeth. "Look what I got," she said, twitching the cord so it made an interesting swirl in the dust behind her.

Crouching down to be on the child's level, Edith said, "Whatever is that?"

Holding it up, Maribel said with glee, "It's a snake!"

Edith was proud of herself for not shrieking in alarm. However, as she toppled over in terrified surprise, she could not claim to have much dignity left.

Both men raced over to pick her up, though Grouchy got there first. He poked his black, wet nose against her cheek. Jeff pushed the hound out of the way and helped her up. He studied her, while his father bent to brush off her skirts.

"It seems to be my day for falling down," she said blithely.

Recovering, Edith pushed away from Jeff's warm body, only to discover naked skin beneath her fingers where her hand rested on his chest. Soft, crisp hair curled around her fingers, and seemed to cling as she pulled back.

"Oh, dear," she said, staring, fascinated by the fact that he wasn't smooth. She never considered that the male of the species might have anything she did not have. The hair spread out across the strong, solid contours of his chest, glinting golden in the sunlight driving in through the barn doors. His arms, tanned brown, supple with muscles, seemed to ripple as he lifted his daughter up.

"Where'd you get the snake?" he asked.

Edith shuddered as the little girl lifted the limp reptile to show her father the sightless head. "I found it," Maribel said proudly. "It's all dead."

"Hey!" Louise's outraged voice sounded from the doorway. She ran in, shouting, "That's mine. I found it first."

Her bare feet sent up puffs of dust as she slid to a stop in front of her father and sister. "Give it back!"

"Won't! I found it!"

"Didn't! I did."

"No, you were looking in the water. . . ."

"But I saw it first!"

Taking advantage of Maribel being still in her father's arms, Louise grabbed the tail end of the snake and began to tug. Maribel gripped tighter, howling, "Mine, mine, *mine!*"

"Hold it!" Jeff bellowed. Two pairs of identical eyes switched onto him. "Leave the poor critter in peace. Dad?"

Sam took the flaccid creature from the girls and measured him out. "He's a good three feet, son. Wonder how he came to give up the ghost."

"Feel like tanning him, Dad?"

"Sure thing. Make a fine pair of snakeskin belts for a couple of young hellions I know tell of."

"Me, Grandpa!"

"No, me, Gran'pa!"

Jeff let the squirming Maribel slide down. "Unless you'd like it, Cousin Edith. Guests should have first choice."

Edith swallowed. "No, thank you."

"All yours, Dad."

Casually, Jeff reached out to shrug on his chambray shirt. He left a few of the top buttons undone, and Edith saw the diamond glints of sweat beading the hollow of his throat. The gentle hands that had roamed her body now rested on his narrow hips. She realized the latent power of his form. His wide shoulders and flat stomach seemed to be the most perfect shape a man could take. For some reason, her lips were dry again.

The milk cow lowed. "Care to make another effort, Edith?" Jeff said, jerking his thumb toward the sound.

"No, thank you. I'd better prepare to go . . . freshen up. Get the hay off my skirt. . . ."

She stumbled blindly toward the exit. All she could see was Jeff, as though he were imprinted on her inner eye. The sunlight dazzled her but didn't conquer the afterimage Jeff had caused.

Troubled by her reactions, Edith sought the sanctuary of her room. Yet even here, thoughts of Jeff pursued her. She'd lain awake for an hour last night, acutely aware that this was his room. As soon as she began to feel sleepy, she'd roll into the hollow in the center of the mattress made by his body. The thing that frightened her most was that she fit so well into the space. It seemed far too intimate a thing for an unmarried lady to experience.

But Edith knew that the difficulties of the night before would pale before those that would keep her awake tonight. For now she knew what it was like to be held by him.

Peering into the mirror propped on top of the dressing table, she sought for an outward change in her appearance. She looked just the same—"like a pickled calf's head," she murmured.

The curl Jeff had adjusted had once more fallen into her eyes. She withdrew the long hatpin and laid her hat aside. Her long hair fell in untidy waves to the crest of her bosom. She attacked the waves with her brush.

Someone knocked at her door. It couldn't be Jeff, she thought. He never waited after a knock to come in.

At Edith's summons, Louise poked her head around the door. "Ooh, how pretty!" she said, and bounced into the room. Standing slightly behind Edith, she looked at her in the mirror. "Did your hair take a long time to grow like that?"

Edith couldn't help being flattered by the child's gaze of open admiration. "Not very long. It was cut very short a few years ago, when I had an illness."

"Short as mine?"

"Much shorter." She ran her hand around her head at the level of her earlobes. "Like that."

"I don't like mine this short," Louise said. "All the other girls wear theirs in two long braids with big bows."

"But yours is such a pretty color."

Louise yanked on a piece of it. "It's straight as a board, Grandpa says. Maribel's is all curly."

"Many babies have curly hair," Edith said, aware that she was speaking out of a vast *in*experience. "I'm sure yours curled too when you were very young."

Louise looked doubtful. Edith hurried on, "Besides, smooth,

straight hair is all the fashion. Ladies even put special compounds on their hair to make it like yours."

"Really?" The young girl stood on tiptoe to see herself more fully in the mirror. She ran her hand over the bright golden hair that hung on either side of her face. Licking her hand, she flattened the sharp fringe above her eyebrows.

Edith thought the hard angles of the little girl's hair rather unbecoming to her pointed face. She would not say so, however, not for all the world. Even now, she could feel the unblunted pain of overhearing a visitor saying, "What an ill-looking child! Why ever did you pick *her*?" Though Aunt Edith had put the impertinent person in her place swiftly and succinctly, the shame of being thought unlovely remained with Edith to this day.

"You know," she said, getting up. "I have a ribbon here somewhere that would be so nice on you."

"Grandpa doesn't hold with ribbons. He says they take too long to fool with 'em. String is just as good."

"Oh, but all little girls like a pretty ribbon to set them off." She rummaged through the drawer she'd filled with her new undergarments. "Here," she said, pulling the ribbon from the bodice of a nightdress. "Let me put it on you."

Her hands shaking a little, for she'd never dressed anyone's hair but her own, Edith tied the blue satin band around the child's head, hiding the ends under her hair. The broad ribbon softened the severe hairstyle instantly.

"Look how blue your eyes are now, Louise."

The girl bit her lip as she leaned forward into the mirror Edith held low for her. "It does look kinda . . . okay." She turned her head from side to side, trying to see the whole effect. Her smile was wavering. "Do I look funny?"

Jeff's warm voice flowed over them from the open door. "You look like an angel, honey."

"Look, Daddy," Louise said, racing across the plain pine floor. "Cousin Edith tied it for me, an' everything!"

"Pretty as a picture," he said, dropping a light kiss on the ribbon itself. His daughter glowed at the praise.

"Maribel'll be sick as a dog when she sees. Huh, who needs any old snake?"

She ran down the hall, with Jeff watching to be sure she didn't slip on the long rag runner. Then he turned back to Edith. "My daughter didn't say it, so I will. Thank you, Edith."

"It's nothing. I now have so much that a ribbon won't . . ."

"I'm not thanking you for the ribbon. It's for caring enough to help her with it. Believe it or not, Louise doesn't think she's pretty."

"No woman ever really believes that she is. Except if she's vain, of course." She'd picked up her hairbrush again but could not use it with him watching. That would be another step on the road to intimacy, and she must remember every moment that she'd be on her way at the end of the week.

"She's beautiful to me. Both my daughters are beautiful. I try to tell them that but . . ." He shrugged.

Edith pictured his unclothed shoulders moving while the muscles in his back worked beneath his brown skin. Suddenly, her high collar was too tight.

Jeff leaned against the post at the end of the bed. "I guess it's like I was telling you before. They need a woman in their lives. Now that you've met Miss Climson, Miss Albans and Mrs. Green, what do you think of them?"

"As I said, I really can't judge so quickly. I'm used to letters. Meeting these people in reality, well, it puts my concentration off."

"How?"

Edith made a futile gesture with the brush. "Two of them are going to be disappointed. They may get their feelings hurt. If it were just a matter of choosing among a stack of letters, then the personal element doesn't enter into it. It's just yes or no, this pile or that. I don't get entangled."

"Your emotions, you mean."

"Yes. Now, I shall be imagining two of them hurt, and that makes me uncomfortable."

"What about that couple you were telling me about? The girl who had to really like cows."

"That was different. I knew as soon as I read Miss Fiske's letter that she would be the perfect person for Mr. Hansen. There was no question of choice."

"What do you mean . . . you knew?" Still leaning against the post, Jeff crossed his arms and gave her a hard, straight look.

"I . . . knew."

From downstairs, she heard Sam Dane shout, "Come on if you're ready, Miss . . . Cousin Edith!"

"Just a minute, Dad!" Jeff yelled back, only just turning his head. He fixed his eyes on Edith to compel an answer.

She sought for one, something believable. As though he read her thoughts, he said, "Don't try to lie. You can't deceive me."

"I wasn't going to," she answered, stung. "I'm just trying to think how to . . ."

A sound of heavy boots came clumping up the stairs, and Sam appeared in the open doorway. "Come on, Edith. If you two start talking, it'll be Christmas before we get going."

"Just a moment, while I pin up my hair."

"No time," Sam said. "Got to get to the depot so I can sign for the goods that are coming in."

"What goods?" Jeff asked.

"Never you mind, son." His father lay his finger alongside his nose. "Just get your hat on, Edith, and let's go."

"But I must put my hair up. It isn't decent . . ."

"Ah, heck! I've never seen a woman yet that wouldn't primp if she got half a chance."

"That's true, Dad. Do you remember how Gwen and Mother would keep us waiting? First one would come down and then the other and then they both trot back up because they'd forgotten something, or the other one would notice something wrong with the first one's hair or dress."

"Yep, that was it. We were five minutes late to church every single Sunday."

By the time they'd finished their complaints, Edith was waiting by the door, her dark red hair smoothed into its dull bun. "Well, come on, if you're in such a hurry," she said.

The Dane men exchanged a wink. Then Sam followed her.

Jeff lingered a moment. It made him feel warmly sentimental to see the brush and comb sitting on the dressing table, while a green ribbon, caught when the drawer was closed, peeked out. It had been a long time since a woman's dainties had adorned this room. He liked it and hoped it wouldn't be long before such things were here to stay.

He could trust to Edith's sense of responsibility. She'd stay, he knew, just as long as it took to find him a suitable wife. In the meantime, he'd have to keep his hands to himself. Soon enough, he wouldn't have to be so careful. There'd be a nice woman here to warm his bed.

After all, it was only celibacy and Edith's nearness that made such a dangerous combination. He couldn't, in honor, do anything about the first fact, but he could keep her at arm's length. He'd simply have to manage not to be alone with her.

Glancing at the white coverlet, he wondered how well Edith had slept. Probably she slept like the virgin she was, peacefully, dreamlessly. Her sleep could only be restful, untroubled by any ardent dreams.

He hadn't slept well at all. He woke himself shivering in the cool breeze that blew through the windows his father left open year-round. His father tended to take up more than his fair share of the mattress, and he was a cover stealer as persistent as Paul Tyler, his partner of the Trinity gold days. Jeff shook his head ruefully, remembering those wild, carefree days.

The nights had been wild too. Edith, shocked by the thought of him taking an occasional drink, would be horrified by those all-night poker games that had been carried on in an atmosphere of heavy smoke and easy virtue. On occasion, he'd paid for his pleasure, for there were no respectable women near the gold fields.

Yet no kiss, not even from the most expert and wanton woman, had aroused him the way naive Edith Parker's had done. Perhaps it was knowing that it had been her very first. He'd never tasted lips so sweet or so innocently responsive. Not even with Gwen, for she'd been wildly popular with the boys since her girlhood and had kissed a dozen boys or more before he'd come back into her life.

Jeff supposed he should be ashamed of himself for stealing

that kiss from Edith, without, after all, having honorable intentions. Yet he didn't regret it. As a matter of fact, he wondered when he'd have the chance to do it again before remembering that he had vowed not to.

11

AS SOON AS they'd driven away, Sam said, "You know, my wife and I met through a professional matchmaker."

"Is that so?" Edith asked. "I have never met anyone who owned an agency like mine, although I believe they are very popular in the West. One sees advertisements for brides to come out and get married in almost every paper."

"It's a gamble."

"Especially if one knows nothing about the man except that he wishes to marry. Why, at least with my service, I have had the chance to judge, to some extent, the character of the man. I don't simply take whoever walks in off the street."

"It's a gamble for both, I reckon," Sam said, giving a little grin. "The woman can't know much about the man from three thousand miles away, but then, he doesn't know much about her. She could be a nag or crabby."

"Or one of them could be married with the intent to deceive. I always ask for a letter from a good reference, like a pastor, before I send any information on prospective brides or grooms."

"The one that matched up Louise and me . . . her style was a little different from yours. I was living in Boston at the time. Before that, I lived in Atlanta. The southern girls are the most beautiful in the world . . . present company excepted, of course."

Edith dared to tease a little. "Were you this gallant as a young man? I can't believe the girls of Atlanta let you leave."

Sam chortled. "I was awfully shy, then. Louise . . . my wife . . . cured me of that. She walked right up to me, the first time we saw each other, and said flat out, 'If you want to marry me, you're going to have to talk more.'"

"How bold!" Edith said, trying not to smile.

"Yes, she was bold with as brave a heart as a . . . as a lioness. She wasn't from Boston either. She was from Connecticut, staying in Boston with friends. It was kind of like fate, our both being there on the same night."

"And this matchmaker?"

"What was her name?" Sam squinted up at the sky. "Miss Eudora something. I remember her first name because she looked just like an Aunt Eudora a childhood friend of mine used to have. Both of 'em vinegary old maids in loose purple gowns."

"Purple is not very old-maidish, is it?" She'd once seen a woman in a purple silk gown all spangled with gold braid like a military uniform. At sixteen, such a showy garment had had definite allure for her, though her aunt had sniffed and talked coldly about "a certain type of woman."

"Lots of old maids keep a purple dress for special times. That kind of dull color, like widows wear when they first come out of their mourning blacks."

He murmured under his breath, "Pratt, Pryor, Pringle . . . no, I can't remember. She ran a dancing place where young bachelors could go to meet nice young ladies. My friend Ross dragged me along one night. God, Louise was beautiful," he added reverently. "She wore white gardenias in her hair."

"What were you doing in Boston?"

"I was clerking for a dry goods firm."

"Then you haven't always been a farmer."

"A rancher," he corrected gently. "No, not always. I worked in a stuffy old office until the War. Afterwards, the doctors said

I had to get out into the air more. Louise decided that we should move to Missouri as the Armstrongs had moved here. She'd known Mrs. Armstrong when they were girls and not even the War could stop them corresponding."

"I have no such friends." Edith feared her tone was wistful.

"Well, you have 'em now. Even after Jeff marries one of these girls, I'll write you. Maybe you can find a nice wife for me, after you solve Jeff's troubles. I miss Louise. I miss having a woman in the house. Mostly, I hate to cook biscuits."

Edith laughed. She pretended to make a note on her sleeve. "Must bake biscuits. I'll let you know, if I can find someone to fulfill your stringent requirements."

"You know, you talk like you're from Boston yourself."

"My aunt always insisted on correctness of speech. She said that a lady could always be known by the way she spoke."

"My granddaughters must be a shock to a lady like you. Jeff hasn't had the heart to scold them much since their mother died. I try, but I don't know how to raise little girls."

"I think you've both done a wonderful job. They are sweet, loving little girls and, after all, that is what a parent strives for, isn't it?"

"You seem to know a lot about children."

Edith gave him a warm smile. "I was a child myself, once. For a while, anyway."

They drove past the church and many neat homes. Soon they entered the main business district. Richey, Edith was learning, was more than a single-street town. As the county seat, it had an imposing city hall, a round pocket-sized park with a military statue standing strictly to attention, and at least three rival general stores. As Sam drove by, several ladies waved and most of the gentlemen tipped their hats.

"Some people," Sam said, lowering his voice, "think Jeff ought to run for mayor. But I think an older, wiser head should run things right now."

"Oh, yes. A mayor must be a man of distinguished record and mature judgment." Edith didn't have to be a mind reader to know that Sam wanted to be asked to run. She only hoped father and son would not be competing against each other.

"That's Miss Albans' shop down there," Sam said, nudging

her elbow. "Be careful with her. She's an unusual girl. Bright and cheerful on the outside, but I think she has a tender heart."

When Edith got down, however, she did not march immediately into Miss Albans' hat shop. She'd been so interested in talking to Sam that she hadn't had the chance to work out what she was going to say. After all, she couldn't possibly walk up to a pleasant, cheerful girl and say, "Marry Jeff Dane, yes or no?"

Remembering a bench in the tiny park, Edith walked back to where the green grass glowed in the summer sunshine. As she sat on the bench, she closed her eyes to think.

Obstinately, however, her thoughts centered around one subject only. Why had Jeff kissed her? And what a kiss! Her toes curled and she found gooseflesh rising on her arms from just remembering the way his mouth had felt on hers.

She blushed to recall her own behavior. Did it take so little to overthrow the constraints of lifetime? Just the slow slide of a man's hands, or the mere velvet touch of his lips?

Edith rubbed down the renewed gooseflesh. She tried to concentrate on how to approach Miss Albans. Perhaps she could lead up to the subject by mentioning how Jeff was so attractive. If Miss Albans agreed that a man should be tall and strong, that his hair should be so thick that it looked like an animal's pelt, or that there was something pleasant about the soft abrasion against her cheek where his beard . . .

Closing her eyes again, Edith put her hand to her throbbing temple and tried almost desperately to think of something beside Jeff Dane.

She'd awakened at dawn with the sunlight dazzling across her pillow with shifting beams. She had stumbled up and tossed her dressing gown over the shade, which was too narrow for the window. For a moment, she had peered out at the golden light of the rising sun, but it had been too brilliant for her bleary morning eyes.

She had found it easy to fall back asleep—only to be awakened half an hour later by Sam, whistling a merry air as he made breakfast. Giving up in defeat, Edith had stepped out of bed, and uncovered Orpheus. The little bird sang out at once.

Now, her tiredness caught up with her. Keeping perfectly

upright, her head sagged onto her shoulder. Between one blink
and the next, she went from sitting in a pleasant park to talking
with some aggrieved insects. Fairy laughter gathered around
her, and then, breaking her dream, a desolate sob.

Waking up at once, Edith was instantly ashamed. Sleeping in
public? Her aunt would have pressed a hand to a palpitating
heart and ordered an explanation. How Edith hated explaining
herself! She would stumble over the words, wishing that her
aunt would punish her severely rather than insist on knowing
why she had been guilty of some unforgivable lapse.

Edith glanced around to be certain no one had observed her
lack of moral fiber. The only person near by was a very little
boy. He stood a short distance away from the park bench,
obviously trying not to cry.

Every other breath would catch in his chest and be exhaled
raggedly. He stuck a grubby fist in his eye, rubbing tears away,
but a few escaped to mark his cheeks.

"Are you all right?" Edith asked. "Can I help you?"

His babyish blue eyes met hers in a look of mute misery. The
round chin quivered. In a rush, his fat little legs pumping, he
ran over to her and buried his head, still wispy with baby curls,
in her lap.

Taken aback, Edith hardly had enough presence of mind to
pat the boy's shaking shoulder. She noticed a large, uneven
darn in the yoke of his shirt. His hair had not been brushed for
some time, as it was terribly tangled in the back.

"There, now," she said, the comforting sounds limping off
her tongue. "There, now. Don't cry. Are you hurt?"

Though still hidden in her lap, the little head shook.

"No," Edith answered for him. "You're not hurt. Are you
hungry?"

He looked up, his face all slobbered with tears. Edith
reached for her bag and took out a clean handkerchief. With a
silent gulp, she gingerly wiped his running nose and eyes. "You
are hungry."

Nodding, he said, "An' losted."

"Losted?"

Once again his chin started to quiver. "Sister'll be mad."

"Now, don't cry. I'm sure no one will be mad at you."

She held out her hand for her handkerchief but the little boy held on to it. Rubbing the white square of cotton against his cheek, to the ruin of its whiteness, he said, "Smells . . ."

Edith didn't know what to do. He was lost and hungry and so very small.

Sam wouldn't be back for some time, he had said, so he was no help. Miss Albans' shop was just down the way. She might know who the boy belonged to. But on the other hand, Edith didn't think Miss Albans would know any more about comforting a small lost boy than she did herself. And he was in need of a kind of motherly comfort no maiden lady could give.

He was rocking back and forth, the handkerchief wadded up in his cupped hand, as he pressed his cheek into it. His eyes were closing. "Mama?"

That decided her. There was one person in Richey who not only could but undoubtedly would take care of this child.

"Come along, little boy," she said. He clutched her hand with all the trust in the world, even smiling as she towed him along. The little nails were too long, and black. Edith only hoped he wasn't carrying anything alive on his person.

A few minutes later, Edith knocked at a house she'd visited before. She knocked twice more before she heard Mrs. Green yodel, "Come in!"

Feeling like an intruder, Edith pushed open the door and went in, the little boy still in tow.

"Why, Miss Parker. I didn't expect to see you again so soon! Not that you aren't . . . who's that?"

"I found him in the park."

"Park? Oh, the square."

"He says he's lost."

"Oh, I'm sure you can't be." Mrs. Green knelt down and looked the little boy in the eyes. Her smile was motherly. "You're not lost at all. You're here, with me."

The little boy didn't even glance at Edith. He jerked his hand out of hers and barreled into Mrs. Green's arms. Talking rapidly, he seemed to be telling her about an open gate and a dog he had followed. Edith hardly understood one word in ten, but Mrs. Green didn't seem to have any trouble.

"Then I got losted." He heaved a big sigh, as though he'd

dropped all his fears and worries onto this comfortable woman's shoulders. Edith tried not to feel envious of the boy's instant faith in Mrs. Green. He'd even dropped her handkerchief. Yet a certain yearning had been born when she'd felt his little fingers clasped in her own.

It was similar to the feeling she'd had when Jeff had kissed her, as if the two were related. Her lips tingled at the memory of the way his mouth had felt, moving eagerly over hers. She'd wanted more, just as she wanted a deeper joy than holding the child of a stranger. But what did kissing a man and holding a baby have in common? Except that they were things she'd never before imagined herself doing.

Edith said, "I think he's hungry."

"That at least we can mend. Right now!" Lifting the boy up into her arms as she stood, Mrs. Green stepped into her pantry. A moment later, she came out, the little boy still in her arms. In each of his hands, however, was a doughnut, with one already missing half of its circumference.

Mrs. Green, smiling maternally down at the tousled head, glanced up when Edith said, "I didn't know who to bring him to. I thought as you have boys of your own . . ."

"My boys! They'll be sure to know who he is. As it's almost dinnertime, they'll be back soon." She hefted the boy in her arms into a more comfortable position. "Woof, you're heavy."

"I'm a big boy," he said, stretching his mouth around the second doughnut.

"Yes, you are. What's your name?" He mumbled something that Edith couldn't catch. "Well, Rudy," Mrs. Green said, "do you know where you live? Who's your momma?"

"Ain't got a momma."

Mrs. Green sighed. "No? Then what's your daddy's name?"

"Daddy."

"I think," Edith said, "that's he's too little to know."

"He's old enough to have learned things like that, if anybody ever took the time to teach him. Somebody's not taking proper care of this child," Mrs. Green said, her full mouth becoming tight. A fire blazed in her green eyes. Edith realized that whoever was responsible for little Rudy wasn't going to enjoy meeting Mrs. Green!

Edith wanted to be there when they did meet. Looking at the boy, who was falling asleep on the shoulder of Mrs. Green's print wrapper, his lower lip pouting out, she also wanted to give someone a piece of her mind. She only hoped Mrs. Green would give her a chance.

"Where are my manners?" Mrs. Green asked. "Would you care for a glass of lemonade, Miss Parker?"

"Never mind about me. Why don't you sit down? I'm sure Rudy must be heavy."

"Lord, I'm used to it. One of my boys wouldn't go to sleep 'less I walked him for an hour by the clock."

"But your sons are grown, now, aren't they?"

"Not yet. But it won't be long now," she said wistfully. "They're thirteen and near twelve. Seems like yesterday they were no bigger than this." She cuddled the sleeping boy more closely against her body. Very carefully, she lowered herself into a well-worn, much loved rocking chair.

"Help yourself to lemonade, if you want any. Once those boys are home, that'll be the first thing they'll clamor for. 'I'm dry as a bone, ma.' 'I'm plumb thirsty, ma.' It's the same story every day. Just as if there wasn't a pump in the yard."

Edith filled two glasses. As she brought them into the parlor, she heard Mrs. Green singing "Lorena," the unforgettably sweet and sad song of the Civil War soldiers. Her memory turned back to long ago, when a dimly recollected figure, whose presence meant enfolding love, had sung that song to her.

Shouts, whoops and a shriek that struck terror into her soul caused Edith to look toward the open door. Were Indians attacking? She saw two savages leap the closed gate. Finding some cause for argument, they fell to the ground, pummeling one another.

"That'll be them," said their complacent mother, without turning around.

"Should I separate them?"

"You just try. They'll stop in a minute."

Each seemed to pull the other up. As though they were being assaulted by every fly known to man, they ran wildly about the yard, now tumbling, now leaping in the air. At last, they ran up the steps as though they would raid the house, sparing neither woman nor child in their recklessness.

"Are they always like this?" Edith asked, in the seconds before the hellions entered.

"Oh, no. They seem kind of peaceful today."

The last boy slammed the door. Little Rudy never stirred, not even when they hollered, "Hey, ma! Got anything to drink?"

Though she was sitting only a yard away, they repeated their demand, even more loudly. Edith, not used to the noise, hastily handed them each a glass of lemonade. Giving her surprisingly friendly smiles, with a variety of missing teeth, the two boys drained the glasses in a few seconds. One uttered a loud burp.

"'Polergize, Hank." The slightly bigger one cuffed his brother's head.

"Cut it out! Sorry, lady."

"Boys . . ." said their mother.

They clumped over to her. "Hey," Hank said. "That's the kid everybody's been looking for."

"Yeah," his brother added. "He's got some dumb name . . . Rhubarb or Randolph . . ."

"Rudy," his mother said. "And those who live in glass houses shouldn't throw stones, Aloysius."

Hank looked at the ceiling and began to whistle idly. His brother tried to dig a hole in the carpet with his big toe. "Yes'm," he muttered.

Edith, embarrassed, asked, "Who does this boy belong to, Hank? Aloysius?"

"He's one of the butcher's kids, and, if you don't mind, ma'am, it's Al."

"Excuse me, Al."

"Pleasure, I'm sure." His round green eyes were grateful.

"Well!" Mrs. Green said with decision. "Mr. Huneker's going to have me to deal with before he's an hour older."

Carrying the boy to Edith, she laid him down gently on her lap. The sleeping boy sagged into a comfortable new position, instantly numbing Edith's arm.

"I won't be a minute," Mrs. Green said. "I'll change into my dress. Boys, wash up. Soap!" she added as they tore out of the room, shouting, "Heap Big Mother Squaw on warpath! Ugh!"

"Make'um stew from Butcher," Al said, poking his face back into the room. He winked hugely before running off again.

A few minutes later, a questionably clean pair of boys with slicked-down hair, followed two impeccably dressed ladies. The boys kept themselves from the temptations of rain barrels, cooling pies on windowsills, and a dead blackbird. They knew that bigger fireworks than the Fourth of July were bound to explode when their mother met the butcher. Also, they were determined to defend their mother's honor, if any of the Huneker clan looked like they might start trouble.

Edith trailed slightly behind Mrs. Green who, despite her clean dress and large hat, insisted on carrying the still sleeping child. Edith had never seen anger before, at least not as a manifestation, but she could almost see it flickering around the edges of Mrs. Green's attractively full figure. As they stopped before a gate, Edith began to feel distinctly apprehensive.

"Hmph, he's having trouble keeping his yard neat, too. Nothing but dirt. Look at those flowers—haven't been watered since the Flood. And that swing is broken right across." She clicked her tongue. "It's a shame to give a baby like this back to a father who takes so little care of him."

Hank said, "Want me to roust 'em out, Ma?"

"Certainly not. We'll knock like Christian folk."

As the party stepped up the warping steps and onto the peeling porch, Edith heard the murmur of a voice. Mrs. Green raised her hand to knock at the unpainted front door when she paused. The voice had gotten louder. Accented with a slight German flavor, the man prayed aloud.

". . . Thee to return our wandering son, to guide his steps homeward to his family. He is just a small boy, Heavenly Father, and must rely on Thee to see him safe home, as Thou guidest all the lost to their rest."

An amen sounded from half a dozen voices. Edith sniffed, choked by tears. Mrs. Green echoed the sound, her fine jade-colored eyes were sparkling now with moisture rather than anger.

Without knocking Mrs. Green stepped into the threadbare, but scrupulously clean front room. A large family of children, hands clasped, stood around a mild-looking gray-haired man, who was just folding up his spectacles. He looked nothing like Edith's conception of a butcher.

"Mein Gott," the man said, rising. Holding out trembling hands, he hurried around the table, stepping around children ranging in age from adolescence to a baby crawling on the floor.

"Rudy. My Rudy." Mr. Huneker took his son from Mrs. Green's arms as though the boy had floated in under his own power. The small blond head lifted. "Papa?"

The man rocked back and forth, clutching the child tightly, while his other children clustered around. There were two boys and two girls, and the infant, whose sex was not clear. All were handsome children who looked to be wearing each other's clothes. By the time the shirts had reached the youngest child, they were nowhere near flawless.

Tears shone in the gray eyes of the butcher as he kissed his son's head. Rudy had gone to sleep again.

"Poor thing's worn out," Mrs. Green whispered to Edith.

She was about to agree when she was struck into silence by Mr. Huneker's expression. He had looked up when Mrs. Green had spoken, but whatever he'd meant to say never passed his lips. As though he'd been turned to stone, he stared at the red-haired woman, his jaw slightly open.

Edith had read about love at first sight. She had never thought she would actually see it.

As though the sun had sent its first rays straight into a crystal chandelier, Mr. Huneker threw off beams that bounced and sparkled, not only about his person, but about the rest of the room. Like a prism, he transformed the white fire of true love into dancing rainbows. Every one of his facets reflected back a portion of his heart to make a whole too dazzling to look at with the naked eye.

"I'll put him in his bed," Mr. Huneker said, stuttering a little, his accent becoming more pronounced. "Please stay. . . ." He added something in German. To Edith's surprise, she saw Mrs. Green blush as though she'd understood what he'd said.

She turned to Edith and said softly, "I worked for a German family before I married Mr. Green. They're very . . . poetical."

As if compelled, Mr. Huneker glanced back as he carried his son out. He repeated, "Please stay. . . ."

After he'd gone, the tallest girl dropped a bobbing curtsy. "I'm Friederike, ma'am. Where did you find him?"

"This lady found him," Mrs. Green said. No one looked at Edith for more than a moment. Even the infant stopped playing with his brother's bootlaces to smile toothlessly at Mrs. Green.

Hank and Al peered around the room. "Hey, Gerardine," Al said, flipping a hand at a girl about his age.

"Is she your mother?" the young girl asked. When Al nodded, she transferred some of her awestruck interest to him.

The other boys introduced themselves as Bing and Konrad. They pulled forward their father's chair and escorted Mrs. Green to it with considerable ceremony. She sat down like a queen, only to cluck like a mother hen at the tear on Konrad's jacket. "Does anyone have a needle and thread?"

"I do." Friederike bobbed another curtsy as she brought out a needle wrapped round and round with coarse white thread.

Edith was charmed by the way Mrs. Green didn't display the slightest discouragement at the wrong color for the repair of a faded blue jacket. Instead, she began to stitch the sleeve, while Konrad still wore it. And, by taking the stitches on the wrong side, she managed to repair the tear without too much of the white showing through.

Just as she was biting the thread with her strong, white teeth, Mr. Huneker came back. "He didn't even move when I laid him down."

"I imagine he's pretty tired," Mrs. Green said with a nod. "He told me he was chasing a stray dog and was lost before he knew what was what."

"And you find him?"

"No, it was . . ."

"Ah, you are so good. And these smart boys knew who little Rudy belongs to?"

"Why, yes. Say how-do-you-do to Mr. Huneker, boys." Mrs. Green seemed to recall with what intentions she had come. She took a deep breath and said, "Now, Mr. Huneker, about Rudy . . ."

"He is a good boy. Never have any of my children been lost before. Gerardine comes running to my shop as soon as she knows he is gone. I never even put the sign that I am closed in the window. Many, many thanks for bringing him back to us."

"Oh, really . . . it was . . . that is . . ."

As Mrs. Green stumbled along, softened by the power of the man's prayer and his obvious guilt, Edith slipped quietly out of the house. As she headed back toward Miss Albans's place of business, she was thinking, It will be much easier for Jeff to choose between two women than between three.

12

THE BELL ABOVE Vera's door tinkled merrily when Edith came in. At once came an answering bell-like voice from the curtained area at the back of the store. "Be with you in a minute!"

Edith hardly had a second to look around before Vera, her clothes protected by a white muslin apron, came bustling out. Her pretty face lit up when she saw who it was.

"Oh, hello, Miss Parker. I didn't expect to see you again so soon. What can I do for you?"

"Nothing. That is . . . I wondered if you had a few minutes just to talk. I don't really know anybody . . ."

"Me either. I've only lived in Richey for about six months and it takes a while for them to get used to you. You're lucky to be related to the Danes. They pretty much *are* Richey."

"Are they?" Edith hadn't gotten that impression.

"Come on in the back and talk to me while I finish this hat. I'm hoping to sell it to Mrs. Judd. She'll look a fright in it, but she's crazy for lavender."

The workroom was scrupulously neat, the rolls of ribbon and

sprays of feathers all tidily shelved, the blank straw forms hanging from hooks behind the workbench. A round hat with a small brim sat on a black, featureless head projecting up from the center of the bench. A lavender ribbon, as wide as the crown, encircled the hat, while a spray of Persian violets sat beside it.

"She's got about twelve dresses in varying shades of light purple," Vera said after showing Edith to a stool. "If I put this in the window, she'll want it—and she should be going by at about four-thirty. Hand me that pot of glue behind you, please?"

Trying not to breathe in the strong fumes, Edith held it out. "Will it dry in time?"

"Oh, yes. I don't usually use glue, of course, as it's not reliable in the rain, but it won't rain for at least a week."

Edith smiled at the devil-may-care tone. Yet she saw with what guilt Vera glued the ends of the ribbon to the hat. Plainly, the milliner did not like failing to do her best work.

"Who is Mrs. Judd?" she asked.

"My landlord's wife. I figure that if I charge her two dollars fifty for the hat, I can pay my rent and eat, all with my landlord's money." Shamefaced, Vera shifted her eyes from Edith to the violets she attached to the side of the hat. "I suppose you think that's pretty mean-spirited of me. But people with money can't know what it's like to be so poor."

"But *I'm* poor, too," Edith protested. "I haven't any money at all, you know."

"Oh, sure. With that hat and those shoes and Jefferson Dane for a cousin? Nobody knows how much he brought back from his gold claim but it's enough to keep you and his entire family in comfort for eternity."

Twisting viciously, Vera added a loop of tulle, in a shocking shade of green. Though it went with the silk violets' green foliage, it clashed vividly with the cool tones of the hat's main theme.

Sympathetically, Edith knew that Vera Albans spoke out of a great jealously and fear. Well she remembered pacing back and forth in her tiny room, praying for freedom from her stagnant life, battering against the walls like a caged beast.

She realized with a shock that she had just admitted the one thing that her aunt would have died rather than confess. Namely, that she was utterly without money. Edith felt as though something inside her had broadened, if only her view of herself. She was poor and it mightn't be wonderful, but it was survivable. Even if she went back to St. Louis tomorrow, she would find some way to survive. Perhaps she *would* make paper flowers.

"Is that what you meant to do?" Edith asked quietly, nodding toward the tulle.

Vera glanced at the hat and chuckled, her voice mellowing. "Yes, it really is. You see, Mrs. Judd is never quite satisfied unless she can put her two cents worth in. She'll narrow her eyes, like this, and tap her chin with her forefinger, like this"—Vera Albans' pantomime made the woman come to life—"then she'll ask me if this green tulle is meant to be 'artistic.' I'll answer, yes, of course."

"Of course," Edith echoed politely.

"Then she'll have it removed and go away happy, convinced as always that she would have risen to great heights had she ever entered any profession."

"Did she?"

"What?"

"Enter a profession?"

"Oh, no. She believes a woman's place is in the home, doing the washing, the cooking and the rest. She also thinks a woman should be able to juggle her housework, husband and children, with good deeds and a generous contribution of time to charity."

"She sounds admirable." And formidable, Edith thought.

Vera added another loop of tulle. "Of course, she's admirable. It's easy for her, she has Selma and Clyde to cook and do the garden. And the washing and the cleaning, light and heavy both. And their daughter, Garnet, she looks after the Judd children, except for an hour in the afternoon Mrs. Judd watches them while they nap."

"Sounds like a boring life."

"Believe me, I'd trade mine for it in a minute. Well, no, I guess I wouldn't. Not if it meant being married to Mr. Judd."

Taking a look at her handiwork, Vera said, "Maybe I'll recommend she take a facial massage. I've been studying how to do it in a magazine. If the ladies of Richey could be convinced to lie in a chair while I do something to make them look younger, that could bring me in a few extra dollars."

"I've never heard of facial massage."

"Oh, it's easy. I put a little oil on my fingertips—something that smells nice—and rub it in. The thing I read says it increases circulation, 'imparting a youthful glow.'"

"Sounds wonderful," Edith said wistfully. How nice it must be to have the money to pay someone for the express purpose of "doing something" to your face. And it couldn't hurt to look younger, not so drawn and pale. What would Jeff think if he saw her glowing? With a flutter behind her breast, Edith knew that all he had to do if he wanted to set her cheeks afire was kiss her again.

After primping out the tulle bow to flirt becomingly on the back of the hat, Vera went on, the bitterness returning to her tone. "'Course, I'd probably have to go to her house for that. After all that hard work, the only thing Mrs. Judd wants to do is lie down on her comfy sofa. It sounds like laziness to me but ladies like that can do no wrong, as I'm sure you must know."

As she put the completed hat in the window, Vera said, "I'm sorry. I don't know what your circumstances are and it's unfair to lump you together with the uncaring rich."

"Would you call Jeff . . . and Sam of course . . . uncaring?" Perhaps there was a side to Jeff that she hadn't seen. She definitely wanted to understand all of his personality.

"No," Vera admitted, perhaps grudgingly. "They're not uncaring. Far from it."

She got up to open the back door. "It gets kind of warm in here after a while. You look flushed."

Edith knew it wasn't the smell of the glue or the heat that made her heart beat like this or caused her hands to tremble. He'd kissed her once, no doubt for the first and last time. What astonished her beyond anything was realizing how much she wanted him to repeat his outrageous action. And repeat it. And repeat it until she learned exactly how to kiss him back to sweep his senses away, as he had stolen hers.

Vera continued arranging the petals of the violets, but absently, as though long habit made it possible for her to work without much thought. She smiled perfunctorily when she looked up, as though she'd forgotten Edith's presence.

"I think they care very much. They know how to be generous without making people feel obliged. For instance, Sam loaned me the money to open here when the bank wouldn't. Jeff cleared up the mess when the railroad couldn't find me to make deliveries. And I know the Danes have done as much for half a dozen people in this town . . . including Mrs. Green and Miss Climson."

"Miss Climson?" Edith repeated. "She seemed so self-reliant today. What did they do for her?"

Vera shook her head and stepped away from the window. "Only helped her get the school. Some people said it was because Jeff and . . . but there, gossip does a lot of harm. I promised myself I wouldn't do it any more and here I am chattering about everybody in town. And not very charitably, I think."

Filled with understanding, Edith touched the other girl on the sleeve. "You haven't said anything so bad. But sometimes it's so hard not to let your hurt show."

"What hurt?" Vera asked, holding still.

"You know. Watching other women with their children, with their husbands and wondering, Why them? Why not me?"

"They're no prettier than I am, no smarter," Vera whispered.

Edith nodded. "And yet they have everything and I have nothing. Nothing but hard work and hunger."

Suddenly, tears overflowed Vera Albans' dark gray eyes. "You *do* understand. How can you understand?"

"I told you. I'm poor, too. So miserably poor that until Jeff came along I didn't have the price of a meal. I was living on crackers and looking enviously at my canary's birdseed."

Vera laughed, and wiped her cheeks with a trembling hand. "I think . . . I think we're going to be good friends, Edith."

For once, Edith didn't feel uncomfortable embracing someone. It was as if Vera were her sister. Vera said as they separated, "I'm sorry I was so rude. But you're right. Sometimes it just gets to be too much. Mrs. Judd really is a nice woman, plump and kind, almost as kind as Adelia Green, who is a genuine saint."

Returning to her bench, she stood on tiptoe to reach the top shelf. Bringing down a round tin, she pried off the lid to reveal shortbread cookies. "Want some? It's my secret hoard."

As they munched cookies, Vera said, "It's not as bad as you might think, though. I could have all the money and things I want if I'd just give in."

"A wealthy suitor?" Edith asked, sitting up straight in attention. With her curling golden hair and heavy-lidded gray eyes Vera looked like the heroine of a romantic tale. Though she wasn't a great beauty in repose, her lively expressions and quick speech gave her such animation that she seemed beautiful.

"No," Vera said. "A despotic brother. He made a fortune on the stock exchange, but his methods were underhanded to say the least. Now he sits in his big house on the Hudson and expects the whole world to leap when he snaps his fingers. And I don't leap for anybody."

She tossed her head proudly. Edith copied her motion a moment later but with one reservation. She couldn't be a hundred percent sure, but she thought she might leap if Jeff snapped his fingers. Not that he would. He wasn't the finger-snapping kind.

"So what does he want, this despotic brother?"

"Me. Under his thumb. He likes to have people at his beck and call. Oh, he's generous. As long as you do what he wants. The minute you show a little mule, though . . ." She brought her hand slicing down through the air. "He makes a scene about how much money he's spending on you, when you've never asked him for anything. Or he brings up things that should be forgotten. I might stand for it from a father, but not from Porgie Albans."

"Porgie?" Edith asked, spraying shortbread crumbs.

"Yes, you know. Georgie Porgie, Pudding and Pye? That's him. Right down to running away when the boys come out. Oh, he's a heroic figure, Porgie. He sends me a check every six months which—now that I have my own business—I spend on whatever would make him angriest."

"I imagine you get a lot of fun out of that."

"I do. Once I endorsed it over to those railroad strikers. Porgie must have had an apoplectic attack after that one. Almost as bad as the time I sent his money to the suffragists. I read in the paper that a delegation called to thank him that time."

All too soon, the doorbell tinkled again. Edith followed Vera out, for she wanted to see Mrs. Judd. But it was Sam, his hat in his hands.

"You ready to go, Edith?"

"Yes." Quite naturally, Edith embraced Vera again. "I'll come and see you again tomorrow if I may."

"Any time." Vera turned her smile Sam's way. "How are you?"

"Doing fine. Got that little problem with the bookkeeping straight. Thanks for the tip."

"My pleasure."

The two stood in silence for a moment, Sam turning his hat brim around in his hands and Vera's smile fading a little, but still there. Edith, watching, saw no aurora flash between them. Yet she felt certain there was some emotion here, if only she could give it a name.

Vera said, "As long as you're here, I wonder if you'd mind taking a look at my sink. I think water must be seeping through somewhere when I pour it away, because there's a big water mark underneath it."

"I can't right this minute. I got a special guest out in the wagon."

"A guest? Is he the 'goods' you had to pick up at the station?" Edith asked.

"Paul's an old friend of Jeff's. It a secret. Jeff doesn't know anything about it, so I told him a little white lie. I picked Paul up at his aunt's house. He got in yesterday, and I'm lucky to pry him away from them. They dote on the boy."

"Is that who Jeff went to California with?" Vera asked.

"That's the one. He stayed out there and struck it rich. He hasn't been back to Richey since, and now he's only going to be in town for a couple of days. He's heading East."

Edith suggested, "Why not look at Vera's sink? I'll go out

and keep your friend company until you're finished. What's his name again?"

Edith could hardly believe that she'd volunteered to talk to a strange man. Yet she had a strong feeling that if Vera and Sam were left alone together for a little while, there might very well be an explosion of light that would serve as a beacon for the future.

As she parted again from Vera, she thought, That's three friends I've made. Vera, Sam and Dulcie. Yes, I think Dulcie's a friend.

She frowned as she crossed the street. Dulcie was still a problem. After seeing Mr. Huneker's reaction to Mrs. Green, she was more certain than ever that Dulcie entertained no feelings for her fiancé. If they'd agreed to marry after only knowing each other a very short time, the girl should have been giving off rays of love like the sun's. Why wasn't she?

By the time the wagon drew up in front of the house, Edith and Paul Tyler were on the road to becoming good friends. Though his sharp clothes and fine leather luggage showed that he was used to the best things in life, he rode on the hard seat of the wagon as if he did it every day. Sam discussed people they'd known years ago, yet Paul was careful always to include Edith, explaining who the people were behind the names.

She was laughing at something he'd said about the hills of San Francisco when he lifted her out of the wagon. As his hands supported her, she looked past his head to see Jeff standing on the porch. The golden beams of the late afternoon sun played over Jeff's stern expression. He looked like the only thundercloud on a bright blue horizon.

He barreled down the steps, placing each foot firmly on the ground. The set of his shoulders was belligerent. Then Paul turned around and, at the sight of his old friend, gave a war whoop. Jeff stopped dead.

A slow grin spread over his face. Edith, standing to one side, thought she'd never seen such a swift reversal of mood. One moment, he was looking murderous, and the next moment, as impish as a schoolboy.

"Wah-ha-ha-hooo!" he yelled. The girls came running out of the house behind him, wide-eyed.

Paul yodeled back. Together, they made the very air ring. Maribel put her hands over her ears, while Louise laughed. Then the two men were shaking hands, pumping up and down like a derrick. Twin grins enhanced their faces. They couldn't, however, have been more different in appearance.

Paul was stocky in build, with an olive tint to his complexion. His hair was in keeping, being smooth and a rich brown, through which the tops of his ears peeked. Jeff chaffed him about that, saying that in all the years between them, Paul still hadn't found time for a haircut. Paul fired back that if he'd known his friend was going to turn into a giant, he'd have brought him an Englishman to grind into bread.

"They're all over the place in San Francisco. Uh . . . come to see the savages, don't you know?" he asked in an affected accent. "What, no redskins?"

Finding Sam at her side, Edith looked up. He explained, "They were closer than brothers from the minute we moved here. Louise used to say it was as if she'd finally gotten the second son she'd always wanted. 'Course, they had to go off on their big adventure together."

Edith nodded as she watched the two long-parted friends grin at each other. Then Jeff threw his arm about Paul's shoulders and turned him around. "These are my girls," he said.

The pride in his voice made the two children stand up straight. Louise stepped forward and held out her hand. "How do you do?"

Paul smiled as they shook hands and Edith saw Louise fall in love. A bright tide of blush rose in the little girl's cheeks. He said, "I'm glad to meet you, Louise. I knew your mother."

"Mine too?" Maribel asked, and then turned shy. She took two steps to the side. Hiding behind her father's leg, she stared around it at the second stranger to enter her life in a few short days.

It was an evening filled with memories. The two friends talked over their boyhood days in Richey, reminiscing about the wars they'd fought with the other children, the apples they'd stolen, and their explorations of the Cave of Mysteries.

"What cave?" Edith asked.

Louise answered, "We're only allowed to go in there during the fair."

"That's right," Jeff said, shaking his finger at her. "And then only with a guide." He looked across the table at Edith. "There's a limestone cavern above the fairground. It's a great place but dangerous."

The two men exchanged a glance that seemed to be made of compressed secrets, sent across from one memory to the other. Jeff said, "Paul and I did a lot of wandering around in there, but even we don't know all about it."

"I've come at the right time," Paul said. "I'd like to take another look down there. We had some good times, down in the cave, before . . . Well, I haven't seen anything that spectacular in California."

"Surely the gold . . . ," Sam said.

"You know how I discovered gold?" They all shook their heads. "It was the summer after you left, Jeff. I was looking for blackberries. You remember how they grew down the hillside, great tumbling masses of 'em, like amethyst beads?"

"Sure, they were the best thing I found there."

"When I waded into 'em, I caught my shirt on a big thorn. Well, the more I thrashed around, the worse I got tangled and scratched. So I just got mad and ripped the whole plant out of the earth. And at the root was this big ol' chunk of gold." He held his hand out as though he clutched the nugget, fingers spread wide. "The whole hillside was like that. No veins to speak of, just chunks of gold like God had gotten tired of 'em and left 'em in a heap."

Jeff chuckled. "Better than the way we used to do it. Breaking our back with panning."

"Do you remember . . . ?"

The men began to remind each other of the wild characters they'd met and the fights they'd shared as well as the deprivations of life in a gold camp. They made even the hardships sound like a fantastic escapade out of a storybook.

Edith sat enthralled, her elbows on the table, copying in every detail the attitude of young Louise, right down to her chin propped in her hands. But where Louise never took her eyes off Paul Tyler, Edith watched Jeff, mesmerized.

She saw a reckless youth, eager for adventure, change to a man tried in the furnaces of experience. As the hours passed, she heard his voice deepen as he talked about the child he had delivered, the wounds he'd bandaged and the single time he'd stood up against a bully who held a gun. And when, at last, he'd decided to end the endeavor and come home, she heard nothing but satisfaction with his decision ring in his voice. Not even as Paul described the life he'd been living after his stroke of good fortune did Edith feel any regrets coming from Jeff.

"I'm not running through my money like there's no tomorrow. A lot of fellows strike it big and go buying everything in sight—big houses, jewelry for their . . . wives, you name it. I'm being careful. My investments have done well. I can't complain." Paul accepted another cup of coffee from Sam. Maribel had long since been carried off to bed by her grandfather and Louise's eyelids seemed to be growing heavy.

"So what are you going to do now? Move back to Richey?"

Paul gave a half-laugh. "No, I don't think so, though I'm sure my aunts would love it if I did. Tell you the truth, I don't know what I want. But whatever it is, it isn't in 'Frisco. After you left the Trinity, Jeff, I got to know old man Crawder."

"Crazy Crawder?"

"Yes, that's what we used to call him. I'd forgotten. You know, he had books in that cockeyed cabin of his, tons of 'em. Books on everything from history to philosophy to science. Even a couple of law texts that had 'Harvard' on the flyleaf."

Edith whispered, "Reading is a great comfort," but neither man heard.

Paul asked, "You remember how long those nights are out there?" Jeff nodded in answer, lost in thought. Almost to himself, Paul continued, "You think the stars aren't moving, that the earth's stopped moving. The whole heavens seem about ready to fall in on you. And every minute you pray that dawn's going to come, and it never seems to make it.

"Well, it's worse if there's nobody around to talk to. So I started to read. It struck me after a while I was as ignorant a body as ever drew breath. Since then, I've had a couple of

years of everything money can buy but I can't shake the feeling
that I'm just as ignorant as I ever was. Maybe worse."

"Couldn't be worse," Jeff said, with his wicked smile.

Paul pushed his fist into his friend's shoulder, slow and easy,
smiling back. "So I made up my mind that what I ought to do
is travel. See some of this big old world and make sense of it.
And not just in the States. I'm going to Europe and maybe even
farther. I've read about these pyramids in Egypt and a big wall
in China. There are forests in South America where whole
tribes of people live like nobody ever invented electric light or
the telephone."

"Heck, we've got places like that here. Richey, for one."

Paul shook his head. "I want to see everything before I settle
down permanently. There's a palace in Russia with domes like
onions and a whole city that was buried by a volcano in Italy.
I read about it in a book by . . ."

"Pliny the Younger," said a new voice from the doorway.

Everyone turned. Miss Climson stood there, a book clutched
to her chest. "I knocked," she said, "but I guess you couldn't
hear me."

13

L OUISE LAY AWAKE in a patch of moonlight. Next to her, Maribel whistled in her sleep as her breath rose and fell. The sound coaxed Louise toward sleep but she fought the call. She had a big prayer to deliver.

Though she knew she should get out of bed and kneel on the floor, she always found the best way to pray was to lie very still, looking at nothing. Her arms crossed behind her head, she stared past the ceiling, past the attic, past the roof. Soon she reached the vast sky above. The stars were pale beside the moon. As Louise fell into the sky, her mind opened up, one door after another, until she knew God was listening.

One day soon, her father would marry again. She saw his loneliness and had overheard him and Grandpa talking about it. Also, there had been whispering around town, and whatever the adults said today, the children would say tomorrow. So many adults seemed to think children's ears were made of wood, at least until their conversations turned interesting. Then they'd chant, "Not in front of the children."

However, Louise knew the names of the women most likely

to become her new mother. She told God that none of them would do. So long the envy of the schoolyard for her liberty, Louise knew she couldn't give that up for just *anybody*. Her new mother had to be just right, for her sake and for Maribel's.

Miss Climson? She tried to be stern but the children knew she was soft as butter inside. For that alone, Louise might love her. Yet, she did want to teach, all the time. She'd even corrected Mr. Paul when he'd been talking, his words just like poetry, about countries far away.

Louise let her thoughts drift to Paul Tyler. Almost as handsome as her father, he seemed like a dream prince. He'd actually brought her and Maribel presents, all the way from California. Only someone wonderful could have known exactly what to bring for two girls he'd never met.

Without looking, she reached for the little doll, dressed like an Indian maiden right down to her long black braids and white doeskin boots. The tiny bells sewn on her dress tinkled faintly. Maribel stirred in response.

Glancing over at her sleeping sister, Louise saw how tightly Maribel clutched her new stuffed toy sheep. She hadn't understood why Daddy had groaned or why Paul Tyler had grinned when he'd pulled a sheep out of his bag.

Louise hadn't understood either, exactly, though she'd heard that sheep and cows didn't get on. However, she'd pretended to laugh when the adults did while Maribel just looked confused. She was just a baby still, really. But she could be useful, for she always did as her big sister said.

No, Miss Climson wouldn't do. Correcting Mr. Paul! As if it mattered where Madrid was, when he was so happy to be going there. Louise relived the sound of his voice and the shine of excitement in his eyes. She would think of that, even when he was far away.

Miss Climson had to be teaching all the time. Louise didn't want that. She liked school, and was good at it, but she liked to leave learning at the schoolhouse when she heard the bell. How horrible it would be to find education at home as well!

Miss Albans was pretty, the prettiest girl in town, everybody said so. Maybe if she came to live here, Louise could capture some of that beauty for her own. She would like to be able to walk without her knees making her skirt billow and puff. And maybe she could learn to smile in that way, as if it only took seeing you to make a day perfect.

But the benefits of having the prettiest woman in town for a mama were overwhelmed by becoming the daughters of the dressmaker. Who was to say that Miss Albans wouldn't decide they should be walking advertisements for her business? Louise considered the one dress her grandpa had Miss Albans make for Sundays and special days.

It was a pretty blue, with a deep full skirt, ruffles and real lace on the sleeves and neck. But she had to wear about nine million petticoats underneath it and every time she sat down the skirt flew up. Plus it had tight elbow sleeves, giving her fits. And it was so hard to sit still in it!

Then again, when she wore it, she couldn't play at all, let alone as hard as she usually did. To be the daughter of the dressmaker would mean keeping clean all the time, not just on Sundays. So, no, Miss Albans was out.

Louise's eyes fluttered closed. Tossing her head to keep awake, she thought of Mrs. Green. If she could have changed just a few minor things, Mrs. Green would have made the perfect new mother. She was warm and understanding. She baked terrific cookies. But she'd never seen her father laugh in Mrs. Green's company. And then, there were those two boys.

They were noisy and too often teased her about all the things that bothered her most. Like the time they'd spent the whole recess imitating her, Al with a mop on his head. It wasn't until she punched him in the stomach that they stopped.

Louise hated Al. Hank could be nice sometimes but Al was the worst boy in the whole school. No way was she going to be a sister to him! Not while she had her strength!

Also, Maribel didn't like the way Mrs. Green smothered them both with big kisses every time she saw them. Once she'd even shed a few tears, calling them poor motherless lambs. Al had spent the rest of the week "baa-ing" at her.

No, Mrs. Green, Miss Climson and Miss Albans all had their good points, but they weren't perfect. Louise abruptly rolled on her side. With one hand, she groped under her pillow and brought out a length of blue satin hair ribbon, neatly folded. She thought about Cousin Edith.

From the front porch beneath their room, she could hear the voices of the grown-ups. It was a restful sound, punctuated by quiet laughter. As it rose and fell, Louise felt safe and very sleepy. She held the ribbon tightly.

Yawning, she finished her prayer. "Cousin Edith might do, God. I'd like to wait and see, but Daddy said she'll only be here a week. That's not much time so I'm just going to try my best. I'll leave whether she's the right one or not up to you. Bless Daddy and Grandpa and Mama in Heaven. Oh, and Maribel, too. Amen." She yawned again and snuggled down beneath her light blanket. Sleep took her away.

Down on the porch, as the clock in the parlor rang the half hour, Miss Climson said, "Goodness, it's late. I'd better be going."

"Me, too," Paul said, standing up. "I'm so tired I won't care if I have to sleep on a plank tonight."

"If I know your aunts . . . ," Jeff started to say.

"Actually, I think they've given me every pillow in the house and enough blankets to outfit an Eskimo army. I guess I'll be suffering tonight, but we've slept in worse places, hey, Jeff?"

"That's right. The biggest danger at your aunts' is from overeating. You remember to watch out for their pancakes. They're light as a feather and trick you into thinking you have room for a second double stack."

Miss Climson let a bubble of her delightful laughter escape. "That's very true. When I board with them, I limit myself to four, though they're good enough to live on by themselves."

"You board there sometimes?" Paul asked.

"Why, yes. As the schoolteacher I board with all the families in turn, one month at a time. Even though your aunts have no children in the school, they very kindly take me in every May. I'm always sorry to see June."

Sam said in the slight silence, "Better be going."

Miss Climson stood up, saying, "Thank you again for your

hospitality, Mr. Dane. I'm sure Louise will improve her studies this year. I look forward to having Maribel, too. She is a very sweet-natured child."

"I'll have a talk with Louise, but I'm hoping by the time the school year starts that she'll have a mother to help her."

There was enough moonlight on the porch to show Edith that Miss Climson was perfectly sensible of Jeff's meaning, if a little embarrassed by such plain speaking. She wondered how much gossip there'd been about his choices for a new bride. Did all three women know they were in the running?

Sam said, "There's room in the wagon for you, Miss Climson."

"I do enjoy walking, but . . ."

"Please do come," Paul said. "I'd rather talk to you than to ol' Grouchy."

"Is that any way to talk about me?" Sam said. The three of them chuckled as they stepped off the porch to go around to the barn. Edith and Jeff could hear Paul asking Miss Climson eager questions about English history. Her answer came back to them faintly, "I've heard that story. To me, Beckett was a . . ."

"They like each other," Edith said softly.

"Yes, they do." Jeff looked up at her, standing in silhouette against the moon.

She couldn't look at him. "Well, it's late, so I'll say . . ."

"Don't go in yet." He caught her hand as she stepped past his chair. "Sit with me and look at the moon."

Slow heat rolled up her arm. "Some other time."

"Won't be another time. The moon's always different. Look at it now. As big and bright as a new cent piece."

Edith glanced over her shoulder. But the steep pitch of the porch roof cut off her view. "I'll look at it from my window."

"You can't. Your window faces the other way. Can't you see it from where . . . no, of course you can't. Here . . ."

He tugged suddenly on her hand. She stumbled, though under his control, ending up right where he wanted her—on his lap. His thighs were hard beneath hers. Struggling to gain her balance, she thrust at his chest, protesting, "Mr. Dane!"

"Hush. . . ."

His arms closed around her, cradling her backward. Their faces were but a sigh apart. Edith held very still, though her blood raced maddingly. Abruptly, her need to escape him left her, though she knew how important it was to evade this kind of incident. But surely, she argued with herself, once more couldn't hurt. The years ahead are going to be so lonely. . . .

"Look," he said, nodding toward the vast golden moon.

She looked, but not at the gilded planet. With the unearthly light on his face, he looked haunted until he smiled. Even then, his eyes were lost in deep hollows, yet she knew their intense gaze was fixed on her.

"Edith . . ." His head dipped lower.

"Why?"

Jeff stopped, his thoughts dazed. "Why what?"

"Why did you . . . kiss me?"

"I haven't yet."

"Yes, you did. Before. Why did you do it?"

"Because I wanted to. I'd wanted to since the first time I saw you, I think. I wanted to know if you would taste as good as I thought you would."

"The first time you saw me you thought I was my aunt."

"Believe me, I wouldn't want to kiss your . . . oh, never mind."

His arms tightened, raising her up. She didn't need to remember the smooth muscles of his upper arms to know how strong he was. She felt content to be helpless before his strength and did not try to evade his kiss.

His breath whispered over her lips, tasting of the coffee he'd drunk. A deep trembling took hold of her. Trying not to give way, she whispered, "Am I tempting you again?"

"God, yes." His voice was rough but his kiss very gentle. "Edith, you're delicious."

He kissed her again, tiny pecks that stole her response rather than demanded it. He brushed kisses over her throat and up again to her mouth, never staying long enough to let her kiss him back. Edith longed for him to slow down, to linger. Shifting restlessly on his lap, she tried to tell him her need without words.

Raising her arms, she let her fingers tangle in his hair. Touching the soft, thick strands aroused her hands unbearably. Every part of her body seemed to come to life the moment it touched his. If only he'd kiss her as he had this afternoon, that might help ease her jangled nerves.

Grasping harder, she held his head still. "I want . . ."

"Yes?" Jeff raised his head as if to see her words.

Edith felt her skin burn. "I want you to . . ." Her voice sank to a whisper. "Kiss me."

He smoothed back the hair from her forehead. The moonlight played over his satisfied smile. "I thought I was. Am I doing it wrong?"

She sighed, frustrated. Was he really going to make her come right out and say such an unladylike thing? Glancing at his delighted face, she realized he was. She summoned up her courage and failed.

"Please let me go."

Insultingly, he made no attempt to hold on to her as she wriggled off him. With her feet on the floor, she felt she was herself again. Except that Jeff stood up with her and her mental balance was once more profoundly tilted.

With the porch roof blocking the frivolous moonlight, Edith could be more serious. "Mr. Dane," she said firmly, "perhaps I was unclear, out of a sense of gratitude for your coming to my rescue in St. Louis, that I . . . oh, dear, what was I saying?"

"That you weren't clear about something." His arm slipped around her waist, his hand splayed against her side. His thumb nudged the fullness of her breast and Edith swallowed hard, scrambling to collect her scampering thoughts.

"Yes. Ah . . . perhaps I wasn't clear about my place in your house. I am here simply to do a job, to see you safely married. I think . . ." He squeezed her waist and she lost her breath.

"Safely married? Am I unsafe while single?"

She would have given worlds to confess he was most definitely a danger to *her*. But she dared not, for fear he would prove her right!

"You should remember that I am trying to perform my duty

and stop . . . well . . ." She pulled at his hand. "Stop doing that."

"Doing what?" She'd never heard a more innocent tone. If she hadn't known better, she could have believed he had no idea what she was talking about.

"That! And stop catching me."

"Catching you?"

More softly, she said, "Kissing me. You must stop."

"But I haven't even started."

Less moonlight made her more serious. And it did the same for him. There was nothing lighthearted or silly about the kiss he gave her now. It sought her out, giving her no place to hide.

The tiny sounds she made in her throat sent Jeff's self-control careening. Edith pressed tightly to him, her eyes closed, her mouth open and seeking beneath his. He ached to bring her closer still.

Without breaking their kiss, he guided her hands beneath his coat and felt her nails prick lightly through his shirt. With a voiced sigh, he urged his fervent body against hers, remembering how eagerly she'd responded to him before. Yet even when she moved as he wanted her to, it still wasn't enough.

Images flashed through his mind, of the passion they were about to share. He had no doubt that this was the right moment for them. But where could they go? Not into the house, they might wake the children. The barn? Right here on the porch, the moonlight gilding her exquisite body, and him kneeling over her to make her his?

"God, Edith!" The cry broke from him against his will. He didn't want her to think even for an instant that this was her fault again. But she couldn't possibly understand what she was doing to him, pressing against him, moving as she did.

"This is so wrong," she sighed raggedly, her face buried in his shoulder. "Why can't I be strong?"

"You don't have to be strong," he said, his voice hoarse. "I should be. I should protect you, even from me. Especially from me. But I can't. I can't."

Her hair smelled of juniper and spices. Jeff pressed a kiss to her temple, smiling as a tiny curl tickled his lips. The fire that burned in his body hadn't dissipated, but he forced it back within bounds.

"I'll go," Edith said.

"No, stay." He didn't want her to move away from him, though he swore he wanted just to hold her. Of course, even sacred vows had no power over him when she was so close to him.

"I mean, I'll go back to St. Louis." She turned her cheek onto his collar. "I know it won't be long before you . . ."

He felt her stiffen, and the pressure of her hands as she pushed away. Reluctantly, he let her go, if only to arm's length. He had to keep touching her, if with no more than his fingertips.

"Jeff, I think . . . is it possible that you're attracted to me because you don't want to get married again?"

"How do you figure that?" His eyes had adjusted enough to the darkness to see that she wore that puzzled frown he found so endearing. He knew already that the sweet puckering across her forehead meant Edith was working out the mysteries of the universe to her own satisfaction.

"It makes sense. It's obvious I won't be looking for a bride for you if you seduce me."

"Edith!"

"Haven't you been trying to seduce me?"

He stepped back and rang his hand through his hair. Somehow he knew that soon he'd be pulling it out in handfuls. "I don't know why I'm attracted to you. Yes I do, though. You're lovely. You're the loveliest woman . . ."

"Miss Climson is far prettier than I am."

"Miss Climson?"

"Yes, when she was here tonight, I thought she looked very handsome. Mr. Tyler certainly seemed to think so. Once she came in, he hardly looked at anyone else." She'd seen no fireworks, like the ones Mr. Huneker had given off. Yet Edith had been conscious of a certain glow, though she hadn't really *seen* anything.

"All right, she is pretty, I guess, if you look behind the glasses and get her hair down. . . ."

"Good, you have been thinking about her in the right way. And Miss Albans is certainly most attractive. From what I have read, the Plantagenet royal family was supposed to have hair just that color. And, of course, she is a very amusing person to talk with. She has a unique point of view."

Jeff clutched his hair more tightly. "How on earth did we get onto this subject? Next you'll be telling me Mrs. Green is my ideal mate because she has proven that she can have sons."

"I don't think you need concern yourself with Mrs. Green any further." Edith retreated slowly, as though she were walking past a sleeping bear. Her pulse had slowed to the point where she no longer felt as though she'd just run a race. It would only take a touch from Jeff, however, to send it speeding again.

"No? What happened to her?"

"Mr. Huneker happened."

"The butcher?"

"Oh, yes." Edith pressed her hands together as though in prayer. "It was wonderful. He took one look at her and it was so beautiful. A genuine case of love at first sight."

He didn't know what she was talking about. What was so beautiful? And love at first sight only happened in women's silly books. First passion meant nothing. Real love came only after a long time of knowing each other, after growing together. He and Gwen had been working on that kind of love when she died.

Edith said, "But it's strange, now that I think of it. They must have met before, often. I mean, she must buy meat."

"Not much," he said, rubbing the back of his neck. "I give her a side of beef every spring."

"You do?"

"Yes, I do. Green worked for me. He was killed on the job, struck by lightning."

"Miss Albans was right. You are generous."

"I can afford to be. Edith . . ." He reached for her hands. After five minutes without a touch of her, he felt like a man dying of thirst in Death Valley.

Edith moved back again, until she pressed against the porch

railing. "Anyway, you should concentrate on Miss Climson and Miss Albans. I shall be most surprised if some interesting news is not heard from Mrs. Green very shortly."

"You mean she might marry Huneker right away? They don't even know each other. Is this more of your 'female intuition'?"

She gave him a serene, all-knowing smile that irritated the heck out of him. Then, she grew somber. The look she fixed on him then was unnerving. She seemed to be looking at him, through him and past him all at the same time. Her frown returned, deeper and sadder, as if she'd not seen what she wanted to.

Jeff reached again for her hands. When she swept them behind her, he growled, "Fine. If that's how you want it . . ."

He wrapped his arms around her, trapping her. Edith felt his heart hammering wildly, and for a moment she swayed, ready to surrender. But she endured his kiss without giving in, though it was a struggle she was within a heartbeat of losing.

With a groan of frustration and misery, Jeff ended his onslaught. Resting his forehead against hers, he closed his eyes and said, "I'm sorry. You've every right to resist me. I'll leave you alone, or at least I'll try."

He opened his arms and stepped away, freeing her. Edith walked past him. On the threshold, she said without turning, "It's only lust, Jeff. Which is a deadly sin. I think I can overcome mine, if you'll try to do the same for yours."

"I'll try."

It was only after her door opened and closed that Jeff realized what she'd just confessed. Lust, it seemed, ran both ways in this case. The thought elated him and depressed him at the same time. Edith wanted him for a lover, but her principles wouldn't allow her to have him. He felt the same, but his principles were turning out to be a whole lot more feeble than he'd thought.

Though the chiming clock in the parlor had long ago sounded nine times, Jeff knew he'd never sleep as long as thoughts of Edith swirled in his head. Exhaustion was the thing. He entered the house and crept up the stairs.

Rapping softly at her door, he murmured her name. "Come on," he urged through the white panel. "I've got something to say and I can't speak loudly or we'll wake the girls."

Edith hadn't had time to get undressed, only enough to take the pins from her hair. The rippling waves crimped by her hairstyle sprang free to frame her face and tumble freely to her breasts. Jeff's eyes were drawn to her mouth. Knowing what pleasures could be had made it harder to resist. But the hurt suspicion in her twilight blue eyes kept him from stealing another kiss.

"I'm going for a walk," he said. "Will you listen in case one of the girls needs anything?"

"Certainly. I should be happy to."

"Thank you. Dad'll be home soon. He'll take over then."

"Are you going to be gone a long time?"

"No, not long."

"All right." She began to close the door, her eyes still fixed on him. He heard her gasp when he stopped the door with a stiffly outstretched arm.

"I just want to say . . . I won't ever hurt you, Edith. There's no reasonable explanation for the way I . . . I leap at you. Just one of those things, I guess. But I want you to know . . . you're absolutely safe with me."

"I know I am, Jeff. And I promise I won't tempt you."

Slowly, as he tried to remember how, Jeff smiled. "That, I'm afraid, is a promise you can't keep. Everything you do tempts me. But that's my problem, not yours. Remember that, will you? It's my problem."

She nodded and closed the door. Jeff stood outside it for a long moment, wishing he felt as noble as he'd sounded. Then he heard her shoes hit the floor, one after the other. Realizing he was going to be unable to keep his imagination in check, he whipped around. Heading down the stairs as though something were after him, he knew it would have to be a long walk.

His steps led him to the Red-Eye. On the plate glass window in the front some traveling artist had painted a representation of the name—a wide-open eye, jagged veins darting out in all directions from a bilious green iris. Whether the artist had intended it or not—perhaps he'd had too much of Lashy's whiskey—the eye had a menacing, even evil, expression.

"Hey, Lashy," he said, walking in.

The bartender-owner gave him a yellow gap-toothed grin. "Hey there, Mr. Dane. Haven't seen you in here in a while."

"I've been in St. Louis. I'll take a beer."

"Sure, sure. Have a seat."

The other customers looked up as Jeff took a seat at one of the sticky tables marked with white rings. He recognized some of the faces, the ne'er-do-wells and drifters that even a decent small town collected.

The saloon itself wasn't much, a few tables, an out-of-tune piano, and a grubby bar. Yet it was nowhere near as serious a sink of degradation as Richey could show. Jeff imagined that Edith, however, would think it was just that.

There'd been an attempt or two to clean up Lashy's, mostly promoted by the Armstrongs. The bar had survived even the Women's Christian Temperance Union that had every woman and child in Richey wearing white sashes for two weeks last summer.

Jeff crossed his legs, sitting back. He remembered how Louise had held out against the pressure to pledge that she would never touch alcohol, though Mrs. Armstrong herself had tried to persuade her to sign. Jeff hadn't interfered, leaving the matter to Louise's conscience and good sense.

Her only reply to Mrs. Armstrong's pretty description of the Lord and his angels waiting for her to sign the pledge was, "My daddy goes to Lashy's. How bad can it be?"

His daughter's simple faith had kept him out of the saloon ever since. Sam sometimes stopped in for beer and gossip. As long as Sam brought home the gossip, Jeff felt he wasn't missing much.

Lashy brought a mug of beer over. "St. Louis, huh? Mighty nice city. Got a brother-in-law there, don'tcha?"

"Yes, that's right." He sipped the amber beverage. "Say, has Sullivan been in here tonight?"

"Sullivan?" Lashy, with a straggling gray beard and a habit of blinking rapidly, wiped his hands on the once white apron that hung under his low-slung belly. "Sullivan? Don't know him."

"Sure you do. He's new in town. Engaged to marry the preacher's daughter. Quick worker."

"Yeah, quick worker." Lashy chuckled, but his eyes blinked faster still. "Look, Mr. D. Don't tell him it was me told you he was here, okay?"

Jeff lifted the mug to his mouth and spoke swiftly before he drank. "Why not? Is there a problem?"

"Uh, no, no problem exactly. And I don't want there to be none. He just asked me to keep quiet if anybody comes around asking questions."

"Sounds kind of shifty to me."

Lashy looked uncomfortable. "Uh, I don't ask no questions but I figure he don't want Preacher to know he comes in here."

"Which one is he?"

"Over there, by the pianny."

Jeff glanced over. A young man sat at a table, repeatedly shuffling a deck of cards. He had fast, clean hands. His shiny nails, catching a gleam from the lamplight, matched the gloss on his shoe-black hair. As though aware of Jeff's scrutiny, Sullivan looked up. His eyes darted around, checking the faces.

Catching Jeff staring, Sullivan raised his hand in half-greeting. Moving leisurely, he stood up, tapping his cards together. He put them in his pocket and sauntered over.

"Evening. You got a problem, friend?"

Jeff didn't like him. Put all together—the fancy weskit, the shiny nails, the nasal voice—Victor Sullivan impressed him as a nasty piece of work. And this was Dulcie's fiancé?

Jeff interrupted Lashy's fast apologies by standing up. Toe to toe, the stranger came off second best in height and musculature. "No problem at all. I'm Jefferson Dane."

At once, an ingratiating smile spread over Sullivan's face and he held out his hand to be shaken. "Ah, yes. Dulcie's told me so much about you, I've been jealous. Let me introduce myself. I'm Victor Sullivan, her fiancé."

Jeff looked Sullivan up and down, purposely insulting. The other man just grinned. Jeff longed to haul off and wipe that smile off with his fist, but he had no right to. His reaction startled him for he had never been of a violent bent. Could Edith's "intuition" be correct? He dismissed the notion. Every right-thinking male would feel the same longing faced with a smooth-talking scoundrel like this.

14

JEFF DIDN'T STAY long at Lashy's after meeting Sullivan. There was nothing he wanted to say to the son of a bachelor, not now anyway. He had to think about whether it was right to meddle at all. He had no real duty to Dulcie, who had many friends and a family to look out for her. And now she had Edith too.

Walking along the road, he tried to talk himself out of his half-belief, growing all the time, in Edith's intuition. After all, she hadn't even met Sullivan, only Dulcie. It didn't make sense that she could know anything about one person by meeting another, however closely they were involved.

The wind picked up, driving before it the smell of rain. A low rumble sounded, less loud than a heartbeat yet capable of dominating the air. The rustling leaves showed pale undersides as though in surrender to the coming storm. Jeff began to jog in his boots, for he had livestock to get safe under cover.

He liked to run, to shut his mind of everything but the pounding of his feet and the hurrying of his heart. Figuring he had about half a mile to go, he kept his pace easy for he didn't want to be too beat to work when he got home.

From behind him a voice called, "Hey, son!"

Jeff stopped and looked around, his hand on his rapidly expanding and collapsing ribs. His father halted the horse, so Jeff could climb up into the wagon.

When he got his wind back, he said, "You're getting in late, Dad. Not that it's any of my business."

"It's on your behalf that I'm late. I stopped in to see Miss Albans. Seems she's got a little problem with her sink. I told her you'd be out to fix it before the end of the week."

"Is it a big job?"

Sam shook his head.

"Why didn't you do it then?"

"Don't know. I reckon it's better if you do it. Give her a good reason to be grateful . . . well, more grateful. A woman likes a man who can be handy 'round the house."

"You're handier than I am. Remember, I'm the fellow who stepped through the bedroom ceiling while flooring the attic. Scared Mother half out of her wits."

"Well, anyway, it'll give you two a chance to be alone. She'd make a choice armful, if you're still thinking that way."

"Yeah." Another shiver of thunder in the sky. "Looks like it'll be a good rain."

"We can sure use it. Been hotter than the hinges of hell. Everybody's complaining about the crops." Sam squinted up at the sky. A few clouds hid the moon, only to be blown around like the veil of a beautiful woman. "Are you still thinking that way?"

"Sure. What other way could I be thinking?"

The rumble drowned Sam next words but the lantern light showed his mouth moving in the syllables of "Edith Parker."

"What about her?" Jeff asked.

"Come on, son. It doesn't take a genius to figure it out . . . not after Maribel comes running into the kitchen to holler the news that you're kissing Cousin Edith."

Jeff groaned, covering his eyes. "She saw us?"

"They saw you. Maribel wanted to know if it meant she'd

have a baby brother tomorrow. Don't worry—Louise set her straight. Where that child comes by her information . . ."

"Look, Dad, about Edith and me . . ."

"You don't have to explain to me. I'm not her father."

"No, but you're mine."

"So your mother said. . . ."

"So listen. I'm not denying that Edith had an effect on me. A mighty powerful effect. But how could it be serious . . . matrimony-type serious?" He looked at his father but saw neither approval nor censure.

"She's a nice girl," Sam said levelly.

"But she can't do the things I need a wife to do. Can she cook for a passel of ranch hands? Birth a calf? Mother the girls? She's city-bred and more . . . she's a natural-born spinster. I'll take my dying oath no man ever laid a hand on her before."

"Before you, you mean."

"That's right. Nobody before me." All his masculinity called out, "and damn well no man after me either," but Jeff fought the need to say the words out loud. Only Edith should hear that, preferably in the long afterglow of lovemaking.

The horse pulled them along faster and faster as he scented the rain blowing in. This time Jeff saw the flash, a brief flare on the horizon, showing the clouds greenish pale like the belly of a vast fish. He counted until the dull roll of thunder echoed.

"We've got a little time before it hits."

"Yep," his father said, pitching his voice above the gusty wind. "I agree with what you say about Edith, Jeff. But I don't think it's her fault she's so . . . so . . ."

"Innocent? I know. That blasted aunt of hers. I never heard of the woman until a few days ago, but I'd like to . . ." He made a impotent fist. "She ruined that girl for any kind of life outside of politeness and prayers."

"Sounds like it." Sam pulled back the reins while his son got down to open the barnyard gate. He leaned over to say, "I'm just wondering . . . if that's how you feel, why'd you kiss her?"

Before Jeff could do more than stare at him in surprised inspiration, Sam drove the wagon through to the barn. As a lightning flash sundered the sky, Jeff realized there wasn't another moment to waste in talking. There was much to do, and the wind was urging the storm to violence.

The two hired men had rolled out of the bunkhouse to round up most of the cows and half-grown calves. The young bulls lowed at the gate, eager to get into their shed. Circling dogs kept them from panicking as the moist wind blew over their backs. Behind them, stately and slow like the dim-witted king he was, came Black Prince Edward, the founder of Jeff's herd.

His deep chest and thick neck flowed seamlessly into his smooth, square sides. He'd sired a dozen prizewinners, though he'd been a scrub bull when Jeff had come back from the Trinity. Jeff found his prosperity on this animal's procreative powers.

Now, swinging the door of his stall across, Jeff knew a moment's jealousy. If only he could treat his affairs as casually as the bull did. If only Edith could be as content as a cow with as little thought for the future. But he wronged the beasts, he knew. At mating season, each cow was more beautiful than the last to the Black Prince, and each cow yearned for her master. No doubt they pledged eternal fidelity to each other, at least until the rutting instinct was satisfied.

Hard raindrops splattered Jeff's shoulders and back as he ran the last few feet to the back door. His father had cared for the horses and chickens. He'd gone to bed some time ago, as had the hired men. But it was Jeff's responsibility to see that everyone and everything was safe before he retired. Even to the cats in the barn, snuggled in the hay, sound asleep.

The next crash of thunder was so close and so sudden that Jeff grabbed for the banister to keep from falling down the stairs in surprise. The house shook. "Jesus!" he whispered.

A burst of lightning brightened the windows, followed after only a few seconds by another rolling explosion. Thinking the girls must be cowering under their bed by now, Jeff finished the stairs two at a time.

Their door stood open. Jeff peeked inside, not wanting to wake them if by some miracle they'd slept through the artillery barrage outside. The covers were rumpled but there were no feathery blond heads on the pillows. He bent to look under the bed. No little feet peeped out from under the coverlet.

Combing back his damp hair with his fingers, he looked around in the next lightning glare. Edith's door stood open too. Following his curiosity as much as his inclinations, Jeff walked down the hall.

With a grin, he counted three heads on a pillow. As he might have guessed, Edith wore her rich dark hair pulled into a prim braid. He noticed that Maribel had tight hold of the end of the braid in one hand while with the other she clung to her new toy sheep. Louise was curled into a ball which reminded him of the cats asleep in the hay.

Despite the noise and the flashes which broke the sky with the intensity of day, his girls were sleeping like angels on a cloud. Jeff's smile faded as he recalled that Gwen never let Louise crawl beside them when frightened in the night. It had been her firm rule that once the child was put to bed, she must stay there until morning. Often Jeff had crept up the stairs to comfort his crying daughter, knowing that Gwen was undoubtedly right but unable to bear the sound of his child's sobbing.

Neither treatment had done any harm, he decided as he scooped Louise up to take her back to bed. She was a bright, self-sufficient little thing, despite his doubts about a future with no mother to guide her. Thinking of Edith's aunt, he decided too much self-sufficiency was not good. Had she ever needed anyone? Had she ever loved anyone? She could not have taught Edith any of these things. How could he?

Edith had needed him once, he thought in triumph. Instantly, however, a doubt nagged at him. Would she have found some way to survive even after a devastating fire destroyed everything she had? Who had needed whom more?

He made a second trip for Maribel, though he had to pry open her fingers to get her to let go of Edith's hair. Like a baby, Maribel rode limply against his shoulder and dropped bonelessly onto her mattress. He pressed a kiss onto each girl's warm face and closed the door as he left.

The rain rattled like needles fired against the windows as Jeff made one last trip down the hall. He told himself his hands had been too full with Maribel to close Edith's door behind him.

But when he got there, he stepped inside her room, to take a picture of her face on the pillow into sleep with him.

"What the . . ." Her bed was empty.

She stood by the window, the curtain caught back in her hand. Jeff looked at her and forgot to breathe. Her beauty of form showed clearly against the rain-silvered window. Her nightgown gathered over her breasts and flattened across her stomach, leaving much to his imagination but not nearly enough.

"I thought the rain would never start. All that booming and crashing but no water 'til now. It's already cooler." She put the back of her hand to her forehead and then to her temple.

"It'll come down until morning," he said, recovering.

"I stood here and watched it come. It was terrible, exciting and terrible. The rain in St. Louis wasn't like this. You'd look up between the buildings as a shadow crossed the sun and there'd be rain falling. The clouds were never green there, only ordinary gray."

Jeff sat on the foot of her bed, his bed. "How could anything be ordinary if you are there?"

She quivered as though she would look toward him. Controlling the motion, she went on staring out the window. "Maribel came in when it began to thunder," she said.

"And Louise?"

"I went for her. Do you know she is terrified of thunder?"

"No, I didn't," he admitted to his shame. As though in punctuation, another crash sounded, a little further off now.

"Well, she is. And she wouldn't ask me if she could cuddle up here, I had to invite her."

"My wife . . ."

"She told me."

He felt her smile, rather than saw it.

"Louise wouldn't join Maribel and me until I told her we needed her, that we were frightened. She takes after you, doesn't she?"

"Does she?"

"Yes, very much so. She can't give herself to people unless they ask and you . . ."

Jeff crossed the few feet between them. He didn't touch her, didn't pull her into his arms as he longed to do. After all, the only thing he could give her was the security of his word. He'd promised to leave her alone. He must keep that promise.

"And me?" he prompted softly.

Edith had never felt so aware of another person. It wasn't just that she knew the taste of his lips, the hot urgency of his hard body. She knew every nuance of his breathing. She could tell, not what he was thinking or feeling, but how his frame of mind changed from moment to moment. Right now, he was determined to be chivalrous. She felt a purely feminine wish to break the will that kept him from touching her.

She looked at him over her shoulder, knowing that her eyes must look black and deep in the darkness. "You're the most important man in town, the leading citizen. What you want to have happen, happens."

"Is that so?"

"Everybody says so."

He said, "Not everything happens as I want it to, Edith. Not by a long shot."

"No?"

"Not even close. If it did, you'd be . . ." He glanced at the bed, the sheets softly rumpled and still warm. It would be so easy to make love to her now. From her response to his kisses, from her confession of desire, he knew she'd put up no resistance to him. Worse yet, she'd assist him in accomplishing her own seduction. He could imagine her smiling at him like a goddess while she let her nightgown drift to her feet.

He coughed. "I should tell you that the Armstrongs hold prayer meeting Wednesday nights. Do you care to go?"

"I'd like that. It will give me the chance to see Dulcie again, and the others. Do you usually attend?"

"No, but I'll go with you tomorrow."

"Thank you, Jeff. Dulcie's intended will be there too, I suppose?"

This was the moment to tell her he'd seen Sullivan himself. But he didn't want to argue about whether she'd been right about the city slicker, even though such an argument would keep him close to her for another few minutes. That would be a sweet torture, too much to stand. If he couldn't kiss her as he wanted to, deep, lingering kisses that would send them both tumbling over the edge of desire, then he couldn't bear to stay.

"Good night, Edith," he said abruptly. He left the room as quickly as he could without running.

It was about an hour later that Sam kicked Jeff out of bed.

"Go and do your tossing and turning in the barn, son. I'm an old man and I need my sleep."

"But Dad . . ." He didn't know whether to laugh or holler.

Sam turned up the dimly glowing lamp by the bedstead. His graying hair stood in spikes. He rubbed his hand over his sprouting cheeks and said, "Okay, we'll talk."

"Thanks. What do you think I should do?"

"I don't know. But until you decide, it's pretty obvious I'm not getting any sleep."

Jeff stared at the blanket over his knees. This was like the long late talks he'd had with his father as a boy. He hadn't enjoyed one since he came home—a man—from the gold rush.

"The problem," he said slowly, "is Edith."

"Congratulations on the blinding inspiration." Sam rubbed his eyes. "Sorry. I'm always sarcastic in the middle of the night. Your mother could have told you that."

"I know it myself. I once woke you up coming home late from some hell-raising and you blistered me with a dozen words."

"What were they?"

"'If you were visiting a lady, she sure must be disappointed.'"

"Were you visiting a lady?"

"No, sir. A woman—and she didn't complain. Not that I heard, anyway."

Sam chuckled reluctantly. "Sometimes, when you were raising that kind of hell, I envied your opportunities. There was never any woman for me but your mother."

"I envy you your fidelity. And you had the time to prove your faithfulness. I didn't have near long enough with Gwen."

"No, son, you didn't. But right now 'the problem is Edith,'" Sam prompted.

Jeff thought about Edith. Was it just physical, this attraction between them? The kind of heat that would burn itself out after one or two encounters? Or was it the imperishable flame of two people destined for one another?

He flinched away from the thought as though it were a knife's blade against his skin. Love was not something he wanted ever again. He'd seen what pain it could cause when, for no good reason, Gwen died.

That was why he wanted to marry a woman he liked, one he could respect, but one for whom he'd never felt the slightest frenzy. Miss Albans, Miss Climson or Mrs. Green . . . any one of whom he could take to his home as an ornament. Sex wouldn't be a problem as he was young and healthy. Those responses depended more on the moment than on love.

"The problem is Edith," he repeated again. "She's different from anyone I've ever met. She seemed so helpless when she appeared at my hotel, carrying nothing but that canary. And yet, if I hadn't been there for her to come to, why do I think she would have managed to get along?"

"Probably 'cause she would have, somehow. Most people manage to survive even the worst calamity. I survived when your Mother died, though I sometimes hoped I wouldn't." Sam ducked his head in embarrassment. "Ah, heck. You know what I mean."

"Yes. I do know. It's a terrible thing to be left alive when the one you love has died."

Sam coughed to hide his emotions. "What do we keep talking about them for?"

"Maybe because the subject's marriage and we don't know anything about it 'cept what we've done so far." Jeff tossed the covers off and stood up. Pulling on his jeans over his drawers, he said, "Okay, Dad. I'll sleep in the parlor."

"Good. But listen, Jeff . . . maybe the reason you keep thinking about Gwen is Edith's got you thinking about marriage."

"Marriage has been on my mind for a year. You know that."

"Not marriage with Edith Parker.

Instantly, Jeff protested, "Are we back to that? I've already told you . . ."

Sam held up his hand. "All right. You told me. Now tell

yourself, 'cause I swear you keep circling 'round and 'round this business like ol' Grouchy looking for the scent."

Jeff knew his father was right. He couldn't be thinking of Edith as a wife, but at the same time, he wanted no one else. But that was just his body talking, and a man had to be ruled by his head. His head told him he'd only known her for a very few days. After a moment, he heard from a part of himself that very rarely spoke up. His spirit said very quietly, You have known her for always and always.

"The problem," he said as his mind began to work again, "is Edith's sense of duty. She has come here to see me 'safely married' to use her words."

"Married to one of those three gals."

"That's right. Now I could delay making my choice and keep her here that way. That would give me more time to know if she really is . . . the one."

"Sooner or later you'd get tired of living like that. Hands off all the time," Sam said, stifling a yawn.

"I'm already tired of it. Or I could come right out and ask her to marry me." He found himself grinning daftly at the idea. "I could marry Edith, Dad."

"No, you can't."

"Why not?" Quick as a lightning bolt, Jeff's merriment vanished. His frown would have made a lesser man back off instantly. But a father is a father forever.

"Because the problem is Edith's sense of duty."

"Isn't this where we started?"

"Hey, you want to talk about her, that's fine. But don't expect me to make much sense at this hour of the night." This time Sam didn't bother to hide the yawn that cracked his jaws.

"You mean she won't marry me because her duty is to see me married to one of the others."

"Right at last."

"Then what am I to do?" I sound as frustrated as I feel, Jeff thought with a growl.

"Well," Sam said, "for tonight . . ."

"Yes?"

"Tonight you sleep in the parlor." Suddenly, Sam hurled one of the pillows at him. Before he could pick it up, Sam had turned down the lamp and rolled over, producing a raucous snore.

"You're my father and I love you, but I've got to tell you . . . you're one lousy actor, Dad."

Leaving, he pretended not to notice the second pillow his father shied at his head. He went to find, as best he could, sleep on the parlor settee. Between the torments of passion and horsehair, he stole little rest. Dawn found him heavy-eyed and grumpy, not at all Edith's eager, yet patient, lover that he had planned to be at their next meeting.

15

THE RAIN CONTINUED. Until dawn and beyond. The little girls moped listlessly, for it was far too wet to go out. Sam shooed them out of the kitchen, where he was trying to get a cake to rise against its will.

Edith hadn't seen Jeff. He was gone before she'd come down to breakfast after a restless sleep. She wanted to go into town to talk to Miss Climson. Sam, however, was too busy cursing like a sailor to be interrupted, and she hadn't the right boots for walking. Besides, the road was most likely nothing but mud by now.

Entering the parlor, she saw Maribel on the floor, jumping her toy sheep over a wall made of blocks. Louise sat in the window, her chin propped on her hand, heaving heavy sighs at regular intervals. The air was close, sticky with humidity, and Grouchy added the strong fragrance of wet dog.

"What are you doing?" Edith said, crouching down next to Maribel. She checked carefully for snakes and other creepy things before she did so, however. She felt that being in the house was no protection.

"Baa, baa," said Maribel. "I'm a sheepdog."

From the window Louise said in a bored tone, "Sheep dogs don't baa. Dogs bark. Woof-woof, like that."

"They do so baa!"

"Do not!"

Edith put her hand on Maribel's shoulder to keep the little girl from flying at her sister. "Maybe the sheep is half a dog. That would make him a sheep-dog. Or a dog-sheep."

Maribel giggled and said, "Baa-baa. Woof!" She bounced the sheep over the carpet, making him come down on his little black legs and bound once more into the air.

"Baa-woof!" Edith said. "Or, if you prefer, woof-baa!"

Grouchy woofled, tilting his head at their nonsense, but thumping his tail good-naturedly.

Louise shook her head and stared at the drizzling sky. "Some people are too silly. . . ."

Edith and Maribel played for a few minutes. The child seemed to take it as a matter of course for the grown woman to kneel beside her on the carpet. Yet Edith remembered how her aunt would stand above her as she played, a grim tower in her straight smooth skirts, the only friendly sight Edith's own face reflected in her aunt's polished, high button shoes.

Before long, Louise turned her attention from the outside to the action beside her. In a moment, she too was sitting cross-legged on the carpet, reaching for the blocks, saying, "Not like that . . . like this. Put them on top of each other."

The back door slammed, shaking the windows. "That's Gran'pa," Maribel said, not looking up.

"He's gone to throw the cake to the pigs," Louise added. "I 'spect that baking powder wasn't any good. He should of stuck to Borsun's and not try any new stuff. Gran'ma only used Borsun's."

"You remember your grandmother?"

"Oh, sure," Louise said.

"Oh, sure," her sister parroted, nodding briskly.

"You do not! I remember Grandma and Mama and you don't remember nobody."

"Yes, I do! Mama was pretty."

"Daddy told you that. You don't remember her." Louise

looked up at Edith. "She was pretty with green eyes and long silvery hair. I remember her brushing and brushing it, a hun'ert strokes. Sometimes she'd let me brush it. Daddy cried for three days when she went to Heaven."

"Daddy cried . . . ," Maribel said like an echo, though her baby face was bewildered.

"You must miss her very much," Edith said to both girls.

"Not so much any more," Louise answered matter-of-factly. "That's a long time ago. I'm eight now . . . I was a baby then, like Maribel is now. Daddy still misses her, I guess. Well, being married . . . you know."

"Oh, yes. I see." Obviously Jeff had not yet gotten over the death of his beloved wife. His attraction to herself was merely an attempt to distract her from the performance of a duty he no longer wished her to complete. Naturally, he wouldn't come right out and admit that, not after all the bother he'd been put to in order to get her here. Yet Edith remained steadfast.

These children needed a mother. Even she, a spinster, was fairly itching to run an iron over the girls' wrinkled pinafores. She wanted to banish the wary look in Louise's eyes forever. And the sweet, trusting way that Maribel rested in the curve of her arm awoke some maternal sense she hadn't even suspected she had.

Edith felt sure Jeff would come to love whomever he married—in time. It might be far from perfect at first, yet his kisses proved that he was ready for at least part of marriage. She did not imagine that with his loving heart he could spend any time in company with a wife without offering her affection. Then he would initiate his wife into those mysteries of marriage that wives and husbands never discussed with anyone but each other.

Edith thought about this future wife. For some reason, this woman refused to take on the appearance of either Miss Climson or Miss Albans. Surely this faceless someone must be happy with such a wonderful husband. Jeff was startlingly handsome. Edith knew how kind he was firsthand. He was prosperous, generous, and physically as well proportioned as any Greek statue.

Shifting a little on the carpet, Edith tried to focus on Jeff's other good qualities but kept returning to contemplation of the splendid physique that had been revealed while she was recovering from being frightened by the dead snake.

How smooth his body had looked, gleaming in the afternoon sunlight. Her fingers curled into her palm as she recalled how his chest had been so firm and hard when her fingers brushed over it. The sunlight had picked out the gold glint of the hair that spread across the division of his chest muscles. With her mind's eye, she followed the trailing line over his flat stomach and down into the waistband of his jeans. Licking her lips unconsciously, she found herself wondering what existed behind those silver-toned buttons. If a man's body was so different from her own in so many ways, how else might it differ?

"Is she okay?" Maribel asked Louise in a whisper. "Her face is all red."

Edith realized she'd closed her eyes. "Yes, I'm fine," she said, snapping them open. "I'm just not used to sitting on the floor. I think my legs . . . limbs have fallen asleep."

She stood up, exaggerating her stiffness. She thought savagely, In future, my imagination had better feed off fiction alone!

"Come here, my dears," she said, seating herself on the window seat. The air off the glass felt deliciously cool on her hot cheeks. "I'll tell you a story, if you like."

"What story?" Maribel pulled herself up onto Edith's lap with a grasp of her full skirt.

"Is it from the Bible?" Louise asked, her eyes narrowing suspiciously.

"Don't you like Bible stories?"

"They're all right. I like the ones in Daniel, like Neb . . . Nebu-can-sneezer's dreams. But . . ."

"But what?" Edith asked.

"Well, nobody will tell me what 'beget' means. Al . . . someone says it means 'found' but why were all those people lost?"

Edith recalled being sent to bed without supper for wanting to know how she should begat, since her aunt told her to always behave as the Bible instructed. "Begat just means father. One man is father to another man, so they say, A begat B."

"Oh, I see. Quicker."

"That's right. You see, a long time ago, people didn't have printing presses and lots of people to do work like printing a Bible. So the whole Bible from Genesis to Revelations was written out by hand."

"Golly," Louise said, impressed. "I had to write a twenty-five-word essay last spring and it almost killed me."

"And every word had to be right. So they used some shorter words like 'begat' instead of 'father of' again and again."

"I can print," Maribel stuck in. "I can print real good."

"You cannot," Louise said automatically. "Only the first couple of letters in the alphabet. I can print them all. I can do script too, some."

Maribel's lower lip began to quiver. "Can too print. A—B—C. And G too."

Edith's arm tightened around the little girl's shoulders. "That's a lot," she said. "Before I go, I'll help you with some of the others. You've got all the hard ones already. Can you say the whole alphabet? Let's do it together."

"What about the story?" Louise wanted to know.

"Alphabet first, story after."

She told them a shortened version of *Ivanhoe*. Then she told them about Lochinvar and even recited some of Scott's narrative poem. To her amazement, Louise repeated the lines back to her although half an hour had passed since she heard them. After the children pleaded for one more story, Edith described some of the adventures of Robin Hood, whom she'd mentioned during Ivanhoe. Her throat was sore by then, and she was glad when Sam announced lunch, even if without cake.

Jeff came in late, and dropped down into the chair next to her without speaking. His sleeves and shirt were wet and molded to his form. Crystal droplets hung in his light hair. He pushed back a damp hank that hung in his eyes. Edith had to force her gaze away from him.

After helping Maribel reach the jam, Edith asked, "Jeff, you said something about church today?"

"Tonight," Sam answered after a little silence. "Wednesday

evenings Mr. Armstrong runs a prayer meeting. They're so popular a couple of the other churches have started them."

"So Mr. Armstrong isn't the only . . . ?"

"Lord no," Louise said. Under her father and grandfather's austere glances, the little girl hastily apologized. "Sorry, Cousin Edith, I spoke without thinking."

"That's all right." How had her aunt reacted to Edith's taking the Lord's name in vain? She didn't want to recall the coldness she'd had to endure. Her aunt had never struck her. She'd never needed to. A simple "I see" could raise welts.

"In about the last five or six years, we've had a couple of new churches start up. There's even one for the black folks, those that don't go where their white families go. For a while there, the churches looked like they were going to get awful competitive, but they straightened out their territories. God help any new families who come to town, however."

"You make it sound like competing businesses."

"Isn't it?" Jeff said, lifting a fork to his mouth.

"We don't go to church much," Louise volunteered.

"I like the singing," her sister put in, and began to warble "From Greenland's Icy Mountains," softly but very clearly.

Jeff looked sheepish. "We go," he said. "Sometimes."

. "I see," Edith said.

"When we want to," he responded, glancing at her with a rising anger in his eyes. .

"You don't have to explain."

"I'm not explaining. I'm telling you we go to church when we feel like it. But if it's Sunday and the sun is shining, I think there's better ways for children to learn about God than sitting in a pew!"

"I spent every Sunday in a pew," Edith said. She sipped from her glass of cloudy lemonade. Then she raised her eyes to his angry ones and said simply, "I agree with you."

"Oh." Jeff took another bite of chicken. "Oh."

"Why are they arguing?" Maribel whispered to Louise.

"I don't know." Louise turned to Sam. "Why are Cousin Edith and Daddy arguing?"

"'Cause they like each other would be my guess."

The little girls nodded, obviously approving of this answer.

Edith colored. Jeff kept on eating, only the burning tips of his ears giving away his emotions. "Really good chicken, Dad," he said in a few minutes.

"Excellent," Edith said. "I can't remember when I had better. And there's so much of it."

Jeff turned in his chair to look into her face. "Eat all you can while you're here," he said bluntly. "You're too thin."

"I beg your pardon?" She was not used to hearing comments on her appearance. And such an unflattering remark was not at all what she hoped to hear from Jeff Dane.

"Scrawny, spare, skinny. Take your choice." He leaned closer to her. His thigh pressed against hers. Her jerked back. "I know you haven't had enough to eat for a long time. So fill up, every day, three times a day or more."

"Mr. Dane, what I eat and when are none of your . . . I am your guest and I thank you for your kindness to me, but if you'd be so good as to . . ."

"I don't want you to thank me for my kindness. Here," he spooned up an extra helping of mashed potatoes and plopped them on her plate. "Put some butter on that and get it down."

"Mr. Dane!" Edith tossed her napkin on the table and stood up, all in one seamless motion. "Please excuse me!"

"Nice going, son," Sam said as Edith stalked out of the room.

"Nice going," Maribel echoed.

"Skinny!" Edith fumed as she closed her bedroom door. Even as angry as she was, long training kept her from slamming it.

"Scrawny!" She sat on the bed but couldn't stay still.

"Thin!" Catching sight of herself in the mirror, Edith frowned. This far away, she could see all of her person.

The full-skirted dress, the prettiest thing she'd ever worn, had been a pleasure to put on. The muslin, embroidered all over with tiny blue flowers, had a soft sheen and skimmed over her body without any sensation of weight. Edith had practically skipped down the stairs this morning, just to feel the fabric swaying around her.

Now, however, she saw that the looseness of the fit emphasized her slender waist, while the rest of it hung about her like a sack. Her bony wrists emerged nakedly from the ruffled sleeves. Beneath the full skirt, her ankles looked too frail to support her. Not to mention that the new, less harsh hairstyle she'd tried today only made her cheekbones stand out, turning her eyes into saucers.

Edith acknowledged in shame that she had hoped to please Jeff by these changes. She writhed to remember how she had primped in this mirror, trying her hair this way and that, and pressing her lips together hard to make them pinker. It seemed only right that her pathetic efforts to ensnare Jeff had brought his censure down upon her.

Approaching the mirror, Edith shook her head at her folly. It seemed so typical that she could not tempt him when she wanted to. For she confessed to her reflection that she had indeed been trying to rouse the brute beast that supposedly slept in every man's soul. All she'd managed to awaken was his pity, something she could very well get along without.

A rapping at her door made her call, "Come in." Realizing her eyes were wet, she knuckled away the tears just before the door opened.

Louise stood there, agitation plain in her twisting hands and stuttering voice. "Please, C-Cousin Edith. It's Maribel."

"What's the matter?" She began to grow anxious, pushing aside her misery.

"She's in the root cellar and I can't budge the door."

"The root cellar? What on earth is she doing there?" Edith hurried down the stairs.

"She wanted an apple. Grandpa told her she couldn't but she wanted one awful bad. . . ."

"Where *is* your grandfather? And your father?"

"Please, hurry! It's awful dark in there."

They rushed outside, Edith's skirt trailing across the wet grass. She gave no thought, however, to her beautiful kid shoes. The important thing was to reach Maribel.

Two doors of wooden planks lay across the opening. Earth had been piled up and then faced with boards to make an entry. A latch had fallen across the two handles. Leaning forward, Edith slid the latch away.

The door wasn't that heavy, but Edith supposed it must have seemed so to Louise. It was awkward, though, swinging crookedly to the side. Putting her foot on the first step that lead down into the darkness, Edith called, "Maribel?"

"She must be in the back, where the apples are," Louise suggested. "At least she won't be so frightened. Maybe if you go down there . . ."

Edith nodded. Slowly, watching her footing, she descended. "Maribel, dear. Come out now. There's nothing to be afraid of."

She wished she'd brought a lamp. There was only dirt underfoot but the floor was uneven. Her voice fell strangely flat as she moved farther away from the shaft behind her. Looking up, she called, "I don't see . . ."

Abruptly, the light went out as the cellar door slammed down. "Louise!" Edith called.

"Yes, Cousin Edith?"

"Are you all right, dear?"

"Oh, yes, Cousin Edith. But I still can't move this door."

"Where's your father?"

"I don't know."

"Where's your grandfather?"

"I don't know."

Edith uttered a sigh of vexation. How like men, she thought. But then she smiled, for it struck her suddenly that she sounded like a woman with a thousand years' experience of their sex, rather than a girl with but a week's knowledge.

"Well, go and find them, like a good girl," Edith said.

"You'll wait right there?"

"Absolutely." What choice did she have?

After a moment or two of silence, Edith called again, "Louise? Are you still there?"

Silence was her only answer. Edith crossed her arms across her chest. The air in the cellar was dank and cool. The temperature chilled her like a cool cloth dripping on her skin. It was refreshing, compared to the heat and humidity of the day.

The smell, however, reminded Edith of the fresh earth of a

burial. She shivered, not entirely from the cold. Remembering that Maribel was supposed to be down here, she called her name.

As her eyes adjusted to the little streamers of light that filtered through the slats of the door, Edith peered around her. A few large barrels took up some of the room, and these had two or three smaller ones resting in the spaces between their rounded sides. Strings of onions and bags of potatoes hung from pegs driven into the supporting floor beams.

Moving farther into the darkness, Edith realized this was a larger space than she had first thought. It must run under half the house.

That gave her an idea. Perhaps there was a way into the house from the cellar. It made sense that Sam's wife and Gwen hadn't wanted to tramp all the way around the house every time they wanted a carrot or a turnip. What about in the winter? They must surely have rebelled at the thought of getting all bundled up just to obtain a few vegetables.

After bumping into two dirty partitions, Edith decided she would recommend a few things to Jeff's next wife. It was just as she was deciding that electric lighting was really a necessity for mankind that too much light suddenly filled the cellar.

Once more Edith found her eyes watering. She stumbled toward the opening. A broad-shouldered figure fell across her vision like a shadow.

"Sam?" she asked, stepping blindly forward.

"No, it's me. Edith, are you all right?" Jeff dashed down the rickety wooden stairs to take her hand.

"Don't trouble about me. Maribel is down here, and she won't answer when I call her."

"Maribel? But she's out . . ."

Once more, the light was cut off with a slam. Jeff and Edith jerked around with one accord. Releasing her hand, he climbed the steps determinedly.

"Louise," he called. "Are you playing a trick on your old dad?"

"No, sir."

Faintly, Edith heard the inevitable echo. "No, sir." So Maribel was outside all along.

"Are you positive about that?"

Two little voices. "No, sir."

"All right then. You've had your joke. Now open the door, Louise."

"I can't. It's too heavy. I'll go get Grandpa."

"You'd better. And then we'll have a little talk about this, young lady."

Edith put her hand on the railing and looked up at Jeff, crouching like Atlas. "I didn't think they disliked me so much."

"They don't dislike you at all. This is just a practical joke. All kids do it. Didn't you?" Looking down into her face, lit palely by the sifted sunlight, he answered his own question. "Of course you didn't. You probably played sedately with your dolls and never got your tucker messed."

Responding to the note of pity in his voice, Edith tossed back her head. "That's right. I was never a wild animal like other children."

"Your aunt saw to that. I'm really going sour on . . ."

"It has nothing to do with my aunt. It's just the way I am. Why, even before I left the orphanage, I . . ."

"Orphanage? What orphanage?"

"The one I lived in until I was . . . I must have been about Maribel's age. The papers never gave a clear birth date."

"You're adopted?" Jeff sat down on the top step.

"Of course. My aunt never married."

"She wasn't your mother's sister? Or your father's?"

Edith lifted her shoulders. "Neither. She really wasn't related to me at all. She told me to call her aunt. I never knew who my real parents were until after Aunt Edith died. My real name, believe it or not, is Jessica Hawes. But I can't imagine answering to it. It belongs to a stranger."

"Jessica's a pretty name. What else do you know?"

"The details were in the papers she left behind." Her gaze sank to the floor. "They were burned with everything else."

"Do you remember your parents?"

"No. That is, not really. Sometimes I think I remember

something. A song, or a smell will make me think . . . that was my mother. But it's never any stronger than that."

She glanced up again toward him. The light behind him, reflecting off his thick, fair hair, gave him a halo. "I've never told anybody else about my adoption. I don't know why."

His voice was deep as he said, "Maybe because between us, there should be no secrets."

16

❧❦

JEFF PACED BACK and forth at the bottom of the stairs. Edith, watching him, thought of a pendulum clock. Then she sank again into a fantasy.

From her chains, Lady Jessica Hawes listened to the slow drip of water from the goatskin bag upon the wall. Clever Lord Ivor, to torture her thus! But she would never yield to his foul demands, though her life pay for her stubbornness.

The deep-barred oaken doors at the top of the slimed stone steps creaked open. The smoking torches set in high brackets around the dungeon walls flickered in the rush of cool air. Was this her deliverance? The chains cut into her wrists as she strained forward to see.

A dark hulking figure stumbled over the threshold, held up by the cruel arms of her jailers. A sharp shove and the figure fell, tumbling down the steps, helpless to save himself. He lay at the bottom, in a tangle of soiled straw. The guards laughed harshly and clanged the great doors shut.

After a moment, the figure raised his head and Jessica looked upon the features, cut and bruised but yet defiant, of

Jeffrey the Dane. He said, "I don't know where those kids are, but I'm going to have something to say when I get out of here."

"I'm sure it's only a joke, as you said," Edith told him, jolted into reality.

"Well, they're taking it too far. They should have brought Dad by now, unless he's in on it."

"Why would he be?"

Jeff began pacing again. "He might think it was funny."

"Your father hasn't struck me as a man to make silly jokes."

"Not any more. He was once." Jeff wondered if locking them together in a cellar was his father's ideas of matchmaking. He realized it might very well be Louise's idea of it. Push two people together in a situation like this and they could wind up in each other's arms. Especially if the woman has shown herself to be scared of snakes.

"You know," Jeff said, stopping again in front of her. "I don't want to alarm you, or anything, but . . ."

"Yes?" How handsome he was with the light on his face! She didn't know what he had been doing when Louise brought him to rescue her, but he had a hardworking, windblown look about him as though he'd been wrestling with the earth and sky.

Jeff struggled with his baser self. He lost. "You know, sometimes snakes creep into cool places like this to wait out the heat of the day."

"Do they?" Her tone was calm but she drew her skirts together around her ankles.

Darn! he thought. He'd been enjoying the glimpses he'd had of those delicate underpinnings. "Yeah," he said. "But I'm sure you're safe there. I don't think they can climb stairs."

"I won't budge."

He went back to pacing. Edith returned to dreaming.

The big, blond god of a man inched his way over to her like a lowly worm. Every motion caused his brow to contract and his lips to set hard against the pain of his bindings. Tears flowed freely from Lady Edith's crystalline eyes as she suffered each pain with him. At last, he could lay his head in her lap.

"I came to rescue thee," he said. A bitter laugh broke from his throat. "A fine hand I have made of it."

" 'Twas bravely done."

"Nay, 'twas folly. But when I learned what had become of thee, my brain was fired. I listened not to the counsels of my cooler friends, nor heeded any call but that of my love for thee. And now, what can I? Only die with thee."

"That is enough," she whispered brokenly. "For I would die gladly with thee."

"What are you crying about?" Jeff asked, one foot on a step. He leaned forward to take her hand. "It's not so bad. They'll be along. Or listen . . . I could try to break the latch again. I'm pretty sure I felt it give a little before."

"I'm a fool," Edith said vehemently, pulling her hand away. "Don't take any notice, please."

"What do you mean, don't take notice? If you're upset about being down here . . ."

He sat on the step beside her and put his arm around her waist. Snugging her against his side, he said softly, "Come on, darlin'. It'll be all right."

"I know," she protested, sliding away from his warmth. She couldn't accept his comfort under false pretenses. "The thing is . . . you see, I make up . . ."

"What?" he asked after a long pause. She was blushing as though she were confessing a secret fondness for blood sacrifice at the height of the full moon.

"I invent stories. Awful lies."

"Lies? Or stories? There's a big difference."

"No, there isn't. A lie is an untruth, a falsehood. And a story is the same thing—making up people who never existed and who do things no one has ever done." She hung her head. "I've always done it in secret."

"That's not so terrible," he said, laughing a little at her air of utter disgrace. "Who ever told you . . . ? Let me guess. Your aunt."

Edith made a further confession, not trying at all now to disturb his comforting arm. "Ever since she died, I have been . . . sneaking novels out of the library."

"Is that some sort of a crime?"

"It's unfair," she said, surprised he didn't understand. "And it might be illegal, I suppose. It was her subscription and she would never take a novel home. To her, they were the devil's books. Do you suppose it really is against the law?" Her blue eyes, looking black with dilated pupils, went round at the idea.

She shook her head over her own wickedness. "It's like an illness. I have tried to stop, to read only wholesome works—travel and biographies—but I always wind up taking home Dickens and Twain and Verne."

"Three dangerous men." He grinned at her and cuddled her closer in a teasing way, telling himself he was behaving just like a big brother. "Whose company I enjoy myself, when I'm not working on the stud records or the accounts. It's not a crime or an illness to love to read great stories, Edith. I don't care what your aunt told you. She was wrong."

His face was so sincere that she was reassured. She said, "But you must admit that there is a difference between reading stories and making them up. That is a vice equal to drink."

"Now how did you decide that?"

"When I am reading, I can put down the book and be Edith Parker again. I can do my household tasks and carry on rational conversations, when there is anybody there to talk with."

Thinking of the squalor of her boardinghouse, Jeff hoped she had not talked much with the people he'd seen there. Drunken landlords and neighbors who looked to him like women for hire were not fit confidants for this gentle, intuitive girl.

"But when I make up stories," Edith went on, "then it is a very different thing. My food burns, my bed isn't made . . . and I talk to people without knowing what they said or how I answered." Her voice dropped to a thread. "Some people in St. Louis thought I was crazy. But I was only thinking I was someone else."

"Who?"

She shook her head and wouldn't answer.

"Have you ever written any of these stories down? I'd like to read . . ."

"Oh, no! I mean, I could never let anyone read any of my stories. I just couldn't. Besides, they are all gone now."

"The fire?"

"Yes. Everything I knew about myself and all my dreams . . ."

Jeff cupped her soft cheek in his rough hand. Bringing her

head up, he met her gaze. "You haven't lost a thing," he said, his thumb moving gently next to her quivering mouth. "You still know who you are. And you can find new dreams."

What might have happened next haunted Edith's thoughts. But just as she thought Jeff was about to kiss her—her eyes had even begun to close—there was a loud thump on the boards behind them.

"Hey, son. You down there?"

Jeff's arm dropped from Edith's shoulders. "Yes, sir. We sure as heck are!"

"Why?"

Half-laughing, Jeff shouted back, "What do you mean 'why'? Get us out of here!"

"Yes, please, Sam, do," Edith added.

"How in tarnation did you get the bolt across is what I want to know," Sam said after wrenching open one of the doors. The prisoners emerged into the light, blinking and squinting.

"Those fool . . ." Jeff began, but Edith put her hand on his arm to stop him.

"I'm so glad that the girls found you, Sam. We might have been trapped down there all day."

"Better you than me," Sam answered with a shudder. "Always hated damp, enclosed places. The very idea gives me the jumps."

"I don't blame you! But I do thank you for rescuing us."

"My pleasure, Cousin Edith. Always wanted to rescue a damsel in distress. I just never expected her to be in my root cellar with the big bohunkus I call 'son.'" Sam headed off, his limp slightly more noticeable than usual.

"He must have run all the way," Jeff said fondly, watching him go. "Thanks for stopping me telling him everything. He'd be awfully disappointed in the girls." He turned toward her. Except for some dirt around her hem, she looked not a hair the worse for her confinement.

"I felt it was between you and them."

"And you too. You're in this discussion, all the way in."

"Oh, but as a stranger . . ." Edith said, hanging back.

"Even a stranger has rights. You were locked up without a trial—that's against the Constitution."

"Are you a lawyer, too?" Edith asked as she followed reluctantly along.

"Heck, no. Paul is, though. He told me he'd taken an apprenticeship in the law while he was in San Francisco, though he could have bought and sold the fellow that schooled him. That's why he's only now getting around to coming back to Richey. And points East."

"Miss Climson doesn't know Mr. Tyler's a lawyer, does she?"

"Not unless he told her last night. Dad said Paul asked to be dropped off where Miss Climson's boarding this month. He seemed to think they might have stayed up late talking." Jeff glanced back. Her face was so alive with speculation that he could almost read her thoughts.

"Now, look," he began. "If you're getting any ideas about matching Miss Climson up too . . ."

"Too? But I had nothing to do with Mrs. Green and Mr. Hunaker. It was . . . a force of nature. Like a tidal wave or an earthquake. Just because I was there doesn't mean I caused it."

"I don't know 'bout that," Jeff said, mock-seriously, as he tapped his boot on the ground and his fingers against his chin. "Stands to reason that anybody who's made as many matches as you have just might not be able to help herself."

Catching his mood, made up no doubt of the sun peeking through the silvering clouds and the fresh breeze that seemed to fan the heat away, Edith said, "You may be right. Maybe it's not under my control anymore. My astral self might just be matchmaking without my knowing anything about it."

She pressed her hand to her brow and swayed as though in a mystic trance. "Yes . . . yes . . . ," she sighed. "I can see it all so clearly. The past . . . the future . . . Paul Tyler . . . Miss Climson . . . yes . . . yes. . . ."

Hearing those "yesses" on her sighing breath sent Jeff's temperature up to the top of the mercury. He could easily imagine his kisses calling forth those provocative murmurs. Nevertheless, he made a real effort to hold on to this light-hearted mood.

"Oh, wise Madam Edith, never mind those other folks, tell me my future. Will I marry the woman I adore?"

"Describe her to me and I shall consult the spirit guides."

"Oh, I'm on fire for her. She's three feet tall, and moon-faced. Has a cast in her right eye and a hairy wart on the end of her nose. And, oh, how could I forget, a wooden leg."

"That's pretty vague. Left or right leg?" Edith couldn't keep back a gurgle of laughter.

She snapped her eyes open as he pulled her against his hard chest. "You should laugh more often," he said, his brown eyes intense. "It suits you."

Edith wondered later if that was the moment she fell in love with him, or afterward when she saw him being stern yet gentle with his daughters? He held them each on one knee and made it clear that he never wanted them to play such a trick again. He never raised his voice nor his hand but he let them see his disappointment.

Maribel began to sniff and cry very soon after he started to speak. Louise, made of sterner stuff, kept a stone face. When her father excused them, however, she flung her arms around his neck and whispered something against his shirtfront.

Then both little girls crossed the room to where Edith sat, feeling very much in the way. "We're sorry, Cousin Edith," Louise said, her eyes more than her face betraying the depth of her feelings.

"Very sorry."

"We won't do it again," Louise stated. Maribel looked mournful and shook her head.

"That's all right," Edith said, feeling as bad as they did. "Don't cry any more, you're good girls. I'm not angry. I was just worried about you."

She glanced at Jeff to see if he approved of what she said. He returned her look with a smile and a thumbs-up. Warmed, she reached out to gather Maribel into her arms. Edith kissed the child's soft, warm cheek. Maribel shyly touched her lips to Edith's cheek in return.

Letting the younger girl wiggle down, Edith looked up and surprised a wistful expression passing over Louise's face. Standing up, Edith quickly bent to hug the other girl tightly. It was a bit like embracing a doll carved from a single piece of wood. Edith pressed her lips to Louise's smooth forehead.

"It's all right, dear," she said as she stepped back.

Louise nodded, her eyes as startled as a deer's. For once, it was Maribel who spoke first. "Can we go play now, Dad?"

"No," Jeff said. "I think you should go to your room and think over everything I've said. You can come down for dinner and then an early night."

"Yes, sir," the two said, dragging their feet over the rug.

Edith couldn't bear their woebegone faces. "That's too hard, Jeff. Louise, Maribel . . . come with me to church tonight?"

Their faces did not exactly light up. Obviously weighing the rival merits of their room and the church, Louise visibly came to the conclusion that church had ever so slightly an edge.

"Can we, Dad?"

"You'll come too, Jeff, of course."

Glumly, he answered, "Of course."

Sam was no more cheerful about the idea than the rest of the family. Finally, he gave in to majority opinion. "Do I have to put on a stiff collar?"

"You should be used to them," Edith said. "You must have worn them as a young man."

"I hated them then too. But I guess you can't go to church in a flannel shirt, no matter how comfortable."

"Certainly not!" Edith smiled and hurried up the stairs. She'd promised to give the girls their baths and wanted to use the fine soap she'd found packed in some of her undergarments. It had a sweet lily-of-the-valley fragrance that made all her things smell so fresh. She was sure the girls would revel in it.

Edith had little time to think about Jeff until she was sitting beside him in the buggy. Yet he was always at the back of her mind, even while she was bathing the girls or learning how to bake biscuits by watching Sam. Sitting beside him now, she knew that she was already far too deeply in love with him to save herself.

He looked again like her rescuer from St. Louis, wearing his fine tan suit, his low-crowned hat tipped over one eye. Leaning back, she watched his face covertly from behind her veil. His firm jaw showed a scrape where he'd shaved too closely. A slight smile tugged at the corner of his mouth, while his keen eyes stayed upon the road, never flicking in her direction. Yet, after a few moments he smiled and said, "What?"

Startled, Edith also said, "What?"

"You're staring at me."

"No, no, I wasn't."

"Sure you were. Or were you looking past my nose at the scenery?"

"I wasn't even looking in your direction."

"Sure?"

"Absolutely."

His smile widened, showing his white teeth as though he'd like to take a bite of her. Realizing she was staring again, she glanced down at her white-gloved hands. But when he said, "Whoa!" and pulled back on the reins, her gaze snapped up to his face as though it was drawn there by magnetic force.

"What are you doing?"

"Stopping. . . ."

"But you can't!"

The wagon, carrying Sam and the girls, stopped beside them. Even their horses turned their heads to see what was the matter. "Something wrong?"

"Nothing at all," Jeff said. "I'm just waiting for Edith to tell me . . ."

"Yes, I was," Edith said quickly. "All right?"

"Sure thing." He motioned for his father to go on ahead.

"It's extortion. That's what it is." Edith bit her lip to keep from smiling. She didn't want to encourage him in his outrageous behavior, but at the same time, she hoped he'd continue to say reckless things.

"Now where did a nice girl like you learn an ugly word like extortion?"

"A city can be an ugly place," she said, looking at the trees. All the leaves were shiny, as though Mother Nature had passed through the woods with beeswax. A fresh smell permeated the air. Edith breathed deeply, for she'd never known such an exciting fragrance before. It spoke of the mysteries at the heart of the green woods, far from brick walls and stone streets.

"I know." Jeff untangled his hand from the reins and

dropped it lightly over her knee. "Have you thought . . . you don't have to go back. You could make a good life in Richey."

"A good life, but not a good living. There isn't much call for a matchmaker here."

"I found a use for one. Besides, you do all your work through the mails, remember? Just list your post office as General Delivery, Richey, Missouri, until you get settled."

"Now you're tempting me, Mr. Dane." Daringly, she patted his hand, very quickly, afraid of being burned. How could she possibly stay after he married someone else?

The church doors were open, a sign of welcome. Many buggies and wagons, even a four-person surrey with a fringed canopy, were parked in the green churchyard. The horses, some with nose bags, waited patiently for their masters in the glow of the setting sun. A few stragglers were climbing the church stairs.

"Are we late?" Edith asked anxiously. "I hate walking into church late. It makes such a poor impression."

"No, we're not late."

"Then where is everyone?" Now the only people in sight were Sam and the girls.

"The service hasn't started yet," Jeff assured her.

"Oh, we'd better hurry though." She wondered what the difference was to him between walking in late during the service or walking in late before the service. Everyone stared either way. Perhaps it was a distinction only a man would understand.

Maribel and Louise both slipped their hands into hers when they met crossing the grass. "We want to sit next to you," Louise whispered as they entered the church.

No one noticed them. The citizens of Richey, all that attended here, were busy talking amongst themselves, a musical whispering punctuated by laughter. As Edith followed Sam and Jeff to an empty wooden pew near the back, she saw that the church, though simple, had been decorated with care. A few pictures were hung beside the red and blue windows, showing sentimental scenes from the Bible. Nearest her was one of Christ ministering to the little children.

To keep the girls from fidgeting, Edith told them the story.

Maribel was interested enough to stop banging her shoes against the pew in front. Louise, however, didn't seem to be attending very closely. She had poked a finger into her ribs and was scratching vigorously.

"What is it?" Edith asked, interrupting herself.

"It's this danged dress. It itches something fierce and I can't ever seem to make it better."

Edith considered reproving Louise for her language in the house of God, but having suffered through itchy dresses in her own girlhood, she understood perfectly. Not that she'd ever known the word "danged."

"You must have on a horsehair petticoat."

"I think it's wool."

"In the summertime?" Edith shook her head sympathetically. "We'll find you a nice muslin one tomorrow."

A peculiar wheezing followed by thin organlike notes stilled the congregation. Edith could just see the back of Mrs. Armstrong's head as she played the harmonium by the pulpit. With a concerted rustle and the thumps of feet hitting the floor, everyone stood up and began to sing the Twenty-third Psalm. Knowing the words well, Edith also sang, blending her voice with Jeff's bold baritone and his father's surprisingly lyrical bass as well as the piping voices of the girls.

When she sat down again, Maribel climbed onto her lap. Edith caught a gleam of admiration in Jeff's eyes. She cast her gaze downward. A pretty situation when a smile from him made her insides feel all squeezed. She peeked to see if he was still looking at her but he was attending to Mr. Armstrong who mounted into the pulpit.

He wore his dark suit, and looked as though he were a lumberjack doing an imitation of a preacher. He spoke, however, with the true faith of a Christian ringing in every word. From his opening words, "The night is far spent, the day is at hand: let us therefore cast off the works of darkness, and let us put on the armor of light," the preacher had the full attention of the assembly.

The women ceased to fan themselves with their paper fans bearing advertising mottos. The men sat up from relaxed attitudes, or leaned forward. Even the children stopped squirming, though they were the first to resume.

Mr. Armstrong went on, telling them that now was the time to consecrate themselves to Jesus, that soon there would be no more time for any repenting, for the Second Coming was surely now at hand. They had to be ready. Some people were nodding now, while a woman in the middle kept saying, "Amen!"

Edith felt the tension building in the little church. The intensity of feeling which Mr. Armstrong wrought from the people began to frighten her. It was like sitting next to a keg of black powder as the fuse dwindled, headed toward an inevitable explosion. She wanted to sink to the floor and cover her head.

Then the harmonium started again and the moment passed. When Mr. Armstrong began to speak after the hymn, he persuaded more gently, like a father encouraging a wayward son, rather than as an avenging spirit. The fans began waving again, languidly, stirring the stifling air.

Edith became aware that some heads had turned in her direction. Unable to believe anyone had a reason to look at her, she glanced over her shoulder. Vera Albans stood in the doorway, closing the door discreetly behind her. Her face flushed beneath her gaily decorated hat, she began walking as quietly and as quickly as possible up the aisle.

Sam sat at the end of their pew. He had also turned around to see the milliner creeping in late. As she approached, he signalled Jeff to scoot over. Edith had already moved the children down. She smiled a welcome when Sam snagged Miss Albans's hand as she tiptoed toward her regular seat.

Miss Albans gasped at the sudden touch of his hand, and more heads swiveled in the Danes' direction. Sam stood up, a tall figure in his checked suit, and let Miss Albans pass in front of him. He gave her a grin that was very nearly a duplicate of the one Jeff used when he wanted to fascinate. After they sat down, Miss Albans began to whisper to Sam, obviously offering explanations for her tardiness.

Few people seemed to be attending to Mr. Armstrong anymore. Most of the children were whispering. Some of the men were yawning, and Maribel was very nearly asleep.

Everyone woke up instantly, however, when Mr. Armstrong said, "Most of you know already that my daughter Dulcie is getting married soon. I reckon this would be a good chance for you all to meet her intended. Victory? Victor Sullivan? Come on up here. You, too, Dulcie."

With some good-natured grumbling, and a nervous giggle from Dulcie, the happy couple stepped up onto the slightly raised platform at the end of the church. Edith leaned forward to peer at Dulcie's fiancé. She interfered, accidentally, with Vera's view. "I beg your pardon, Vera, I just want to see . . ."

He had a lean body, a handsome face in a pretty way, and a wide, friendly grin. His pale, pasty skin looked as though it had never been exposed to sunlight and he must put something on his hair to make it so shiny. Edith disliked him at sight. She glanced at the young lady next to her to see what she thought. No doubt that irreverent mind must have some comment.

What she saw shocked her. Vera Albans was white, literally as white as the lace collar of her dress. Some beads of sweat had appeared at the edges of her red-gold hair, and she bit her lips until Edith thought she must be tasting her own blood.

Instantly, Edith transferred Maribel to Jeff. She touched Vera's arm. "Are you all right?" she whispered.

"Air . . . please . . . outside . . ." Her eyes were eloquent with misery. Edith could not resist the plea.

Supporting Vera's elbow with her hand, she said, "Excuse us, Sam. Miss Albans is unwell."

Once again the tall man stood up. Jeff at the other end of the pew stared worriedly past Maribel's head on his shoulder. Edith waved at him as she assisted Vera out of doors. Sam remained standing, staring after the two women until his son tugged him down.

17

Before they'd reached the bottom step, Vera began to sob, dry sobs that wracked her from head to foot. It was a terrible aching sound that started Edith's lip quivering in sympathy.

"I . . . I'm sorry," Vera gasped.

"No, now, don't be," Edith murmured, fiercely ordering herself to remain collected. Vera needed strength, not mere feeble sympathy.

Feeling the other girl sagging, Edith put her arm around Vera's waist and helped her over to a gravestone in the shade. She pulled her softly scented handkerchief from where it hung over her belt and gave it to Vera. "Sit here. Do you need a drink of water?"

"No . . . no, I'm better now." Vera pressed the handkerchief to her eyes. Her voice still shook as she said, "It was just such a shock . . . seeing him . . . I . . ."

She gave herself up to tears, but only for a moment. Straightening, she shook herself as if she were coming out of deep water. Edith could only admire her self-mastery. "There,

I'm perfectly all right. It must have been the heat. Thank you for your help, Miss Parker."

Her smile was as brilliant and false as the purple rhinestones in her brooch. Edith did not want to press her, but she felt very strongly that she ought to. It was a compulsion as strong in its way that which drove her to talk to strangers about the people they loved.

Choosing her words carefully, she said, "If you don't want to say anything more, that's all right. However, you know I will be gone from Richey in a few days. If telling me your troubles would help you bear them, I would be happy to listen."

Vera sank slowly down once again onto the granite stone. "I don't know what you mean. . . ."

Looking up into the deep blue sky of twilight, Edith said, "You know, the first morning I was here, I woke up twice. The second time was when I heard Sam in the kitchen. It is a strange thing that so pleasant-spoken a man cannot cook without swearing. He uses words I have never heard before, and don't know what they mean but they sound terrible!"

"Sam . . ." Vera rubbed her forehead and looked miserably at the ground.

"Anyway, the first time I woke . . . I don't know exactly why, but I went to the window. The curtains were moving in the breeze. They looked just like watered silk, so much so that I had to touch them to be sure they were still just cotton. When I looked out the window, the whole sky was silver. I'd never seen a silver sky before but there it was. Then the clouds turned pink, so faintly at first that I couldn't tell them from the sky. They became brighter and brighter, becoming orange, and the whole sky flushed with pink. And when the sun came up, I was astonished to think that this sun has been rising over the world for so many thousands of years I couldn't begin to count them all—and I had never seen it before. It makes me wonder what other miracles I have wasted."

"Miracles . . . ," Vera said, and gave a little mirthless laugh. "All my miracles have been ominous, like the bears eating the children who laughed at Elijah."

Edith looked into Vera's gray eyes, now darkened with misery. "Are you sure *all* your miracles have been so grim?"

"No, you're right," Vera admitted. "It isn't always like that, but sometimes do you ever get the feeling that something . . . maybe just the world . . . is out to get you?"

"Out to get you?"

"Yes, you know. A dark menace pursuing you and all you can do is run and run like in a nightmare, never getting away."

Edith shook her head. "No, even when things go badly for me, I don't feel that way. Why do you?"

Vera paused, plainly considering how much she should reveal. "All right," she said, "it's like this. That man . . . Victor Sullivan . . . I knew him, only that wasn't the name he was using."

"I knew it!" Edith nodded, far from happy that her intuition had proven itself. "I knew there was something wrong with that man."

"Wrong is right. To state the facts briefly and baldly, he met me at a party. I was shy, naive and as stupid as any girl could be. My brother was introducing me to society, trying to impress everyone in New York with his culture and gentility." Vera's face showed her disgust, as though she were reading a page from a sordid novel aloud. "They came all right, but I could tell they were laughing at him. And at me. Then I met Tate . . . that was what he called himself then. He won my heart at once."

She laughed bitterly. "I can't say I made it very difficult for him. Heavens, what a perfect idiot I was! Anyway, he soon convinced me to agree to marry him, but my brother wouldn't hear of it. He called Tate a fortune hunter. George swore he'd refuse to support me once I was married. I 'persuaded' Tate to elope with me, though he kept putting off our marriage. I know now he was expecting George to change his mind and send money. He even wrote George letters, begging letters."

"Did your brother change his mind?"

"George never changes his mind. Tate left me. I was all alone in this miserable boardinghouse in Boston. He'd even taken the few trinkets I'd brought along. The landlady kicked me out. The only thing to do was to go home."

"You must have hated that," Edith said. She could imagine returning, disgraced and despoiled, to a stern, righteous brother.

All she had to do was substitute him for her own aunt. "Did he say 'I told you so'?"

"Only about every hour on the hour," Vera laughed again, more warmly. "I couldn't stay. George was right about that too. If I stayed I might drag him down. They're very hard on girls who 'slip' in that society."

"What did you do?"

"I wandered around, staying in hotels." She shrugged. "I couldn't stand to be in one place for very long. Then, one day, I came here. I was out of money and George wasn't supposed to send another check for several weeks. The milliner had gotten married and moved West, and I've always been good with frills and furbelows. They've been nice to me here, but if they knew . . ."

Vera stood up. "I shall probably dislike you very much tomorrow, Edith. But I can't help being grateful today. I've been carrying around this secret like a lead weight. It's a little lighter now."

"I'm glad you feel better," Edith said. "But aren't you forgetting something?"

"Victor?"

"No, Dulcie."

Vera blinked and turned back. "Dulcie?"

"You can't let her marry him. Not knowing what you know."

"Maybe he's changed. People do change."

"Do you believe that he has, so much as to make Dulcie a good and loving husband?"

"I can't think why else he'd want to marry her. She doesn't have any money he can take."

"What are you going to do?"

"What can I do?" Vera demanded with sudden passion. "I've built a life here . . . I can't just throw it away. I've done that once and the consequences were terrible. I can't do it again."

"What about Dulcie?"

"Dulcie has made her bed . . . no, I don't mean that. Of course she mustn't marry him. He's as cruel as . . . the letter I found after he left me. . . . But what can I do?"

"Go to Mr. Armstrong. He would never let Dulcie . . ."

"No, I'd have to explain to him. He might kick Tate down the church steps but he'd also denounce me."

"He wouldn't. . . ."

"Yes, he would. He'd pray for me publicly, naming names and announcing exactly how I've strayed. I couldn't stand it. All those people staring and whispering at me."

"I know how you feel," Edith said, shuddering. Thinking of how intensely the pastor had exhorted his flock to cast away their sins and make their souls white again, Edith could believe that Mr. Armstrong would act as Vera had said. Also, the outraged father in him would likely overcome whatever assurances of secrecy he might promise Vera.

"We must do something," she repeated in a determined tone.

Vera shook Edith's sleeve lightly between her fingers. "It's not your problem, Edith. It's mine, and I'll think of something. If I have to, I'll go to Mr. Armstrong before Dulcie gets married. Milliners are supposed to be wicked, abandoned women anyway. They've been whispering about me since I came, so what's the difference?"

After a moment, she answered her own question. "The difference between a lie and the truth, that's all. Well, I can start all over again, but . . . God, I don't want to!"

"Don't want to what?" said Sam, coming up to them. They'd been so absorbed in their conversation that they hadn't heard him until he spoke. Now both girls whirled around as though caught in some petty wickedness.

The instant Vera saw him, she began to back away. One hand went out to him, but with the fingers splayed as if to warn him off. "No," she said, in a gasping voice, "I really can't."

Edith once more put a supporting arm around Vera's waist. "Don't fall," she said, stopping her short of the tombstone.

Again, Vera fought for her self-control. "Thank you." She turned a trembling smile toward Sam. "I'm not feeling very well. I shouldn't have tried to come to church today . . . I felt so strange when I woke up."

"Maybe you should have the doctor come by," he suggested.

"Yes, yes, I will. Funny, I felt fine yesterday, but I think maybe I overdid things. Got too tired. I was sicker than a dog last Sunday with that head cold that was going around."

"I know. I missed seeing you in church."

"You did?" Vera frowned as if his confession annoyed her.

"Let me drive you home," Sam said.

Vera stepped free of Edith's restraining arm. Her bright smile once more firmly pinned in place, she said, "No, thanks, Sam. I appreciate it, but no, thanks."

Twitching her skirt to the side so she could pass Sam without touching him, Vera walked away without a backward glance. Her back was straight as a soldier's going to face the enemy's firing squad.

"She's a funny woman," Sam mused.

"You like her?" Perhaps her matchmaking fervor showed in her voice for he looked around at her and grinned.

"I like everybody. Always have. That's why I get along so well. Never argue, never fuss."

"Yet Jeff tells me . . ."

"You can't believe a word that boy says. Where he gets such ideas . . . you don't know the half of it."

"Are you warning me, Sam?" Not that she intended to listen. The moments she had with Jeff were too precious to let a harsh reality come between them.

"Heck, no. You're a sensible woman—I saw that as soon as I met you. But that boy of mine . . . the stories he tells about me would shame a politician." He started walking toward the church, and Edith matched her speed to his crooked gait.

"Like what?"

"Like how he tells people he doesn't know what side I fought on in the late war. Did he tell you that?"

"Well, he mentioned . . ."

"Now see! See!"

"Which side did you fight on?"

Sam stopped and ran his finger around under his tight collar. "All right, so maybe I did wear gray for a little while . . . but it was sheer force of circumstances that made me do it. I was captured, you see. And a more raggle-taggle bunch of half-wits you never saw in your life. They were all city boys out in the middle of the swamps. Why, only Lucifer himself knew. They sure didn't have any idea."

"So you . . ."

"I had to help 'em out or the lot of 'em would have died standing up. Though I wasn't a webfoot myself, my uncle and I spent a lot of time fishing and camping on rivers, so I knew a little bit—which was whole encyclopedias more than they did." He kept his smile in place, but his eyes sobered. "Not a one of 'em was older than twenty. I saved them in the swamp, but I couldn't save them from the madness of a nation at war with itself."

He blinked and gave her a wide grin. "Now what call does my son have to tell people I couldn't make up my mind which side I was on? Course, I had to sign up with the Confederate Army, or those boys would be in trouble. And if I was getting pay from both sides, you can't say I didn't earn it. Besides which, I paid the North back . . . but I'll tell you about that some other time."

"Please do. I can't wait to hear more."

"Really?" Sam looked surprised and pleased. "Nice of you to say that, Edith. Awfully nice."

He quietly led her back into the church, the singing of the congregation covering their entrance. Jeff was the only one to frown at them. She patted his hand reassuringly as she sat down. Maribel immediately wiggled her way back onto Edith's lap.

By the time the last hymn had been sung, the little girl was a dead weight on Edith's shoulder. While the rest of the congregation, including Sam and Louise, went out into the cool blue twilight, Jeff and Edith stayed behind. He held out his arms for his daughter.

"I don't mind," Edith said, shifting the child higher.

"No, come on. I know she's got to be heavy on you."

"A little, but never mind."

He reached for Maribel and the little girl half-woke up to look around. Then she slumped limply, trusting her father to catch her. She clung to his broad shoulder, settling easily down again into sleep.

"There's a lot of hay in the wagon," Jeff said as he moved out into the aisle. "She'll get a good nap and be full of beans later on."

Paul Tyler was waiting at the door, two elderly ladies beside him, their mittened hands tucked in the crook of his elbows. There was a strong family resemblance between the two ladies. They were on the short side, but broad in their black silks. Like Paul, they had brown eyes and their hair was still dark.

"I don't have to ask you," Jeff said, "I can tell you're glad to have your boy back again."

"So happy," Miss Minta said. "But he's hardly staying a week, bad boy." The adoring look she turned up to her nephew's face belied her querulous words.

"That's youth for you," Jeff answered. "Always on the go, these young whippersnappers."

"Will you listen to Grandpa!" Paul scoffed. "I don't know, my darlings, maybe we shouldn't invite him to supper. He looks like he could use a nap instead!"

"Will there be some of Miss Minta's crullers?" The little lady nodded. "And Miss Hetty's potato salad? Then get out of my way, whippersnapper, there's work for men!"

The aunts giggled as Jeff pressed past them. Edith noticed that both ladies looked up to Jeff with affection which, if not as glorified as that showed to their nephew, was still strong. As the three women fell into step behind the men, Miss Hetty said, "Dear Jefferson has been so kind to us, Miss Parker. He fixed our shed roof last spring and . . ."

"Don't forget all that wood he brought us in the fall. We never had to pay a penny to have it chopped, either." Miss Minta raised her eyes to heaven. "Surely he'll be rewarded. In the meantime, however, if he wants my crullers, he may have as many as he wants."

Miss Hetty nudged her sister and said, "You must be thinking us rude as pigs, my dear. We hope you'll be able to join us for supper too."

Edith yanked her attention back to the aunts. She had been listening more to the bits of Paul and Jeff's conversation rather than to the women who walked with her. She thanked them and said, "I'd enjoy that, but, you know, Sam has the children. Why not invite him? I'll stay with the girls."

"Oh, we spoke to Mr. Dane when he left the church," Miss Hetty said. "He has something to do tonight."

"He didn't say what," Miss Minta added.

"We're having Miss Climson, too. Paul insisted."

"He insisted most strongly." The two aunts looked at each other and giggled as though they were no older than Louise and Maribel. Then they caught Edith's eye and forced their faces to be solemn. Except that bubbles of laughter kept escaping Miss Minta.

Having heard a snippet of Paul's conversation, Edith felt she understood. "She's a remarkable girl," he said. "Astonishingly well educated, too. Almost makes me an advocate of higher education for women, though I'm not sure it's right for every girl."

Jeff's reply had been muffled. "Maybe," Paul replied. "But living here I can't blame her for being a little sharp. God knows I wouldn't have amounted to much if I'd stayed. Richey's no place to live if you're ambitious."

Edith felt reassured after she took a hard look at Paul Tyler. His face gave away his admiration and respect for the school-teacher, but there was none of the white soul-incandescence of love immeasurable. Edith hoped this meant there was still hope for Jeff.

He shouldn't have *all* choice taken from him. Miss Albans, to Edith's mind, was still in the running. The seduction she had hinted at need not cast her out from the bonds of matrimony and indeed might even make her a more desirable prospect. After all, men cheerfully marry widows every day.

Edith accepted the ladies' invitation gratefully. She tried pretending that the ride home in the dark, with Jeff beside her, was not the chief attraction of the evening ahead. He was not for her, and that was how it should be. Edith only wished that knowledge was not so deeply depressing.

"Are you making up another story?" Jeff asked as he drove the buggy to Misses Tyler's house.

"No," Edith said, coming out of her reverie. "I was thinking about Miss Albans."

"Yes . . . Miss Albans . . . was she all right?"

"She really didn't look well."

"If you want to, we can stop by her place on the way home." Edith smiled at him. "You're very thoughtful."

"I'm being selfish. You wouldn't want me to marry a sickly woman, would you?"

"No, of course not."

"I've been thinking . . . if I'm serious about this marriage thing, I ought to do something about it, don't you think?"

Edith placed her hands in her lap and put on her most businesslike expression. "What had you in mind?"

"Formal calls. Hair slicked, clean shirt, bouquets of flowers maybe. What kind do you like?"

"Oh, I like . . . all sorts of flowers. Daisies always seem cheerful and don't commit one to anything the way roses would."

"Roses commit you?"

"Oh, yes, certainly red roses . . . they indicate an undying passion. Pink roses are safer, and yellow roses are a mark of warm friendship. White roses are, naturally, a token of purity."

"I bet they're your favorite," Jeff grumbled under his breath. "What about violets?"

"Surely you can't get violets at this time of year." Edith considered deeply as they passed the houses and shops, yellow lamplight revealing and concealing their faces as they drove along. "Definitely daisies," she said in judgment. "Especially if you are going to be courting more than one at a time. Or are you planning to begin with one and then go on to the next?"

"One at a time is less confusing," Jeff said, as they turned into the yard. "Let's see how Miss Climson strikes me tonight."

As he helped Edith down, he said, "I'm glad I made you come to Richey. Imagine, I might have given red roses to Miss Minta and be committed for life. You saved me from a bad blunder."

"My pleasure," Edith answered. She hid her disappointment well. Jeff's hands hadn't tightened for even one instant as he lifted her down. Perhaps he was seeing reason. Edith stifled a wish that he'd still be blind.

18

EDITH REACHED FOR another cheese-filled roll. As she leaned closer to Jeff, she whispered, "Have you noticed Miss Climson?"

"Yes," Jeff answered. "She looks nice. I told her so."

"You said 'nice'?"

"Yes. What else should I have said?"

He filled his eyes with Edith. She wore a blue suit embroidered with white, a kind of a drapery effect hanging from her waist to about where he figured her knees would be. She'd done something different to her hair — it was softer, giving her the gentle appearance that suited her nature.

Jeff would have liked to see her in red, about the color of the sofa they sat on. Red silk for instance, tight enough to show off her body, with her hair falling richly over her shoulders and the half-revealed curves of her breasts.

He moved restlessly on the sofa, trying to remember what they'd been talking about. Miss Climson . . . that was it.

"Nice isn't something I should have said, I guess."

"Well, it isn't very emphatic. And you want to charm her, don't you? You should say something more . . ."

"Are you enjoying those, Miss Parker?" Miss Hetty bustled into the room, balancing a tray with a dark blue bottle and some glasses. "Be careful not to spoil your dinner, dear."

"They're wonderful." It was obvious that neither aunt considered any of their guests to be older than about fifteen.

As she set the tray down on the piano, Miss Hetty said, "We'll give you the recipe for the filling. It's the sort of thing every young girl should know how to make. Husbands do entertain their friends and expect their wives to be prepared."

She looked around archly. "Where have Miss Climson and Paul gotten to?"

"They went out to look at the stars," Edith explained. "He seems to know all the constellations."

"Oh, yes. He was always interested in things like that. He's come back to us full of cleverness, hasn't he, Jefferson?"

"Yes, ma'am. He always was smart as a whip." He watched the lady pour out a bright red liquid from the glasses. "Don't tell me you're giving us your famous strawberry cordial, ma'am!"

"Oh, just a taste, just a taste. Even Mr. Armstrong doesn't disdain to take a glass when he calls."

"What beautiful glasses," Edith said. They matched the decanter, a dark cobalt blue that was cut with white glass showing through in a pattern of flowers.

"Our grandmother brought them from Europe." Miss Hetty took a healthy nip from her glass. "I'll go call Paul and Miss Climson in. It's nearly time for supper and Minta gets so cross if we're late."

As Edith lifted her own glass to her lips, Jeff said, "Be careful with that stuff. It's lethal."

"Lethal?" Edith sipped cautiously. It was sweet as the ripe fruit of which it was made and it filled her mouth with the taste and fragrance of summer. "It's delicious."

As she raised her glass again, Jeff pressed her hand gently down. "I'm telling you that raw whiskey would be less dangerous. This cordial doesn't taste like it but it's pure alcohol. I don't know how they do it . . . there's not another woman in town that makes it the same way. Last year that cordial put Mr. Armstrong's district superior right under the table. But before that, he was laughing and singing off-color songs. And he's supposed to be one of the toughest birds in these parts."

"That's dreadful! They're teetotalers, aren't they? Didn't Mr. Armstrong get into trouble?"

"No. Seems this Mr. McCauley just thought he was extra tired from his trip. He never connected it with what he'd been drinking. But I'm telling you . . . watch out. . . . "

Miss Hetty came back, a frown between her thick brows. She looked pointedly at Jeff and then at the burl-wood clock on the crowded mantel.

He stood up, putting his glass on the table. "If supper's about ready, I guess I'd better get washed up."

"How grown-up of you to remember without being told, Jefferson. You remember where the pump is?"

"Yes, ma'am." He winked at Edith, half-turning so he wouldn't hurt Miss Hetty's feelings.

Miss Hetty took his place. Sitting down she sighed heavily.

"Is something the matter?"

"How kind of you to ask. Not really. It's just that time flies so." She lowered her voice and said, "I couldn't mention this in front of Jefferson. Somethings you just can't talk about in front of boys. They will laugh and make silly jokes."

"Jokes about what?" Edith took another tiny sip of the cordial. It really was very good.

"You know. Boy and girl romances. You won't believe it, dear, but Paul had his arm about Miss Climson's waist just now. Oh, he pretended it was to show her a star or a planet or some such, but I think it was . . ." She coughed. "Hanky-panky."

Edith couldn't help being tickled by Miss Hetty's tone of darkest disapproval. However, she was concerned. Paul Tyler had made it clear that his visit to Richey would be fleeting at best. Edith hoped he didn't mean to amuse himself with Miss Climson.

"Of course," Miss Hetty went on, "Miss Climson is as nice a young lady as one could hope to find, and if they were each just a *leetle* bit older . . . well, Minta and I have always hoped that one day Paul would settle down again in Richey. It is a terrible sad thing to have no relations near you."

"I know," Edith said. "I'm an orphan myself."

"Are you! My sister and I are orphans too. Our dear father died only last year. We felt lost for so long. Fortunately, we always had dear Paul's letters, though it isn't quite the same. Oh, listen to me running on. A young thing like you doesn't want to hear an old woman's maunderings. Let me just refresh your glass, dear."

Miss Hetty rose and went to the piano. She came back with the decanter, but was a dash too liberal. "Oooh, sip it! Sip it or it'll will overflow!"

Almost before Edith had put her glass down, Miss Hetty had refilled it a second time. "It will put roses in your cheeks."

Paul entered with Miss Climson. "Now, Aunt Hetty," he said. "Be good. Miss Parker may not like your cordial."

"Oh, no! It's delicious, really." To prove it, she took another gulp.

Edith never knew she was such a wit before. She kept the table in one long roar of laughter as she described little incidents of keeping up appearances on a poverty-pinched budget. None of the incidents she related had been amusing at the time, but she could make funny stories out of them now. Only the thought of Jeff's probable reaction kept her from telling about Mr. Maginn's continual pursuit of her in lieu of rent.

As Miss Minta brought in the roast, she said, "I do hope this won't be tough. Mr. Huneker didn't seem to hear a word I said today, not a word. And he is usually so polite."

"Arnie Sloan said . . ." Miss Hetty began.

All the hearers leaned forward.

"But then, I shouldn't pass along gossip, should I? More potato salad, Jefferson?"

"Oh, how can you be so provoking, Henrietta?" her sister asked. "Don't start a sentence and not finish it. Arnie Sloan said what?"

"Just a little something about Mr. Huneker and a lady . . . I'll tell you later." She glanced around the table as though to say, "not in front of the children." Immediately, all their guests tried to look as though they were interested in anything but the latest gossip from the station master.

"And I hear the Uffizi Gallery in Florence is not to be missed, Mr. Tyler."

"What works are there, Miss Climson?"

"Botticelli's finest works. 'The Adoration of the Magi' for one. I have a good etching of it in my room. I have collected quite a few etchings. Perhaps you'd like to see them later?"

"I'd like nothing better," Paul said eagerly.

Miss Climson colored ever so slightly under his pleased respect. Edith noticed it and frowned.

"Oh, very well," Miss Hetty said, "if you must know . . ."

"Get on with it, dear. . . ."

"It's about Mr. Huneker and Mrs. Green. Arnie Sloan said she was at his house until long past midnight last night. And that he came calling this afternoon . . . closed his shop and he was dressed *very* nicely for a widower."

"Did he bring her flowers?" Jeff asked.

"He did. An enormous bouquet of pinks."

"I heard it was tiger lilies," Miss Minta said. Coughing, she covered her slip by saying brightly, "More roast, anyone?"

Jeff whispered to Edith, "What do tiger lilies mean? Animal passion?"

She didn't know what was wrong with her. Instead of reproving him with a gentle look, she giggled lamentably and even growled. Then she hiccoughed. Covering her mouth on the second try, she said, "'Scuse me."

During dessert, he poured her out a cup of coffee. "I think you'd better drink this," he said while the aunts were in the kitchen and Mr. Tyler was discussing ancient architecture with Miss Climson.

"Oh, I couldn't," Edith said. "My aunt . . . my aunt warned me about coffee. Something . . . oh, yes, it stirs unhealthy cravings in young ladies."

"Then I insist you drink some." He grinned at her and her insides tilted. Very quietly he said, "Edith, my dear one, you're a little bit drunk. I told you that cordial was deceptively mild."

Aghast that he should even for a moment believe her to be

drunk, she sipped the coffee and held it out for a refill. Better to take chances with coffee than to have him believe the worst of her. Though the brew bit at her throat and she came close to gagging, she found that she rather liked the taste after her second cup, especially when he added cream.

Her head cleared for a moment. She glanced at Jeff sitting beside her and knew it was not entirely what she'd been drinking that gave her this funny feeling. It was Jeff himself. He seemed to give off torrid waves that buffeted her body, lifting her off her feet. She met his eyes and his wonderful smile was gone. A light seemed to burn in his eyes as he dropped his gaze to her mouth. Edith knew what he was thinking. Her own eyes closed slightly and she felt warmth spreading from her center.

When the aunts came back, they dropped a broad hint that now would be a good time for the men to go outside and smoke their cigars. Paul sat in the porch swing, beating time softly against the floor with his foot. Jeff had refused one of the panatelas the other man had urged on him. He half-sat on the porch rail, one long leg trailing.

"When are you leaving, Paul?"

"Can't wait to get rid of me, eh? Well, can't say I blame you. Nice little hareem you've got around here, Jeff."

"Your aunts love to talk."

"They'd be a bonanza to any police force in the country."

"I am thinking about getting married again," Jeff said. "What's your plan?"

"I'm going off to see the world again. This time, all of it. There won't be corner I won't visit, not a shrine I'm going to miss. It's my oyster. I only wish you could come with me, like old times."

Sitting in the near dark, it was as though there were no years of separation between them, as though they were still both fourteen. Jeff wouldn't have been surprised if Paul had leaped off the swing and proposed they go play pirates in the woods, as they used to.

"Do you remember Black Sprigo and Plague-y Jack?"

"Black . . . oh, yes, the Terrors of the Spanish Main! Weigh-hey, my hearties, and ho for glory!" Paul set himself to swinging in the slatted chair. "What those boys would have given to know that one of them would one day discover a bonanza? Do you remember how one whole summer we dug for gold before we learned they kept it all in California?"

"We worked harder that summer than we did on the real diggings. What made us run off?" Jeff wondered. "We must have been crazy."

"We were young. We hadn't any responsibilities we were willing to acknowledge. I still don't."

"Don't you? Miss Climson, for instance?"

"Have a heart, man! I only met her . . . was it yesterday?" Paul looked toward the square of yellow light that was the kitchen window. He'd heard her voice a moment since, that smoky, drawling voice. From the first moment, though he'd heard her saying something entirely commonplace, her voice had made him think of unmade beds and abandoned sprawling bodies.

"You want someone to go on your adventure with, don't you? Or do you want to go to Florence and Madrid and Timbuctoo alone?"

Paul glanced at Jeff. Had he spoken? Or was it a voice in his own head that asked him those questions. "It's fantastic," he said aloud.

"What is?"

"That I should take Miss Climson with me on my voyage."

"Hey, that's not a bad idea. It would be a dream come true for her, you can tell that by the way she talks about the things you'll see. If she's not dying to go . . . course, there's the moral side of things. A single man, a single woman, there'd bound to be talk. But you could always say she was your secretary, or something like that."

"My secretary?" He'd had one in Frisco. A lanky fellow in horn-rimmed glasses whose sole interest outside the law was the opera. Miss Climson looked nothing like him, which was a good thing. If he'd ever had these kinds of thoughts about Harrison, he'd have shot himself.

Paul thought about the soft glow Paris reputedly possessed. He thought about making love to Miss Climson in the sitting room of the most luxurious hotel in the City of Light while that glow reflected off her pearl-like nakedness. He thought about leading a trembling Miss Climson by the hand through the dark catacombs of Rome. He thought about the perfumed gardens of England and picnics with Miss Climson telling him, in her velvety voice, all about the passions of long dead kings. Snuggling up with her under the bearskin rugs as their troika raced through Moscow. Pampering her at the spas of Germany. Looking at her through the clouds of incense in a Buddhist temple. Taking her hand as they gazed up at the Mountains of the Moon. Marrying her in Chicago before their journey began.

"It's . . . it's fantastic," he said again, much more slowly. Standing, he pitched his thin cigar over the railing into his aunts' flower bed. "I think I'll go help Miss Climson with the dishes. Say, do you happen to know what her first name is?"

"I've heard them call her S.J. I don't know what it stands for." As his dazed friend moved inside, Jeff called after him, "Tell Edith I'm ready whenever she is, will you?"

Sitting on the railing, Jeff rubbed his hands together with glee. One down, one to go, he thought.

Turning to bid the aunts one more good-bye, Edith nearly fell as she mounted into the buggy. "Isn't the fresh air marvelous?"

"Don't breathe too deeply. You'll go right to sleep."

"It's not that late."

Jeff drove off. "No, but you're not used to drinking. Sometimes fresh air will sober you up faster than coffee. Other times it'll put you under."

Singing an Italian song under her breath, Edith stared at him as they drove through the soft moonlight. She had compared him to every other man she'd seen since they arrived at church and she'd finally reached an inescapable conclusion. Jefferson Dane was physically perfect and mentally far superior to the run-of-the-mill male. In addition, he was the only man in the world she wanted to kiss. And she wanted to kiss him right now.

"Stop the carriage!" she ordered suddenly.

"Why? Are you going to be . . . ?"

"You always stop it when you want to say something. I want to say something."

With a wary, sideways glance, Jeff stopped. They were on the road home, lonely and deserted at this hour, save for the watching moon. "You're a little drunk. Whatever you want to say can wait 'til tomorrow." ·

"I'm not drunk and I want you to kiss me."

"Believe me . . ." Jeff gently pushed her reaching hands away. He managed to remember he'd been raised to be chivalrous toward all women. Especially toward an auburn-haired, slightly tipsy witch making provocative propositions.

Edith asked, "How do you prove you're not drunk when someone says you are drunk?"

"You say something difficult like . . . British Constitution." Nobody unused to alcohol, with a glass of the Misses Tyler's lethal concoction swashing about her insides, could manage that wilderness of syllables without seriously spraining her tongue.

With a bell-like clarity and her eyes looking straight into his, Edith enunciated, "British Constitution. British Constitution. British Constitution. I can say it faster but I want you to kiss me. Please."

She didn't move when he touched his lips fleetingly to hers. Merely a reward for not tripping over her tongue, he thought.

"There," he said, taking up the reins. His hands shook slightly.

"Show me how you do that . . ."

"What?"

She licked her lips. "You know . . .

She was so innocently seductive, kneeling on the seat. "I don't think this is a good . . ."

Then she was locked in his arms, an embrace so tight that Jeff could feel the slightest quiver of her eager body. She opened her mouth to his foray at once, holding on tighter still. He dragged her across his lap.

"Am I hurting you? I'm too heavy . . . ?"

"No. God. Stay still." He gripped her by the hips, forbidding her to move. He hadn't been so close to embarrassing himself since he was an overeager boy. But holding her there was just as bad. Closing his eyes against the sweet torture, he was aware of the roundness of her behind beneath the frilled skirt and the secret delights he now knew she kept just for him.

"Jeff . . . ?"

He opened his eyes to see her gazing down on him with tender worry. "It's just . . ." he began. "Edith, you're so . . ."

The tantalizing perfume of her body surrounded him, filled him with every breath. Resigning himself to the inevitable, he raised his hands to the row of pearl buttons marching down her front. But his hands trembled too much to work them free, for which he was heartily glad. He couldn't take her, not now, not on a flimsy buggy seat, for heaven's sake!

"Edith, I want you . . . I want to make love to you. It's wrong, but I can't stop wanting you. You drive me wild."

"You do the same to me," she whispered, smiling down at him.

With hands that did not tremble in the least, she undid the top button. He watched in wonder as each pearl slipped free of the button hole. The placket that covered her slowly parted, the V widening as she moved her hand lower. A line of lace, not a whit whiter than her skin, showed between the darker fabric. He could see the shadow between the soft plumpness of her breasts, a promise of paradise.

He closed his eyes. Temptation shouldn't be just under a man's nose. "Stop it, Edith. I can't . . ."

"I want you to kiss me," she murmured. She touched her mounded flesh—"Here."

"No. You don't even know where this will lead. It's the cordial talking. You don't think you're drunk but why else . . ."

"I've asked myself what this feeling means, this ache when you kiss me. I guess it's wanting you. Like you want me."

Jeff couldn't think for the pounding of his blood. As though he watched himself in a dream, he smoothed down the concealing lace. Her corset pushed her breasts up and together, presenting her rosy nipples to his gaze as though on satin pillows. Jeff glanced up and saw in Edith's eyes only pride amid a haze of growing desire.

If he'd been on the brink of losing himself in her before, he threw away his compass when he bent his head to taste her.

Edith cried out and buried her fingers in the soft pelt of his hair. Her head fell back as she felt for the first time the wonderful madness of Jeff's mouth at her breast. His tongue, so smooth in her mouth, dragged roughly over her nipple, again and again, until she began to move her hips in concert with his licking. She didn't care how shameless and abandoned her movements became so long as he didn't stop.

She felt him fumble with the edge of her skirt that flowed over his hips and thighs. Then his hand was sliding over her leg from the ankle, up and up, until his fingers were under the loose band at her knee. Then he stopped.

Edith uttered a sound of protest as he withdrew. But a moment later, through the thin lawn of her drawers, he placed his hand at the exact spot where her ache was strongest. For a moment, she froze at the intimate touch.

He murmured her name. "Go on. Move like you just did. You'll like it. I promise."

Tentatively, she flexed against his hand. It felt so right. She knew he must be able to feel the moisture that had gathered there, but there wasn't room in her now for embarrassment. As he turned his attention to her other breast, more sensitive as though to make up for being second, Edith could no more control the movement of her hips than she could contain the sounds that broke from her throat.

"God!" he said explosively. He turned her so she was cradled in his arm, though his other hand stayed beneath her skirts. Greedily, he kissed her, while increasing the pressure against her hidden cleft. He wanted all her sweetness now and told her so, in hot words that did as much to push her over the brink as his overpowering touch.

As her tumult faded, Jeff held her close against his heart. He touched his lips to the waving curls at her temple, for her face was hidden against his chest. Realizing his hand rested on her thigh, he withdrew it, though his fingers burned with memory. He smoothed down her rumpled skirt.

"Edith," he whispered. "Don't be ashamed. It wasn't . . . you were wonderful."

She didn't look up. Jeff became aware that her breathing was deep and regular. "Edith?"

He shook her a little bit. She sighed, deeply, contentedly, but she did not wake up. Looking down at her relaxed, glowing face, Jeff smiled and shook his head. "Dollars to Miss Minta's crullers, you won't remember a thing when you wake up. But in the name of Jumping Jehoshaphat, what am I supposed to do now?"

Miss Albans bathed her reddened eyes and did up her tumbled hair. Looking at herself in the mirror above the washstand, she was repelled by her resemblance to the girl she'd once been in a Boston boardinghouse. How dare she be so stupid as to weep again for Tate LaRue!

She straightened the waist of her skirt, twisted around when she'd thrown herself on the bed in a storm of weeping. She'd fallen asleep in her clothes and now she felt hot, fidgety, and surprisingly hungry. Glancing at the clock, she couldn't believe it was already after eleven o'clock at night.

Wearily, she slipped down the narrow hall in her tiny apartment above her store. It was an old building, built at the founding of Richey, and lived in by many different families over the years. There was a two-by-four excuse for a kitchen at the end. She had struggled to make it clean and cheery, using only her own hands and imagination. Entering it now, she realized how dismally she had failed.

Lighting the lamp, she thought about supper, keeping her mind resolutely on little, unimportant things. Had she any eggs? There was the knuckle of a ham bone. Could she bear to make an omelette? Neither George nor Tate had ever wanted her to cook. . . . She flinched away from the memory as though it were a glittering knife.

Cooking took her mind off the dull anger. How nice Edith had been! Vera had shied away from making intimate friends but there was something about the strange cousin of Jeff Dane's . . . something that wouldn't let one hide behind social niceties. Vera was glad that Edith had forced her to confess her past.

As she ate her omelette, she wondered why the other girl hadn't been more horrified and shocked by what she'd said. She couldn't think of another woman in this town, even the nicest, who wouldn't have flaunted a tiny bit of moral superiority over their fallen sister.

As Vera carried her plate to the sink, she heard a rattle as someone climbed up the back stairs. They were rickety things, assembled of scrap lumber when the store was built years ago. Vera was afraid to use them, but whenever she had, she'd heard the warped and cracking boards rattling at each step, held down only by squared-headed nails.

Instinctively, Vera turned up the lamp. She wanted light when she opened the door to Tate. "What do you want?"

"Why, to come in."

"Do your talking where you are."

"Now, do you want everyone to see me? I thought not." He seemed to skulk in without her opening the door any farther.

Vera immediately put the table between them. He looked hurt. "Aren't you glad to see me? Old friends and all . . ."

How well she remembered with what skill he could color his tone to make her feel whatever he wanted her to. Now he was playing the wounded friend, whose motives had been terribly misunderstood. Vera knew it was all a trick, yet she still wanted to respond with kindness. She hated herself for it.

"Say what you have to say," she snapped.

"May I sit down at least?"

He'd already drawn back the chair when she said, "No! I'm sure this isn't a social call, so you can stand."

"You were never so rude before." He sighed sentimentally. "I remember with what tender care you waited on me before our unfortunate parting."

"You left me," she said coldly. "You stole from me."

"Some things I stole," he admitted with a reminiscing smile. "Other things you gave me, willingly. Come now, you can't still be mad. We had a gay time. You had few complaints of your treatment then. Why, you used to tell me . . ."

This was intolerable. "What do you want, Tate?"

His hand lashed out, catching her across the cheek. The slap echoed off the stove she'd bought herself, off the dried flower wreath she'd won at a bazaar, off the china she'd painstakingly painted, breaking the peace she'd thought she had found.

Shocked more by the sound than the pain she couldn't yet feel, Vera touched her face with trembling fingers.

"Victor. Remember that it is Victor now." His eyes, never warm, were like two black pits. "A name that you would think would bring good fortune, but it hasn't. An unlucky turn of the cards and I had only enough money left to ride the railroad to this one-horse town. And I had to leave Memphis when I did. You wouldn't think they'd still be as fussy about cardsharping down South as they were before the War."

She remembered when he'd hit her before. He'd always been so sorry, even weeping afterwards. And yet, she knew now that he'd never meant it, that his sorrow was just another way of controlling her, just as the slaps and kicks had been.

"What do you want?" she whispered, for the third time.

"Your silence, Vera. Nothing else. You'll keep quiet about me. About you and me. Have you told anyone?"

"No."

"What about that girl you left the church with? A stupid thing to do, drawing attention to yourself that way, but you always were a stupid girl. Did you tell her?"

"No. I said I was ill." The sight of him, so cool, so unruffled, really did make her stomach clench and roil.

"Good. Well, this has been fun." His eyes wandered insolently over her. "You're still a fine looking gal, Vera. Dulcie doesn't have your . . . shall we say enthusiasm? But she'll learn. Sometimes the ugly ones are the most grateful."

"Why Dulcie?" she asked. Let him strike her again if he wanted to for her curiosity.

"I need money. Of course."

"But Dulcie doesn't . . ."

"On the contrary. Don't tell me you haven't heard about her little windfall? The hundred and fifty dollars a distant relation left her?"

"But that's hardly anything . . . I mean, what good . . ."

"It's exactly a hundred and forty more than I have at the moment. And a man like me can't very well live on ten dollars. I had a few dollars more but I had to buy the girl an engagement ring. Only rolled gold, of course."

"Of course."

"I know," he said, polishing his nails on his shirt front. "I should probably settle down to some grubbing job, but there are golden futures for the man who knows how to take advantage of them. And I'm just the sort . . ."

He shook his head with dry amusement. "At first, I had hopes of this Dane character, but all his daughters are mere babes in arms. And my talents have always been best employed on young ladies. Especially of a certain artistic bent. I find them so readily fascinated by a man of the world. Isn't that what you find to be true?"

With the smile she once would have traded her soul for, Victor Sullivan opened her kitchen door. Once more he let his eyes stray over her. "Perhaps I'll call again, Vera. After all, I can't devote all my time to Dulcie."

When she said nothing, he chuckled and left. She heard the rattle of the steps as he all but danced down them. Praying for them to break beneath him, she listened for a crash and a cry. But the devil was looking out for his own.

19

EDITH DIDN'T AWAKEN when Jeff carried her up the stairs. He laid her carefully on the bed after taking off her hat. Though he considered loosening her clothing, he knew he couldn't trust himself, not while his body was still ablaze.

A cold bath for you, right now, he thought. But still he stood over her, gazing at her rose-colored cheeks and crumpled clothing. Just one more to go, Miss Edith Parker, and then you're mine. I've got 'till Sunday to get Miss Albans paired off. So far, this matchmaking business hasn't been that hard. Maybe we'll have more than one kind of partnership before we're done.

She stirred, rolling over onto her side. Her smile was that of an angel, if an angel slightly tipsy on cordial and pink with loving. He wondered if she were dreaming of him, or of one of her fantasies.

Using powers he hadn't acknowledged until she entered his life, Jeff sensed mysteries at the heart of this woman that a man could spend a lifetime exploring. Modesty in word and speech mated with the unrestrained ardor she gave him when he kissed her. Her deep sensuality mated with a deeper innocence, not just of men but of the world. And yet she lived in a world he could not touch. Endless paradoxes, strange conundrums that he knew he would never solve but would never tire of trying to unravel. It would take so little for him to fall endlessly in love with her.

As he admitted that, he knew it was too late. He already was drowned in love for her. Love at first sight, probably, though he couldn't tell for sure. All at once, Jeff surrendered to his love, unable to fight anymore. In surrender, he found a great peace that for now, ended the war between his head and his spirit. His body was delighted too.

He had to get out of there. But it was too late. Edith's lashes fluttered. She stared for a moment at the candlewicking that decorated the spread; then her focus took him in. "Oh," she said, pushing up. "Did I fall asleep?"

His voice came from his boots. Would she remember? "Yes."

"How rude of me. I'm sorry, Jeff. Perhaps you're right and that cordial was stronger than I knew." She ran her hand over her disordered hair and glanced around for her hat. The sight of it hanging by its ribbons from the back of the chair reassured her. "Thank you for carrying me up here."

She was obviously waiting for him to go. "Well, good night," he said.

"Good night."

He got as far as the door before his reprobate body made a demand. "Edith, could I kiss you good night?"

"I don't think that's a good idea, do you? After all, soon you'll be courting other women."

She didn't remember. Jeff knew by her calm response that she had no memory of flinging herself at him, or of going wild in his arms. "I know," he said. "But I'm kind of out of practice."

"I hadn't noticed." Edith tightened her lips as though she regretted saying that. "After all, you've kissed me twice."

Jeff noticed that her hands clasped the bedspread. "Third time's the charm," he said, crossing back to her.

His weight made the mattress list toward him. Edith sat very still. "Just . . . a good night kiss?"

"That's all," he promised.

He brushed her lips with his own, as delicately and lightly as a caress with a flower petal. "Was that so bad?"

"Is that it?" she asked. "Is that all?"

"Just a good night kiss. Like between new friends or old married people."

"It was nice." She tilted her chin up. There was no reason not to do it again.

Jeff could imagine kissing her like this after a hard day's work, or after a long night's sleep. It was a kiss to be given after a bouquet of flowers, or before he went to the general store. Jeff could imagine all these kisses, but he couldn't imagine these being the only kisses he'd give her.

There'd be others. Deep kisses in the night, swallowing up her wanton cries. Kisses when he'd catch her unawares, pressing her into the wall while the fried chicken burned on the stove. And gentler ones, too. When she held their first child in her arms, he'd kiss her with all the joy in his heart. Should death threaten them, his kiss would keep it at bay.

Perhaps something of these thoughts showed in his face when he lifted his head. Edith stared up at him in wonder, her eyes the color of wild violets. "Jeff . . ."

"Go to sleep, Edith."

After he'd gone, Edith lay on the bed thinking for a long time. Only after the little clock chimed twelve times did she realize that she was lying there with all her clothes on, even her shoes. She got up, but her knees were curiously weak. She had a low ache in her back and she greatly feared she needed a bath to wash away a certain immoral moistness.

With shame, Edith knew she must have had one of her peculiar dreams. Though she never recalled the details, she had often awakened feeling this way, even before she'd begun reading novels. Edith only hoped she hadn't made any noises while she slept. What if Jeff had guessed that her dreams were wicked?

The thought of Jeff was like a sudden magnesium flare in the darkness of her dreaming mind. He'd been part of it, she was certain. She seemed to hear his hot, urgent voice saying things he'd surely never say in the waking world. Something about how she should move or not move. . . . They must have been dancing, she decided abruptly. Though why that should leave her feeling limp and curiously contented, Edith dared not guess.

She began to undress. But her fingers paused on her blouse. She glanced down at the row of mother-of-pearl buttons. They were all skewed, the second button in the third hole. Had she been walking around like that the whole evening? One of the other women surely would have mentioned that her button was open, revealing her undergarment. Edith hoped that since they hadn't mentioned it, they simply hadn't noticed.

After she was in bed, Edith realized she was hungry. Though the Misses Tyler had pressed huge amounts of food on her, Edith had been too busy talking to eat very much. Now she thought about biscuits spread with sweet butter and jam like the ones Sam made for breakfast. Wondering if there were any left, Edith put on her pretty ginham Mother Hubbard and opened her door.

"Now wait a minute," she heard Jeff say. "Where are you going with that, Dad?"

"I'm going to shoot a weasel. A walking, talking, two-faced, low-down weasel."

They must be in the front hall for their voices carried clearly to where she stood. She walked to the head of the stairs. Though she couldn't see their faces, she could see that Sam carried a long rifle, its wooden stock bright with polish.

Stunned by the thought of gentle Sam with a gun, Edith watched and listened, trying to understand.

"Now, hold on a minute, Dad. Who's got you so riled?"

"Better you shouldn't know . . . but he deserves what's coming to him. What have I always told you to do if you see somebody picking on someone not up to their weight?"

"Knock 'em down and sit on 'em."

"Well, I mean to knock him down. Let the undertaker sit on him."

Once again, Jeff caught at his father's sleeve as Sam turned to head out the door. Sam shrugged off his tall son as though Jeff were a pesky fly. Edith decided it was time to intervene.

She walked quickly down the steps, nearly tripping in her hurry. "Sam, wait."

"Sorry, Cousin Edith. Got a weasel to hunt."

"At least, tell me . . . that is, doesn't Jeff have the right to know why his father is suddenly turning into a murderer? What will he tell the girls?"

Sam stopped, halfway out the door. Jeff stepped forward, knowing a good thing when he heard it. "That's true, Dad. They're bound to ask. After all, the kids at school . . ."

"Ah, hell!" Sam said, leaning his rifle against the wall. He grimaced at the couple staring after him. "You've taken all the fun right out of this."

"Fun?" Edith asked. Would she ever understand men?

"Not fun, exactly, but when a fellow gets his blood up for vengeance and then somebody comes along talking about his family, the anger drains out like his plug's been pulled. And here I was really looking forward to scattering Sullivan's guts all over creation." He glanced at Edith and his eyes were human again. "Beg your pardon for swearing, ma'am."

"Not at all."

Jeff asked, "Sullivan? You mean Dulcie's fiancé?"

"That's right, I forgot about that part of it." The red tinge had faded from Sam's face but his voice got hard again. "That low-life piece of horsesh . . ."

Edith interrupted before he had to apologize again. "Has Mr. Sullivan done something to Dulcie? Or to . . ."

Sam measured her with his eyes. "I guess you and Miss Albans had a nice long chat this evening. All the same . . ." He turned to his son. "Come on into the parlor, Jeff. What I have to say isn't for a nice young lady to hear."

"Please!" Edith said, stepping between the men and the door. "If there's trouble, I want to know. After all, I am part of this family."

She hadn't known she was going to say those words until they came out. Quickly, as they stared at her in surprise, she amended her statement. "I mean . . . for the time being . . . until Sunday . . . Sam, you said you'd write me after I left here. I don't want to get letters from jail. What would my neighbors think of me?"

Surprisingly, it was Jeff who answered, his wide grin making her head spin. "Oh, probably that you're a dutiful . . . cousin."

Why was she so certain he'd nearly said something else? She swept him with a puzzled gaze, before saying to Sam, "I think I have the right to know everything. And if something is wrong with Miss Albans, a woman can be of more comfort than a man."

"You've made your point, Edith," Jeff said, "though I'll argue with you about 'comfort' some other time."

"If you two are done flirting . . ."

"Flirting!" Edith squealed.

"I'll tell you what I saw at Miss Albans'."

"Is that where you went when we came home?" Jeff said as though a guess had been proven.

"Yes. She was having a problem with her sink, remember?" The red tinge had returned to color Sam's slightly bristly cheeks. Edith didn't need any special sight to realize the older man was abashed. His gaze dropped before their combined gaze and he looked shiftily off to the side.

"I thought I'd just sneak in the back way and fix it before she woke up. That way . . . well, she wouldn't have to be grateful. It'd just be done."

Jeff said with heavy sarcasm, "Did you want her to think the fairies had done it?"

"Hush," Edith said, laying her hand on his arm. "It's a wonderful gesture, Sam. So romantic in a practical kind of way."

If anything, her praise only embarrassed him more. "I didn't mean it to be. It was only . . . Lord Almighty knew when Jeff'd get to it. He's got a lot on his mind lately. Don't know when I've seen you more distracted, son."

Edith didn't understand the broad wink Sam threw at Jeff. She only saw that the blood had risen in Jeff's face too. "Go on,

Dad," he said quickly. "So you're fixing her sink. Why should that have you in a dither?"

"'Bout eleven, I heard her moving around. I didn't think she'd be awake so it kind of threw me for a loop to hear footsteps. So I gathered my tools and got ready to slip out. Then . . . I heard somebody creeping up those shaky stairs that run up to her apartment. So I stayed, just in case." His mild brown eyes began to grow hot. "For all the good I did, I might as well have stayed in bed."

"Was it Mr. Sullivan?" Edith asked, clutching the base of her throat. "I was afraid he'd seen her when we left the church. Naturally, he'd recognize her too."

Sam looked as though he'd like to spit to rid himself of a foul taste. "The things he said to her . . . if a man said 'em to me, he'd be worm food inside of a minute. But that isn't the worst of it. It was the way he said 'em. Like she didn't matter, like she was nothing, less than a dog."

Sam's bright eyes were suddenly wet. "And she didn't do anything! How could she hear him talking like that and not do anything? She just took it, like it was his right to do it." He jerked around to grasp Edith by the wrist. "They're not . . . tell me she wasn't crazy enough to marry that devil?"

"Careful, Dad," Jeff said, freeing Edith's numb hand from Sam's grasp.

"No." Edith rubbed her wrist, already forgiving Sam for his severity. "She said she didn't marry him, although they eloped."

"All right then. She's not his, not permanently. I'd sure hate to make a widow of her. At least, not *his* widow."

Jeff wondered at his father's agitation. Though there had been times in the past when his father had thrown himself bodily into battles that were not his, the heart for fighting seemed to have gone out of him when his wife had died. Since then, he'd been content to poke about the ranch and to care for the girls. Jeff was willing to butter Sullivan all over Richey just to see the fire in his father's eyes again.

He noticed that Edith was looking at his father very strangely. It was the look he'd seen before, as though she were staring so deeply at a person that she could see inside. Her eyes seemed unfocused, but intense enough to burn a hole. Then she blinked and shook her head slightly as though puzzled by something inexplicable. Maybe she was tired. He wouldn't be surprised, he thought with a guilty smile.

"It's late, Edith," he said. "Shouldn't you . . . ?"

She waved off the suggestion. "You mustn't shoot Victor," she said to Sam. He started to protest. "Or strangle him, stab him or in any other method end his life."

"What about drowning?"

"No. You must think of Dulcie too, you know. If you murder him, she might never recover. And if he is as unworthy as I believe him to be . . ."

"You can count on it."

"Then it would be a waste for her to mourn him for any length of time whatsoever. No, we must think of a way to be rid of Mr. Sullivan without resorting to murder."

"What if the body were never found?" Sam asked. "Then it would look like he just skipped town."

Jeff said, "It's not like you to be so bloodthirsty, Dad. Is there something else you're not telling us?"

"Nothing. 'Cept that he's only interested in marrying Dulcie because of her hundred-fifty-dollar inheritance. He told Vera Albans that he's broke."

He never would tell a soul about the slap he'd overheard. As it rang in the air, he'd gripped the newel post at the bottom of the inside stair so hard he still bore the imprint of the leaves carved around the support. More than that, it was as if his own cheek burned from the impact.

It had taken every ounce of his self-control to keep from running up those stairs and pitching Sullivan down them. But, he wanted to keep Vera from knowing he was aware of her abuse. That was one injury he could spare her.

Jeff said, "If he's broke, we can pay him to leave town. If a hundred fifty dollars is enough to make him face the altar, then two hundred ought to see him clear into Kansas."

"And Dulcie?"

"She wouldn't care a thing about him then, Edith. Her pride would be so hurt . . . oh, I see what you mean."

"What?" Sam asked, returning to the present.

Edith explained. "If he leaves her, she'll be terribly hurt. The one man who has overlooked her so-called imperfections only did it for money."

"We can keep it a secret," Sam said.

"In Richey?" his son replied. "No, Edith's right. We've got to get rid of Sullivan in such a way that Dulcie's not hurt and Vera's not exposed."

"That's a tough one, all right." Sam eyed his rifle lovingly. "I still say . . . no, you're right. I won't do it, but it'd sure make me feel a hell of a lot better. I beg your pardon, Edith."

She didn't answer. She stared out the parlor window, but she could not see anything but her own reflection. Jeff stepped beside her. He'd taken off his coat and vest. He wore only his white shirt and tan trousers. Edith couldn't but admire his strong shoulders and trim waist, but it was not his attractiveness that was in doubt. With him beside her, she took another look at herself, trying to see herself through his eyes.

He found her pretty enough to kiss. That had done more for her morale than he would ever know. Moreover, she supposed her hair had reasonably attractive reddish gleams, and it was just barely possible that her figure was alluring enough to make her story believable.

"Are you okay?" Jeff asked, putting his hand on her shoulder. As though his touch had set off a firecracker, Edith gaped for a moment at an illuminating flash. He'd kissed her in the buggy on the way home. How could she have overlooked it? Was she so abandoned now that embraces meant nothing to her?

She stammered, "Yes, I'm . . . I'm fine. I think I've come up with a plan."

Shortly afterward, Jeff roared, "No! Absolutely not!"

"Hush." Edith put her forefinger to her lips. "Don't wake the girls."

"Edith, it's out of the question."

"But why? It solves both our problems in one . . . er . . . fell swoop. And furthermore, it means Miss Albans will have no stain on her character. You'll be free to court her without everyone imagining the worst."

Sam said dryly, "No plan is that good."

"And as for Dulcie, if she's the sort of girl I believe her to be, she'll send Sullivan packing immediately."

"What about her money?"

"I won't say anything about that motive—merely that I recognized him yesterday in church as the libertine who soiled me in . . . where should I say he soiled me?"

"How 'bout Saratoga Springs?" Sam suggested.

"Dad! You can't let her . . . damn it, talk her out of it!"

"It would solve our problems."

"And ruin her life. This kind of thing gets around. Do you want to go through the rest of your life being pointed at?" He glared at Edith.

"It won't matter. I'll only be staying in Richey for a very short while after this."

"I thought you were thinking about settling down here."

She admitted, "I did think about it after you'd mentioned it. Though I am tempted . . . I'd like to continue getting to know Louise and Maribel, as well as Mrs. Green and the others. . . ."

"Well then. Don't do this. Stay."

Edith realized that if he'd only ask in his own name, she'd be rooted here in an instant. But she was not what he wanted in a wife. She remembered his requirements well. Sassy, smart, experienced with children. She could perhaps be thought intelligent, except where he was concerned. But sassy? And her experience with children extended only to the few hours she'd spent with Maribel and Louise, and they'd enjoyed it so little that they had locked her in a cellar.

"No, I can't," she said calmly, though her heart cracked. "Besides, once I tell Mr. and Mrs. Armstrong about Mr. Sullivan, I won't be able to stay."

Sam said, "Wait a minute. Won't Sullivan just say he never met you before?"

"Naturally, he'll deny everything. But I'll have enough details to convince the Armstrongs. The great danger is that Mr. Sullivan will get so angry that he'll say it wasn't me, but Miss Albans he ran off with. However, if he says that, then . . ."

"He's convicted himself!" Sam said, rubbing his hands. "It's a real risk to Miss Albans, though. I think we ought to get her permission before we go to the Armstrongs."

"That's only right," Edith agreed.

"Yes, we will," Jeff added. "Maybe she'll be able to talk sense and stop you two lunatics!"

20

JEFF DIDN'T SLEEP that night. He wanted Edith too much to rest in any bed that didn't have her warm body curled up against his. After he changed out of his fancy clothes, he dragged out the books and began to bring the records up to date, hoping to dispel the heated images that filled his thoughts. It worked until he reached the stud records. Then he had to put them down and go for a walk in the night air.

Edith saw him from her window, as he headed toward the barns. She knew he wasn't convinced that her plan was the best way to be rid of the troublesome Mr. Sullivan. Hustling into her pretty gingham wrapper and shoes, she hurried down the stairs.

Reaching the barn, she stood still, peering into the darkness. The moon was very low to the west, but still gave off enough light to see by. Edith thought she'd lost Jeff until she heard a splash.

All her instincts urging caution, she tiptoed around the barn. At first she didn't see him. Then, surprisingly, a seal-slick head emerged from the large wooden watering trough. Jeff came up for air, gasping, shaking glittering droplets from his thick hair. He wiped his face with his hand and sank back into the water with a contented sigh.

"Much better," he said, floating.

Edith watched him, delighted by a chance to watch him unseen. It seemed a strange hour to be taking a bath, however. And surely the water must be unpleasantly cool. Sam told her that all the water on the ranch came from an underground spring.

Her musings fled when Jeff stood up.

She stared in openmouthed wonder as he arose from the water, like Neptune coming on land to ravish a maiden. She didn't have to wonder any more if his whole body was as muscular as his back and chest. His firm torso ended in a carved V between his lean legs. A thicket of hair grew low. Edith squinted. Then she had to lick her dry lips. Men were *very* different from women. Wonderfully different.

As she watched, his body seemed to change. Perhaps it was the night air, slipping over his skin as it did over hers, like a warm caress. Then, before she could be sure, Jeff turned his back to pull on his jeans. She sighed in frustration as he drew them up over his taut buttocks.

Jeff froze and turned his head as though looking or listening for something. Edith shrank back into the shadows beside the barn. If he knew she was there spying on him, she'd be so mortified she'd just die where she stood.

"You might as well come on out, Edith."

She considered running. There was something exhilarating in the thought of fleeing across the night, while he, with his powerful stride, pursued her. But what good would it do? He'd only catch her. That was an even more exhilarating thought.

Then Jeff said something intriguing. He said, "Aw hell. Quit fooling yourself, Dane. What you got in the buggy's all you're going to get. So cool down. Just cool down."

He sat on a concrete block to pull on his boots. The moonlight danced over the sinews and hollows of his back. A memory of his madly arousing touch flooded Edith's mind. At once, she knew exactly what had happened in the buggy. How he'd touched her, how utterly abandoned she'd become.

She felt driven to walk out there to him, wanting to complete what had begun between them. But shame held her back. How could she face him? She'd reached a wild ecstasy in his arms and probably made a total idiot of herself by crying his name and moaning. She admitted that she'd enjoyed every instant, perhaps too much. Surely such utterly selfish pleasure had to be wrong and dangerous. Edith knew her aunt would say it was.

Jeff stood up, his shoulders slumping. Astonished by the force of her need to go to him, Edith still hesitated, balanced on the thin edge of a blade. She longed to soothe his disappointment by wholeheartedly surrendering her body and soul. Yet she was frightened by the irrevocability of such a step.

He picked up his shirt. As he drove his arms through the sleeves, he began to whistle a spritely tune. Edith raised her eyebrows. Maybe he wasn't dejected after all.

Humiliation overwhelmed her, followed quickly by anger. He *should* be frustrated, not whistling cheerfully as though he'd been granted all his desires. Maybe putting his hand up her skirt had been all he wanted. Next, no doubt, he'd be boasting in the local den of iniquity about how he'd had her writhing.

Edith now wanted to go out and slap his face. She mastered that impulse by the only alternative. She spun around and ran for the house, as she'd not run in years.

She was careless over the cobblestoned runway. Jeff spun around as the sound of pounding footsteps echoed around the barnyard. Instantly, he followed.

When Edith became aware that he was pursuing, she tried putting on a burst of speed. But her heart was already hammering, her throat already dry and tight. Then she tripped, over nothing more than her own feet, and went sprawling on the ground. She grunted as she fell headlong into the sweet grass.

Instantly, she rolled over, only to see him above her, his hands resting on his hips. Jeff's face was stern, but she could see it was the severity of implacable virility, rather than anger. He wasn't even breathing hard, until he looked at her. She felt

very small and helplessly feminine, a harem slave at the feet of
her master.

That thought was intolerable. Even in her stories, she'd
never relished that setting. She might be obedient; she'd never
be submissive. "Don't just stand there," she said, thrusting out
a hand irritably. "Help me up."

It seemed as if he'd never take her hand. When he did, his
strength was machinelike, hauling her upright. She tried to free
her hand when she was upright, but he pulled her closer.

"No," she said, twisting. "Absolutely not."

"Absolutely not . . . what?"

"I'm not letting you kiss me again."

"I don't want to kiss you."

"You don't . . . ?" She looked at him with suspicious eyes.

"No. I'm just going to hold you . . . like this."

She was wrapped around by his warmth, her cheek against
his bare skin. The scent of clean male filled her breathing. The
sprinkle of damp hair over his chest tickled her chin, a madly
arousing sensation. His fingertips massaged her back lightly,
right up to the sensitive nape of her neck. Edith discovered she
was pressing more tightly against his body than the strength of
his arms alone could explain. She was aware of his every
breath, almost his every thought.

Her hands slipped around his taut waist. She grasped the
distinct columns of his back either side of his spine. Looking
dreamily up into his eyes, she murmured, "I'm not giving in,
Jeff. I'm not. . . ."

"Hush."

He didn't kiss her lips, the fiend. He kissed her cheek, her
fluttering eyelids, the tip of her nose. He nibbled his way, with
light, fleeting nips along the soft, sensitive edge of her jaw and
down to the tender cord in the side of her neck. There he bit
harder, with a suddenness that had Edith shivering. Calling his
name, she demanded that he kiss her.

The throbbing note in her voice and the rigidity of her
nipples against his chest told Jeff how ready she was. Her
defenses were down. She was so ripe for the taking. And the
grass around them was soft and thick.

He had no sanity where Edith was concerned. None. Gwen

had never made his head spin like this. He'd never once considered making love to his wife out-of-doors, no matter how bright the moonlight. But then Gwen had never clung to him like this, never called his name so hotly, so urgently.

Edith reached up and caught his face between her hands. He instantly answered her kiss with his own, as she strained up against his body. She moved her hips against him, mindlessly aware of the hardness behind his jeans.

"And you won't talk to the Armstrongs," he said, as he filled his hands with her breasts.

"Wh-what?" Couldn't he see there were buttons down her front? Why hadn't he undone them yet? She guided his hand to the small buttons. A tension began to coil in her mid-section, and she knew he could release it.

He drew his tongue from her mouth to say, "You won't talk to the Armstrongs. You won't tell them that ridiculous story about you and Sullivan."

Edith slapped her hand down flat over his, stopping him from pushing the buttons through their holes. The sexual haze still dimmed her thoughts but an alarm had rung in her head. "Are you trying to . . . Oh, you are despicable! Lower than . . . lower than . . . I can't even think how low . . . how contemptible!"

"Hey!" he protested as she shoved him.

"You can't win this argument with seduction, my friend." That her knees had melted was unimportant. "I'll do . . ."

The sound of a window sash sliding up cut her off. "Hey," said a very sleepy little girl. "Who's yelling?"

The adults exchanged a guilty glance that asked, How much do you think she heard?

"Nobody, Louise," Jeff said looking up. "Go to sleep, baby."

Louise gazed blearily down. "I had a bad dream, Daddy."

"I'll be up in a minute to tuck you in, okay?"

She nodded. Propping her elbows on the windowsill, she cradled her chin in her hands. Edith saw that the girl was nearly asleep sitting there. She dared to venture a last word.

"I'll see you tomorrow. Good night, *Mister* Dane." She spun about sharply and marched away.

Try as she might, however, she couldn't sleep. Even the

weight of the sheet over her was unbearable. She stared up at the plain white ceiling and demanded to know how she wound up so deranged. It was all Jeff's fault, of course. He would have to be amazingly good-looking, impossibly likable and over-whelmingly lovable. Who taught him how to go from arousing her right down to her soul and then, just like that, be able tenderly to comfort his daughter's wakefulness?

It's just not fair! she complained, raising up to punch her hapless pillow once again. She should have picked someone ordinary to fall in love with, someone easy to leave. If she'd been smart, she would have fallen for Mr. Maginn. She would have looked forward to forgetting him!

Edith feared that her restless night showed on her face the next morning. She said down to a breakfast she didn't want.

"Well," Sam said at the end, looking at her nearly full plate. "Seems like nobody's hungry around here this morning. Not you—that's a first—and Jeff didn't want breakfast either."

"I do, Gran'pa," Maribel said, with a hopeful air.

Sam stood up. "We've eaten up all the pancake batter, darlin'. But if a split biscuit with honey'll do you . . ."

"Yes, please," both girls said loudly.

"All right, all right." He fixed them the addition to their breakfast and then said, "Go on and take it outside. Pretty day today . . . might pretty."

He sat down again after pouring himself another cup of his special thick coffee. "Okay, so how you want to work this?" At her blank expression, he said, "You know . . . the Arm-strongs? Now if I were you, I'd talk to her first. Millie's always been strong and a lot less likely to get riled than Ezra. He kind of loses his temper and doesn't pay much attention to what he damages. Though he's always sorry afterward, it doesn't do much good to mend the broken heads and bruises. And there's nothing in the world that'll rile a man faster than learning his daughter's intended is a scoundrel, a hound, and a no-good liar."

Sam drained his coffee mug. With an impatient flick of his arm, he threw it against the wall. Edith flinched as the mug smashed into thick white shards.

Grouchy started to his feet with a muffled woof. Then he left the room, looking reproachfully over his tan shoulder.

Sam went on as though he'd done no more than put the mug in the sink. "But Millie's different. She burns down low. If I guess right, she'll have Sullivan's hide off him and hung out to dry before he knows what hit him. Dulcie takes after her father more. We may have to hold her off Sullivan, or we'll be tripping over pieces of him clear to the county line."

"What about you, Sam?"

"Me? I've got nothing to do with it."

"But last night . . ."

He waved his anger away. "I guess I was kind of sore. Who wouldn't be? But it's really nothing to do with me."

Sam reached out for his coffee. When his fingers closed on empty air, he seemed confused. Turning his head, he saw the white fragments scattered widely with splatters of coffee slowly dripping down the wall. Unable to meet Edith's eyes, he pushed himself out of his chair. "Ought to clean that up," he said.

With a greater effort than usual, Edith achieved a state of relaxation. Using her inner sight, she gazed fixedly at Sam. It was obvious to the meanest intelligence that he had strong feelings for Miss Albans. Yet Edith saw no sign of the radiance that surrounded people who loved. Even to her most searching, intense gaze, Sam remained unlit.

She must be wrong. There was no love in Sam for Vera. His looking after her must just be the responsibility that the Danes seemed to naturally accept for everyone. Even Jeff's protection in St. Louis could be seen in that light.

"I'll go get ready," she said, rising.

Soon after, she came down, looking neat and honest, she hoped, in a brown seersucker skirt and waist. It was her least favorite of the four outfits she'd been given. Her little straw hat with the plain silk ribbons gave her an innocent air that Jeff took exception to.

"If you're determined to go through with this," he said, leaning on the buggy's big rear wheel, "you ought to be wearing tight black satin. Or maybe scarlet."

Edith didn't have a chance to be shy with him. "You would

know more about that sort of thing than I would, Mr. Dane," she shot back. "Or have you forgotten your friend Sabrina?"

"No, I'm not likely to forget her. I wonder what she's doing now?" He smiled reminiscently. "Bet I can guess."

"Bet you can," Edith muttered. Then she looked angelically toward the sky as though such a vulgar reply must have originated from some otherworldly source.

"Get in," Jeff said, holding out his hand.

She hesitated. "I thought Sam . . ."

"I'm driving you. Get in."

Wordlessly, Edith took his hand to step up. Before she was ready, he took his support away. Edith sat down harder than she had expected. It was as if he couldn't bear her touch.

They drove in silence all the way to town. When he would have stopped before the Armstrongs' house, however, Edith said, "Would you drive on, please?"

"Are you scared? Or have you changed your mind?"

"Neither. But I promised Louise I'd find her a muslin petticoat. She was wearing a wool one yesterday and it was much too hot and itchy. You saw how much trouble she had sitting still in church."

"I never sat still in church," Jeff said, "and I never wore a petticoat either."

"Guilty conscience, then?" She gave him a look that told him soulless brutes often had that trouble.

In the dry goods store, Edith compared children's petticoats while Jeff rocked back and forth on his heels. "How many are there?" he asked.

The lady clerk answered, "Oh, we have a wide selection, Mr. Dane. Ranging from the simple muslin at thirty-seven cents to the fine cambric with the lace at one dollar."

"The fancy one," Jeff said.

"No." Edith picked up the simple white underskirt. "This one will be easier for Sam to keep clean. Wrap it up, please."

As the clerk unrolled brown paper, Jeff said, "I thought you were trying to make Louise feel pretty. You know, I found that hair ribbon you gave her under her pillow last night."

"I do want Louise to feel pretty," Edith said, moved. "But the girls told me that Sam ruins lace by washing it incorrectly.

They were resigned to losing their nicest things because he just doesn't understand that lace is different from denim."

"Oh," Jeff said, rubbing the back of his neck. "I didn't know that."

The clerk came back. "On your account, Mr. Dane?"

"Thanks." He took the package and stood back for Edith to pass in front of him. Edith was aware of his eyes tracing over her from top to bottom and wondered what he was thinking.

As they walked down the steps, Edith heard someone call, "Miss Parker?"

Squinting in the bright sunshine after the dark shop, Edith peered across the street. A woman, her lower body hidden behind a cloud of children, waved to her. Looking both ways, cautioning the children not to run in front of a hay wagon, she crossed.

"Hello, Miss Parker, Mr. Dane," Mrs. Green said over the children's heads. Some were laughing, at least two were arguing, and the littlest one in her arms just stared around a fat fist. They were all neat and clean, with the patches in their clothes well mended and even a few new items gleaming here and there. The baby was wrapped in a beautifully ironed shawl, while the oldest girl wore an apron hand embroidered with the fancy stitches Mrs. Green had used at the sewing bee.

"I'm sorry I didn't have a chance to thank you for bringing little Rudy to me the other day." She looked down fondly to where the blond boy was hanging on her skirt. "He really was frightened, poor lamb."

Edith gazed around at the children and then again at Mrs. Green who chortled charmingly. "Oh, yes. I'm taking charge of them all. Stop it, boys." She spoke without looking at Al and Konrad, obviously plotting some mischief against the girls. Instantly, they looked innocent as angels.

"Then Mr. Huneker and . . ."

"I suppose there's no point in keeping it a secret. We'll be married very soon. He keeps saying . . ." Mrs. Green glanced up at Jeff and then twinkled at Edith. "He's awfully romantic, more like a schoolboy than a grown man. He keeps saying that every day that goes by is a day wasted. So far as he's concerned he won't be really living until we're married."

"That is romantic," Edith agreed, not without a small sigh.

"And I wanted to thank you, Miss Parker. If you hadn't brought Rudy along that day, I might not have met Ernst for months. You'd figure in a town this size it would have been impossible for us to miss each other, but somehow we did." She began to sway back and forth as the baby in her arms went gradually limp, the waxy lids falling over big blue eyes.

A voice called, "Adelia!" Mrs. Green turned at once, her smile mingling tender affection and exasperation. "God love the man," she said. "I've only been gone five minutes."

The gray-haired meat cutter came hurrying up, with eyes only for the plump widow. "I remembered what else was needed. Scissors. Bing used them last to pry up some nails and they became very dull and dented."

"For goodness' sake, Ernst. I have scissors. Big ones and little ones. I'll bring them along when I move . . . after we're married. Don't forget your manners. Say hello to . . ."

Mr. Huneker grasped Edith by the hand and shook it vigorously. "The so-nice young lady who guides my Adelia to me! Like a saint."

It was hard to tell which women he meant by his last comment until he turned his gaze once more on his future bride. Edith prepared herself to see a renewed outflashing of the halo that surrounded true lovers. She saw nothing.

While Mr. Huneker greeted Jeff, saying he knew him well, Edith rubbed her eyes. The sunlight was very bright but nothing could be brighter than the fire that melded two hearts.

Frowning, she looked more intensely, concentrating her heart's gaze on Mr. Huneker. Even if Mrs. Green were not completely in love with him, he was certainly mad for her. Edith still saw nothing but two people smiling giddily at one another.

Slowly, Edith said, "I wish you and Mr. Huneker every happiness."

"As do I," Jeff added.

"She has already made the children happy," Mr. Huneker said, not taking his eyes off her. "And I am always happy now."

The oldest girl took the baby from Mrs. Green's arms and said, "Don't forget to ask them, Adelia."

"Oh, thanks, Friederike." Mrs. Green said to Edith, "You must come to the wedding. It's going to be a small, mostly just us, though . . ." She chuckled again. "Though we're a crowd now all by ourselves. But since you're really the cause of it all, Miss Parker, we must have you as a witness. And you too, Mr. Dane. Maybe you'd like to bring your girls and your father?"

Jeff said, "We'd enjoy that. What day?"

"Next Wednesday. Goodness, is that only a week off?"

Apologetically, Edith said, "I'll be gone by then, Mrs. Green. But I do thank you for the invitation."

She walked past the children and got into the buggy without waiting for Jeff. He stayed for a moment and said something to Mrs. Green, something that brought the laughter once more into her face. All the children waved as Jeff and Edith drove away.

She was frightened, feeling as lost as Rudy had been. If only she could run home! But she had no home to go to. She began to tremble. The world was so big—without her special gift, how was she to make her way in it?

"Edith?" Jeff said, as though he'd said it before. "Edith, what's the matter?"

He glanced at her as he drove. Even after the fire when she'd appeared in his hotel, grimed and exhausted, owning nothing but a bird cage, she hadn't looked this distressed. She was white to the lips. Her fingers worked restlessly in their smooth leather gloves, and she had a haunted look in her eyes.

"Edith," he said again, worried now. "I'm stopping."

She placed a hand over his as he began to draw on the rein. "No, don't. I'm . . . I'll be all right."

"Was it Mrs. Green? Did she say something to . . ."

"No." She forced a smile. How could she explain to him? He'd only say she couldn't have lost something that didn't exist in the first place. "Don't worry. I'm all right."

"Like hell you are."

He pulled back on the reins, and the patient bay stopped in the shade of some elm trees. Not caring that half the idlers in Richey were probably watching, Jeff reached across to take

Edith by the elbow. He demanded, "Now tell me. What's wrong?"

"Really . . . ," she protested. "There's nothing."

Jeff pulled her into his arms and kissed her ruthlessly. He paid no attention to her pushing against his chest or her whimpers of protest. Only when those noises changed to ones of pleasure did he let her go.

"Now tell me."

Edith blinked foolishly. "I can't . . . see anything."

"You're blind?"

"No, I mean . . . of course I can see with my eyes, it's the other thing . . . I've lost it."

"Maybe I kissed you too hard. You're not making any sense."

Edith nodded. "I know. But what can you expect from me? Jeff, I'm . . . different."

"Why do you think I . . . Okay. Let's have it. What's the matter with you? Wait, don't tell me. You're a Sioux squaw. No, a dancer from some hootchy-kootchy show?" He squinted at her. "I've got it. You shaved your beard but you're really Robert E. Lee."

"Don't joke." The misery that set her lower lip trembling and filled her dark blue eyes with tears silenced his raillery. "It's a terrible thing, a secret I've always kept. My aunt knew, but she hated for me to speak of it."

Jeff gripped her hands, hard. "You're not married, Edith? Never mind. I know you're not. And even if you are, there are such things as divorces. I'll spend every cent I've got if that's what it takes. I'll get you a divorce."

He looked so terribly fierce that Edith couldn't bear it. She laid her hand against his cheek and forced him to meet her eyes. "Of course I'm not married. But I am . . . abnormal."

"What? How?"

"I . . . see things. Or, rather, I saw things."

"What things? Some people see spots that aren't there; it doesn't mean anything."

Edith shook her head, tiredly. Telling him was harder than she had guessed it would be. He wanted so much to explain away her dismay, to make all her troubles light enough to float away. The only thing to do was to tell him straight out, no beating around the bush. Then he'd know what to make of her.

"I can look at someone and know about them. At least, I can tell if they are in love, or if someone is in love with them."

Jeff stared at her. "You can . . ."

"The desk clerk at the hotel, the porter . . . I told them about their true loves. It's also how I know that Dulcie isn't in love with Mr. Sullivan. She couldn't be because there was nothing to see."

"What are you trying to make me believe?" His frown was black.

Now that she'd opened her heart, the words poured out. "I can't explain it very well. It just happens. I'll look at someone and I understand. Only love, though. I can't tell who you hate or respect. Take you, for instance. I knew as soon as I saw you that you weren't in love with anyone and that no one was in love with you."

"You could tell all that from a glance."

The disbelief in his voice was enough to wilt her. "I hoped . . . I guess I should have known better. Take me to Vera's, Jeff. Then I'll catch the first train back to St. Louis."

He caught her hand. She struggled for a moment, then let it lay passively in his grasp. "Edith, forgive me. This is a lot to throw at a fellow all at once. If you believe it, honey, that's good . . ."

"No. It's better if I go. I couldn't stand for you to start looking at me as if I were crazy . . . but I can see it's too late for that." Edith pulled her hand free. "All I can say is that I've always been able to do this thing. Except . . ."

"Except?"

"Just now I couldn't do it." She told him about Mrs. Green and Mr. Huneker, how they should have out shone the sun, but that nothing had happened. "I can't imagine what has changed or how it happened. Even when I concentrated . . ."

"I know what changed."

"How? You don't believe . . ."

"I happened." He had a funny look, half-ashamed, half-boastful. "The ride in the buggy happened. You were so sweet, Edith. And a little drunk, I guess, on Miss Minta's wine. One thing led to another. You don't remember what happened next. You . . ." He hesitated, as though looking for a gentle word.

"I remember," she said, putting her fingers on his lips.

"You do?" He kissed her fingertips. A familiar gleam came into his bright eyes. "That's a pretty overwhelming experience for a girl, especially one like you who's never had a whole lot to do with men. I was your first kiss, wasn't I?"

Edith was blushing painfully. "You could tell?"

"There's nothing crazy about you. Oh, maybe you think too much, and imagine too much, and you definitely talk too much sometimes . . ."

"But . . ."

"But that doesn't mean you're crazy, honey. Though I don't suggest you go telling anybody else in town what you just told me. Not everybody has seen as much of the world as I have."

"Then you . . . believe me?"

He tugged at his earlobe as he looked at the ground. "I believe *you* believe it. But . . ."

"That will have to do, I guess." She could face the next ordeal, now that Jeff hadn't rejected her utterly. The world seemed to shine a little more brightly, compared to the despair she'd been thrown into a few minutes since. She wondered if Jeff was right. Had the physical pleasure she'd known overthrown her mental powers?

Straightening up, Edith said decisively, "I think we must stop at Vera's first, as Sam isn't here to talk to her as we agreed. I didn't think he'd back out."

"You're still going ahead with this?"

"Unless you've thought of another way to save Dulcie and Vera."

Jeff reached for the reins, with a fatalistic shrug. "I guess we're about out of options."

Driving down the street, Jeff nodded toward a familiar-looking wagon. "Dad hasn't backed out. Look. He's there now."

"But the girls?"

"They're all right. He'll have taken Mrs. Jackson to stay with them by this time. The girls love Ida. She spoils them rotten. She wants to spoil Dad too, but he's not having it."

He pulled up in front of Miss Albans' building. Dropping the reins, he turned toward Edith. He tried to take her hands, but Edith clasped them tightly in her lap.

Shrugging, Jeff said, "While Dad's up there talking her into it, I'm going to try one more time to talk some sense into you."

"You can't. I mean, I'm determined to do this."

"But why?"

"We've been over that. Mr. Sullivan is . . ."

"A lousy excuse for a human being and a waste of fresh air. I know. I agree. The first time I saw him I thought . . ."

"When did you see him? The other day you said you'd never . . ."

"I went down the saloon the other night. He was there."

"Oh. I didn't know that. That was very good of you, Jeff."

He said, "Maybe it was kind of feudal of me, checking out Dulcie's intended that way. But I didn't like the looks of him then, and I don't care for them much more now."

"Now?"

Jeff nodded toward a sharply dressed figure walking down the street. "If he's heading for Vera's, there'll be trouble."

Just then, Sam left the building through the front door. He was dressed in a long black frock coat with straight-legged trousers—very fancy for a weekday. He'd even put on his second hard collar of the week. With his graying hair and proud stance, he looked every inch a distinguished gentleman, and a very handsome one too. Vera stood smiling above him, holding the door open to add a few parting words. She glanced past Sam and saw Victor.

Coming to a stop at the bottom of the steps, the dapper man touched the brim of his straw hat and gave an entrancing smile. Even from the street, Edith could see the color drain from Vera's face, leaving her haggard.

Sam turned slowly around. His voice was deep, slow, and unaccountably dangerous. "You want something here, mister?"

Jeff jumped down from the buggy. He reached for the whip standing in its socket. Idly, he began to trace patterns with it on the boardwalk.

His toothy smile broadening, Victor said, "Merely to speak

with Miss . . . Albans, isn't it? I want to buy something for my fiancée. Is that allowed in Richey?"

"There are other stores that might take your money," Sam said. "Get your . . . self away from here."

"No," Vera said above him. Edith noticed that her friend's hands gripped the edge of the door so hard the white bones showed through her skin. "It's all right, Sam. I'll wait on him."

"That's right," Mr. Sullivan said, putting his gaitered shoe on the first step, though Sam still stood in his way. "Money's money, after all."

"Is it?" Sam reached into the pocket of his long coat. He withdrew a handful of gold coins and weighed them in his hand.

"I guess I must have about a hundred dollars here, give or take a little. Pretty things too, twenty-dollar gold pieces."

With a careless flick, he sent them rolling and bouncing down the steps. They glittered in the sunlight, flashing as they rained down.

Victor stared at the coins, his mouth hanging open, wet with greed. Suddenly Edith wondered how anyone could ever have thought him handsome. Sam's voice was cold as a wintry wind as he said, "You go ahead and pick 'em up, boy."

The younger man stooped, but Sam's voice came again. "I warn you though. For every one you grub up out of the muck, my son there will lash you. Now you ask yourself if money's the most important thing in the world, or not!"

Victor glared at Jeff, a trapped creature. In his eyes, Edith saw a hatred born of envy and fear. "Easy for you," he snarled. "You've got everything! But one day, you'll be brought down, you fine gents. One day!"

He ran then, as he must have run when he stole apples off barrows. They watched him run, and Edith saw that the sole of one of his fancy shoes flopped. Suddenly, she felt bitterly sorry for Victor Sullivan.

"Good riddance." Sam glanced up at Vera. "You're crying?"

She shook her head. Her smile was as heartbreaking as her tears. Unable to speak, she stepped back and closed the door. Sam looked up at the sky and said, "Women!"

Jeff coiled his whip. "I don't know," he said, following

Victor with his eyes. "I almost feel bad for that fellow. Sure, he's a bad egg, but what sent him bad, I wonder."

"I don't give a damn," Sam said. "Beg pardon, Edith. But if he comes around Vera again, or any other decent woman, I'll give him that whipping all right."

He pulled out his watch and flicked it open with his thumb. "We'd better be getting along to the Armstrongs before they take their lunch. Not they'll have much stomach for it afterward."

Making up her mind, Edith climbed down from the wagon. "I think we should wait."

"Wait?" Jeff demanded. "I've been trying to talk you into . . ."

"And you're right," she said, stealing his thunder. "You're right. I'm going to talk to Mr. Sullivan."

"Oh, no," Jeff said. "That's a bad idea."

"Bad idea," Sam echoed.

"All the same, I'm going to. I'll see you at home. I mean, I'll walk back to your house."

"No," Jeff said again, crossing his arms.

"Well, if you want to wait for me . . ."

"You're not going, Edith and that's final."

She just patted him on the arm and started walking.

21

I T WAS NOT difficult to follow Sullivan. At first, she could trace him by the startled looks on the faces of the people he'd pushed out of his way. Soon, he slowed to a walk, his hand pressed to his side. He did not look around but led her deeper into parts of Richey with which she was unfamiliar.

After riding with Jeff, she'd been lulled into believing she understood how the town was laid out. But this part of Richey was different from the neat houses and respectable storefronts. Even though the day was still bright, the narrow streets seemed darker, dirtier. The citizens here did not take as much care to keep the sidewalks clear of garbage and waste. Many of the windows she passed were broken or boarded.

Keeping the nattily dressed man in sight, Edith began to close the gap between them. She did not like the way loafers stared after her or the mutters she heard after she passed.

The music of an ill-tuned piano floated out of the doorway Sullivan entered at last. Edith looked up at the three-story building. Dingy lace curtains hung in some of the windows. Across others, peeling shutters closed out the daylight. The building had a neglected, resentful look as though it were scowling at the uncaring world.

The scarlet-painted door was ajar. Edith stepped up the splintered stairs and pushed the door open. A dingy hall with steps along one wall with a shadowed well beneath, a gold-and-black beaded curtain across the entrance to a large main room, and a plush sofa met her wondering eyes. The piano music continued to crank away, a maddeningly circular tune.

The smell of cooking cabbage reminded her powerfully of her former boardinghouse. Yet there was something different about this house. Maybe it was the odor of cheap perfume, overlaying the cabbage. Maybe it was that the entire household seemed to be asleep in the middle of the day. Maybe it was the photographs on the walls, of half-naked women reclining on plump cushions or of wholly naked women standing up, with one foot on a hassock. All had coy expressions as though pretending they didn't realize they'd carelessly forgotten their clothes.

Deciding to find the pianist to ask some questions, Edith put out her hand to push aside the clacking bead curtain. But the piano music stopped. Then she heard a familiar voice and halted, stunned.

"If that don't beat all! Somebody gives you a sideways look and you're shaking in your boots. Just calm down, Victor. It's not like you've done anything so terrible. So you saw Vera Albans and scared her some . . ."

"Guess I didn't scare her enough."

"Don't bother doing anything else to her. The minute we're married, I get my money. Then we'll get away."

"But what if your folks find out? They'll never let you and me get married then."

Dulcie laughed, a hard, cold sound. In a flutteringly sweet voice, she said, "Just tell 'em how you've reformed. Cry a little over your sins, if you can manage it. They'll buy that genuine gold-plated kind of repentance very time."

"I don't know. . . ."

"Come on, don't you want to shake the dust of this place off your feet as bad as I do?"

"Yes, but . . ."

"Are you still worrying about that bigamy stuff? Haven't promised once we're out of here you're a free man?"

"I've been thinking about that. . . ." Sullivan's voice dropped into a huskier register. "We could go places, you and me. There's some big scams waiting for a couple of clever . . .'

"Keep your hands to yourself!" Dulcie snapped. "I've told you before, quit grabbing me!" There was a crash as something fell over. "All I want from you is a quick marriage. Then I give you what's yours and we leave Richey for good. 'Til then, you keep your hands off me!"

"Ah, but, baby . . . ," Sullivan said, wheedling. "Let me just . . . you sure got some figure on you. . . ."

"All right," Dulcie said, obviously bored. "But keep your hands where I can see 'em. Don't even try anything else."

Edith's stomach turned. It was as though she were hearing a younger version of Mr. Maginn and Mrs. Webb, whose low and unclean souls expressed themselves in every word they uttered. She couldn't believe that gentle Dulcie could talk in such a way.

"Edith!" Jeff said in a low, quick voice behind her. He walked up to her. "Don't you know any better than to . . ."

"Shush," Edith said, taking his hand and listening hard. There was silence from the parlor. Then Dulcie said, "Did you hear something?" Only a low moan came from Sullivan. "Hey, I thought I heard somebody say something."

"Some of the girls," he said. "Oh, Dulcie, can't I . . . ? Just a little more . . ."

"No. It wasn't a girl. Go see if anybody's there."

Jeff tried to push Edith toward the door.

She shook her head and tugged on his hand. Waving him to silence, she made him follow her into the well beneath the stairs. It was dark and close under there, with a musty smell like old clothes. Picking up on her disquiet, Jeff pressed back against the wall, holding Edith within the circle of his arm. Leaning forward the least bit, he saw Sullivan part the curtain and look up and down the hall.

"Nobody there." He turned around and the whole set of his shoulders showed disappointment. "What'd you have to go and button up for? I was just getting started."

"Started is as far as you're going. If you're lucky, maybe I'll be grateful after I get my money and let you do what you want. In the meantime, though, a taste is all you're getting."

Dulcie appeared in the doorway, her lightweight plaid shawl crossed in front over a chambray blouse. With her plain hat and pink cheeks, she looked like any prim young lady out for a morning's shopping. "Be at the house early, about six. Dad's going to talk to us about the duties of marriage. It's his usual speech; lasts about half an hour. And don't dress so flashy. Leave the diamond ring and stickpin here."

"Somebody'll steal 'em!"

She threw him a contemptuous look. "Then stick them in your pocket. See you tonight. Remember, show up early. God!" she said explosively. "I can't wait to get where they don't preach morning, noon and night!"

Dulcie didn't wait for Sullivan to open the door. She swept out. He watched her with a twist to his thin-lipped mouth.

After a moment or two had passed, putting her safely out of earshot, he muttered, "Give orders now, sweetheart. You'll be taking 'em later. Oh, yeah." He rubbed his hands together. "You'll be singing a different tune soon as we're hitched."

He walked up the stairs, whistling. Edith shuddered at each footfall over her head. She rested her forehead against Jeff's chest. He was safety and sanity in a wretched world.

He murmured, "I think it's time to go."

As soon as they were a reasonable distance down the street, she asked, "What was that dreadful place?"

"A whorehouse," Jeff answered absently.

"What?"

"Uh, I mean . . ." He pushed his hat back with his thumb. "Dang it, don't look at me like that. *I've* never been there before. But I know about it—everybody knows about it. Even Dulcie, apparently."

"I didn't." Edith put her hand on his sleeve. "And I'm not thinking anything about you, Jeff. After what I overheard, I can realize the worth of a good man."

He smiled at that, pleased beyond words. Then he remembered that he was annoyed. "All I can say is, next time you want to chase some bravo with dirty work on his mind . . ."

Squeezing his arm, she said, "I know. You have every right to be angry. I just thought . . . maybe I could do some good." Sighing, she said, "Poor Dulcie."

"Poor Dulcie? Save your concern for her folks. When we tell them about this . . ."

"We can't do that!" Edith said, stopping.

Jeff urged her on, not liking the looks of the loiterers, they were men he didn't know. "Dad's waiting around the corner."

"Good, I want to get home and take a bath. I don't know why, but I feel . . . unclean." The antique word fit her feelings precisely, yet it conjured up images of lepers and disease that made her all the more eager to scrub herself thoroughly all over.

"I know how you feel," Jeff said, scratching his arm.

"Even though you had a bath last night?" She glanced up at him with a flirtatious gleam, reminding him how much she had seen. At that moment, they reached the wagon, so Jeff couldn't very well say the things he wanted to. As he boosted her up, however, he gave her curving rear a little squeeze, then looked offensively innocent when she squeaked.

"So what happened?" Sam wanted to know.

She told him briefly, Jeff taking over from the point he'd entered. Sam whistled. "I always wondered if they weren't raising those kids too strict. Isn't natural to reject all vain adornment, you know. Everybody likes to be well-turned-out."

"It was more than that," Edith said. "It was as if she were a trapped animal, desperate to escape. Yet, to me, Richey seems such a peaceful town. All except the part I was in today."

"You've had a wider experience of the world, Edith," Jeff said. "You can see the value of peacefulness. For someone like Dulcie, the very things you like most would drive her crazy."

"And not just Dulcie," Sam added, glancing at his son. "Seems to me I recall a certain pair of wild cards who couldn't wait to light out for adventure, once upon a time."

Jeff nodded ruefully. "It's different for boys. They may get knocked around some . . . it's good for 'em. But for a girl . . . there's too many men who'll take advantage. Even Dulcie, who's asking for it, has found more trouble than she bargained for."

"Your daughters have an excellent father," Edith said.

Jeff looked bashful, then said, "I still say, we've got to tell her folks about this."

"No," Edith said again.

"Now just a darned minute. You were bound and determined to tell the Armstrongs all about Sullivan, but now you say . . ."

"Jeff, Dulcie can't be all bad. She's going out of her way to make this look like a love match. Now, why would she do that unless she was trying to spare her parents pain?"

"I think you're wrong, Edith. I think Dulcie is all bad. And getting worse."

"Sounds like it," Sam agreed.

"No, I don't believe it. I'll talk to her . . . make her see reason. She can't throw her life away on this man."

"Not to be crude, Edith, but he did have his hand up her shirt . . . at least her shirt."

"Well, you had yours . . . that doesn't necessarily make her a bad person." She felt as though she'd been painted scarlet. Fortunately, Sam seemed to have missed what she'd said.

He said, "I don't much care what happens to Dulcie, though I wouldn't want any girl I knew going off with that Sullivan. But you've still got to keep Miss Albans out of it."

Jeff looked his father up and down. "You're awful particular where the young lady's concerned."

"Course I am." He met his son's gaze steadily. "Now that Miss Climson's going off with Tyler, she's my best bet for a daughter-in-law. When do you mean to start courting her?"

"One trouble at a time, Dad, please."

"He's right," Edith said. "Miss Albans should be courted, if only because she must be feeling very low right now. I should be, if Mr. Maginn came back into my life."

"Who the heck is Mr. Maginn?" Jeff demanded, his hands clenching into fists.

"My old landlord. The one who wouldn't let me keep a dog."

"How old was he?"

"I meant, my former landlord."

"So he wasn't old. What did he want?"

"My rent, mostly," Edith said. She gazed out at the flicking ears of the horse. "Sometimes other things," she added. "I never gave in, but I was so tired of his insisting that sometime I thought it would be easier to give him what he wanted. I can understand Dulcie, pretty well, you know. And Miss Alban, too. They're like my . . . sisters in a way."

She looked up at Jeff, her eyes perfectly serious. "You mustn't ever mention to Vera that you know anything about her past. Let it be buried and quietly forgotten."

"Do you think I would remind her of it? Honestly, Edith, what do you think I am?"

They would have gone on arguing, if Sam hadn't drawn up before the preacher's white house, the riotous garden brilliant in the sunshine. "Look," he said. "I've been listening to everything you've been saying, and I agree with Edith." He held up his hand to silence Jeff's exclamation.

"Let her talk to the girl, woman to woman. Maybe Dulcie's got some explanation. If she doesn't, if she's just bad, then we let it go. It's not really our place to meddle, is it?"

"Yes, damn it! The Armstrongs have been your friends, mother's friends, for thirty years or more. Mother was there when Dulcie was born, for God's sake."

"Yes, she was. And Millie cried on your mother's shoulder when she couldn't have any babies for all those years. Hell, we even went with 'em to pick up Gary from the orphanage, so you might say I have a long time interest in this family. But Dulcie's a grown girl, son. She's got a right to make her own decisions. And we're not princes. It's not up to us what she does or doesn't do with her life."

"Dad . . ."

"Look, the way I see it, the Armstrongs are going to be miserable if what we think is true. But don't force me to be part of the cause. We've been friends too long."

As the two Dane men escorted her onto the porch of the Armstrongs' home, Edith felt like a criminal between two guards. Their faces were equally stern, branding them with family resemblance. She hadn't realized that fair brows could look so stormy or that brown eyes could be so cold.

"We'll be right out here," Sam said.

Jeff put his foot down with a thump. "No way is she going in there alone, Dad. God knows what Dulcie will do."

"I'm not in any danger," Edith said gently. "I feel she won't do any violence, if that's what you're worried about."

"You feel . . ."

"I was right about Mr. Sullivan, Jeff. And about Mrs. Green and Mr. Huneker." She had been inarguably right, though whether her intuition had completely failed was something the next few minutes would show. Edith could only hope some trace remained; if not, she was indulging in wishful thinking that could get her into trouble. Just in case, she stopped resisting Jeff's efforts to accompany her.

One of the children answered the door. At Edith's request, she went to find her sister. Waiting in the neat parlor, Edith saw that the campaign chair was again in its place. "Oh, good," she said, going over to look at it. "They fixed it. I bet Gary did it. He's very good with wood."

"And other things." Jeff stood by the mantel, holding a small objet d'art in his hands. He had such a strange expression on his face that she walked over to him to see what he held. A bas-relief head, in silhouette, emerged from a thin circle of clay. The woman's mouth was curved in a tender smile while the hair tumbled carelessly down her back.

"Isn't that pretty! It looks . . . familiar. Who is it?"

Jeff raised his eyes to her. "It's you."

"It can't be." Edith peeked into the mirror above the mantel, half-turning her head to catch a glimpse of her profile. "I don't look anything like that."

"Yes, you do." Jeff spoke with calm assurance. "But how did Gary . . . ?"

A shadow across the doorway heralded Dulcie's entrance into the hall. Dropping an armload of parcels on the hall table, she called, "Mama? I'm back. They didn't have Calder's Dentine, so I got Tooth Soap instead. Oh, and Mrs. Judd wants to know if you have any purple flowers in blo . . ."

She saw Jeff and Edith waiting for her. She hesitated, her eyes subtly shifting left and right as though searching for a trap. Plastering a smile on, she came forward. "Oh, hello. I didn't know anyone was . . ."

"Jeff wanted to speak to your mother about something." Edith gave him a glance that compelled and appealed at the same time. "Go on, Jeff. Dulcie will keep me company."

Grudgingly, he said, "Yeah. Edith, call me . . . when you're ready to go."

His cold eyes traveled over Dulcie as he passed. Her hand crept up to rub the base of her throat, her eyes dropping under his gaze. "Is he all right?" she asked when he'd gone out.

"Naturally, he's disappointed in you."

"In me?" She half-laughed incredulously. "Why should he be?" Half-turning away from Edith, she seemed ready to spring out the entry, heading for safety.

Edith approached her and looked into the girl's frozen face. "I know everything," she said as kindly as she could.

"What do you mean? You can't . . . I mean, there's nothing to know about."

"Not even your plan to leave Richey with Mr. Sullivan? Then I don't know about your splitting the money with him, either. Or are you going to keep it and leave him somewhere high and dry?" The girl's eyes evaded hers. "You can't dupe him, Dulcie."

"Sure I can." Her voice hard, Dulcie jerked up her head to stare defiantly at Edith. "I got that skunk right where I want him. All I got to do is get married. Then Pa gives me my money and I go to live with my 'husband.' Only I don't. I drop him somewhere along the line and take my money to start over some place new. Someplace exciting."

"But Mr. Sullivan . . . you don't know what he's really like."

"Don't I?" She tossed her head contemptuously, her dark eyes flashing. "He's bad, but he's also stupid as a drunken dog. I've been waiting for someone like him for months, ever since I inherited that money."

"But surely one of the boys in town . . ."

"Them? I wouldn't give them the time of day. Farming's all they ever want to talk about. If you only knew how sick I am of crop prices and manure! And God. I'm sick to death of hearing about God! Morning prayers, evening prayers, grace before meals, grace after meals! I've prayed enough to last me forever. I want off my knees."

Edith shook her head sorrowfully. "You'll be praying more than ever if you marry Sullivan. You know about poor Vera?"

"Yes. She was stupid, too. Letting that idiot tell her he loved her. What kind of fool believes a man like that?"

"Yet you believe he's going to do what he says. That'll he'll marry you and then let you walk away."

"He thinks he's going to be paid well for it. Seventy-five dollars for half an hour's work. He's broke; he'll do what I want him to."

"And afterwards?" Edith shook her head again. "I happen to know something about the laws that govern marriage, Dulcie. It's part of my work. A woman has to be terribly careful whom she marries. Because he'll own her labor, her wages, even the clothes on her back. And the children belong to him too."

Dulcie blinked at the inexorable truth in Edith's tone. She tried to bluster, "Well, oh, well! Sullivan won't have any of those rights. He's already married in New Brunswick."

"Who told you that?"

"He did, of course. He was scared I really wanted to marry him. Once I told him the truth, he got over being scared."

"But you believe him about his 'wife.'"

"Sure."

"Then aren't you a fool, too? How do you know he's really married? How do you know he won't keep coming back into your life the way he has into Miss Albans's?"

"That . . . that was a coincidence. He'll never find me again. I'll see to it."

"Are you safe from coincidence?" Edith asked. Dulcie bit her full underlip with her slightly prominent front teeth.

Edith pressed her advantage. "Dulcie, if you are so eager to leave Richey, then find a way to do it without tying your life to this evil man's. No good can possibly come of it."

The moment passed. Tossing her head again, Dulcie said with a tense laugh, "You're awfully nosy, Miss Parker. What business is it of yours what I do and who I do it with? You're not my mother, you know."

"Can a brother speak?"

Dulcie flung around. When she saw Gary in the entry, she put up her hands to hide her face. As though struck blind, she retreated. "No, Gary. Go 'way."

Forgotten, Edith watched as the dark young man come into the room, his footsteps firm. He caught Dulcie by the waist, though she flailed her fists against his chest and tried to kick. Gary murmured to her, even as he grappled with her. Capturing her arms, he held her against him with caring strength until she went suddenly limp, weeping against his shoulder.

"Hush, now, my lovely . . . my lovely." His voice was rough yet warm. "What a little ninny. If you want someone to marry, marry me. You know I've been in love with you for years. And you love me, too. Did you think I couldn't tell?"

She said something, the words too muffled for Edith to hear. It could have been a confession of love. Dulcie shook back her blonde hair and said more loudly, "But Mama and Papa . . . they'll say it's a sin. Better I should just . . ."

"A sin for an adopted brother and sister to fall in love? I don't believe it. There's no real reason against it. There's not a drop of blood we have in common but I'd give every drop of mine for you."

Then he kissed her blotched face and her hands crept up to touch his face. "But it's wrong," she said, in a tone that gave away her utter acquiescence.

"No, it's right."

Realizing this moment was not for vulgar eyes, Edith studied the toes of her shoes. After a moment, however, she realized she had to look. If she saw the coruscating radiance, the pink and golden light of love, then she would know that the bright sun alone had kept her from glimpsing it about the forms of Mrs. Green and her lover.

Edith looked straight and unequivocally at the entwined couple. Nothing. Not a gleam, not a glitter, not a glow. Nothing more than any casual observer would see. At her heart, she felt a great, draining loss. She pressed her hand to the place that ached and swayed, biting her lips to keep back a moan of pain.

Edith wanted to run away, to nurse her emptiness in secret. Where was Jeff?

Raising her arid eyes, Edith saw the young couple sigh, smile at each other, and change position. As their kiss continued, Edith realized that one spinster making a quiet exit would not begin to disturb them.

However, the first shriek from Mrs. Armstrong broke them apart like a hammer blow. "Dulcie! Gary! What are you . . . ?" To the daughter who trailed behind her, she said, "Run for your father, quick!"

Dulcie edged farther away from Gary, but he caught her hand and held it tightly. "Mama, we're going to get married," he announced recklessly.

"Married!"

"Yes, ma'am. And there's nothing anybody can do about it. If we . . ."

"Excuse me," Edith said, feeling she ought to interrupt before unforgivable things were said, "but, if you don't mind my asking, how do you feel about that, Mrs. Armstrong?"

"It's what I've always dreamed of!"

Her children, one by birth, the other by affection, stared at her. "Mama," Dulcie said. "You don't . . ."

Tears collected in the corners of Mrs. Armstrong's hazel eyes. "Ever since you were little . . . I hoped that some day . . . that's why we never formally adopted you, Gary. Oh, we were going to and then I knew I was going to have Dulcie and then all the others started coming and . . ." She was crying in earnest now, and the two went to her.

The big preacher appeared in the doorway, sweat-stained and dirty, a double-bitted axe in his hand. Jeff was right behind him with Sam standing on tiptoe to see over his son's shoulder.

At the sight of Jeff, Edith let her hand drop from her heart. She held out her hand to him and he walked right over and took it, as though it were the most natural thing to do.

"What's the matter?" the preacher asked.

"They . . . they want to get married," Edith stammered, her brain whirling. She'd known she loved Jeff, but she hadn't realized that his touch could make her feel complete again.

Mr. Armstrong put his meaty hands on his hips. "Well, it

sure took 'em long enough to make up their minds. That's
wonderful. And to think, we won't have that ugly city slicker
sitting down to table with us anymore."

"Oh," Dulcie said, putting her fingers to her mouth. "I
forgot. He's supposed to come to dinner. . . ."

Sam and Jeff said, in one breath, "I'll take care . . ." They
grinned at each other, their resemblance even more marked.

The preacher said, "Let us pray. Heavenly father . . ."

With barely contained laughter sparkling in their eyes as
they glanced at each other, Dulcie and Gary bowed their heads
obediently. Jeff tugged on Edith's hand.

They slipped out, while the family prayed. Jeff had to grab
Sam by the arm and tug him too to get him to move.

"I'm confused," his father said on the porch, lifting his
creased soft hat to scratch his head. "Isn't Dulcie immoral? Or
did I miss something?"

Edith smiled, feeling her heart beating again. She liked
Dulcie and when she'd thought the girl was evil, she had
worried that her picture of the world as a generally pleasant
place might be a fiction. She was happy to know she was still
right.

"No," she said. "Dulcie's not wicked. She was just confused.
Her feelings were for Gary all the time, but she told herself
they were wrong. She hid them away very well. So well even
I . . . Well, of course, she got angry at herself and wanted to
do something notorious."

"I don't get it," Sam said. "Maybe it's something only a girl
would understand."

"Well," she said, trying again. "If you think you're evil,
you're going to try to prove it, aren't you? And since she
thought being in love with her so-called brother was evil, she
wanted to do something even worse, like run away with
Sullivan."

"Never mind," Jeff said, still holding her hand as they
crossed through the garden. He winked at his father. "It makes
sense to me, Dad."

"It does?"

"Just as much sense as Mrs. Green falling for Mr. Huneker.
Or Paul Tyler deciding to marry a girl he's known for less than

two days. This kind of thing happens when you bring a matchmaker to town."

Edith returned Jeff's grin shyly.

Sam climbed up into the wagon. "Well, it passes me," he said. "But next time you want to make a change in your life, son, let me recommend dynamite. It's safer."

22

WHILE VERA WENT into the kitchen for coffee, Jeff slicked his hair back with one spit-licked palm and looked around the tiny, comfortable parlor. Somehow picking up his buggy from her store had become an invitation to supper. The galling part was how Edith had nodded and smiled, all but answering for him, as though she hadn't a jealous bone in her body. She thinks a lot of you, Dane, Jeff jeered. Yes, sir, you Casanova you.

Vera came back and Jeff hastily rearranged his features into a smile as he got up to help her with the tray. "Yes, ma'am. That certainly was the tastiest pork chop I've ever eaten."

"I thought you'd enjoy a change from beef." Sitting down, they smiled with nervous grimaces at each other over the coffee cups. They'd already discussed dinner twice already, and the subject of Victor Sullivan was too tender to touch upon a second time.

Casting around for something else to say, Jeff nodded toward the decorative stenciling of flowers that adorned the plain mantel. "Did you do that?"

"When I first moved in, I added some of my own touches to these rooms—painting, and so on. They were awfully shabby, but you remember, I'm sure, from when you helped me move in."

"I remember Dad and I knocked the plaster off your hall trying to get this sofa in." He sipped his coffee, still glancing around at the gleaming furniture and hand-hooked rugs. "Yes, you've certainly done a lot to the place. You ought to come over to our house. I'm sure it could use freshening up."

"I think you and Sam have done a fine job keeping up your house. So many men would have let everything go to wrack and ruin. Do you remember the bachelor that lived in these rooms before I moved in?"

"Old Satcherly. How the women used to chase him! But he went to his grave single." Jeff decided to ride out of this dangerous territory. The last thing he wanted right now was a discussion of the pleasures and pains of matrimony.

He finished his coffee at a gulp. "Thanks again for supper. I sure appreciate it."

He stood up and stuck his hands in his pockets. She had no choice, even if she'd wanted one, but to rise and accept his farewell. "I'll show you to the door," she said, stepping ahead of him down the narrow hall.

Looking out through the open doorway at the stars, Jeff commented, "Nice night. Cooled down some."

"Jeff . . ." Vera put her hand flat against the doorframe and examined her splayed fingers. "I want to say . . ."

"Never mind. You've said thank you enough. And like I said, it wasn't me. It was all Edith."

"I like her. I like her a lot. She's changed things in Richey. Haven't you noticed?"

"It does seem as though a lot of people have suddenly found each other." He counted them on his fingers. "Mrs. Green and the butcher, Paul and Miss Climson, Gary and Dulcie . . ."

Regret drifted into Vera's eyes. "If only . . ." she sighed.

Awkwardly offering comfort, Jeff patted her on the shoulder. "At least you won't have to worry about Sullivan. My dad and I will be paying him a little call tomorrow. If there's anything left of him after he went to the Armstrongs' this evening."

With sudden flash of an idea, Jeff said, "Hey, let's walk on over there and see what happened."

"Yes, lets. The house seems . . ." She cast a glance behind her. "Let me get a shawl."

Mrs. Armstrong was glad to see the milliner. "Goodness, but this is good of you, Miss Albans. I was going to come see you tomorrow. What do you think of tulle?"

"Tulle?"

"For Dulcie's veil, of course. She wants nothing but a few flowers tucked into her hair. Come in and talk to her."

Jeff trailed along behind but a whistle and a wave from the back of the hall drew him into the kitchen. There Mr. Armstrong sat in his shirtsleeves at the pine table. Gary held the door open for Jeff. He met his eyes with whimsical resolution.

"Only thing to do is hide when Mama and Dulcie start talking clothes. And bridal clothes seem to be even worse than the ordinary kind."

Jeff asked, "Didn't they settle all that when she was going to marry the other fellow?"

Mr. Armstrong shook his broad head. "Doesn't seem to me they discussed it much."

"Of course they didn't, Pa. Why make plans for something that wasn't ever going to happen?"

Jeff sat down and refused the pie Gary offered. "So what did you do when Sullivan showed up?"

Flexing his meaty hands inward and outward until his knuckles popped like firecrackers, Mr. Armstrong said, "We had a little heart-to-heart chat. Told him that Dulcie had changed her mind and wasn't planning to change it back. He demanded to see her but he didn't press the point."

"He's a coward," Gary said curtly.

"And the boy was itching for a fight, too. Seems a pity." Mr. Armstrong chuckled suddenly with a rattling sound. "He would have turned that pretty boy into something fit only for sausage."

"Well, you taught me everything I know," Gary replied, looking fondly on his father.

Jeff stood up. "I'm glad everything's worked out so well. If Sullivan's smart, he'll be on the next train out of town."

Gary followed Jeff out of the kitchen. "Listen, Mr. Dane," he said, catching up.

"I don't want him coming around Dulcie again," Gary said.

"Without her money, he doesn't have much reason to stay," Jeff said. "But if you want my advice . . ."

"Please, sir."

"Marry her at once, without the frills and nonsense the women want. Marry her and take her away from Richey if you can. Once she's seen what the rest of the world has to offer, I'll lay you whatever odds you name, she'll want to come home again."

"I hate to keep her from the wedding she wants . . . ," the young man said hesitatingly. "But I'll see what good putting my foot down will do."

Just then, Vera came out. Catching sight of them, she said, "They've agreed on a flat round hat, worn low on the brow with a floating veil behind. Dulcie doesn't want to cover her face at all, because she thinks people will laugh if she does."

Gary glanced at Jeff who gave him a nod of encouragement. "Sorry, Miss Albans," the younger man said. "I don't think Dulcie will need a new hat. Excuse me." With the air of one who goes to beard lions in their den, Gary went into the parlor.

On the road back, Jeff and Vera strolled as old friends do, not speaking, not touching. He was thinking of Edith, wishing she were here beside him instead of at home. If she were here, he could have taken her hand, stopped for a kiss, whispered heated words in her inclined ear. He decided to refuse more coffee if Vera should offer it. He wanted to get home quickly to Edith before she went to sleep.

The late sunset had turned the few clouds into candy mounds of pink and gold. The luminous twilight flowed relentlessly across the sky. A cool breeze whispered of coming relief from the heat of the day. Except for a cat momentarily turning luminous eyes toward them, the road was eerily deserted, though the moon, like yellow lamplight, showed comfortingly through the shades and shutters of the clouds to the east.

"Hush," Vera said, stopping and catching Jeff in the crook of his arm. "Did you hear something?"

"Like what?"

"I don't . . . footsteps?"

He didn't hear any thing but the creaking of branches and the lonesome hoot of an owl. "There's no reason to be on edge," he said, moderating his volume out of respect for her nerves. "Why shouldn't someone be walking along here, just like us?"

She returned his smile. "Oh, you're right. It must be nerves. Or the cat's wife."

But as soon as they walked on, paradoxically, Jeff began to feel jittery himself. The footsteps were like an echo, but the rhythm was wrong. They seemed to be coming from behind them, but the sound bounced strangely in the close air. He couldn't be sure. This time, Jeff stopped Vera.

"Hold on," he said loudly. "Your shawl's caught a button." While he pretended to free the imaginary tangle, Jeff listened hard, filtering out the sighing of the breeze and the rustling leaves.

The footsteps were closer. Listening, Jeff picked up an unevenness in the way those booted feet struck the hard packed road. "It's all right," Jeff said. "Somebody's coming out from town. Drunk, maybe, by the sound of it."

"I thought they were following us. . . ."

"Your nerves can play tricks on you in the dark, Vera. Why, once I . . . listen to me, I sound like my father."

"That's not such a bad thing," Vera murmured.

They could see the man now, strutting along with a military air. Catching sight of them, he began to whistle "John Brown's Body," and to swing his arms and legs in time to the music. The slight drag of his left leg and something familiar in the set of his shoulders told Jeff this martial figure's identity.

"It's Dad," he said, hurrying forward. Vera caught up her skirts and sped along behind.

Stopping at attention, Sam snapped off a salute. Instantly, however, he half-crumpled, catching his right hand in his left and pressing it to his chest. "Damn it to tarnation," he rasped.

"What's wrong?" Jeff asked in alarm. He laid his hand on his father's back, leaning down to see his face. The purple swelling of his father's cheekbone and the trickle of blood at his swollen lip were black and sinister in the moonlight.

"Dad!"

Sam straightened up, giving him a beatific if lopsided smile. "Don't worry son. Those'll heal up in no time. What's worse is I think I broke my hand on the bastard's jawbone."

Edith was waiting up for them when they came home. Her eyes widened at the sight of the gaudy silk sling Vera had rigged for Sam. It was bright stripes of green and orange with a wiggly figure like a tadpole in the weave. But more startling than the sling was the air of triumph about the battered older man. He seemed to strut as proudly as a general returned from victory.

"Vera cleaned him up some," Jeff said, coming down again after he'd helped his father to bed. "I haven't seen Dad this elated since Maribel was born. You would've thought he'd done the whole thing himself. Mother said he was even worse when I came into the world."

"I assume then that he vanquished Mr. Sullivan?"

"According to Dad, the other fellow is still lying in an alley somewhere, broken and bleeding. And I believe him. Dad's fist doesn't travel far, but he could knock down my Black Prince with it, if he put his mind to it."

"He hasn't killed Mr. Sullivan?" Edith thought she sounded too hopeful, and added, "That is, he hasn't really killed him?"

"I doubt it. But it'll be a long time before he wants to come back to Richey. Dad left him money for the train ticket before he pounded him."

"Isn't it strange?" Edith mused, picking up her candle from the mantel. "He's so concerned for Miss Albans and Dulcie that he'd actually put himself in harm's way for them. Mr. Sullivan is, after all, a much younger man."

Jeff glanced at the ceiling. "Seems to me Dad's getting younger all the time. Hey, you're not going up to bed already?"

"It's very late." She traced the porcelain candleholder with an idle finger. "I am curious to hear how you spent your evening with Miss Albans. She is a lovely woman, isn't she?"

She dared to risk a glance at him. Her heart hoped to see dislike or, better yet, indifference on his face when he spoke of

Vera. The worst would have been an expression of adoration, but mild admiration was bad enough. Yet, true to her code, Edith civilly wished that Vera and Jeff had a most pleasant evening.

"Yes, she's pretty in her own way. Makes a very poor cup of coffee, however."

"She can cook, though?"

"Sure. The food was terrific. And she keeps her house nice and neat. You ought to see what that girl can do with furniture somebody else junked."

"Old furniture can be very fashionable, I hear."

"Yeah." Jeff began to advance on Edith. The house was quiet, except for the soft tick of the clock's swinging pendulum.

Edith retreated, slowly. He reached out suddenly and took the candlestick qway from her, placing it on a table as he passed. She said nervously, "I wonder if she could show me what she's done. I'll have to buy my furniture secondhand too."

"I'm sure she would."

"What about paint?"

"You shouldn't wear it. Your cheeks are pink enough." Spreading his arms out, Jeff grinned as he herded her into a corner. "I like pink cheeks. They make a girl looked like she's been kissed. Or is about to be kissed."

She turned her face abruptly away. Though his mood was playful, she had ample experience by this time to know how quickly wildfire could consume them both.

Jeff shrugged. "I'll take what I can get," he muttered.

As she felt the warm touch of his mouth roam over her cheek and throat, she wanted to grab him tight. Feeling the heat move from the surface of her skin to inside, she begged, "Oh, please. Please, Jeff. Stop."

She pushed against his shoulder, wondering how her hands had come to be clutching his coat. He gave her a half inch of breathing space, just enough so he could look down into her eyes. "I don't want to stop, Edith. You and I . . . we were made to be together. Can't you feel it? You feel so many things. You make me feel so many things. New things—wonderful . . ."

He swayed forward, his hands gliding over and around her to pull her against him tightly. For the last time, Edith allowed her better judgment to be overruled. She kissed him with all the passion of a lonely woman who could see a pit of wretchedness yawning before her feet. When they parted, Jeff was smiling as happily as a bridegroom.

"Edith," he said. "When are you going . . ."

"Sunday. After church."

"It's a little soon but . . ."

She pushed a little harder this time and he let her go. Filling her lungs with a quavering sigh, Edith said, "I can go back to St. Louis with a clear conscience. There's only one young lady left, after all."

Picking up her candlestick, she held the white wick to the flame of the lamp. By concentrating only on the sparkling flame, she could keep from looking at Jeff. "I'm sure you and Vera will be very happy. She deserves happiness. So do you."

"Edith . . ."

He sounded so hurt that she took a step toward him before she commanded herself. "Good night, Jeff."

"No!" He was in front of her. "This is crazy, Edith."

"I know."

"You . . . you like me, I know you do. And I'm so much in love with you . . . that's right. Flash those big eyes of yours. I want them and all the rest of you too. Now stop telling me I'm going to marry Vera Albans. I wouldn't think for a minute of marrying Vera Albans. Not so long as you're around."

As he pulled her against him, her candle fell to the floor. He ground out the sputtering wick with his boot toe without taking his eyes off hers. His kiss was a seal set to a promise.

"When are you going to marry me?" he whispered. "Make it soon, darlin'. I'm dying for you."

In Edith's dream, she became aware that two of the rose bushes in the garden were whispering to each other. She wanted to hush them because the gardener was saying something very important as he flourished her corset—stolen from her by sleight of hand. Edith tried to listen to the gardener but the roses were whispering very loudly now.

"I told you it will be okay."

"But why's it taking so long?"

"They're grown-ups. You know what they're like."

Edith frowned and tried to hush them. But it was too late. She knew she'd never get back into her dream. Whatever the gardener had wanted to say would remain unexpressed. Opening her eyes, the first things she saw was two flowerlike faces, regarding her no less somberly for being upside down.

Maribel and Louise's worried expressions faded. "We didn't wake you up? Gran'pa said we shouldn't wake you up."

"No you didn't." She blinked in the morning light and sat up, rubbing the sleepiness from her face.

"It's just that the sooner we get to the fair, the more we can see," Louise said.

"I want to see the baby sheep," Maribel announced.

"A fine thing for a cattleman's daughter to want," Jeff said from the open doorway.

Instantly, Edith pulled the sheet tight against her breastbone. Her gaze lifted to his face and then jumped away. He wanted to marry her.

Last night, he'd asked and teased, making her laugh, never taking no as her last word. He had sworn to keep her up all night unless she promised to give him her answer later today. To escape before she surrendered, she promised. Edith knew what she must say, but how precious this last day with him would be.

"I'm glad they got you up. Time's wasting. And today's a big day," Jeff said with a significant glance. He leaned against the doorframe as though he had all day just to look at her.

"We didn't wake her up, Daddy. We were quiet as mice," Maribel declared. "She opened her eyes right away."

"That's right," Louise said. "We only whispered a little."

He chuckled. "Only loud enough to wake the dead, I'll bet."

"They were very quiet," Edith said defensively. Glancing at the girls, she added, "But really, if you all want to go to the fair as soon as possible, you'll have to let me get dressed. And I want to take another bath before we go."

"Aw . . ."

"All right, girls," their father said. "Git."

As Maribel and Louise left, Edith dared to add, "You too."

"Oh, no. I claim special privileges."

He kicked the door closed as he came in. A naughty thrill skittered through her. He looked very tall. She shrank back against the headboard, trying to be stern and failing.

"What 'special privileges'?"

"Just a good-morning kiss." He strove for a light tone, but he had to clear his throat before he spoke. One of his knees sank into the mattress as he reached for her. His hands burned through her thin lawn nightgown, branding her shoulders. Edith braced herself for an onslaught of her senses that would leave her weak and trembling for nameless pleasures.

Yet his kiss was a mere, gentle brush of lips. Edith murmured a vague protest and reached for him when he would have pulled away.

He pushed her hands down. "Not . . . not a good idea."

"Oh!" Edith hastily caught up the sheet a second time.

Standing up, Jeff said ruefully, "Really not a good idea. Hurry up and take your bath, though." He let his gaze wander over the rumpled bed linen that imperfectly concealed the outline of her body. Holding up his hands as though to show he had nothing in them, he said again, "No, not a good idea at all."

After her bath, and wearing her nice gray dress, Edith went down to eat a catch-as-can breakfast. Sam was arranging and rearranging the long stems of his roses in a blue milk-glass vase, muttering to himself.

"They're beautiful, Sam," Edith said, caressing an apricot bud. The fragrance was as intoxicating as wine.

"I only hope Fred Grant has aphids and thrip. Did I tell you how he nabbed first prize last year? As underhanded a piece of skullduggery as any train robbery!"

"Yes, you told me."

"He set his stems down on a slab of brick inside the vase—used one of those thick Wedgewood things from England so the judge couldn't see through it. They were six inches above everybody else's blooms. And I 'spect he put a little red dye in the water to keep the color up."

Jeff called from the hall, "I've got your crate ready, Dad."

"Well, come here and help me, dang it. You think I can do it with one hand?"

Under a flurry of orders from his father, Jeff lifted the vase as carefully as though it were a sickly baby. Sam danced around and fussed like a worried mother.

Edith trailed behind the men. She couldn't quite meet Jeff's eyes. Had he known how she wanted to keep him in bed with her? Had he felt the eagerness of her hands or the way her body had lifted against his?

After Jeff lowered the roses into the crate, he packed it with straw. Edith returned to the kitchen for a broom to sweep out the mess they had made. While Sam fussed some more with his display, letting the straw drift from his good hand over the blossoms one strand at a time, Edith went ahead and swept the porch too. When she was finished, Sam was still at it.

"Come on, Dad. They'll be all right," Jeff said.

The girls came in, Louise balancing the box of chicks that she would show at the fair. Maribel looked at her grandfather's roses and listened to her sister boasting of how she was bound to take first prize. The little girl's lower lip began to tremble and two perfect crystal tears overflowed her lashes.

"What's the matter?" Edith asked, crouching beside her.

The words were muffled but the gist was that everybody had something to show at the fair but her. Louise heard and said, "You should have thought of that before."

"Don't even got a snake," Maribel sniffed.

Edith wiped away the tears with her handkerchief. "You should have something to show. What else is there, beside livestock and flowers?"

Jeff stood above the little group. "There's a prize for cooking or fancywork. There'll be a display of farm machinery. Usually Roger Randall shows his mineral collection. Oh, and the kids have a pet-judging event."

"Pets?"

"You know. Dogs, cats, rabbits . . ." He was dazzled by the smile on her face. But it wasn't for him, it was for Maribel.

"Would you like to show Orpheus?"

The little girl's eyes shone like river-washed stones. "Could I?"

"That's not fair," Louise protested. "He doesn't belong to her."

"I've been giving him his seeds," Maribel stated.

Edith bit her lip but didn't hesitate. "Orpheus is yours, if you want him."

The embrace of two chubby arms was reward enough for giving up her only friend. "Come on," Edith said, gathering Maribel up in her arms. "We'll go get him."

23

"TODAY'S MOSTLY FOR the exhibitors to set up," Jeff said, helping her down when they arrived at Richey's Meadow. Two big marquees had been erected at either end of the field, while booths and smaller tents created an avenue between them. Narrow banners snapped in the breeze, and concertina music started and stopped as someone tried to catch hold of a tune.

A creek wandered through the wildflowers, bubbling a song. Above the fairground at the far end of the meadow, a gentle hill rose against the sky. Its side was marred by a white scar, from where, once upon a time, the slabs of stone piled at the foot of the hill had fallen. Jeff saw Edith looking that way.

"Just below that mark is the Cave of Mysteries," he said. "It goes deep, right under all of this, even where we're standing. We'll be running tours of it tomorrow. Mostly to keep the kids out of it the rest of the time."

"Who's we?"

"Me and some of the other men, Paul for one. I guess he and

I know it about as well as anybody, but nobody's ever explored it all. You run into deep water, for one thing."

Edith looked up at the white mark of the cave and shivered despite the sunshine. She could imagine the dripping depths of a lightless hell, worse than a dungeon. "How awful," she said.

"Wait 'til it's ninety degrees at noon. You'll be glad to get into the cave then. As a matter of fact, it's so cool up there we keep the ice cream in it."

Sam said, "Quit talking about it. You're giving me the willies."

"You won't be giving tours, I imagine," Edith said gently.

"You couldn't pay me to go in there. I don't even like getting the ice cream down, to tell you the truth." He glared at his son. "Are you going to stand there gabbing all day, or are you going to help me with this crate?"

Jeff winked at Edith and went around to the back of the wagon to lift the crate out under the faultfinding supervision of his father.

His prediction for the heat came true very shortly. No one seemed to mind, however. The children raced around and played with shrieks of abandon no matter how high the mercury climbed. Outside the livestock tent and looking down the fairway, Edith saw a bright array of parasols, in every shade from white to black with red predominating. She wished she had one, but that was the single item the kind ladies in St. Louis had forgotten.

"Miss Parker?"

Edith turned to see Mrs. Armstrong and Dulcie standing a few feet away. They came over at once. "Isn't it hot, though? I declare there isn't a breeze stirring," Mrs. Armstrong said, patting her forehead with a handkerchief.

"It was a little close in the tent." The ordure of the cattle combined with the heat had turned her faint. Jeff didn't seem to be affected by the smell or the temperature. Grouchy, by his heels, seemed delighted by the different smells. Jeff had nodded when she whispered to him about going out, and he went on discussing the merits of Black Angus versus the Shorthorn with a group of men.

"We're going to get some lemonade at the Methodist tent.

Come along," Dulcie invited. She had a calm, relaxed air about her today, completely different from the wound-up wildness of the day before.

"Thank you," Edith said, falling into step beside them. "Where's Gary?"

A blush augmented the heat-induced pink in Dulcie's cheeks. "He's entered a whittling display. He's there now, hovering."

"You were there yourself," Mrs. Armstrong said. "You won't believe it, Miss Parker, but I had to practically drag her away. It seems like only yesterday that carving was too dumb for anyone but hayseeds to trouble with."

"Mo-other . . ."

As Jeff came to the tent exit, he caught sight of Edith moving off with the Armstrongs. He grinned happily as she stopped to talk to Louise, who had raced by her like a wild creature. More and more, he was growing confident that he'd made the right choice. Edith fit in here. Soon she'd give up her foolish notion about mysterious powers beyond mortal ken and settle down to life with him.

"Hey, Jeff!" Arnie Sloan came trotting up to him, flapping a piece of paper. "I'm awful sorry about this. Seems like a mailbag done fell open while Minnie Grable and me were moving it to the post office. We thought we picked 'em all up but here was this one under the bench when I swept up the depot this morning."

"It's all right, Arnie. These things happen." Jeff looked at the superscription in the corner.

"Hope it isn't anything important—I mean, you know, like somebody dying or something." Arnie lifted up on his toes to look at the envelope through his rimless cheaters.

"Mighty pretty handwriting. I've been studying up on handwriting, you might say. Got a book on it. This feller says you can tell everythin' 'bout a person by the way they write. Now that big O there, that means a generous nature. And the way she crosses her T—it is a woman, ain't it? S. Carstairs. You can always tell when it's a woman."

Jeff stuck the letter in his coat pocket. "Thanks again, Arnie. See you later."

"Sure thing. Don't know how I come to overlook . . ."

This must be the letter Sabrina had said she'd sent him. Obviously, Arnie didn't believe in sweeping the station too often. Jeff thought about ripping it up unread, but his curiosity got the better of him. Stopping off the main fairway, he opened the letter.

What he read there sent him hotfoot after Edith. She'd been right about Sabrina and the waiter. They were deeply in love, hoping to marry and move West. Then Sabrina inserted a sly request for money, hinting that she'd never trouble her old "friends" again. Jeff vowed to send her a hundred dollars just for proving that Edith really could tell lovers at a glance.

But when he reached the Methodist tent, he found only Mrs. Armstrong and Dulcie at one of the little tables by the entrance.

"Edith? She went to take some lemonade and cookies to Maribel. Louise went too." Mrs. Armstrong studied Jeff's face. "Are you feeling all right? You look like you've seen a ghost."

"Where did they think they'd find Maribel?"

"Over at the little tent next to the livestock. Where the kids are keeping their pets until the judging tomorrow."

As Jeff raced off with his long-legged stride, Grouchy lolloping along side, Dulcie turned to her mother and said, "What a strange family!"

There seemed to be a lot more people on the fairway now than even a few minutes ago. Jeff careened off heavyset women, tripped over children who appeared out of nowhere to run between his legs, and brushed past men he'd known for years without a greeting. But when he bumped into his father and put him aside without apology, he found his arm gripped.

"Hold on, son. Gol-durn it! Isn't it bad enough Sullivan got in a few licks without you adding to 'em?"

"Sorry, Dad. I'm looking for Edith."

"I saw her a few minutes ago, but I don't think she heard me call. She was heading . . ." He jerked his thumb toward the hill. "Figure somebody shanghaied her into handing out the ice cream. Better her than me."

Jeff ignored the sharp tug on his coat skirt and Louise saying, "Daddy . . ."

"How long ago did you see her, Dad?"

"I don't know. Five, maybe ten minutes. *I'm* looking for Vera Albans. Have you . . . ?"

"Just a minute, Louise."

"But Daddy . . . Miss Edith said . . ."

"I have to say, son, you look like you've got a real burr under your saddle. What's up?"

"Nothing, but I have to find Edith. I was wrong . . . about something important . . . and I think I owe it to her to say so."

"Daddy, please!"

"What is it, Louise? You want some doughnuts or something?"

"No, Daddy. Miss Edith said I should find you and tell you Mr. Sullivan's taking Maribel to the cave."

Out of breath and overheated from the climb, Edith hesitated an instant at the gaping mouth of the cave. She felt the cold air it exhaled like the slithering touch of a snake over her skin. A lantern, unlit, sat on one of the dripping boxes of ice cream just inside the entrance. Edith picked it up, the oil swishing inside the bell.

A bobbing light ahead in the sloping darkness showed her how far ahead Sullivan had gotten. Like an echo, Maribel's light voice floated back to her. Though the words were indistinct, the tone was happy. She had no fear of the man who held her by the hand, though his replies were monosyllabic at best.

Edith hurried over the threshold between the sanded entrance and the hard stone of the cave, her breath still short and rasping dryly in her throat. She mustn't let the others' light get too far ahead. Already the dark was closing in. A few feet beyond the entrance, all the daylight was swallowed up.

Like in a nightmare, Edith hurried on, but always the light bobbed too far ahead to catch. She began to feel that something was behind her, breathing down her neck. Glancing behind her at the entrance, the lighted space seemed infinitely tiny and remote. The sight brought her no comfort. Suddenly she understood Sam's fear of underground places.

When she turned to go on, the lantern's glow had vanished. She stopped as though she'd run into a wall, the dark like a muffling curtain all around her.

"Wait! Mr. Sullivan!" she called out. "Please wait."

She went on, blindly, her hands before her, her whole body shrinking from an inevitable crash against solid stone. Then the light returned, blessed light, showing Maribel's figure beside the battered Mr. Sullivan. "Who is it?" he snarled, raising the lantern into the air.

"It's me. Miss Parker."

Maribel tugged her hand free of Mr. Sullivan's, though he made a futile grab to recapture it. "Cousin Edith," Maribel said, running up to her. "I get to look at the cave by myself! Louise will be so mad!"

In her relief and joy, Edith knelt down on the gritty floor. She embraced the little girl, who wiggled free at once, impatiently. "You want to come too?"

Edith raised her head to look at Mr. Sullivan. From his pocket, he withdrew a knife, the yellow light dancing along the edge. "Yes," he said with a smile. "Miss Parker would like to come on a private tour too, wouldn't you, Miss Parker?"

"I would. But Maribel . . . did you ask permission from your father before you left the tent?"

Though the light was behind Maribel, Edith felt the girl's shoulders slump. "No," she admitted.

"Don't you think you'd better?"

"Now wait a minute. . . ." Mr. Sullivan approached.

"Let her go ask her father," Edith said, crouching at his feet, but not looking up. "I'll go with you, instead."

"I don't want you . . ."

"I'm going to m-a-r-r-y Jeff Dane." Maybe if she spelled key words, Maribel wouldn't become alarmed. "And it won't help you to show her that k-n-i-f-e. You'll only f-r-i-g-h-t-e-n her."

Maribel said on a note of grievance, "You don't have to spell stuff. I know what you're saying. Daddy's going to be mad at me, isn't he?" She sniffed. "I just wanted to see the cave before everybody else."

"No, your daddy won't be mad, honey," Edith said, rising to

her feet, Maribel's hand in hers. She looked Sullivan in the eyes. "Let her go ask him. You'll be able to show me some of the chambers while we wait."

His gaze shifted between Edith and the child. "All right. But no tricks or . . ." He patted the pocket where he'd concealed the knife.

Edith touched the child's cheek with her free hand to tilt her face up. "Now listen to me, Maribel. You've got to walk very slowly and head straight for the exit up there. You'll be able to see your way out without any problem. Then you sit and wait for your . . . for someone to come. There'll be somebody along soon to get the ice cream. Don't go back to the fair. Just sit and wait. All right?"

"All right." Maribel's white face turned from Edith to Sullivan, a look of doubt narrowing her eyes.

"Can you see the way out?"

"Sure." Still the child hesitated. Edith prayed that Maribel wouldn't say anything about the tension between the two grown-ups. It was like the silence before a mighty thunderstorm, when even the earth seemed to cower down.

"Go on then," Edith said.

"Okay." Maribel turned and began walking up the slope toward the exit, her little legs carrying her along with surprising speed. About ten yards away, she suddenly turned and yelled, "But it's not fair!"

Edith studied Mr. Sullivan as the echoes of Maribel's running footsteps surrounded them. One of his eyes was swollen nearly shut and his mouth was bruised and sore looking. He took care to speak out of the other side.

"You think you're smart, huh?"

"Not really. But whatever you're going to do, better I should suffer it than a child, don't you think?"

He stepped suddenly closer and grabbed her upper arm in fingers that bit her to the bone. He twisted. Edith cried out, trying to turn out of his grasp. "That's right," he said in her ear, his voice pleased. "Be scared of me. Be real scared."

He let her go, almost throwing her aside. Edith rubbed her arm, her skin burning from the friction.

"Let me . . . let me get the other lantern," she said, trying
keep her voice from wavering. "We might need it."

"Okay. But I won't light it. Better for me that way."

After they'd been walking for some time, Edith was glad
e'd worn her own shoes. The ones Mrs. Waters had bought
r her were always a little too big or too small. Mr. Sullivan
t a rapid pace and the footing was very uneven. She kept
ose behind him. Though she tried to take notice of landmarks,
e was soon confused.

Sullivan noticed her looking around. "You might as well
joy yourself. You wouldn't have gotten this much of a look
you'd gone with your boyfriend."

"You seem very familiar with this cave, Mr. Sullivan. Are
u from Richey, somehow?"

"Hell no. I was born in Pennsylvania."

"But you don't seem to have any difficulty down here.
m . . ." She rubbed her arms, the eternal sunless chill
netrating to her bones. "I already don't know which way we
me or where we're going."

He laughed pridefully. "No cave can mess me up. I was sent
the mines when I was nine years old. Spent five years of my
e underground, slaving away at the bottom of a coal shaft.
here's nothing I don't know about caves and such."

He held the light to illuminate the ceiling. "See those? We
lled them Devils' Teeth."

Projecting down from the roof were huge, pointed icicles of
veating stone. Edith saw a single drop of water hanging at the
d of the one closest to her. She held out her hand to touch it.
he coldness stung even through her cotton glove.

"That drop could have been forming for a year. Shows you
w long it takes for something like that to grow. And I've seen
m big around as a man. Seen 'em fall too, right through the
est of some guy too slow to get out of the way." He grinned.
'inned him like a bug on a card. Never saw so much blood."

"Horrible!"

They passed through great vaulted chambers that seemed
corated with delicate plasterwork. Edith stopped for breath
a stone garden, with curious pieces of rock petaled like

roses. Tiny castles sprouted on mounds of stone at the botto
of stalactites, like models of European strongholds. Though sl
saw great wonders, all the colors were the same, a ghost
yellow-white in the lantern's glow. And overlaying everythin
was the smell of a vast cellar and the ceaseless rushing of wat
somewhere in the depths.

Edith asked, "Where is all that water I can hear?"

Sullivan's mood seemed to have changed since he told h
about the Devils' Teeth. "Shut up, can't you? That's all wom
are good for. Jabber, jabber, jabber."

Edith's mouth was dry. She felt as though a hundred yea
had passed since she'd sipped lemonade at the Methodis
tent. Though they slopped over a rise that water raced dow
slurried with mud, Edith saw nothing to drink. The sound of t
water became taunting, for it surrounded her, yet the on
moisture she saw was the faint sheen on the walls in t
lantern's glow.

How long they'd been traveling, with their only light t
yellow circle of the lantern, she couldn't say. Time had litt
meaning here, where such things were measured by a slow
swelling drop of water and the passage of centuries. Sl
remembered squeezing through a passage sideways, afra
every instant of becoming stuck. She walked along a narro
ledge, clinging to the slick stone as best she could.

Sullivan abruptly stopped and swore when Edith bump
into him.

"Give me that other lantern." He snatched it. Her finge
were so cold she'd forgotten she was holding it until the weig
was taken away.

"Sit down," he ordered. "Over there." He flashed his lanter
at a large stone slab, tilted out over a mess of small chips li
a drawbridge over a gravel pit. The small stones spurted o
from beneath Edith's feet so that she had to spread her arn
wide to keep her balance. She reached the big slab and hoiste
herself up on it, thanking mercy that she had a small bustle
use as padding.

Sullivan put the second lantern down at his feet. "Now yc
listen, girlie. I haven't brought you all this way for your healt

ot at all. I'm going to go back up there. If your boyfriend does
hat I say, I'll tell him how to find you. If not . . . I'll think
you down here, when I'm someplace sunny."

"I feel confident you will one day find yourself where it is
ways very warm."

He gave her a half-grin, as though pleased by her good
ishes. Then, figuring it out, he snarled, "Be nice. That's the
rt of thing that might make me make a mistake in telling your
oyfriend where to find you. Maybe you didn't notice but
ere's a whole lot of passages running through these caves. A
t of 'em are dead ends. This will be one for you if you're not
reful."

His quip seemed to restore his good humor. "I'm a kind-
earted fella, so I'll leave you this lantern. I guess it's got about
ree hours worth of oil in it. If Dane sees reason, he'll find you
ng before the light goes out. If he tries any rough stuff or calls
the law . . . Are you afraid of the dark?"

Still laughing, he went to the entrance of the chamber. "You
ay put, girlie. Don't get any smart ideas about finding your
ay out on your own. They'd never even find your bones if
ou tried *that*. Be a good girl," he said, his voice a horrible
arody of the tone she'd taken with Maribel.

"Mr. Sullivan?" Edith asked, just before his light faded.

He stuck the lantern back through, the shadows leaping
eirdly across the ceiling. "You want to beg?"

"No. I want to know . . . did no one ever love you, sir?"

"What the hell kind of question is that?" He marched away.
he could hear him grumbling for a long time, the echoes
ouncing down the passages.

Edith wriggled on the stone but soon gave up trying to find
more comfortable position. In the lantern light, she saw no
ore comfortable perch than the one she now occupied. At
ast up here the draft was not so noticeable. She considered
tting down and going for the lantern but was afraid that if she
ipped on the large stones coming back, she'd break it.

As a rule the dark did not frighten her. But she realized here
at what she'd thought of as dark was really always lit by star,
oon, or the ambient glow that is in the sky itself. Here there

was only the feeble light of a lantern and the ear-breakir
silence. Edith shivered, but not from the cold. What if she we
to hear a noise? Who knew that primordial terrors might lurk
the impenetrable darkness just beyond the circle of light?

Edith began to regret having an imagination. It could n
create a fire to warm her, or compel Jeff to find her any mo
quickly. It could only pull up nameless fears to torment he
She could almost see a huge shape detach itself from the mur
the slaver dripping from . . .

Edith crossed her arms to hug herself, to calm the shive
that wracked her. A slight crunch, in the utter silence as loud
a breaking branch, came from her pocket. Puzzled, Edi
touched a rough surface. With a smile, she pulled out one
the gingersnaps she'd been taking to Maribel. There had bee
five or six in the folded calico packet, but now the packet ar
the other cookies were gone, fallen somewhere on their twiste
trail.

Edith nibbled the edge of the remaining cookie. Somehov
the warm flavor of the spices drove back the dark. And, aft
all, she had, as a rule, found an imagination to be a comfort
times of trouble.

Lady Jessica studied the man before her, determined to wip
the triumphant smirk from his rubbery lips. "You think I w
submit to you to save my life? It will never be. I shall sho
defiance with my final breath."

"Brave words, my lady," Lord Ivor lisped. He rubbed h
ringed hands in delicious anticipation of her surrender. "B
you will sing another tune, I fancy, when the choice is marria
with me or death for your lover. Bring in Jeffrey the Dane!

The guards exchanged a look as the tumult outside the doc
reached their ears. "But, my lord . . . there is some distu
bance!"

"All the better. Let him struggle. His exertion will not la
long." When he was not instantly obeyed, the corpulent lor
half-rose from his seat. "Obey me! Let the Dane come in."

The guards lifted the bar across the massive door to Lor
Ivor's Great Hall. Lady Jessica cast down her eyes, unable
shame the Dane by seeing his downfall. But the yelps of th
guards made her turn.

Cries and shouts and the thunderous clanging of swords and shields penetrated the chamber. With a mighty crack, the doors burst inward and the battle surged to the very foot of the dais. Greatest among the warriors, Jeffrey the Dane towered above the rest, doing great damage with his long sword, Diavolo. But before he could reach Lord Ivor's falcon seat, the evil lord snatched a poniard from his jeweled belt and held the razor point against the swanlike neck of the fair Jessica.

24

J EFF LEFT THE organizing of the search to his father and Pa
Tyler. Alone, he leaped up the hillside, Grouchy inte
behind him.

At the sandy entrance to the cave, Jeff stared down into tl
dim first chamber. The dog, on the other hand, went sniffir
along the ground to the ice cream boxes just inside.

Glancing at the dog, Jeff saw the whiplike tail lashing a
the sound of a slurping tongue. "Get by, dog," he said. "Con
out of it."

In no humor for kindness, Jeff went to haul the animal bodi
away from the sweet delicacy. He saw, with a jolt of horror th
twisted his heart, the body of his daughter, laid out behind tl
boxes. Grouchy licked the child's hands and looked around
Jeff's exclamation.

Then Jeff saw Maribel's beslobbered hand move as sh
pushed the dog away. "Yuck! Grouchy!" Sitting up, she wipe
her hand on her skirt.

"Daddy!" she protested as he swept her high into the air. H

ddled her close, leaning his head on hers, unable to believe
r a moment that she was alive and apparently unharmed.

"My God," he said, his voice trembling in thanks. "My
d."

Maribel turned to look up into his face. "You're not mad at
e? For going away with that nice man. Miss Edith said . . ."

"Edith? Where is she?"

"In there. With the nice man." Maribel pointed down the
roat of the cave. "She said I should wait 'til somebody
mes. But I got sleepy."

Jeff glared at the darkness over the threshold, then embraced
s daughter again. "I'm just glad you're okay. I was worried
en I couldn't find you."

"Sorry, Daddy. I won't ever leave without asking p'mission
ain." She crossed her chest from shoulders to stomach with
e forefinger of her right hand.

She obviously hadn't the slightest idea that she had been in
y danger. Jeff promised that he'd let her off lightly for any
ture misbehavior. What could she do that would make his
art stop again as it had the instant he had thought her dead?

"I'm going to take you to Grandpa, honey. Then me and a
uple of other men are going to join Edith and Mr. Sullivan."

As he stood up, his daughter still in his arms, he looked
ound for the hound. "Grouchy?"

He heard a woof, the same happy sound the dog made when
nting rabbits through the pastures. "Come on, boy," he
lled, and whistled.

The tan dog came running out of the darkness, his paws
rambling on the loose surface. He held something in his jaws.
oming to a stop before his master, he laid the slobbery circle
Jeff's boot. Then Grouchy slunk back, his belly to the
ound but his tail thumping with barely suppressed delight.

Balancing Maribel on one hip, Jeff slowly lowered himself
pick up the brown circle. It smushed in his fingers but gave
t the smell of allspice and nutmeg.

With a giggle, Maribel said, "It's a cookie, Daddy. Grouchy
ought me a cookie."

"Hot damn! Lemonade and gingersnaps!"

"Daddy! You swore!"

A few minutes later, Maribel stood in danger of be
smothered by the joyful ladies of Richey. She stood it only
long before saying in an widely audible whisper, "Loui
Let's go see Orpheus."

There was some laughter, and then the ladies went to st
cooking for the menfolk. No one could tell how long
searchers might have to remain here, except that they'd stay
long as it took one way or the other.

Putting Maribel down, Sam said, "We'll go see that bird
right, darlin'. But then we're going to go home."

A woman's voice cut through the children's automa
complaints. "Sam?" Vera Albans stood a few feet away,
though afraid to approach.

With the swiftness of instinct, Sam held out his hand to h
A hesitant smile curving her lips, she took the steps t
brought her to his side and gratefully slipped her hand into h
"I was afraid you'd hate me. This is all my fault."

Keeping a careful eye on the girls, but letting them get o
of earshot, Sam said, "Like hell it is. You didn't tell me to
thrash the sonofabitch. Pardon my language."

"It's all right. I've heard worse." She also looked ahead
the children. It felt so right to be walking hand in hand with t
man. If only there wasn't such a cloud over them.

"Maribel seemed unscathed by her experience," she said

"To her, this is just another part of the fair. At least, Sulliv
didn't scare her. That's the only thing that'll keep me fr
ripping him apart when they find him. I just hope none of t
boys get so riled they hang the bastard before he can tell
where Edith is."

"Surely they wouldn't do that!"

"You better believe they would. You see, they all rememb
the last time somebody got lost down there."

"I never heard . . ."

"Well, you wouldn't. Nobody likes talking about it. It w
fifteen years ago. There was this kid . . . He was one of tho
boys nobody seems to take to much. Always on the outsi
you know? He seemed to think if he explored the ca
everybody'd look up to him as some kind of hero."

"I take it that he didn't."

"We looked for three days and nights. The whole town turned out. Jeff and Paul led a lot of the searches, because they'd spent so much time in the place. They never went back much after the two of 'em brought that kid out on a plank. He'd been crushed by falling stone. Nobody knew if he was killed outright or not."

Vera looked away. "Do you think they'll find Edith?"

"They'll find her. But in what condition . . ."

About an hour and a half after Jeff found Maribel, the girls' elation at the new fair had faded. The day had become hot enough to bake bread, and not a breeze moved.

Mrs. Armstrong came up to Sam, pacing at the entrance of the livestock tent. "Why don't you send the girls home with us? You know my daughters would love to keep them, as long as need be."

"Thanks, Millie. I appreciate that. This isn't good for 'em." He called them. As they went off with the preacher's wife, who was promising them pie and new games, he said bitterly to Vera, "Even if they were both of 'em lost up there, I wouldn't be able to stand going in after 'em. I can't even bear to be up here at the hub of things."

"That's all right," she said, leaning her head on his shoulder. What else could she say?

"I've always been afraid of places like that. I won't even go in my own blasted root cellar. And there's no *reason* for it."

"There doesn't have to be a reason. I'm scared of bees. Actually, it isn't bees. It's the noise they make. That buzz!" She shivered.

"Let's get away from here then. The flies make enough noise to drive you crazy."

As they walked away, Gary came running up. He was marked with clay and candle wax. "Oh, there you are, Mr. Dane. Jeff sent me back."

"Have they found her?"

"No, sir. Grouchy lost the trail. There's this place where the water runs down. They're casting around for a new trail now."

"You go take a rest, son. You look worn to a nub."

Gary passed his arm over his forehead and looked surprised at the amount of dirt and sweat that came off. "It's not so bad

in there. Mr. Tyler said it's about fifty degrees inside. It'
coming out to this heat that knocks you down."

Vera said, "I'll get you a drink, Gary."

She came back at a run, holding her skirt high out of th
way. "I saw him." she gasped out.

"Who? Sullivan?" Sam demanded.

"Yes. He's . . . he's down by the flower-show tent."

"Come on!" Sam shouted to Gary. The two men raced away
Sam's limp not slowing him down a hair. The gaudy silk slin
fluttered to the ground behind him. Heads turned as they sho
past, and in a moment, twenty or thirty people were following

Vera arrived just in time to see Sam's left fist slam int
Victor's face. His head rocked back but already his fist wa
coming up. It began as a slugfest but after the first bloo
showed, dotting Victor's clay-streaked shirt, they fell into
clinch, hammering at each with short, punishing blows.

They rocked and reeled between the tent and the spectators
Not a man stepped forward to stop the fight, the crowd stoo
by in a horseshoe. Looking at their faces, Vera saw stalwar
resolve and knew that if by some chance Sam should down
half a hundred men stood ready to take his place.

The two combatants staggered back and forth before the
broke apart. Sullivan brought in a roundhouse punch that sen
Sam tottering back into the crowd. The younger man turned t
flee and ran into the tent.

The crowd surged forward as Sam broke free of th
supporting arms of his friends. He chased Sullivan, nearl
falling but pursuing like a Fury. Catching hold of his shoulder
Sam spun him around, connecting with a bone-crunching righ
to the jaw.

As Sam hollered aloud in pain, Sullivan slid slowly down
his eyes rolling up in his head. As he fell, he caught the edg
of a table, in a last-ditch effort to stay upright. The table
unbalanced, tipped up. The entire display—vases, roses and
all—came crashing down on Sullivan's unconscious form.

As Sam stood swaying above his vanquished opponent, Ver
rushed to his side. "Are you hurt?" she cried.

"Course. But I feel fine." He prodded Sullivan with his toe
tenderly kicking aside a dark red rose. "At least Fred Gran

can't win first prize either. That's his prize bouquet right there on top of this louse. Only time he's ever smelled this good, I'll . . ."

Still with a smile on his face, Sam dropped to his knees. Vera cradled his head against her bosom. "Somebody get some water! And get Doc Butler. Sam, darling, you're going to be all right. I'm so proud of you."

Grouchy tugged against the rope through his collar and whined. To him, being underground was the same as hunting in the light, though the smells were all long dead. All except one, the scent he sought, snuffling along the shale and limestone.

He could sense his master's impatience and excitement flowing down the rope. Grouchy wanted to please him. Once more he snuffed and sniffed along the dry side of a slight rise where the water ran down. Then Grouchy caught the faintest, shivery whiff of the smell he sought. He dragged forward, his big paws digging into the ground so that he staggered like a fur-bearing iguana. The smell was a bright light reaching through to the back of his head, calling him forward.

"I think he's found it!" Jeff shouted over his shoulder to the searchers behind him. They'd all sat down after Grouchy searched fruitlessly for half an hour. There had been no grumbling, however.

Jeff found himself being towed along behind the dog so quickly that he had to duck to pass under low overhangs almost before he saw them. He didn't care how many bumps or bruises he had to take out of here, so long as he found Edith. Besides, compared to what he intended doing to Sullivan . . .

He tripped and went down. The rope slipped from his nerveless fingers. Free of the dragging weight of his master, Grouchy ran ahead. "No, dammit!" Jeff yelled, scrambling up.

Someone from behind caught his arm when he would have gone running into the darkness. "Slow down, Jeff." Paul's voice came out of the dark as it had when they were boys, reassuring and calm. "We don't want to be lookin' for two of you."

"But without Grouchy . . . "

"He'll come back."

They were struck into silence by the deep baying of a hound
on the scent. It came rolling and echoing back like the roar of
some creature from the distant past. Suddenly changing into a
higher pitch, it cut off abruptly.

Someone said, "You reckon he fell in?" Everyone had the
same picture in his head. They all knew there were pits in the
caves too deep for a man to measure.

"Come on," Jeff said. "We can go a little farther. Grouchy
was heading straight as an arrow when I saw him last."

"Okay." Paul looked back over the other men's head. "Mike,
you stay put. And the rest of you, go careful." Once they'd
gotten beyond the knowledge of any man there, they'd left men
at every crossroads or fork they came down. Mr. Armstrong
sweated impotently on the far side of Fat Man's Nightmare, a
passage no more than three feet wide.

Jeff began walking ahead. Though he knew Edith had only
been down here perhaps two hours, he hated to think of her
alone with Sullivan. His mind obligingly coughed up a dozen
scenes of lurid melodrama, and he fought to keep sane. If he's
hurt one hair on her head . . . , he thought, in but the latest of
futile vows he'd made with God or himself.

"Grouchy," he called. "Here, boy!"

He whistled, but the echoes were too shrill to bear. Straining
his eyes, he peered past the darkness until he saw sparkling
lights when he blinked. The others held the lanterns, high and
low, the yellow circles only making the dark that much more
intense beyond the light.

Jeff tried to fix his mind on anything but his greatest fear. If
she were unable to answer when they called, they might pass
within feet of her and never know she was there.

He whistled again for Grouchy, patting his thighs and calling
in mock excitement, "Come on, boy. Come on!" Silence was
his only answer. Even the echoes failed.

The letter in his pocket crinkled. Jeff touched it. If there
were truth in such things, if he had faith in the unknowable,
then . . .

"Wait there a minute!" he called to the men following him.

"You see something?" Paul called.

"Just wait."

Jeff walked ahead until he was out of range of the lanterns. He could tell that the roof was too low for him to stand upright. He closed his eyes and counted slowly to thirty, thinking, wishing and praying that when he opened them, he'd see something.

When he reached thirty, he pried his eyes open reluctantly, unwilling to be disenchanted, sure he'd see nothing but the appalling dark. In wonderment, he saw a glow, very faint and flickering, like a lantern strangling for want of oil.

With a glad cry, Jeff ran forward. The fissure in the rock lead to a wide chamber, filled with loose stones and slabs of rock. Jeff skidded to a stop, his eyes amazed.

Yet there was nothing there to make him stare in surprised amazement. Only a lovely girl sitting on a rock, a panting dog by her side. She looked up from Grouchy and smiled. "Hello, Jeff. I knew you'd find me."

Then she slid off the rock boneless in relief.

The other men crowded into the opening behind him, swinging their lanterns and gabbling a mile a minute. Jeff picked up Edith's limp, chilled form, Grouchy dancing around him, shivering from doggy happiness.

"Let's get her out of here," Jeff said, gazing at her pale face, the lashes thick on her cheeks.

"Say," said Ozzie, picking up an unlit lantern from the floor. "How long do you reckon she's been sitting in the dark?"

"Dark?" Jeff asked as he moved toward the exit. "One of you must have knocked it over."

"Couldn't be—this lantern's cold."

Jeff looked down at her, a question in his mind that would never be asked. But he could have sworn he'd seen . . .

"Wake up, now, Edith. Come on." He patted her cheek with the back of his hand. She was chilled through.

Her eye lids fluttered and lifted. "And they lived happily ever after," she muttered.

"That's right." Over his shoulder, he said, "Whiskey."

"No," Edith said, pushing away the flask that appeared. "Don't want to sing now."

"Have a little sip to warm you up. You've gotten kind of cold sitting down here and we need you to be able to walk."

"I can walk." She pushed again at his hand, though lying against his chest was a blissful comfort after the cold rock. "I don't need liquor, Jeff. Just the sunlight. It *is* still sunny somewhere, isn't it?"

Eager voices assured her that it was only about one o'clock in the afternoon. "Oh, good, just time for lunch," Edith said. "I'm so hungry the rocks were starting to look tasty."

"Edith," Jeff said softly. "You've got an hour's walk ahead of you." She looked so disappointed that the men began to pat their pockets to bring out their own supplies of portable food.

"Here's some beef jerky the lady can chew on."

"I got an apple—kind of wrinkly but I'm sure it's good."

"Want some penny candy?"

Feeling a little foolish for making an exhibition of herself in front of all these nice people, Edith tried to struggle up, her hand on Jeff's shoulder. She was glad of his support, for her knees wobbled strangely. He didn't take his hand off her—touching her waist, or her arm or her hand—throughout the entire journey upward.

When they at last reached the fresh air, Edith hid her stinging eyes against his chest. She'd never seen anything more beautiful than the meadow and the fair in the summer sunshine.

"No reason to cry now," he said, tilting up her chin.

Edith blinked in the light and the tears that ran down were hot against her cheeks. "It's just . . . I only now realize I might have died without ever telling you . . ."

Jeff pulled her against him and kissed her cold lips. They heated quickly under his treatment. She threw her arms with abandon around his neck.

"Tell me later," he murmured as a cheer went up from the searchers. "Tell me every day for the rest of our lives."

Word spread quickly that she was safe and sound. The people of Richey began to surge up the hill as though needing the proof of their eyes before they'd believe it. Jeff and Edith heard from a dozen simultaneous tongues the story of how Sam had clobbered Sullivan, who was now in the hoosegow. But among all the smiling faces there were four they missed.

Gary fought through the crowd. "I'm glad you're alive," he said to Edith and blushed.

"Me, too. Where are the girls? And Sam?"

"I don't want you to worry about Sam. Doc says he'll be fine if he stops laying into people. Miss Albans is looking after him." He winked and looked knowing. "And the girls are at our place, having the time of their lives. They didn't know anything about all this." He looked around at the clay-streaked and tired men. His eyes lit on his adoptive father. "Lord-a-mercy, wait 'til Mother sees you!"

The massive Mr. Armstrong looked down over his shirt and pants, to the thick-coated shoes. Mournfully, he shook his head. "How the mighty are fallen. Look, boys, last one in the creek is a godless heathen!"

With a shout, the searchers ran down the hill, scattering nervous women and excited children with their speed. Though it had been his challenge, Mr. Armstrong lingered a moment to speak with Jeff.

"We'll convene a committee about closing this cave off. It's too dangerous." He looked between the two of them and grinned. "I hope to see you in church mighty soon, my boy. Mighty soon."

As agile as any of his sons, Mr. Armstrong launched himself down the hill. Soon he'd passed the stragglers and was running in the thick of the pack.

Alone with him and the crates of ice cream, now sitting in milky puddles, Edith looked up at Jeff. "Do I have to wash in the creek before I'm allowed in the house?"

She was so hungry that as soon as they drove away from the fairgrounds she dove into the picnic basket that some ladies gave her from the Methodist tent. Jeff shared the contents. But Edith noticed that he juggled the reins and the food so that he always had one hand on her. It was as if he couldn't bear to let go.

The house was strangely quiet when they got home. Jeff said, "I'll start heating some water for your bath, Edith. Then I suggest you hop straight into bed."

"That sounds wonderful. I'm still frozen through."

About half an hour later, as the shadows began to grow, Edith slipped into her nicest nightgown. She sat down before the mirror and began to brush out her towel-dried hair. It was so wonderful to be warm and *clean*! Behind her in the mirror, the white bed looked inviting but a little lonely.

When she awoke, the darkened room showed only a glimmer of moonlight through the translucent curtains. Faintly, she heard a footstep in the hall outside her door. She looked toward the sound and saw the white china knob of the door turn. A slice of light grew as the door opened. Soft as a whisper, Jeff called her name. "Are you awake, my dear?"

Pleased, for a moment she didn't think to answer. She heard him sigh and the creak as he began to close the door. "Yes, I'm awake."

He came back into the room, closer and closer, bearing a candle. "I thought . . . in case you woke up and thought . . . since it's dark now . . ."

"That was very kind." Edith sat up and looked up at him, knowing her eyes were filled with trust. She patted the mattress. "Don't you want to sit down?"

With a sigh that was nearly a groan, Jeff sat beside her. She put her hand in his. "Jeff, I think . . ." Her heart was too full to say easily all that she wanted to.

"Yes, Edith?"

"There's a nice girl a Mrs. Rivers told me about. Twenty-one, three younger sisters, loves children . . ."

"What are you talking about?"

"Well, I promised to find you a wife. And, as it seems Miss Albans has deserted you for your father, I still have a duty . . ."

Jeff leaned down, his hands grasping the brass posts either side of her head. "Oh, yes, you do."

His kiss began as softly as a feather touch. Edith felt like a cat about to purr. She stretched up to entice him closer. Shamelessly, she put her arms around him and leaned into him, her breasts flattening against his chest.

He caressed the back of her head firmly through the soft clinging cloud of her hair. He sought her eyes. "Edith, we can wait 'til we're married. I don't want to rush you."

"I got very cold in the cave," she answered, her deep blue eyes smoky. "I'm not warm yet. Warm me, Jeff."

He hadn't known her full lips could take on such a beguiling curve. Taking them under his, he lifted her against him. As she closed her eyes, he laid her gently onto the mattress. The feel of her beneath him was enough to make him totally ready for her. But he reminded himself that this was her first time.

Edith gave herself up to the feelings he unleashed with his touch. Her modesty seemed to have fled into the darkness when she'd thought she'd never see him again. She helped him slip free the tiny buttons that ran from the square beribboned neck of her gown to her stomach.

When he parted the fabric to gaze with heated eyes at her breasts, Edith boldly flaunted them. She remembered the way he'd put his mouth there and wanted it again. Telling him so without words, she dragged his hands up to cup her. His thumbs brought her nipples to aching peaks while he plunged his tongue relentlessly into her mouth. She met him halfway, more than halfway, meeting his plunge with a thrust of her own.

They rolled over and over, nearly to the edge of the bed. Her gown twisted around her waist, leaving her intimately open to his gaze. She brought her knees up together, to conceal herself, while a burning blush spread over her face and chest. Maybe she had kept a little modesty after all.

"Edith," Jeff said, dragging his attention from the curls so dark a red against the pure white skin of her thigh. "Edith . . . I don't want to hurt you."

"I've heard . . . whispers about it."

"Then you know. But I'll do my best to make it right." He kissed her, gently again, while his hand slipped down, stroking over her exposed hip and across her smooth, quivering stomach.

"It'll be good," he promised in a ragged voice. "I'll make it good for you."

Edith closed her eyes again, flinging her head back as a strange heat blossomed wherever his rough hands dragged. She moved restlessly, her leg rubbing on the sheet between his. But when he reached the springy curls between her thighs, she froze.

"Don't . . ."

Instantly he withdrew his hand, returning to stroke the

gleaming satin of her shoulder. He nibbled her neck, and scattered tender kisses over her neck and face. Edith reached for him, but he was always teasing, never lingering.

Her lips burning for a taste of him, she dragged his head down to hers. Somehow her nightgown had come off, though who pushed it down to the end of the bed was unclear. As Jeff's solid body centered over hers, Edith bit back a cry of pain.

"What's wrong?"

"I think . . . you've got a broken button on that shirt."

Jeff squinted down at the blue chambray. "Maybe I should take it off then."

She nodded, biting her swollen lip. When he had it unbuttoned, she pushed it off his shoulders. She dared to comb her hand through the golden hairs that spread across his chest and downward. She followed the trail, felt his hard stomach muscles dance as he sucked in his breath. His eyes closed, and Edith realized how much pleasure she could give him. She found the knowledge as exciting as his touch.

He clapped his hand over hers as it came perilously close to his belt buckle. "That's enough."

"But, your buckle is cold. I can feel it on my stomach."

"Should I take it off?"

"I think so. And you . . . might as well take off everything else too." She couldn't meet his eyes when she said that, though she watched him covertly under her lashes as he stood up and impatiently jerked his belt open.

"You might as well look," Jeff said. When she glanced at him with wondering eyes, her mouth fell open. Jeff forced himself to think cold thoughts as he knelt on the bed.

Edith stared in open astonishment at the intimidating size of him. "What is that?"

Jeff chuckled despite his desire. "That's . . . hard to explain. Didn't anyone tell you how a man and a woman come together?" She shook her head. "I'll show you. But I've got to touch you."

She knew where he meant. "Will it feel like last time . . . in the buggy?"

"Better. Much better."

He hadn't lied. Edith couldn't be frightened of what he

thought of her when he found her ready. When he slid one finger between her legs, he said on a throbbing note, "Oh, God, you're so perfect."

He moved his hands, weaving a spell that stole her heart and her senses. She couldn't hold herself still, she had to move in concert with his wonderful hands. Hot words whispered in her ear urged her to give in fully to the sensations that promised to carry her off.

If the first time he'd ever touched her she had felt lightning, now she felt a whirlwind rise. She cried aloud, but not with fear. When it ended, she was clinging to his shoulders, breathless and limp. She opened her eyes to see him smiling down at her with infinite tenderness. "I told you it'd be good."

Somehow it felt very natural to be naked together, though she had been told a lady never undressed except to bathe. Edith knew she was too thin, that her ribs still showed despite Sam's cooking, yet she had no fear that Jeff found her anything but beautiful. He told her so repeatedly, as he touched and caressed every part of her body and urged her to do the same to him.

His groans when she touched him made her withdraw at first for fear she was hurting him. But Jeff brought her hand back to press against the resilient, velvet flesh. "We don't have to do another thing," he promised raggedly. "We can stop right here."

"What else is there?" she asked. But she'd known the truth the moment he opened her with his hands.

"I don't want to rush you. . . ."

"We've got until morning." She bent her head and breathed across his flat nipple. Her dark hair tumbled forward to brush his sex and Edith smiled in delight when it leaped in response. Deliberately, she let the heavy locks curl and drift over him.

The world turned upside down as she found herself on her back, her feet flat on the mattress. The tip of him demanded knowledge of all her secrets. She slid her hands along his slick back. "I want you to," she whispered. "Please."

He pushed slowly, slowly, his forearms trembling with the strain of control. When she stiffened, frowning with distress, he stopped. "Do you want me to . . . ?"

"Go on," she gasped. "It's all right . . . I think." Her hands slipped down to cup his firm buttocks.

Her tightness was almost too much. He wanted to plunge madly, to drive her over the edge and to fall with her. The hardest thing he'd ever done in his life was to continue to go slowly. But when Edith rose to meet him, the sensation was incredible. He lunged deeply, unable to stop now, though she caught back a cry that could only have been from pain.

Incredibly, after a moment, she answered his rhythm with her own. He wasn't in charge of this seduction, he realized, as the liquid warmth of her drove him wild. This was an act of pure creation, as they established together a new whole, a new identity. He heard her cries, now unmistakably of passion, mingle with his own roar of completion.

When Jeff raised his head from the junction of her neck and shoulder, the first thing he saw was a single tear falling from the outside corner of her closed eye. "I'm sorry if I hurt you. I couldn't stop myself."

"I didn't want you to." She turned her head to look at him from inches away. Her eyes glowed with happiness. "I couldn't have stood it if you had stopped."

They kissed playfully now, light nips and transient nibbles. After a minute though, Edith pushed lightly against his shoulder. "Are you going to lie on top of me all night?"

"Hmmm, it's a thought."

"You're heavy."

"You're beautiful. But, I suppose, if we're getting married tomorrow, I should let the bride get some sleep." He rolled off her. She followed at once, to lie on her side, cuddled against his warm body.

"You'll sleep here?" she asked.

"Well, it is my bed. But I don't mind sharing."

"Big of you."

"Yes, it was." He caught her hand against his chest when she would have playfully slapped. "This finger," he said, touching the third one. "That's where the ring goes."

"So I hear."

"You will like being married to me, won't you?" he asked in sudden doubt.

She counted on his fingers. "I'm not sassy, I'm not voluptuous—you do like women who are a little that way don't you?—I haven't any experience with children . . . need I go on?"

"No, you're right. You're absolutely wrong for me. What was I thinking?"

Once again she tried to punish him, but he caught her hand. Rolling on his side, he carried it to his lips and began tenderly biting each sensitive pad in turn.

"What could possibly make me change my mind and keep you around, Miss Parker?" he asked, as he moved her arm to lick into fire the ticklish nerves of her wrist.

"I can't think of a thing . . . Oh, unless . . ."

"Unless?" His mouth was only an inch from hers. She could feel that he was ready to love her again. The warmth growing in her lower body told her that she too could revive quickly.

Looking into his eyes, Edith said, "I love you. Is that reason enough?"

"That's the best reason in the world."

Epilogue

THE AUTUMN NIGHT brought a fog with it. Cold, Edith began wriggling upright, preparing to haul herself out of the armchair in the parlor. Instantly, Jeff left his record keeping.

"Here," he said, offering her a hand. He had to pull hard to tug his highly pregnant wife to her feet. She playfully put her hands up to fend off his chest.

She thanked him, trying to fasten her gaping blouse. "I hope Dr. Butler's right and it won't be long. Nothing fits decently anymore."

"I kind of like it," Jeff said. He tilted his head to get the best view of her augmented bosom. "I know I can't do much else right now, but . . ." His hand curved to steal inside her blouse and cup the warm breast within.

Edith closed her eyes, savoring the momentary pleasure. "Stop," she said, when he began to open the rest of the buttons. "I can't remember whether I covered the milk pails."

"I'll go," he volunteered with a last gentle squeeze.

"No, I need the air. Just let me get a shawl."

As had become usual during these last months, Edith and

Jeff went together. The fog garlanded the yard with misty streamers. There was a promise of winter in the air. The quilts she'd received the year before as wedding gifts would be used tonight.

Edith was glad the girls were sleeping in town tonight. Vera was not nearly so far along as she was and could better cope with the two girls, wildly excited as they were by the impending birth of their brother or sister. The extra rest was a blessing.

They were halfway across the yard when Edith stopped, a preoccupied look coming to shadow the contentment on her face. "What's the matter?" Jeff demanded. "It's not . . ."

"I don't think so. Believe me, Jeff, I'll tell you when. No, I just had a strange feeling."

"Oh?" He didn't always believe, but he could never entirely disbelieve either.

"Like someone's coming to visit." She turned to look at the drive. For a moment, she stared hard at the swirling mist. "It can't be," she said wonderingly.

The woman coming toward them, striding along with her large sensibly shod feet placed just so, bore a startling resemblance to Edith's late aunt. So extraordinary was the likeness Edith thought for a moment that it *was* her aunt.

But when the woman came closer, Edith saw that this woman was younger, slightly more attractive, and with the addition of temple pieces to her pince-nez. Her pale blue eyes flicked over Edith's swollen abdomen.

"You are Edith Parker?"

"No," Jeff answered. "She's Edith Dane."

The eyes flicked over him too and dismissed him. "Mrs. Dane, I'm here on behalf of the Sugar Hill Matrimonial Bureau of Kansas City. You are the heir of the late Miss Edith Parker?"

"That's right, Miss . . ."

"Pettibone. Miss Eunice Pettibone." She lifted the case she held. "There are few papers to sign, Miss Par . . . Mrs. Dane."

Her smile was stagnant, as though it was rarely aired. "I have a pen," she said, when Jeff moved impatiently.

"I wasn't getting one," he replied. "Look here, Miss Pettibone, my wife isn't signing anything."

"It's all right, Jeff," Edith said, putting her hand on his arm. "Miss Pettibone and I understand each other. She wants to buy the matrimonial service."

"That's right. We understand of course that all your records were burned in the boardinghouse fire." There was the faintest hint of a question, whether in Miss Pettibone's voice or the cock of her head.

"Yes, completely destroyed. As well as all my aunt's personal papers. There weren't very many."

"I'm sure. That is . . . I'm sure it must have been a great loss. You know, you should have let someone know where you were. We had to trace you though your forwarding address, and it is so time-consuming dealing with the post office."

The two women eyed one another. Edith suddenly understood what her place in the world had been before she'd met Jeff. She would never regret all that she'd unwittingly surrendered, for it was far better for her to belong to this one man. Miss Pettibone had chosen the other road. Edith had great respect for her.

She smiled in welcome. "Won't you come in for a cup of tea, Miss Pettibone?"

"Thank you, but I must catch my . . . my train."

"There's no other train tonight," Jeff said gruffly. "There's a good hotel in town." Somehow he didn't want this woman to stay in his house. She was too starched, too critical. Too strange for all she looked as normal as any spinster aunt.

"Ah, quite." She coughed. "Getting down to business, we want to buy the name, copyrights and goodwill of the Farmer and Maid Matrimonial Service. As you are obviously not planning to operate the business yourself . . ."

"No, I have other things to think of now. Edith placed her hand on her protruding stomach and felt the little knee that pressed up from within.

"Excellent. If you'd sign here . . ." Miss Pettibone withdrew from her case a short document and a surprisingly frivolous pen topped with a long curling pink feather.

"Wait a minute," Jeff said. "You'd better read that."

"I'm sure it's only the standard contract."

"You know?" Miss Pettibone asked with a note of surprise.

"Not until you came. Then it sort of leaps to the eye. Will the name be used again?"

"I doubt it. It's rather old-fashioned now. But it had a good long usage and will always be thought of with respect."

Aware that Jeff was fuming beside her, Edith signed the paper as Miss Pettibone supported it. She gave him a smile as she straightened up. "Thank you, Miss Pettibone."

"No, thank you, Mrs. Dane." She put away the pen and the paper seemed to roll up by itself. "Ah, yes. There is one last thing. Payment."

She took out a folder. "Here you are. All present and correct."

Edith opened the folder and turned toward the light. Jeff tried to read over her shoulder. When they turned to ask Miss Pettibone what she'd given them, the yard was empty except for the swirling mists.

"Maybe we'd better go in," Jeff said, touching her middle back.

Edith sat down again in her rocker, the folder on her lap. She did not open it again immediately. She listened with an air of absorbed interest as her husband scolded her for not reading a contract before signing it. "Yes, you're absolutely right, dearest. I'll never do it again."

Mollified, Jeff sat down next to her. "It's just that I worry, Edith. There are so many dangers . . ."

"But did you ever think how much disinterested good there is in the world? People devote their lives to good works, never reaping any reward. It seems almost incredible, but it is right to remember it. Sometimes people do good."

"What did she give you?" Jeff asked. He was still uncomfortable when her eyes got that far-off look. Remembering how close he'd come to losing her, he grasped her hand to bring her back into the present.

"Oh, yes." She opened the folder, freeing the slightest, vaguest scent of smoke. Her hands trembling with wonder,

Edith withdrew a sheaf of papers tied together with pink ribbon. "My stories!"

"What?" Jeff scooped up two pieces of paper that had floated free when she'd pulled out the papers.

"My stories. All the things I wrote down, my dreams, my fairy tales. Oh, I thought they'd been burned up!"

Jeff read the paper. He put his hand over hers to silence her raptures. "Look at this, honey."

It was a scrap of paper, hardly as big as Jeff's hand. Scrawled on it as though with an unmanageable pen were the words, "Born to Jefferson Michael Dane and Jessica Hawes Dane, October 15th, Samuel Hawes Dane."

"That's today, isn't it?" Edith asked.

"That's right. And according to this," he flourished another piece of paper, "today is also your real birthday."

"Oh, I've always wanted to know that!" She put her hand on her abdomen again, in a different way. "Jeff, could it be . . . ?"

Jeff met her eyes for a fleeting instant. "I don't know what to think right now, Edith. I'd like to think that . . ."

"Oh!"

She lifted the papers high, afraid that the water coming from her body might soak them. They were precious, but she knew she wasn't going to have a chance to look into the past right now. Not with the future coming any minute.

Jeff put the box on a shelf in the pantry while he was shut out of the bedroom. He tried to sit down but the sounds coming from behind the bedroom door seemed to make every chair red-hot. His father tried to make him drink some coffee.

"Calm down, son. It's not like you haven't been through this before."

"I was just as nervous then, Dad. I don't think it ever gets easier."

Finally, a wonderful sound broke the tension. The sound of a baby crying.

Dr. Butler came out, rolling down his sleeves. "Ah, Dane. Mother and son doing splendidly. Strong woman that. Much stronger than she looks."

"She's all right? She's really all right?"

"Of course, of course. Fine."

"Did you say . . . ?" Jeff felt the blood rush to his head. "Son?"

"Yes, a fine, healthy boy. Loud too."

Jeff wrung the doctor's hand and dashed into the bedroom.

Sam looked at the doctor. "Can I ask you a question, Doc? How'd you know to come out here? Jeff didn't go for you."

"Funny thing about that, Mr. Mayor. I was thinking about bed when this woman knocks on my door. Don't know who she was—and I thought I knew pretty much everybody in Richey. Anyway, she tells me to hightail it out to the Danes place 'cause the baby's coming. Good thing, too. That kid was in an all-fired hurry."

Sam nodded. "Funny thing. A stranger stopped at our place too. She looked . . . familiar. I might have known her in Boston, but she looked kind of too young for that." He shrugged. "Just one of those things, I guess. You want some coffee? Or something stronger?"

"Something stronger."

"Then you'll have to come to my place, but don't tell the voters. Edith doesn't keep much in the house but Miss Minta's strawberry cordial."

Jeff knelt by the bed, gazing in wonder at the exhausted face on the white pillowcase. The small, red bundle in her arms gazed interestedly at nothing. "Did you see he has dark hair?" Edith whispered.

"The girls are going to go crazy for him." Jeff smoothed the damp auburn tendrils back from her forehead. "If it had been a girl I was going to call her Jessica Edith, after you. Strange, wasn't it . . . ?" he let the thought go unspoken.

"We don't have to call him what was on that paper."

"We'd talked about calling him Sam anyway."

"But if you want . . ."

"No, Samuel Hawes it is. I think it'll be a lucky name for him."

"Very lucky."

She was sleepy now, and happy. As though he knew that the tricky question of his name had been solved, little Sam whimpered and turned in search of her warmth. As Edith drifted off into sleep, she whispered, "All my dreams have come true. . . ."

"Mine too," her loving husband replied, as he closed his eyes in a thankful prayer to the powers that be. "Mine too."

FREE

Romance

(a $4.50 value)

Send in the Coupon Below

To get your FREE historical romance and start saving, fill out the coupon below and mail it today. As soon as we receive it we'll send you your FREE Book along with your first month's selections.
